WHAT THE TRUCK

WHAT THE TRUCK

BATTLE TRUCKER BOOK ONE

TOM GOLDSTEIN

Podium

To JLM, the Jill of my story

This is a work of fiction. Names, characters, places, and incidents are either products of the author's imagination or used fictitiously. Any resemblance to actual events, locales, or persons, living, dead, or undead, is entirely coincidental.

Cover design by Tom Edwards

ISBN: 978-1-0394-4699-1

Published in 2023 by Podium Publishing, ULC
www.podiumaudio.com

WHAT THE TRUCK

CHAPTER 1

TRUCKS ARE OP

Someone drugged my fucking coffee."

Jill MacLeod was not having a good drive. First some shitbag had tried to squeeze her ass at the last rest stop, then the night manager had threatened to ban her for getting said shitbag's blood all over the floor. Then her cell phone had died in a tiny explosion of sparks for no goddamn reason. Now it was past midnight, and there were all these blue-background, computer-like messages popping up in her vision, distracting her just as she neared the pass. It was still early enough in the year for it to freeze; she had to pay attention to the road and not whatever drug trip she was on. If she ever found out who did this, well, there were plenty of quiet spots that a long-haul trucker knew about to stash a body in.

Another window popped up, partially blocking her vision.

> System Integration in 5 minutes. Good luck, humans!

"Shit! Out of the way!"

Jill waved a hand angrily and the box vanished. Somehow, she knew that she could call it back at any time, just like all the other boxes that had popped up over the last hour. Long experience told her that she should pull over. She'd known far too many fellow truckers who'd crashed after pushing themselves to drive when they were dead tired, and being drugged was worse than being tired. On the other hand, this was by far the tamest drug trip she'd ever been on, and her schedule for this haul was tight. It was a long, long road to Boston after all, and who knew what kind of problems might rear their ugly heads.

As it was, Jill would have just two days at home with Ciara before needing to head out again, and that was if she skipped the trek out to her family's homestead to see her father and brothers. She frowned and gripped the wheel just a bit tighter. Not for the first time, she thought about getting out of the trucker business, of selling her truck and finding some sort of work that would let her stay near her family and, not for the last time, she threw that thought aside. She had made her one-woman company from nothing over long years of work, caffeine-driven nights taking her from a contractor stuck in a bad truck lease agreement to an independent owner, and she wasn't going to throw all of that work out on a whim.

The miles and minutes ticked by. Jill neared Homestake Pass, Montana, the highest point on Interstate 90, where the long road crossed the continental divide. Under Jill's hands, Bertha's wheel started to shake, small tremors growing into raw jerks, as if the smooth asphalt of the interstate had suddenly turned to gravel.

"Woah, girl, you okay?" Jill asked her truck, giving the wheel a reassuring pat. She'd been driving the big rig for sixteen years now, owning it herself for the last eleven. She kept her big girl in the best shape she could, but the truck was getting up there in years. Still, Jill knew her truck better than she knew herself, and Bertha wasn't going nearly fast enough for these kinds of vibrations.

> System Integration beginning.
> You have reached Level 0! Select a class to proceed to Level 1!
> Due to your World First discovery of a significant location, you have gained a Perk Point!
> Classes available:
>
> ...

"Shit-tits!" Jill yelled, one hand frantically waving to clear the larger box from her vision. Bertha swerved alarmingly, and Jill feared for a moment that the trailer behind her would jackknife, all eighty thousand pounds of truck coming crashing down. But she'd been driving most of her life; an expert twitch of the wheel brought her girl back under control.

She glared at her coffee again. Murder was too good for druggers. She was going to rip off their—

Wait.

There was something in the road up ahead: something big on four legs, with eyes glowing from reflected headlights. Jill's first thought was that it was a moose, but the creature was too small for that, if only just. Jill grimaced and reached for the chain connected to the truck's air horn. She really didn't want to have to deal with an animal strike this late at night; hopefully, a burst of noise would scare it away.

Bertha screamed, and 150 decibels of deep-throated power blasted out from above Jill's head. She couldn't help but grin. Even after all these years, the sound of a big rig's air horn made her heart stir.

But the creature, whatever it was, didn't budge, and Jill was getting closer to it at an alarming rate. "Move!" Jill yelled, pulling the horn again. She might have been able to avoid it with a sudden lane change or with a hard brake, but on a night like this where there could be ice, it was just too dangerous. She slowed her rig as fast as was safe, but she hadn't started soon enough. With a crashing whomp the big rig hit, the sounds of crunching metal joining a hideously loud yip, then a set of hard thumps as the animal passed underneath Bertha's wheels.

"Fucknuggets!" Jill swore, bringing the rig to a stop. Not only was the inevitable damage going to be expensive as hell to fix, but in the split second before impact Jill had identified the thing: it was an enormous wolf! She wasn't sure what the laws around killing the things were in Montana, but she was sure she was going to have to report this in. The delay on top of repairs was going to murder the already slim profit margin on this run.

She unbuckled and moved to get out, but paused, thinking. The thing had looked awful mean, maybe even rabid, and where there was one wolf there could be more. She twisted around in her seat and reached for her gun rack, choosing the 12-gauge shotgun. It was the work of a moment to get the shells out from under the passenger seat and load it up.

Jill jumped from the cab, and her boots hit the pavement with a dull crunch. The night was silent, save for Bertha's rumbling idle. Twin pools of headlight-lit asphalt and the full moon overhead provided just enough light to see by. She made her way to the front of the truck and groaned. The damage was worse than she'd expected, with the whole grille caved in. It looked bad enough that, if she was unlucky, there might be damage to the radiator too.

She was about to curse again but instead froze in place. A sense of dread squeezed her stomach and she brought the shotgun to her shoulder, spinning around. A faint noise reached her ears, shooting primal fear through her before her conscious mind deciphered what it was: a growl, a shuffle, something dragging itself towards her. She stepped sideways with care, gun held tight in her hands, trying to get a clear line of sight past Bertha.

A dozen yards away, the wolf was still alive! Head twisted to the side with an eye ripped out, all its limbs broken, and compound fractures popping shards of bone through skin, but alive and dragging itself towards her, growling. There was fire trickling from its jaws, boiling the blood that flowed alongside it into a crackling brown sludge.

A notification popped up in front of Jill, hovering above the creature. Thankfully, this one was faint enough that Jill could see through it.

Lesser Firewolf, Level 12
Status: Maimed

Jill stared at it in shock for a single second before her American instincts kicked in. Her shotgun roared as she poured lead into the beast, pulling the chamber and racking a new round as fast as she could, over and over. The third blast caved in its skull with a splatter of gore and flame. Another blue box bloomed in her sight.

Lesser Firewolf defeated. Bonus experience awarded for: monster kill above your level (+1.2); monster kill significantly above your level (x2); World First monster kill (+1).
7680 Experience Gained!
World First monster kill: 1 Perk Point gained!
Class upgrade required to proceed.

"What. The. FUCK!"

CHAPTER 2

SYSTEM INSISTENT

She stared at the dead wolf, shotgun going slack in her hands. She'd killed plenty of game animals; any woman who grew up in a hunting family did, and her father and brothers were rabid hunters. But she'd never seen anything quite like this. The animals she'd killed had been with a single humane shot, maybe two if she'd messed up the first. The animals went down clean and quick, and there was a certain respect to it even if she didn't really go in for the full spiritualism business.

There was nothing clean about when she hit animals with Bertha head-on though. The last time she'd hit a deer it had, well, exploded. Meat, blood, and partially digested grass splattered everywhere and did a couple grand in damage to the front. A big deer could maybe survive if she clipped it but only at very low speeds. This had been no low-speed hit: the damn wolf had thrown itself at Bertha like it was going to chew through the engine block. No normal animal could have possibly survived the impact.

Jill brought her shotgun back to ready and stepped closer. Sticky looking fire kept leaking from the wolf's mouth in a way that just couldn't happen.

When she got within a few feet another box popped into her vision:

Collect loot?

"What the ass does that mean?"

> System Inquiry detected.
> Loot is a physical reward generated by the System from monsters, related to their physical body or elemental affinity.
> Collect loot?

"My drug trip is listening to me huh? Freaky."

> System Inquiry detected.
> The System observes all events at all times.
> Collect loot?

"Aaarg!" she waved away the box. The messages couldn't be real, they just couldn't. But there was some sort of crazy magic fire wolf dead in front of her, and she really didn't feel drugged. She felt like it was midnight on a cold night, that she was stressed out of her mind, and that the smell of gore might just make her puke. She took a deep breath in, then out. She needed to be calm. Calm like getting home after a two-week hauling route. Calm like the dawn breaking over the desert on a drive east.

> Collect loot?

"For fuck's sake, I'm trying to meditate here! Fine, collect the loot!"

A golden light pulsed over the wolf's body and condensed into a glowing red gem, which flew over to land at Jill's feet. The fire in the wolf's mouth went out. With a trembling hand she reached down to pick up the gem; it was hot to the touch and flashes of fire sparkled in its depths. Her hand clenched involuntarily around it, knuckles white.

"It's real," she whispered. "The stupid messages are real." She stumbled, leaning hard against Bertha to keep herself upright. Her truck was slick and sticky. "Oh, goddamnit!" she said, recoiling in disgust from the wolf's splattered blood, now all over her side. That was real too.

"Ok, fine. Fine! I can deal with this," she said. "I've dealt with every other shitty thing! You, System! Tell me what the fuck is going on."

> System information inquiry detected.
> Direct infusion granted. Standby.

"The fuck's that supposed to—"

Jill screamed and clutched her head, her shotgun clattering to the pavement, as information slammed into her mind.

The system was the end of life as humanity knew it: the coming of magic, filled with wonder and death. Monsters were coming, both mutated animals like the lesser firewolf she'd killed and stranger things coalesced from raw mana. Infused with magic, they wouldn't obey any natural laws that humans knew of. They would be faster, stronger, and tougher, with powers over the elements or even stranger things. That's why the wolf had survived a dead-on impact with a tractor trailer at speed: its hide and bones were infused with mana, making them supernaturally tough. While some would act like the animals humanity was familiar with, others would be driven only to consume and destroy. In places where mana was denser, the monsters would come faster and be more powerful, able to effortlessly kill pre-system humans who lacked any magic power.

And the difference between pre- and post-system humans would be extreme. Anyone who gained enough mana inside of them would be akin to a superhero—the mana transforming them just like it would the animals. But unlike animals, humans could direct their own growth and choose what the mana did to them. In order for humans to understand what was happening, the system represented the impact of mana with numbers. The basic statistics of a person could be summarized by three attributes—Body, Mind, and Spirit—each representing one of the ways in which mana altered someone.

"Kneegrinder, that hurt!" Jill said, her head pulsing along with her heartbeat. "What about me, what are my numbers?"

> Jill MacLeod
> Class: None   Level: 0
> HP: 70/70   MP: 90/90   XP: 7680/0
> Body: 7   Mind: 4   Spirit: 9
> Conditions: None
> Class Powers: None

Jill's eyes narrowed as she read her stats. "Great, magic is calling me dumb. Screw you too, System," she said. After a few seconds with no reply, she looked over the rest and focused on the word "class." "I saw that before, you asking about a class. What are they? Oh, and could you not—"

System information inquiry detected.
Direct infusion granted. Standby.

"Balls!" she yelled, as a new spike of pain slammed into her head.

Mana didn't change humans randomly. Instead there was a direction, a purpose, to the magic that made the abilities a person gained work together. In the system, this was represented by a class, which determined both how their attributes would increase as they gained levels and also what "class powers" they could learn. But not all classes were created equal—the same amount of mana was able to boost one person more than another if it was used more effectively. It wasn't easy to get a powerful class though: one had to meet the right conditions so that the mana would form correctly. The system itself could help, but it cost rare "perk points" to do so.

Jill wasn't really a fan of video games, but her various friends over the years had liked them. "This is more than just damn numbers. Why is this so much like a game?"

System information inquiry detected.
Information denied. Classified access request has been logged.

Jill snorted. "Real fucking useful. Tell me about—"

The sound of a piercing scream killed the rest of what she was going to say, as fear plunged a hand inside her chest to squeeze her heart. A pair of round eyes, glowing green, appeared in the darkness. Something was looking at her.

CHAPTER 3

A DEERING ESCAPE

The shakes started with Jill's hands, but they didn't stay there. Before she knew it, she was trembling in a way she hadn't since she was a little girl seeing her first horror film. Fear came from those green eyes. Fear that held her close in its arms and told her that her end would be painful and slow.

A small fluffy doe stepped into Bertha's headlights.

Fear Deer, Level 4
Status: Deer Fear (Active)

"Y-y-you've got to be shitting me," Jill stammered out, fighting her own body for control. It was a normal looking deer, not a gigantic fire breathing monstrosity—she shouldn't be this afraid. But those eyes, those terrible eyes.

It took a single step closer, then another. Slowly, carefully placing its hooves as if walking on unstable rocks instead of solid earth, the monster stalked closer to the petrified Jill. She mustered her willpower, waiting for the right moment. It needed to be close, but not in biting range. Thirty feet. Twenty. Ten feet! Jill pushed through her fear and did what her family joked she had trained her whole life to do: scream obscenities.

"SHITASSMOTHERFU—" was as far as she got before the deer jumped. It landed in a tangle of hooves, broke eye contact, and the illusion of fear shattered. Jill staggered away from it, the sudden shock of being back in control hitting her like a punch to the gut, and scrambled to pick up her gun. Just as she grabbed it, the deer's hooves slammed her in the back, sending her face first into the pavement. The monster screamed in triumph, a multi-chorded shriek of victory, but Jill had managed to keep the shotgun in her hands.

"Celebrated too early, Asshat McGee!" she yelled, twisting to line up the shot while still on the ground. The deer lunged to bite her, its lips bared to reveal a mouth of serrated fangs that had no business being in an herbivore. Jill's shotgun roared into the night; a solitary shot to save her life. The Fear Deer's scream cut short in an instant: its head had been blown clean off, severed at the neck. Its heart must have kept beating for a few seconds because a shower of blood spurted out of the falling body to coat Jill from head to thigh in sticky red liquid.

Fear Deer defeated. Bonus experience awarded for: monster kill above your level (+0.4); monster kill significantly above your level (x2).
1120 Experience Gained!
Class upgrade required to proceed.

Jill lay panting on the ground—hot blood steaming on her in the cold night air, heart pounding against her ribs—staring at the monster corpse. The box said it was dead, and its head was lying three feet from its body. That was good enough. She let her head fall back against the pavement and willed her breathing to slow.

"Ugg, this is so fucking gross," she mumbled, focusing on the sound of her own voice rather than her pounding heart, or the blood seeping through her clothes. "That fight wasn't too bad. Just some mental voodoo shit to make me piss myself. I wasn't in any real danger. Yeah. I'm fine." She was lying, but didn't care. Some part of her knew without checking that her hit points had dropped by six, to sixty-four, when the deer had struck her. Some of the mana inside of her had been spent to shield her from the worst of the damage, though she still felt a wicked bruise forming. The number ticked up to sixty-five. It seemed that it regenerated quickly, at least, even if the protection it offered wasn't perfect.

Her heartbeat slowed bit by bit, and the frantic pounding settled to a steady rhythm. Jill started shivering—not from fear, but from cold. No matter how pretty the stars above her were, or how much she needed to process what had happened to her, lying wet on the ground on a cold night wasn't the time or place to do it.

She stood, using her shotgun as a prop in a way that would make her dad lecture her about proper firearms care if he found out. The thought of him made her worry for his safety, what with there being actual monsters appearing, but she dismissed it into a locked corner of her mind. He had enough guns to outfit an infantry battalion and the basement of his upstate New York house was practically a survival bunker. She should be more worried about herself than him.

It was time to get back in Bertha and get the hell away. Where there was one deer there were often others, and she had no intention of finding out if they had become monsters too. She eyed the deer corpse warily, then took a step closer. She had gotten an obviously magical gem from the firewolf, so she figured it was worth seeing what the deer would give too.

"Hey system, loot this assclown."

Golden light pulsed over the deer, whose skin peeled off without shedding a drop of blood, revealing muscles, tendons, and organs underneath. The skin hovered a few feet in the air, stretching and morphing until it was an even rectangle three by six feet in size. It rolled itself into a neat cylinder and fell to the ground.

"Wild," Jill muttered, picking up the bundle of what felt like supple, fully cured leather. She almost unrolled it to inspect it further but stopped herself. Distractions like that seemed a good way to get eaten, and not in a good way. She turned and strode back to her truck.

Bertha was still idling away, but the throaty rumble of the big diesel engine wasn't as smooth as it should have been. Jill scowled as she looked at the damage done to the front of the truck and hoped that the radiator wasn't damaged. Worse than that potential problem, though, was that two of the tires on the right side of the trailer were starting to go flat. Luckily, they were on different axles, and she wasn't running with a heavy load—with a little luck, she'd be fine making it to somewhere safe she could do repairs.

She paused before climbing up into the truck, wiping her hands on her jeans in a futile effort to stop from smearing blood everywhere. It didn't work: her pants were just as bloody as her hands. She gave a long sigh, resigning herself to a hefty detailing job later, and climbed up to sit in the driver's seat with a viscous squelch. Her eyes tracked over the various gauges with practiced ease as she made sure that Bertha was ready to go, then eased the truck into gear.

A glance in the side mirror showed dozens of glowing green eyes.

All thoughts of going easy on Bertha to save the remaining tires went out of Jill's mind and she hit the gas, hard. The deer charged and for a few gut-clenching seconds they gained on her, their bounding leaps accelerating them faster than what a loaded semi-truck could manage. But it wasn't long until Bertha's roaring engine won out, and the monsters fell behind.

Moments turned to minutes, and Jill lost sight of the deer. If they were still chasing her, they were too far away to see. She eased up on the gas, letting Bertha slow down to ordinary highway speeds. The familiar sounds of engine and tire noise, and the sight of a dark road lit by headlights with stars overhead, were so commonplace to her that if it weren't for all the gore—for the hot gem sitting in her pocket and the rolled up hide on the passenger seat—Jill would have been able to pretend that nothing had happened.

But she couldn't. Magic and monsters were real, and she had almost died. She chewed on her lip. She couldn't be the only one who'd had crazy things happen to her; maybe someone else would know what the hell was going on. She flicked on the CB radio. A panicked voice crackled through the speaker.

"—out there?!? We need help, please! Can anyone hear us?!? Oh, God, they just keep coming!"

CHAPTER 4

SCOOT AND SHOOT

Jill snatched up the mic to her radio and pushed the talk button.

"This is Junkmouth. I hear you," she said. "I'm putting the hammer down eastbound on 90, right off the pass, with a rack full of guns. Where are you?"

"We're nearby, not far past Bozeman!" said a young man's voice. The signal was weak, with static rising and falling, but Jill could hear thumping and shrieking in the background. "Please, help! There's a whole swarm of things attacking us, and I don't know how much longer we can hold out."

Jill scowled, left hand tightening involuntarily on the wheel. One monster she could handle, especially if she got the drop on it from fifty yards away. Two or three would be dangerous, but if she stayed in her cab she would have cover. A whole swarm would be deadly.

"Hang tight, good buddy," she said. "I'm on my way."

She had to go that direction anyways, so she might as well help.

Jill pressed the accelerator all the way down but had to let up just a few seconds later when the normally smooth roar of Bertha's engine stuttered, losing acceleration. There was definitely something wrong with the engine, some sort of damage that was getting worse, but none of the gauges showed any obvious problems. She was enough of a mechanic to do basic fixes on the road; if the old girl died on her, she might be able to get the engine running again, but that would take time—time she doubted the stranded people had.

She crested the next ridge, and her high beams swept from heaven to earth, lighting up a desperate scene less than a half mile away. On the side of a long straightaway, crashed into a tree just off the road, was a twenty-foot U-Haul truck with its emergency lights flashing. Jill made out two people on the roof and at least two dozen small, four-legged, dog-sized creatures scrabbling to climb on top.

Jill gave a single snort of amusement as one tried to jump and only made it a few feet off the ground before falling onto its face, and she relaxed. They didn't seem very threatening, not compared to giant Fire-wolves or terrifying murder deer. Then her amusement died. Bertha's lights reflected just right, revealing that the creatures had massive teeth, oversized to the point of sticking out past both jaws.

A monster scrambled onto the hood and lunged, open mouth leading the way, but was driven back as one of the men swung an actual sword at it, slicing into its snout. It crouched, looking to lunge again, but a burst of fire from the other man's outstretched hand blasted it off the hood entirely.

Jill's jaw opened in shock as Bertha barreled down the hill. That had been magic not from a monster, but from a person.

The mage turned towards her and frantically waved an arm above his head, his other hand rising to his mouth. Jill squinted and could just make out a cord stretched back into the cab, miraculously unharmed by teeth, sword, and flame.

"Is that you?!" his voice crackled over the radio. "I don't think we can last much longer. I'm almost out of mana, don'tcha know!"

Jill clenched her jaw. There were a lot of the creatures. Too many for her to kill quickly by shooting. "I'm gonna ram," Jill said, "and I might scrape some paint! So don't fucking fall off." She tossed the handset down and gripped the wheel with both hands, aiming tons of truck as carefully as she could. Five knuckle-clenching seconds seemed to drag on for eternity as the U-Haul and monsters grew larger in her vision. The corner of her mouth twitched up in satisfaction the instant before impact, when she realized she didn't need to adjust her steering at all.

"Choke on it, you twatwaffles!" she yelled, as Bertha slammed into the monster horde, and the truck's side passed within half a foot of the U-Haul. Shrieks and bangs assaulted her hearing, and she had to violently correct the steering as something pulled her wheel over. One monster spun into the air, crashing into the windshield with a bloody crunch. The tempered glass broke into a thousand shards, but the adhesive center layer held firm. The window only bent inwards by a few inches—a mad spiderweb of cracks streaked red, but holding.

Jill slammed on the brakes, leaning to the side so that she could still see the road around the monster corpse. She must have killed or maimed half of the swarm, but there were still lots of monsters to go. Just before coming to a stop, she brought the wheel over hard to the left, turning the cab so that she could see the monsters out of the driver's side window. Most were still trying to climb the U-Haul, but three had broken off and were running at her instead. She reached for the seat belt release, swearing as she fumbled it, but soon enough she was free and grabbing her shotgun just as the first monster leapt at the cab door.

It didn't even make it to the window—instead, it crunched teeth first onto the metal steps. It immediately leapt again but didn't manage any better. This close, Jill could see that the dog-sized monsters were some kind of rodent with a very short tail.

Dire Lemming, Level 1
Status: Raging

"Well, that explains the stupid," she said, bringing the shotgun to her shoulder and coming to a half-standing, half-crouched, all-cramped position between the two seats. She growled as the long barrel of the shotgun got caught in the steering wheel; she really needed to saw it off if she was going to keep needing to shoot things at point blank range. She spent long seconds getting the gun ready, then reached over and clicked the window down button. The glass of the window slid down, bit by bit.

As Jill leaned over and aimed out the window, she felt strangely let down. Somehow it didn't seem sporting to shoot big mice that couldn't do anything but clunk into her door. But then her eyes flicked up to the men still fighting for their lives without the luxury of such sturdy cover.

"Fuck sporting," she said, and pulled the trigger. Three blasts, three pulped monsters. The roar of the shotgun in an enclosed space was like a hammer blow to her ears—the sounds of monsters faded and were replaced with a high squealing whine.

She shifted her aim to target the monsters clambering onto the U-Haul but hesitated before firing: the range was too long for a shotgun armed with buckshot, and she was worried about accidentally hitting humans.

"Hold your shit together just a bit longer," she thought towards the men, putting her shotgun on the passenger seat and grabbing her rifle from the gun rack. It was only chambered with a .243 Winchester cartridge for deer hunting, but the lemmings were small enough that the light round should still do the job. She braced the barrel on the edge of the window to steady her aim, but still had to be half crouched, and every shot was a spike of fresh agony in her ears. But she hadn't been raised hunting for nothing, and soon every monster lay crippled or dead.

"Who's a hero? This bitch, that's who."

CHAPTER 5

THE BROTHERS BATI

The CB radio came to life, but Jill couldn't make out what was said over the ringing of her ears. She stowed her rifle on the gun rack, then slid back into the driver's seat. She needed to get over to the men, but she sure as hell wasn't going to walk if she could drive. The road was too narrow to turn the big rig around, and her frontal visibility was blocked by the shattered windshield. But the side mirror was still there, if freckled with bits of blood and lemming brain, so Jill threw Bertha into reverse. The back-up beeps started muffled almost beyond audibility but became louder and louder as her hearing came back unnaturally fast.

As Bertha rolled even with the two men, one sitting on the edge of the roof of their U-Haul and the other on the ground giving each downed monster an extra stab with his sword, Jill felt strangely self-conscious. She had never been responsible for saving anyone's life before—dropping off a load early was nice but just not the same—and had no idea how to act. It didn't help that the man on top of the truck was improbably good looking, if thankfully not her type.

"Hey," she said with an exaggerated nod, leaning an arm against the open window. "How you boys doing?" Boys was a bit of an exaggeration, but they looked much younger than her, possibly as young as in their early twenties. The family resemblance between the two of them was written across their faces, but the swordsman was less pretty. What he lacked in looks he made up for in muscles.

The swordsman stared at her with a funny expression on his face. The mage started laughing. "We're surrounded by dead monsters, you're absolutely coated in blood, and it's the end of the world as we know it!" he said. While he looked like he could be from New Delhi, his accent was pure Midwest. He slid off the truck's roof and landed with an easy grace, then picked his way between corpses to get nearer to her. He grinned. "So, you know, just another Tuesday."

"Ignore my brother, please, and thanks for the rescue. I'm Ras Bati," the swordsman said, "and he's Babu. And—ope! One's still alive!" He surged forward and stabbed one last creature that had been dragging itself suicidally onwards with charred stumps of legs.

Dire Lemming (x31) defeated. Bonus experience awarded for: monster kill above your level (+0.1); monster kill significantly above your level (x2).

Your contribution: 60%

4092 Experience Gained!

Class upgrade required to proceed.

"Oh!" Babu cried out. "We let our guard down too early."

"You let your guard down too early," Ras said. "I was ready."

"Bullshit you were! Always acting like you're better..."

Jill just watched, a half-smile on her face, as the two brothers started to argue, each barb louder than the last. The bickering reminded her of her own family and it was oddly soothing; a bit of normalcy to settle the crazy things that were happening. A surge of panic flashed through her guts when fond thoughts of her family turned to worry about whether they were still okay, but she pushed the feeling away. There was nothing she could do from here, and—she checked again—her cell phone was still dead. She'd make her way east, but for now there was no use worrying.

The silence of the brothers putting their bickering on hold startled Jill out of her thoughts. While she'd been thinking, the brothers had stopped talking and were looking at her expectantly.

"Shitbags, I was miles away," Jill said. "What was that?"

"I asked what your name was. You called yourself, uh, Junkmouth?" Babu asked, sides of his mouth twitching. "Seems about right. . ."

Ras shot his brother a dirty look and seemed to be about to tell him off, but Jill spoke before he could say anything. "You're damn fuckin' right it is. The name's Jill MacLeod, owner and operator of Highlander Shipping, and this here," she banged a hand on the door, "is Bertha."

Ras wiped off his sword and tucked it through a sash around his waist. "I hate to ask more of you, but do you think you could give us a ride?"

Jill shrugged. "Better that than let the monsters get you. Your ride died on you?" she asked, nodding at the U-Haul.

"Yup," Babu said. "Right after the system initialized the engine went dead. Even the brakes stopped working! We coasted off the road and then, well, tree."

Jill slapped Bertha again. "That's what you get for using a dinky little rental instead of something reliable!" Bertha chose that moment for her engine to start choking, nearly stalling out, and Jill had to give her a bit of gas to keep it going. "Cockpile!" she swore over the noise. "Look, I can drive you for a while but no guarantees. Where are you heading?"

"We were going out to Butte," Babu said, wiggling his eyebrows. "I had a gig there, don'tcha know. But," he glanced at Ras with a worried look and got a nod in return, "we need to get back to Billings. For family."

"Then hop on in. Oh!" Jill said. "You should grab some of your shit too. I've got some room in the trailer and I need to check out the engine anyways." She reached under the steering column and pulled on the hood release.

The brothers thanked her again and walked back to their U-Haul, an argument soon breaking out about what things to bring and what to leave behind, potentially forever. Jill didn't pay much attention, but after climbing down from the cab she walked to the back of her truck and opened the rear doors of the trailer for them. It was four-fifths full, stacked with palettes of dry and canned food being hauled to a supermarket whose regular shipper had needed to hire Jill as a subcontractor on short notice. Jill scowled. With monsters around, everything was about to go to complete shit. She really hoped she was going to get paid for this run.

Getting the hood up to look at the engine was an ordeal. First, she had to slide a monsterized lemming body off of it, which wasn't too bad even if it got even more blood on her. But the night's repeated collisions had done a number on Bertha's bodywork, and something had bent in the wrong way and jammed. Luckily, she had a repair kit with a crowbar, and it was only a few minutes of prying and swearing to finally free the stuck hood. It hinged forward and up with a squeal.

The engine, rumbling away with an unhealthy broken rhythm that was getting louder each passing minute, seemed physically fine. There were no obvious breaks or fluid leaks, no clogged intakes, no pinched hoses, and all the belts still moved freely. Jill drummed the fingers of one hand on her leg. If she didn't know better, she'd say that the cylinders were suffering from compression failure and misfiring, but she'd had the engine serviced only three weeks before. Mechanically they wouldn't wear out that fast and the electronics controlling the fuel and injector timings were rated for years more.

"Talk to me, old girl," Jill said, putting a hand on her truck. "I'm gonna take good care of you, like always, but you need to tell me what's wrong."

The engine gave one last misfiring bang, then ground to a stop.

CHAPTER 6

KERSNAP

For the first time in as long as she could remember, Jill was running out of swears. She'd spent the last hour poking, prodding, and tweaking parts of Bertha's engine, but nothing she did got the big motor running again. Not only that, but she couldn't even figure out what was wrong in the first place; despite the multiple monster impacts, the engine's internals seemed fine. Every attempted fix and diagnosis proven wrong elicited a new shouted obscenity, and if it weren't for the rapid healing granted by the system, she would have shouted herself hoarse. Whatever power was healing her throat did nothing for her mental energy or mood though.

"Motherbescumber?" she tried, but it didn't have any conviction in it.

"Wow. What does that one mean? Where did you even hear it?" Babu asked with wonder in his voice. He and Ras had finished moving everything they thought worth saving from their dead U-Haul to Bertha after about ten minutes. While Ras had climbed onto the trailer's roof to act as a lookout, Babu was acting as Jill's assistant, handing her tools and trying to keep up with her language. He had also conjured a small ball of white sparkly light, which hovered above the engine to provide visibility. Ordinarily Jill might have been more curious about such blatant magic, but she was too wrung out to care.

"My dad got me one of those word-a-day calendars, only for weird swears and shit. It's. . . ," she said, then shook her head. "You know what, you don't want to know." She sighed and wiped her hand, now covered with grease instead of blood, on her pants. "I can't tell what's wrong with Bertha, but she's not going anywhere."

"Sorry. I know you and she were . . . close," Babu said, giving his eyebrows a waggle.

Jill blinked. "What?"

"I'm just saying, you've been slipping in and out of her every day for years now, right?"

"Are you making a joke? Because you're just pissing me off."

"The feel of Bertha's hard gear shift in the morning, the growl of turning her on. . ."

"Shut your . . . you . . . Fuck!" Jill spluttered, glaring at the grinning man. "Go get your brother, assface!" He was obviously just trying to cheer her up, and she did feel a bit better. But she wasn't about to admit it.

Babu stuck two fingers in his mouth and blew a piercing whistle, then leaned closer so that he could whisper to Jill. "He absolutely hates when I do that, because he can't."

Ras appeared on the edge of the trailer, looking down at Babu with a scowl. "Are you trying to call every monster in ten miles with that? What is it?"

"Told you," Babu muttered to Jill.

"Bertha won't start," Jill said, ignoring Babu. "I can't offer you two that ride after all."

Ras hopped lightly down and Jill couldn't help but stare. The top of her truck was thirteen feet off the ground—way too high to jump casually down from without some major padding to land on. At least not for ordinary humans. Already the swordsman had enough magic in him to push him beyond that limit. From the flash of satisfaction on Ras's face it seemed like the swordsman had the same thought.

"It's a long way to the nearest town," Ras said. "And a lot of monsters must be in the way too." He idly gripped his sword and turned to his brother. "You've got magic now. Can you get a spell to fix things?"

"Let me check," Babu said. His expression grew distant and his eyes flicked back and forth as he read through system screens visible to him alone. "No," he said after a tense minute, "at least not for a long time. It looks like the enchanter's spells are mostly evocation, illusion, and mind based. There isn't very much for objects."

"Sugar," Ras said, real feeling behind the word.

Jill refrained from mocking him for his grandma curse. "I can't even figure out what's wrong with her," she said. "When did you say your ride broke? Right after the system started? It must be magic that's breaking shit. Everything's fucked since those blue boxes started popping up."

"Our cell phones died around then," Ras said.

"And my laptop's not working, though I only just checked, so I can't say when that happened," Babu said. He narrowed his eyes. "Lots of stories have magic disrupting technology. Maybe there's some truth to them."

"How come Bertha lasted so long then?" Jill asked.

"I'm not sure, but," Babu said, "she's old right? Not too many computers in her?"

"Some. She has expensive things I need to replace every few years that probably are. They're all ancient and hard to source."

"Fascinating that they lasted so long. I wonder if the larger feature size of decades old transistors hardens them against magic?" Babu said, his speech gaining in both volume and speed as he theorized.

"That doesn't help us fix her though, does it?" Jill asked. Babu deflated and shook his head.

Jill leaned her forehead against Bertha but didn't say anything. The idea of leaving the truck, her safe, powerful, faithful big rig, behind tore at her and tears welled in her eyes.

"I've got a thought," Ras said, grasping the hilt of his sword and staring at it thoughtfully. "You've been driving your truck for a long time, yeah? You have a deep, emotional connection?"

"Yeah," Jill said. "She's been, well, home more than home is for almost half my life. Backbone of my company. Pulled me out of a lot of scrapes and storms. Definitely saved my life a few times, not even counting this fucked up night." She knew Bertha was really a thing, not a she, but it was hard to feel that in her heart.

Ras nodded. "If the system is what's making everything break, maybe the system can fix it, make it better? I made my kirpan into a soulbound weapon and now it's part of my class."

Babu turned a confused look at Ras. "I thought the system just gave you a sword. Your old kirpan's like two inches long! And what do you mean," his voice turned mocking, "'deep emotional connection'?" He shook his head. "You're full of it, don'tcha know?"

"I'm more connected than you are. You couldn't even find yours," Ras said, shaking his head. "I still wear mine every day."

Jill was completely lost. "What the fuck's a kirpan?"

Babu huffed out a laugh and the anger drained out of him. "It's a tiny religious dagger that makes the TSA stick their little latex-covered fingers up our asses. Don't worry about it."

Ras grimaced, but didn't disagree. He held out his sword; it was slender and single edged, with a pronounced curve. Then it changed, shrinking in seconds to just a few inches in length. "This is what it used to look like. One of my powers lets it change between the two forms, and just by being soulbound, it will repair itself no matter what happens to it. Maybe the same thing can let you fix Bertha?"

"It's worth a shot," Jill said. "Hey, System! Tell me about soulbinding Bertha!"

System information inquiry detected.
A Soulbound object is tied to the Mana that composes your soul. It will grow as you do. Soulbound objects self-repair if they have sufficient Mana, and can be re-summoned if destroyed.
Binding an object consumes Perk Points, with cost increasing based on object size. Cost decreases based on soul compatibility.
Compatibility with object "Bertha": Extreme
Perk Point cost: 1

"You know you don't need to talk to the system thing, right?" Babu said. "Just think at it."

Jill shrugged. "It gets the job done, doesn't it?" But she thought rather than said, "System, bind Bertha to me."

Soulbinding initiated! You have lost a Perk Point.
Object class assigned: Modular Vehicle
Stand by for Mana Integration.

CHAPTER 7

RIDE SO SMOOTH

A golden pulse of light flashed over Bertha, rocking the truck sideways.

> Mana integration complete. Soulbound Modular Vehicle "Bertha" has been integrated with the following features and abilities:
> Class upgrade required to proceed.

"Woah," Babu said. "I'm guessing it worked?"

Jill nodded. "Yup," she said, her eyes fixed on Bertha's windshield. Tiny pops and pings sounded as the glass began fusing together, reforming into its original state one bit at a time. "Hell yeah! She's fixing herself." Jill grinned and punched Ras hard on the shoulder in thanks. "Nice save."

The punch didn't seem to hurt him at all and the swordsman gave a satisfied nod.

"We're back in business boys! Let's get the fuck out of here," Jill said, putting words to action and swinging herself up to the cab with renewed vigor.

There was a bit of awkwardness as the brothers climbed over her to get in instead of just going around to the other side and using the passenger door, but Jill didn't care. She was too engrossed in the changes that were happening to her truck. Mostly, they were repairs. Small dents and dings from decades of hard use, and grime and stains that resisted her cleaning efforts, all faded away. The leather seats were plush and perfect, no hint remaining of the gore Jill must have ground into them over the course of the night. The steering wheel was unmarred, the patches of bare metal that her hands had etched over the years gone, but replaced by indentations that fit her grip perfectly. Even the air was fresh and clean—like new truck smell, only better. Jill twisted around to look at the tiny living area behind the seats. The bed stretching the width of the cab had been adequate enough before, but now it looked positively inviting.

"Shotgun!" Babu called out, slipping past Ras and claiming the passenger seat for himself.

Ras looked around awkwardly and gestured at the bed. "Would it be okay if I. . . ," he trailed off, face flushing, and his gaze not meeting Jill's eyes.

"Where else are you going to sit?" Jill replied.

Babu started gleefully taunting Ras over his "innocent maidenhood," but Jill wasn't paying attention. Bertha's cosmetic repairs were one thing—actually turning on the engine was another. She reached for the ignition but froze when she didn't find a keyhole. Instead, there was a covered switch with a simple *On* and *Off* written under the label *Mana Engine*. No option to turn on the glow plugs or block heater at all.

"Huh," Jill said, looking over the dashboard for more changes. The speedometer was still there, but everything else was either gone or different. The gearshift had no numbers marked on it anymore, instead just having *Forward*, *Neutral*, *Reverse*, and *Park*. The fuel indicator looked much the same, except it was now labeled *Mana Reserve* and, while nearly empty, it was rising by the second. Where the tachometer had been was a gauge labeled *Mana Consumption*, its needle bouncing just off of the zero point, each bounce coinciding with the sound of a metallic ping announcing Bertha's repair of some other bit of body damage. On the consumption gauge was an additional needle labeled *Mana Regeneration* hovering about halfway through the gauge's range.

Jill lifted up the engine switch's cover, then flipped it to *On*. The mana consumption needle immediately rose, but was still far below regeneration. Instead of the usual growling rumble of a big diesel engine, Jill could feel a slight, but powerful, bass hum in her bones. The quiet would certainly make talking easier, even if she would miss the old familiar sounds. She pressed down on the accelerator just a bit, and the truck eased forward, the smooth acceleration reminding her of that of an electric car. Ras and

Babu stopped their arguing as she picked up speed, leveling off at eighty miles per hour.

"Fuck yeah!" Jill said. "Look at that!" She pointed at the mana consumption, which was sitting moderately below regeneration. "We're at speed and the tank's still filling up. Hell, other than switching drivers, we'll never need to stop!" She winked at Babu. "It's not magic, but I could get used to this system shit."

"Everything is labeled 'mana'," Babu said, "it's definitely magic. Now," he shifted his weight forward, excitement in his eyes, "you have got to tell me what class powers this gave you! Ras won't tell me."

"It's personal," Ras said, his tone flat and final. He had stretched out on the bed and had his eyes closed.

"It can't be that personal," Babu said, "you just don't want to share your toys."

"Boys!" Jill snapped, interrupting what she could tell was going to be another spat. "I've been meaning to ask you two: how did you get your classes? What's up with them? The boxes keep telling me I need to upgrade mine."

"I looked through the list right after the system integrated," Ras said. "A box listed the different options I could pick and swordsman looked like the best one, a common class instead of a basic one, which Babu swears is better. After I bound my kirpan, my spirit gain per level increased by one, and it got its own set of powers."

"That puts him at just under uncommon classes for total stat gain, or at least just under mine," Babu said. "I picked right at integration too but got offered enchanter, which is uncommon. I had to spend my perk point on it but," he shrugged, "I got magic! Did you, uhh, not read your list?"

"I was driving."

"Yeah, Ras was too," Babu said. "So?"

"Jesus's taint, your fucking generation," Jill said. "Those boxes are worse than goddamn texting, popping up right in the middle of everything. No wonder you crashed into a tree."

"The truck died first!"

"Suuuuure," Jill said, drawing the word out. She did believe Babu, and the man hadn't even been the one driving at the time, but he was fun to tease. She could see why Ras did it so much.

"So, you don't have a class yet?" Ras asked. "I can drive to let you read through everything, but you should really get one. The stat gains alone . . . well, they're worth it."

Jill hesitated. Driving a big rig wasn't as easy as people thought it was, especially when monsters might pop out at any moment and try to eat your bumper. Then again, Bertha was handling smoother than ever now that she ran on mana, and there weren't any gears to worry about grinding. Plus, as long as they survived, the truck would fix itself after a crash.

Babu nodded. "You definitely should. And tell me what your stat gains end up being! I've tried to ask the system for more details but it only gives basic info, nothing to plan a build around."

"Alright then, let's do it," Jill said. "Ras, get up here." She brought Bertha to a smooth stop and unbuckled. Jill looked meaningfully at Babu, then at the bed.

"I called shotgun though," he said, but quailed under Jill's unimpressed look and gave up the seat to her.

"Ok, crash course," Jill said to Ras. "Don't fucking crash. If something smaller than an elephant steps in front of the truck hit the brakes, but don't you dare swerve out of the way or we could jackknife. I have no idea how fast the old girl can go now but eighty seemed safe. Get it?"

"Got it."

"Good," Jill said. She took a big breath in, then let it out in a rush. Time to see what this magic bullshit had in store for her, and what she could do with it. "System! Show me my classes!"

CHAPTER 8

REAL CLASSY

A blue box appeared.

> You have reached Level 0! Select a class to proceed to Level 1!

> Classes available:

> Uncommon Classes:
> Battle Trucker (++)
> Malediction Bard
> Shotgun Slayer

> Common Classes:
> Gunsmith
> Huntress
> Mechanic
> Riflewoman
> Trucker
> …

"Hey Babu," Jill said, looking away from the blue box. "Uncommon classes are better than common right?" That was what her system-granted knowledge from earlier was telling her, but she wanted to check. He seemed to have studied this a lot more than she had after all, even if it had only been a few hours since integration.

"Yup, if you get one that does what you want. They give better stat gains, at least, but I don't know about class powers. Hey, tell me what you get, okay? I'm going to put a database together."

If Jill was being honest with herself, she already knew which class she'd be taking, but she decided to look at malediction bard anyways, just in case.

Malediction Bard (Uncommon)

The art of self-expression can be a beautiful thing. Or, in your case, very much not. Your invectives have gained a supernatural power to harm and intimidate your foes. Perhaps you study the ancient blasphemies of the Lower Realms, or you simply delight in loudly breaking taboos, but your searing words spare no one. Your Class Powers improve your spellcasting, your performances, and your ability to insult others.

Requirements:

Have an extensive knowledge of, and frequently use, obscenities.

Use the power of your obscenities to help defeat an enemy significantly above your level.

Body per level: 1

Mind per level: 2

Spirit per level: 3

"No fucking way!" Jill said. "You've got to see this." She almost commanded the system out loud again, but caught herself. "System," she thought, "send this class to Babu and Ras."

There was a moment of silence. "It's official," Ras said, eyes forward and hands in the ten and two position. "As dictated by the system, you swear way too much."

"Or just enough," Jill cackled.

"'Defeat an enemy significantly above your level'," Babu quoted. "Aw schnookers, we should have waited before picking our classes, shouldn't we have?"

"If we had, we'd be dead," Ras said. "Lemming swarm."

"Jill survived."

"I had a shotgun," Jill said, "and the first monster that jumped me was a fire breathing wolf the size of a horse that I only killed because this metal lady," she thumped the wall, "weighs forty tons."

"Ok," Babu admitted, "maybe we would have been in trouble. But, shit, you'd have gotten an uncommon class, and I might have not needed to spend my perk point! We missed a lot of optimization."

"Lemming. Swarm."

Jill interrupted yet another fight before it could begin. "Hey Babu, I'm sending you over all my commons and basics. Have fun. I'm not going to bother looking at them." She gave the command to the system, including sending over battle trucker and shotgun slayer, then opened up the obvious choice to read for herself.

Battle Trucker (Uncommon ++)

Most cargo drivers never see combat; you relish it. Perhaps you are a member of a military logistics battalion with a heroic streak, or a star-trader chasing pirates, but you pilot your cargo vehicle bravely into the fray against overwhelming enemies. Your Class Powers improve vehicles you drive, your business dealings, and your combat power.

Requirements:

Extensively pilot a vehicle whose primary focus is transporting goods or personnel.

Defeat an enemy significantly above your level while piloting a cargo vehicle.

(+) Enhancement Requirement: Fulfill base requirements 10 times over.

Bonus to Class Power effectiveness.

(+) Enhancement Requirement: Have a Soulbound cargo vehicle.

Bonus to Spirit points gained per level.

Class Powers that boost vehicles are restricted to Soulbound vehicle.

Bonus to Class Powers that boost Soulbound vehicle.

Body per level: 2

Mind per level: 2

Spirit per level: 2+1

"Well, yeah, that's obviously me. Has bonuses too," Jill said. "I'm going to pick battle trucker."

"Wait! Just wait a second!" Babu said. "You could totally change who you are! You have options for almost anything here. You could be a crafter, or a caster, or a doomguy with a shotgun!"

Jill raised an eyebrow at the man. "Why would I want to change who I am? Something wrong with hauling freight?"

"N-No, but . . . I just," he said, "I just thought you'd want to give it more thought."

"Sure." She paused for half a second. "Thinking done. Time for magic trucker powers."

Class Upgraded to Battle Trucker!
You are now Level 1!
Applying deferred experience.
You are now Level 5!

Heat rushed through Jill's body, filling every inch of her from head to toe. Her muscles grew firmer, her back pain disappeared; all the aches that a woman in her forties, in a physically demanding job, had collected were gone in an instant. Her senses sharpened, and an awareness of the world around her exploded into her mind, but rather than be overwhelmed she simply absorbed it all without trouble. The slight heavy feeling in the air that she'd been noticing all night she suddenly understood to be the presence of mana. It swirled and flowed and pressed against her as if she were underwater in a current, but at the same time it didn't, because that was but a poor metaphor for a much greater truth that her still nascent soul couldn't comprehend. In the center of that flow was a channel connecting her to Bertha, who in her soul's eye was a part of her, but at the same time not. An object but also a soul.

"That is fucking trippy as shit," Jill said. "So much better than LSD, and I feel wicked awesome instead of just hungry. Was it the same for you?"

"Not for me," Ras said. "But I only gain one in mind and two in spirit each level, don'tcha know, so it was more like instant workout gains. Babu got weird."

Surprisingly this didn't start an argument. "Yup," Babu said. "Four spirit per level for me is a rush!"

Jill decided to check her status and see exactly what she'd gained.

Jill MacLeod
Class: Battle Trucker   Level: 5
HP: 170/170   MP: 240/240   XP: 12,892/15,000
Body: 17   Mind: 14   Spirit: 24
Conditions: None
Class Powers: None
5 points available to assign.
(+) Bonus to Class Power effectiveness.
(+) Bonus to Class Powers that boost Soulbound vehicle.

"Heh," she said, eyes flickering back and forth as she read her status. "Lightweights. Try five levels all at one—"

Jill was interrupted by a loud crash and a jolt, followed by the distinct feeling of something large passing under the wheels. "What the fuck, Ras?" she said, closing her status and glaring at the man, who didn't even have the decency to look embarrassed. "I told you not to hit shit!"

"It was a monster smaller than an elephant," Ras said. A few crinkling pops sounded from the front bumper and hood as they repaired themselves; the mana consumption gauge crept up.

Fear Deer defeated.
Your contribution: 15%
75 Experience Gained!

"I guess it was," Jill said. She grinned. "Nice kill, I hate those fucking things."

Babu tilted his head. "You got a notice about it? What were the numbers?"

"Here, see for yourself." Jill ordered the system to send the box over. "Last time I got bonuses to experience for it being over my level, I think? Not this time though."

"Ras, how about you?" Babu asked, a fire in his eyes.

"Eighty-five percent contribution. There was a boost from the level difference for five hundred eighty-five total." He grinned. "I'm almost at a new level."

Babu nodded in excitement. "Coolcoolcool!" he said, tapping his fingers together rapidly. He started muttering to himself under his breath, phrases like "optimal grinding strategy," "aggro tank," and "buff the striker while kiting?" escaping from his mouth in irregular intervals.

"What's he talking about?" Jill asked Ras.

Ras shrugged. "He's trying to figure the whole thing out, treating it like one of his games. But life's not a game, so it's a waste of time."

Jill glanced back, expecting Babu to explode at Ras again, but the enchanter was so wrapped up in his thinking that he didn't seem to have heard. "Little harsh there?" she asked Ras.

He shrugged again. "I could be wrong. Either way, he's not paying attention to the here and now."

Jill didn't answer. If anything, she was thinking too much about what was right in front of her, stubbornly refusing to think about whether her family and friends were doing alright or if they'd been killed. If Babu's theorizing was akin to her focus on doing, on pushing forward to the next step on her journey back home, well, was that really so wrong? Figuring out how to game the system could help them all survive.

She shook her head. Enough with the introspection. Time to open up her class powers and see how they would help.

Available Class Powers:
Hold Together - Active - Spell
Repairs 1400 Durability's worth of damage and increases physical and elemental Resistances by 14% for Soulbound Modular Vehicle "Bertha" for 1 minute.
Cost: 10 Mana

A Deal's a Deal - Active - Spell
The next agreement you enter becomes a System Contract. The other party must be of sound mind to enter into a System Contract. If the other party breaks the Contract, they will receive a Penalty of 12% that lasts for 1 System year. You may waive the Penalty at any time.
Cost: 100 Mana

> Battle Hardened - Passive
> Increase physical, elemental, and mental Resistances by 12%.

> Soulbound Powers:
> Various. See Status of Soulbound Modular Vehicle "Bertha"

Jill read through her available class powers, frowned, and read them again. She felt like she got the general idea, though the only thing she could truly understand without more context was how the mana costs compared to her own pool: "Hold Together" she'd be able to cast very often, though she didn't know whether 1400 durability was a lot, while "A Deal's a Deal" would drain almost half of her mana. For the rest, she'd best get more information.

"System," she thought, "what are resistances? And penalties?"

> System information inquiry detected.
> Resistances reduce incoming damage. Only the highest Resistance applies, with exceptions that apply multiplicatively.
> Penalties reduce the effective value of all Statistics. Penalties apply additively and combine, with exceptions.

That helped somewhat, but she could understand why Babu was so insistent about compiling as much information as he could about the system. The system information messages were helpful but frustratingly light on details. Take Battle Hardened: twelve percent resistance sounded good, but was it? Or was that kind of value eclipsed by some other skill or armor that would render her class power useless? At least the system had told her only the highest value applied, so she could think of the question in the first place.

She sent the information over to Babu with a thought. "Alright theory boy, give me some thoughts on class powers. I've only got three of the things to choose from, but maybe Bertha will have some too," she said, turning to look over her shoulder at him.

"I started with three," Babu said, "but once I picked some of them more showed up. Two that I unlocked require me to be level ten before I can pick them though. I can't tell for sure yet, but I think there's multiple trees of powers for every class. I'd know more if someone," Babu glared at Ras, "would let me see his as well."

Ras clicked his tongue. "Fine," he said, "but I'm not sending any soul-bound information." He glanced at Jill. "You should look through that before you choose anything. Mine is extensive."

"Wait!" Babu was practically vibrating. "You two have almost the same skill, 'Battle Hardened,' though Rassy got shafted, and it's only worth ten percent, not twelve. Could that be your class power boost?" He whistled. "That might add up fast. Anyways, if this part of your tree is the same as his, your next skills in that line will be a magic-infused strike and something to make you faster."

"Fucking badass," Jill said. "But not for me, I don't think." She banged a hand on the dash. "I'm a truck driver first, even if I do kick ass when I have to. Hey, System! Tell me all about my kickass truck."

Soulbound Modular Vehicle "Bertha"
Durability: 24,000/24,000   Mana: 16,937/24,000
Cargo: None
Command: None
Habitation: None
Propulsion (Ground): None

Upgrades Available:
Module Upgrades
New Modules
Customization (0/2)

Jill switched to thinking rather than speaking. "Great, but there's got to be more than that, you ball-gargling excuse for a glorified office assistant. I need details!"

Cargo:
"Bertha" has a cargo bay with base volume 90.625 cubic meters, total volume 90.625 cubic meters, internal dimensions of 14.5 meters by 2.5 meters by 2.5 meters.
Includes: Doors.
Add-ons (0/1): None installed.

> Cargo Upgrades:
> Cargokinesis (0/1): Objects inside of the cargo bay and within 14 meters of the cargo bay doors can be slowly moved.
> Climate Control (0/2): Control the temperature and humidity of the cargo bay.
> Volume (0/5): The volume of the cargo bay is set to 2.4x base volume and 1 add-on slot is added.

"Yeah, that's more like—"
Another box popped up, partially overlapping the first.

> Command:
> "Bertha" has a Command Module with 1 control station and 1 observer station.
> Includes: Seat belts (rare technology), air bags (rare technology), openable windows, mirrors, doors.
> Add-ons (1/1): Close range radio.

> Command Upgrades:
> Captain Speaking (0/1): Jill MacLeod can speak to and receive replies from anyone within "Bertha" or within 14 meters.
> Sensor Upgrade (0/5): Effectiveness of any installed perception devices increased 14%.
> Capacity (0/3): Add 1 control station, 2 observer stations, and 1 Command add-on slot.

"Hey, I didn't get the chance to—"
Yet another box appeared, blocking the others. It pulsed deeper and lighter shades of blue in an insistent rhythm.

> Habitation:
> "Bertha" has a Habitation Module with capacity for 1 in substandard conditions, with life support capacity of 0.
> Warning: Habitation Module not sufficient for long term occupation.

Habitation Upgrades:
Bare Minimum (0/1): Increases the capacity of the Habitation Module to 2, life support to 4, and provides basic amenities with 1 Habitation add-on slot.

"Hey, what are you calling substandard?! You're substandard! And slow the fuck—"

The next three boxes popped up in quick succession, each strobing a new neon color.

Propulsion (Ground):
"Bertha" has an engine that converts Mana to rotary motion, which is then transmitted to wheels. Maximum speed: 250 km/h.
Add-ons (0/1): None (Chains available).

Propulsion (Ground) Upgrades:
Torque Converter (0/1): Unwanted rotation along any axis is nullified and converted into Mana. Requires Jill MacLeod to be at a control station.
Utility Wheels (0/3): Wheels function over a wider variety of terrain. Rough terrain lowers maximum speed.
Need for Speed (0/5): Increases maximum speed by 70 km/h.

New Modules Available:
Armor: Installs armor that enhances the Durability and Resistances of "Bertha." Provides Armor add-on slots.
Turrets (Small Arms): Installs turrets that protect occupants and enhance installed Small Arms add-ons.

Customization (0/2):
The cosmetic and structural configuration of "Bertha" can be slowly changed, as long as module limitations are not exceeded.

"Goddamn twistertwat assnoser!" Jill yelled as the final boxes crowded up against all the rest, and her head split open with a migraine. The boxes immediately turned back to their normal shade and organized themselves in a neat column.

The silence in the truck was deafening.

"Are you, um, alright there?" Ras asked a few seconds later, his eyes flicking to Jill, then to the road, then to Jill again with concern. Babu collapsed laughing, banging a fist on the bed.

"Peachy," Jill said. "Just peachy." Maybe, just maybe, she wouldn't insult the system too much. The thing was getting downright feisty.

CHAPTER 9

RIDING RIFLE

Once her boxes were behaving again, it only took Jill a few minutes to read through the various options.

"These are goddamn insane," she said. "Doubling the trailer for one point? An extra seventy kph? Hell, if those five stack, then she'd go. . . ," Jill paused for a moment, "six hundred kph! We'd flip over in an instant unless, I don't know, the power to never flip fucking ever was also just one point." She shook her head in disbelief.

"You wanted magic truck powers, you got magic truck powers," Ras said. "It's still just a truck."

"You're lucky there isn't an ejector seat option, asswipe. No insulting the Bertha," Jill said. She cranked her neck around to address Babu. "Some of these are too good to pass up, but what do you think? Anything look crazy to you, gamer-boy?"

He shook his head. "It's hard to tell without knowing how the individual power upgrades scale. Linear? Sublinear? Exponential? You said five points in propulsion would get to six hundred kph, but what if each additional skill point isn't seventy? The only way to tell would be to invest some points in everything, but there are so many options!"

"Well, no way to tell but to try! Double the cargo each trip? Yes, please," Jill said. "Pull over, Ras, I need to see what happens from the outside when I give her a bigger ass."

"That might not be the best idea," Ras said, with a meaningful glance to the side mirrors.

Jill had to lean over hard to get herself in the correct alignment to see backward in the mirror, but when she did, she nearly choked in shock. There was a small horde of monsters chasing them. Mostly dog-sized creatures that were probably more dire lemmings, but she could make out a few larger animals as well, including a stag whose antlers had to be clearing twenty feet off the ground. "Flapclaps! How long have they been there?" She pulled her rifle down from the rack and started pulling out extra boxes of ammo from the concealed compartment under the floor. The false panel had been the product of her, her father, her brothers, a handle of cheap bourbon, and a blowtorch, and was a surprisingly good hiding spot for all sorts of things. Like guns and ammo that in some states she technically wasn't supposed to have.

"A while now. Maybe half an hour?" Ras shrugged. "They can't catch us so I didn't think it was a problem. Just, well, no stopping for now."

"For now? When would we be able to?" Babu flicked his brother on the back of the head. "They don't seem to be giving up, so was the plan to just drag a huge swarm into Billings?"

Ras shrugged. "I'd have mentioned it eventually."

"Next time you tell us when there are shitbags trying to kill us, got it?" Jill said, glaring. "But I can't say I'm too worried, at least while the bullets last. As goddamn weird as it is to talk about levels, they're real, so let's get some. There are a lot more dangerous things out there than lemmings." She shivered a bit in anticipation of the feeling of her stats increasing, even if she knew that the high from a single level wouldn't be as intense as five at once.

"I wish we could have started when there were fewer of them," Babu said, still glaring at Ras. "I've been thinking about the experience gains we've gotten, and, well . . . If the system is a game, its design isn't very good. There doesn't seem to be any weighting at all for the difficulty of encounters. Kill one level one monster, get a hundred experience. Repeat as much as you want. Kill ten all at once, get a thousand, despite ten monsters all together being so much more dangerous."

"There's a bonus for monsters with a higher level than you," Jill said, recalling most of her kill notices.

"I know! But no penalty for killing low-level ones! Isn't it interesting?" Babu said with a bright grin. "Anything gamified is just a set of incentives to make the users do what the designers want! So, the system designers don't care about fighting fair, they just care about the monsters dying, with two optimal methods: killing large numbers of low-level enemies that don't pose a threat, or single high-level enemies that you can ambush to get a huge bonus!" Babu coughed and continued in a more subdued voice. "Or at least it seems that way to me."

Jill finished checking her ammo. "Huh," she said. "Interesting." She was by no means dumb—no one who owned her own company in a competitive industry could afford to be—but she'd never really considered that kind of game theory before. "I never did ask: what do you do? Some kind of scientist?"

Babu reared back, shut his mouth with a click, and looked away. "No."

Jill glanced at Ras, but the man's face was blank in the same way that a bad poker player's was when trying not to show any reaction. She shrugged and resolved not to ask about it again. Some people were self-conscious about their jobs after all, even if she thought that was kind of dumb.

"Alright boys, time to thin the herd," she said, reaching for the window control. While before it had been a clunky plastic switch, now it was a smooth chrome toggle. "Nice," she muttered, then clicked it to the down position: the window slid silently into the door. "Drive smooth now, and let them get a little closer," she told Ras.

The wind battered her face and hair as she leaned out the window, rifle held tight against her shoulder. The firing position really wasn't great: not only was the trailer blocking more than half of the horizon behind Bertha, but the constant wind kept tugging the rifle barrel off of where she wanted to point it. It got slightly better as Ras let up on the accelerator and Bertha slowed, but the monster horde seemed quite a lot more dangerous when it was catching up instead of falling behind.

Jill waited until they were in range, then started taking measured, deliberate shots. There were some hits and a few dire lemmings died, with Jill dismissing the boxes before they could form and block her vision. But more of her shots were missing than she would have liked, considering that she was practically shooting at a wall made entirely of monsters. She took another few shots, then drew back into the cab.

"This isn't working," Jill said.

"Let me try!" Babu said, eyes bright.

"Calm your tits," Jill said. "Those things are trying to kill us. Get the shotgun and load it up if you want levels. We're going to need to get closer to do any real damage, so you'll be in range." She glanced at Ras. "You still okay driving if they get closer?"

He shrugged. "As long as I don't have to turn, we can't flip, so I'm good for now. But I would appreciate you taking the wheel later so I can get some kills for myself. I got a portion of the experience for those lemmings, but I'm going to fall behind just driving."

Jill checked the kill boxes for the dire lemmings: she had gotten 90 percent contribution, so the system must have awarded Ras 10 percent for keeping them away from the swarm.

"Ok, I'm almost ready," Babu said as he loaded the shotgun, a box of shells open next to him on the bed. "Uhh, how are we going to both fit out the window? I don't think I'll fit next to Rassy's giant head."

"Yeah, that won't work. I've got a better idea," Jill said. She summoned Bertha's upgrade boxes again, "I wanted to see what these class powers did, so let's fucking use one!" Before she could second guess herself, she spent a point on the turrets module.

Turrets (Small Arms) Module added!
4 Class Power points remaining.
Prepare for Integration.

Bertha's available mana dropped with an alarming surge that sent the mana consumption needle flying to the right, but it stabilized with a quarter of the magical reserves remaining. There was the creaking noise of bending metal and, bizarrely, the smell of lilac in the air, then a metal ladder, rungs coated in non-slip rubber, dropped from the ceiling behind the seats. At the top of the ladder was a hatch.

Turrets (Small Arms)
"Bertha" has 1 turret for Small Arms weaponry.
Includes: Firing station, viewing slits (armored glass).
Add-ons (0/1): None (12-gauge shotgun, .243 rifle available).

> Turrets (Small Arms) Upgrades:
> Mana Substitution (0/1): Unloaded Small Arms may fire, drawing Mana from "Bertha" to generate and propel ammunition. Fired ammunition lasts for 84 seconds.
> Superchargers (0/5): Increases damage and rate of fire of add-ons by 14%.
> Dakka (0/4): Adds 1 turret with 1 Small Arms add-on slot.

Jill eyed the ammo she had stacked at her feet as she passed the new system notification to Babu and Ras, getting noises of appreciation in return. While the several hundred rounds she had left would probably be enough for whittling down this group of monsters, they wouldn't last forever. Better to save what ammo she had for those times she had to leave Bertha behind. With a flicker of thought, she purchased "mana substitution."

"All right," Jill said. "Let's try this one more time."

CHAPTER 10

A FAMILIAR FEELING

It was an easy climb up into the turret, the minor bumps of the road not nearly enough to throw Jill off even with her carrying her rifle. The inside was a bizarre mix of aesthetics that looked as if the whole thing had been made by stealing parts from different movie production lots. In the center of the turret was a leather chair with footrests on a shiny post that could have been taken from any hairdressing salon. In front of it was a series of clamps and cables, all pulsing with glowing golds and blues, leading to a thick window, to which was attached a circular, spoked gunsight that had last seen active service on WWII anti-aircraft guns. The turret itself was all hexagonal panels, every other of which had a small window right in the center.

"Badass," Jill said. It was a bit awkward getting into the chair itself because the ceiling was low, but it was surprisingly comfortable once she was in. "Gun goes under the gunsight?" she muttered to herself, and she tried to slot her rifle into the clamps. The instant the tip of the gun was between them, the rifle slipped out of her hands as if it were a greased magnet.

Integrating add-on to "Bertha" Small Arms turret 1.
Level 3 rifle detected. Mana crossfeed enabled. Mana cost per discharge: 2

The rifle was now held firm by three sets of clamps, a thick glowing cable plugged into where the bolt would normally cycle. Handles stuck out of the stock on either side, first sideways and then down, almost like those on a high-end bicycle, with a trigger on each where her index finger would go. The rifle barrel protruded a good foot past the thick glass of the window, held in place by a flexible looking gasket.

"Fuck me, hope I can get that out."

"That's what she said!" Babu yelled from below.

Jill closed her eyes and shook her head, but said nothing. It would only encourage him. She began to experiment with the turret, figuring out how it moved. Pulling sideways on the handles rotated the turret left and right, a soft whine alluding to some hidden machinery. Pulling up tilted the gun downwards and raised the seat on its pole, tilting as it went to keep Jill comfortably looking down the sights. Easy enough.

"Slow it down a bit, Ras. Let them catch up," she yelled over her shoulder, slewing the turret over to point at the oncoming monsters. She still couldn't fire straight back because the trailer was in the way, but it was a much better angle than before, and she didn't have to worry about the wind pushing the rifle around. She squeezed the triggers. A pulse of gold raced down the cabling in an instant and the rifle barked, its sound muted to being more like a rock hitting a windshield than the deafening bang firing in the cab earlier had been.

This. This would work. She began to fire more rapidly, gentle pressure on the handles altering her aim as she did. It was difficult to see exactly where the shots were going—it wasn't like a little rifle like hers fired tracer rounds—but it was easy to see when a monster finally fell, and to calibrate from that. From there she just moved her aim bit by bit and kept pulling the trigger.

Dire Lemming (x6) defeated.
Your contribution: 90%
720 Experience Gained!
Battle Badger defeated.
Your contribution: 90%
450 Experience Gained!
Lesser Ice Wolf defeated. Bonus Experience awarded for: monster kill above your level (+1.3).
Your contribution: 90%
936 Experience Gained!

> You are now Level 6!

The stat increased pulsed through her, filling her body with fire and her mind with ice. For just a second, she again sensed the world of mana, but it didn't come close to what she had experienced the first time.

"Booyah, bitches! That's a level," she shouted. She leaned forward to check her aim and started firing again, faster this time. The rate of fire wasn't truly limited by the rifle's own mechanisms, which had been invaded by the turret's technomagic, but instead there was a maximum speed at which the pulses of light would travel through the cable to supply ammunition. Pulling the trigger too fast resulted in nothing happening at all, and soon Jill found a rhythm right on the edge. The barks of the gun, the drone of wheels on concrete, and the spurts of blood become her whole world; that, and the kills, and the feeling of experience rolling in. One final enemy took what seemed like a hundred hits to bring down: a mighty crimson elk that was oddly liquid, every bullet sending a spray of glittering red.

> Dire Lemming (x9) defeated.
> Your contribution: 90%
> 990 Experience Gained!
> Lesser Ice Wolf (x3) defeated. Bonus Experience awarded for: monster kill above your level (+1.2/x1.2/x1.3).
> Your contribution: 90%
> 2781 Experience Gained!
> Blood Elk defeated. Bonus Experience awarded for: monster kill above your level (+1.5).
> Your contribution: 90%
> 1989 Experience Gained!

> You are now Level 7!

Jill shuddered as she leveled again, her eyes squeezing shut; the feeling was something she hoped she never got used to. It coursed through her for a quick eternity, then faded. She licked her lips and opened her eyes, aiming down the sights for another kill, another level.

But she didn't pull the triggers.

"Aww, shitnuggets," she said, letting her hands drop to her lap. That feeling—she recognized it. It was the feeling of chasing a high, and she knew exactly where that led. Enough of her friends had paid the price of painkillers, of an escape from reality, and teary funerals had steeled her resolve long ago. She shook her head, banishing bad memories, and stood. Someone else could get some experience for a while.

She slid down the ladder in one jump. "How's everything down here doing?"

Ras shrugged. "That gentle curve a minute ago was the biggest bit of excitement."

Jill punched Babu's shoulder. "You're up, eager beaver. Leave the shotgun; rifle's all hooked up."

"Yes!" Babu cheered. He climbed the ladder in record speed. Awestruck noises filtered down from the turret, oddly muted for how close it was.

"He really loves this stuff, doesn't he?" Jill asked Ras.

Ras nodded. "Yup. He almost joined the army just for the cool toys, but mother talked him out of it." The turret above them started to fire: long pauses between shots at first, then faster and faster, until it played an unsteady staccato song.

Jill slouched into the passenger seat, taking a moment to make sure the shotgun was in easy reach. A minute passed, then another. She watched the mana gauge, trying to tell if she could see a change when Babu fired, but the amount of mana per shot was too low. The miles rolled by, the horde behind them thinning.

She was about to call Babu down and let Ras have his turn, but something caught her eye ahead. "Heads up," she said, pointing. A group of half a dozen or so creatures had charged out of the brush a quarter mile ahead, scrabbling and leaping over each other in their haste. Whatever they were, they had way too many legs. Ras pressed down on the accelerator, pulling them away from the thinned horde behind. "Monsters ahead!" she shouted up to Babu, but by the time he had rotated the turret to position it was too late.

They were giant wolf spiders, with thick hairy legs and fangs dripping with venom, and they leapt for Bertha as if it were the world's largest, juiciest bug. Two went low and impacted the grille with a carapace-cracking crunch before being ground under the wheels. Three leapt to the sides of the truck and disappeared from view, and one leapt for Jill and Ras.

It landed badly on the hood and slid forward, a tangle of legs and swollen body, eyes and fangs pressed up against the windshield, hissing and shrieking.

"Holy fucking shit fuck goddamn!" Jill said. She raised the shotgun to her shoulder but didn't fire. The armored glass was keeping the horrible spider out and she wanted to keep it that way.

"Sugarsugarsugarsugar," Ras repeated to himself over and over, his hands gripping the wheel hard enough to turn his knuckles white.

From the rear of the truck came a scraping, tearing shriek as thin metal panels met claw-tipped legs and lost. "They're digging into the trailer!" Babu screamed from above. The turret began barking again.

"I'm driving. Get your sword," Jill said, hip checking Ras to get him out of the driver's seat faster. With a thought, she purchased the Torque Converter with a class power point, dismissing the accompanying box before it could appear. After a half second, a new control slid out of the dashboard next to the gear shift: a small silver ball with three prongs tipped with glowing green balls coming out at right angles to each other, one pointing forward, one to the side, and one up. Despite there being no instructions for the alien spike-ball, Jill knew what to do; Bertha was a part of her now after all, and you didn't need instructions to use your own body. She grabbed the glowing ball pointing forward, twisted it a half turn, then pulled it. It clicked into place, color changing from green to red, and the hum of the mana engine gained a new note: a mid tone in harmony.

"Hang on, boys!" Jill pushed the accelerator all the way down and pulled the wheel hard over. The cab turned even faster than she expected, and the big rig whipped off the road, pulling her sideways in her seat. For a fraction of a second Bertha started to roll, but the Torque Converter glowed and the truck stayed steady. The same couldn't be said for the spider on the hood. It scrambled to stay on, and while its rear two legs found purchase by punching its claws into the engine cover, its others uselessly chipped at the windshield, sending bits of glass flying but offering no solid hold. Two limbs weren't enough and off it went.

"Bye, stoolsucker!" Jill said, turning the wheel in the other direction in the hope that it would throw some of the spiders on the trailer off as well. But big rigs weren't meant to go off-road, and Bertha had already slowed enough that this swerve wasn't as powerful as the one before. The terrain was fairly gentle, a mild slope from the slightly raised highway down onto a grass and shrub covered flat, but the bumps were harsher and the tires were having trouble getting a strong grip. Bertha still didn't roll—though Jill noticed that the maneuver had caused Bertha's mana recharge rate to rise—but she did slide, with the new wheel direction unable to turn the tons of truck without traction.

Saved class points didn't help if she got eaten; Jill purchased the first rank in Utility Wheels. A beat passed as Bertha integrated the change, the mana cost fighting the bonus from the Torque Converter, and then Bertha stopped her slide, the tires gripping the grass and soil as if it were a racetrack. The turn pulled Jill to the other side of her seat as the truck whipped around the other way.

"One's dead, but two got in!" Babu called down.

Jill gave a few more swerves for good measure, then maneuvered the truck back onto the road. She concentrated, and an abbreviation of Bertha's status popped up.

Soulbound Modular Vehicle "Bertha"
Durability: 23,454/30,000
Mana: 17,499/30,000

As she watched, the mana ticked steadily up, recovering from the upgrade integration, but the durability was falling. Whatever the spiders were doing back there, it was hurting.

"I'll take care of them," Ras said. His earlier terror was gone, replaced by steely eyes and just a hint of a smirk in one corner of his mouth. It probably helped that he had in his hands not a steering wheel, but his soulbound sword, glowing blue with wisps of golden mana curling off of it. "Uhh," he faltered, looking at the sleeper area and realizing there was no way through to the trailer, "shoot, we have to stop, don't we?"

Jill glanced in the mirror. The monster horde was significantly smaller, and had fallen farther back as they'd put on speed, but it was still chasing them. And if it caught them, they'd be in much deeper trouble. "Nah, I have a better idea." Another mental prod, and she purchased the Customization power. Her connection to Bertha strengthened, the sensation like a combination of discovering a new muscle and opening her eyes for the first time. It was a much stronger feeling than her previous purchases—a fundamental shift rather than just a new piece to a puzzle.

She pushed through the strangeness and began the change she wanted: a connection between the cab and the trailer that someone could safely walk through. She imagined how train cars were coupled, a short chamber with a door on either end, only able to bend far further. A single pivot joint then, with walls made of overlapping panels that could slide past one another like the joints on old plate armor. The door started to appear, outlines puckering metal as the features pushed themselves outwards like a movie special effect, but was blocked by her bed. Jill huffed in annoyance and imagined it sinking into the floor. It wasn't exactly ideal, and they would have to step over it to go to the trailer, but there was nowhere for it to go. Not yet.

The power description hadn't lied though: the changes weren't fast, and Bertha's durability kept going down. Those spiders needed to die as soon as the passage was complete. "Get down here," Jill said to Babu. Once he had, she handed him the shotgun and filled the brothers in on what was happening.

Babu surprised her by refusing the gun. "It doesn't reach far, but I've got my own fire" he said, wiggling his fingers and causing little tongues of flame to leap out. "It's only two. I've got plenty of mana for two."

"Try not to burn the freight. There's a penalty for damaged goods," she said. "Or slash the freight. Or let giant fucking spiders tear it apart." She thought for a second. "What the hell am I smoking? Just kill the damn things."

Bertha jerked to the right, and Jill had to pull on the wheel to keep them straight. One of the wheels had locked, dragging with its new superior grip, and the truck slowed. The spiders must have been digging into the floor, going for the pneumatic lines that fed the brakes—or whatever magic bullshit had replaced them—just like a predator would go for the tendons of an elephant. Jill opened her mouth to swear again, but at that moment, Customization finished its job. "Go!" she said.

Ras led the way, the door to the trailer sliding smoothly and silently open as it sensed his approach. He yelled something in a language Jill didn't know as he charged, Babu hot on his heels. A pulse of gold light and the roar and flash of raging fire filled the cab for just a moment, but then the doors closed, and their sudden motion brought a surreal silence. The brothers were fighting for all their lives, but she was stuck driving, making sure the horde didn't catch them.

And then the door opened; Babu leading the way, eyebrows singed but a grin on his face. Ras was right behind him, sword leaned on his shoulder blunt-side down and a relaxed rhythm to his gait.

Jill stole a glance backward and, seeing that they were okay, was filled with relief. The feeling cut into her with an intensity she wouldn't have expected from only knowing the brothers for a few hours, but the stress of surviving, of killing, of adapting to this craziness, had formed a bond in a way she hadn't in years. But she had more important things to worry about.

"For fuck's sake, Ras," she said with a scowl, "you're dripping monster goo on my bed! That better goddamn magic itself out or I'm going to make you lick it up! Git!"

CHAPTER 11

APPROPRIATE LEVELS OF DAKKA

Cleaning up the rest of the monster swarm was as uneventful as blood and death could be. Jill went back into the turret first, but made a point to switch out immediately after she leveled. Ras stuck to driving on the road while Jill shot; the monsters ran behind in a futile and predictable chase. When it came her turn to drive again, the monsters were over half depleted, and Jill decided to experiment. With the ability to go off road with no fear of rolling, she drove a wide loop around the group, corralling the monsters into one place. The only tricky bit was that some of the slower monsters that had fallen behind began to catch up as the truck circled in place, so Jill had to dodge the occasional lunging creature whenever she was in the western edge of her circle.

Babu described the process as "kiting"; to Jill it was making your own barrel to shoot the fish in. The monsterized animals might be strong and have deadly magic powers, but they were also rabid and single-minded in their suicidal pursuit. Where Jill would expect a real animal to run from a threat, or attempt to lay in ambush, these could be led in useless circles.

Just like before, Jill gained a portion of the experience from the others' kills. It seemed that the system recognized that Bertha and the gun were hers and that the others were benefiting from her resources. The experience wasn't nearly as much as getting the kills herself, but it still added up to enough to push her to level nine. She didn't know what level Babu and Ras had gotten up to, but by Babu's several whoops of glee, he at least had leveled up a few times. Or he really liked shooting things. Probably both.

The monster corpses piled up inside the loop, the world's most bloody and macabre crop circle, and it didn't take long for the last stragglers to catch up and be gunned down. While Ras stood guard in Bertha's turret, Jill and Babu spent half an hour looting and carrying their gains back to the truck, pulses of gold mana lighting up the now silent night. Most of the loot was animal parts—hides, teeth, antlers, etc.—but there were also glowing gems like Jill had gotten from the lesser firewolf what seemed like a week before but had been only scant hours prior. Despite the possible value left behind on the road, they decided not to retrace their path west. The trail of blood was many miles long and they all wanted to keep moving east rather than spend hours picking up more of the same in the wrong direction.

They hit the road again, with Babu sleeping in the back on the still recessed bed and Ras drifting off in the passenger seat. Jill was exhausted as well, but she was also very used to long nights on the lonely road. Without any new crises to deal with, the events of the past few hours kept running through her thoughts on repeat, every close call making her hands shake when they popped back into her mind's eye. There had been more danger and blood since midnight than in the past several years combined, if not her entire life. Jill longed to use the quiet of the morning to think about anything else, but her brain wouldn't cooperate. A question kept poking her, making her more and more worried as the miles flew past.

Where was everyone? Jill knew that for a major highway like I-90—even in a sparsely populated state like Montana, even so late into the night that it was early instead—there should always be people driving on it. Whether truckers like Jill, shift workers commuting at terrible hours, or just extreme early birds going about their business, it was rare to go more than ten minutes without seeing another vehicle. But, other than the brothers, the road had been deserted. The only thing she could think of was that everyone else's cars must have acted like the Batis' U-Haul and died immediately. Could they have been so fixated on the monsters chasing them that they'd passed a broken-down car in the dead of night? The thought chilled Jill to the core. If so, they had left people to die.

Bertha rounded a bend and the question of a few people maybe having died suddenly seemed like a small concern.

"Babu! Ras! Wake the fuck up!" Jill said, leaning over to punch Ras on the shoulder.

"Waa?"

"We just hit Bozeman and well . . . look."

Technically they had just entered the outskirts of Belgrade, but it was close enough. The plains and hills surrounding the highway had given way to parking lots and single-story businesses, many of which were on fire. Jill was already slowing the big rig down to get a better look when a suburb came into view next to them. She could only see a few homes from the highway, but half were on fire, and others had great holes in them where some monstrosity had forced their way in. Cars sat crushed in driveways, gasoline pooling under the wrecks and flowing into the street. A herd of fear deer ran past them, their over-large teeth piercing through their own lips and leaving a spattered trail of blood behind them.

Ras pointed not at them, but at where they were heading. "There!" he said. A few hundred yards off the highway, barely visible beyond the houses, was a larger two-story building. Rapid flashes sparked on its upper windows, the telltale muzzle flashes of gunfire bright on a night without streetlights. "Babu, get up top!" Ras said, grabbing the shotgun for himself as he turned to Jill. "Please, we have to—"

"Way ahead of you, hero boy!" Jill pulled the wheel over, a sense of purpose, of doing in the now, driving away her doubts. There was only a thin slat fence between the highway and the surrounding suburban road—one that Bertha crashed through with ease. Slats flew into the air all around them as Jill pulled on the horn, Bertha's roar announcing her dominance to the night. The deer turned towards the sound of the horn, their mouths dripping blood, and Jill accelerated right towards them.

Bertha's new off-road capabilities left her going more than fast enough to crush deer. Monster bones cracked and blood sprayed as the big rig hit the herd like a spiked bowling ball into pins of flesh, then drove right over the remains. Jill felt through her connection to Bertha that the truck hadn't gone unscathed: the grille was almost certainly smashed, and a test swerve on the wheel showed that something in the steering wasn't right, but sharp pops and pings sounding from the front of the cab announced that the truck was already repairing itself.

Jill spared a thought for the armor module that was available; she had the points, and she sure as shooting wasn't going to stop ramming into monsters, if this one cursed night was any indication of the future. She almost bought it, but her attention was broken by the residential street ending suddenly in a T intersection. Jill whipped the truck to the right, the Torque Converter glowing as it prevented a rollover. Babu started firing in the turret, though Jill couldn't see what at. She also couldn't see a clear way forward and, as she fought to keep the truck on the road, the typical maze of suburban streets weren't designed for the speeds that she was going.

"Left, go left!" Ras said, as they approached another intersection, one of his hands gripping the shotgun and the other the handle above the door to steady himself through the turns.

Jill followed his directions, then had to fight the urge to stomp on the brakes. "Oh, shit-out-of-your-mouth, you've got to be kidding!" she yelled at no one in particular, as an absolutely giant spider came into view. It was squatting over a wrecked house, dozens of giant eyes glinting in the headlights, with a human corpse wrapped in webbing held to its fangs. It started to raise a fifteen-foot long leg, covered in hairs that were each wicked and sharp as a knife. Jill purchased the armor module with a thought.

> Armor module added! 3 Class Power points remaining.
> Prepare for Integration.

Reflective fractals raced across the windshield as layers of crystals grew on top of the glass. At the same time, Bertha's outer surface cracked and tilted as overlapping bands of shining gray armor slid out from nothing. The process hadn't quite finished as the spider struck: the blow from a single leg powerful enough to send the big rig screeching sideways, despite the enhanced traction of system tires, and a three-feet-deep dent pounded into the trailer. But the armor had held enough that the truck hadn't been skewered.

"Aaaahhhhh!!!!" Babu's scream echoed down from the turret. But he didn't stop shooting, so Jill gave him a pass.

"Sugar, its level thirty-seven!" Ras said, his knuckles white from his death grip on the shotgun.

"We're not sticking around. Point me to that gunfire!" Jill said, pulling the wheel over hard, and—with a skid and a few ineffectual, panic-fired bullets—they were past the arachnid. Jill spared a quick glance to read the new boxes for the armor that had just saved them.

Armor
"Bertha" has an armored exterior. 14% increase in Durability as Armor; damage to this additional Durability does not damage interior systems. Incoming damage is reduced by 14%. Mass increased by 10,000 kg, modified by external dimensions.
Includes: Transparent Aluminum Viewports.
Add-ons (0/1): None.
Mass increased by 10,000 kg, modified by external dimensions.

Armor Upgrades:
Ablative Armor (0/1): Continuous sources of damage affecting "Bertha" decrease by 14% per second.
Face Hardening (0/3): Incoming damage reduced by 14 after other reductions.
Bulwark (0/5): Further 14% increase in Armor Durability and incoming damage reduction. Each rank increases the mass of "Bertha" by 10,000kg, modified by external dimensions.

"Catbutt!" Jill swore, as she glanced up from the box to see the street was ending in a T intersection. She pulled Bertha into a turn, and the additional weight of the armor immediately made itself known as the truck took the corner wider than she expected. Jill managed to mostly correct, but the cab went up onto someone's front lawn and the trailer lost traction for a moment, whipping out to sideswipe the house. The impact barely slowed them but left the entire front of the house caved in.

"Right, then a jog, then left," Ras said, voice steady.

They exited the maze of suburbia and got onto a road meant to actually go somewhere. Outside of the housing development the land was flat and mostly bare, so their destination came fully into view: a sprawling two story structure made of brick, surrounded on one side by athletic fields and the other by an expansive parking lot. Both had monster corpses strewn across them, with more abominations on their way from all sides. A cheerful sign—only partially marred by bullet holes and the flayed corpse of a moose—read, "River Crest Elementary School."

Silhouettes lined the windows of the second story, and muzzle flashes came at regular intervals. Some were the normal flash of a rifle, but others were colored strangely or lasted too long. Someone inside had gotten neon pink tracer rounds and was firing them at a steady clip too, which must have been magical. But there was a constant press of monsters, and it was easy to see by the broken windows and blood that any monster that managed to actually reach the school could get inside easily enough.

"South side!" Babu yelled down, the turret swerving around to fire in that direction.

Jill squinted, then frowned. The south side of the school was just a field, torn up and muddy in large swathes, with grass rippling in the wind. Then the grass rippled over on top of a muddy patch. Like one of those visual puzzles, where once you see the trick you can't unsee it, what had been grass was now a sea of snakes, the vast majority no longer than a foot. But scattered amongst them, and camouflaged by their tiny brethren, were the enormous exceptions: behemoths as thick around as a tree and dozens of feet long. Jill guided Bertha into a turn and pressed down on the accelerator.

"There's no way they can kill that many! They'll be swarmed!" Ras said, a hint of panic lacing his voice at last.

"They're tiny, we'll run 'em down." Jill eyed the big ones and gulped. "Babu," she yelled to be heard in the turret above, "shoot the big ones!"

"Roll down a window!" Ras said, hefting the gun up to his shoulder.

"Fuck no, are you insane?!" Jill said. "I'm not letting those little dicks slither in here!"

"Ahhhhh—that's what she said!—Aaaaaaa!!!" Babu interrupted his scream briefly.

"You're repeating yourself!" Jill yelled back. She put a class point into dakka. "I'm making a new turret," she said to Ras, "but you better get your ass back down here if something breaks in."

Turrets (Small Arms) Dakka upgraded to (1/4).
Prepare for integration.

This time, as the new turret began to form, Jill tapped into Customization, willing it to guide the process. She felt a massive amount of mana congeal; what had been raw power dispersed through the truck, gathering into a single place, and transformed into something new. It felt a bit like pulling at setting gelatin with her fingers, except nothing like that because it was all in her soul. With a creak and pop that reverberated through the new armor plates, a new turret sprang into existence above the trailer.

"In the back," Jill said, gesturing at the door to the trailer with her head. A glance at the mana gauge had her worried: the repeated integrations had lowered it to under six thousand, and she had no idea what would happen if it ran out. Luckily the regeneration rate seemed to have risen with her level, and the driving she was doing towards the snake horde consumed mana well below replenishment. Even though the guns integrated into the turrets drew some mana with every shot, it was nothing compared to Bertha's total mana pool.

The noise in the cab increased as Ras opened the door to the trailer, carefully picking his way over Jill's still sunken bed, then went back to normal as it closed. Jill had a moment where she was finally alone to consider the insanity of the situation: Bertha was a magic battle truck tied to her soul, and she was driving across a school parking lot into a slithering carpet of killer snakes.

"Weirdest haul of anyone's damn life," she muttered. Babu was firing away, and the snakes were getting closer by the second.

Integrating add-on to "Bertha" Small Arms turret 2.
Level 3 shotgun detected. Mana crossfeed enabled. Mana cost per discharge: 3

Ras was in. The shotgun began to fire; the blast was even quieter than those of the rifle with the doors in the way, just a faint bass pop every second or so. Babu's screaming rose in pitch as one of the monsterized snakes reared up, its head towering over the semi-truck. Jill joined in. And, since leaving her big girl out would just be rude, she pulled on Bertha's horn and let it rip just as she plowed straight into the towering scaled creature.

Armor met scales and won, but didn't survive unscathed. Whole bands of metal sheared off the front as the snake collapsed backward, its center completely incapable of stopping the enhanced mass of an armored big rig truck. Its head snapped down like the end of a whip to impact right behind the cab, the impulse enough to bottom out Bertha's suspension.

> Soulbound Modular Vehicle "Bertha"
> Armor: 4220/5040
> Durability: 36,000/36,000
> Mana: 7194/36,000

Nearly 20 percent of her armor was gone in one self-inflicted blow, but the results spoke for themselves.

> Battering Boa, Level 22
> HP: 47/860
> MP: 131/220
> Status: Stunned, Crippled

The guns kept popping away, and Jill threw the wheel hard over, trying to catch the boa in the tires. She didn't know what exactly was responsible for it, but the snake died.

> Battering Boa defeated. Bonus Experience awarded for: monster kill above your level (+1.3).
> Your contribution: 82%
> 4149 Experience Gained!
> You are now Level 10!

In the midst of battle the rush barely registered, unable to compete with the sheer adrenalin running through Jill's veins. She gunned the accelerator and kept the wheel hard over, putting Bertha into a slide lubricated by pulped snakes. With each kill another little jolt of experience flowed into her, each with its own little box that she—by now instinctually—willed to not appear and distract her.

For a minute of splattering blood and spines, she kept the big rig doing massive donuts in the snake swarm, each rotation bringing them closer to the school and its defenders, as its guns on top kept up their fire. Jill tried to avoid the largest of the snakes so that the guns could do their work, but it wasn't to be: one had been hiding low and letting the smaller snakes flow over it, biding its time in a show of unusual intelligence compared to the previous monsters they'd encountered. As they passed close, it sprang its trap: shooting forward and up in an impossible display of agility for such a titanic snake, it slithered over the top of Bertha and down the far side. Jill was thrown forward in her seat, the belt biting hard against her chest, as the monster somehow managed to slam Bertha to a dead stop.

Elder Battering Boa, Level 29
HP: 1296/1410
MP: 112/320
Status: Giant's Snare (Active), Constrict

Metal groaned and creaked as the boa began to constrict, its power enough to slowly overcome the new armor. Babu was swearing now from above as he poured fire into the coil at blank range, but it was obvious that the little bullets weren't penetrating far enough to do more than superficial damage. Jill stomped on the accelerator, her eyes fixed on the snake and its status box. Its MP ticked down fast, spending its mana to keep the truck still and in its clutches.

The rest of the smaller snakes weren't idle either. They leapt onto the hood and crawled over the windows, giant fangs that boas really shouldn't have biting but failing to find any purchase. But Bertha's armor was falling too, each bite whittling it away just a little bit. Jill's heart raced and dread pooled in her stomach. They were caught and, should those things break through, they would eat her alive. Maybe they would deplete the elder snake's mana before it was too late. Maybe it wouldn't even matter if they did, and if they started to move, the snakes would just hang on, chipping away until they cracked her truck open like a coconut and burrowed fangs-first into her flesh. The only thing Jill could do was press on the accelerator and stare her death in the face.

She was snapped out of her paralysis by the sound of hail slamming into the truck. Armor chipped and shattered with each hit, but the elder battering boa suffered far worse, as a solid glowing beam of tracer-laced explosive shells pierced the night, erupting from the roof of the school. Standing there was a woman, dwarfed by the chain gun she maneuvered with a shoulder strap and both hands. The gun sucked down an ammo belt from a crate next to her, huge bullets pulled in at a blinding pace and shot out in a never-ending torrent.

For a few seconds, at least, until the ammo ran out. The belt finished, and the woman struggled to get another one out and loaded into the chain gun's empty receiver. But a few seconds was enough, and the severely wounded snake ran out of mana. Bertha leapt forward, and Jill piloted it out of the swarm—or at least tried to. So many had crawled up the sides that it was more like pulling the swarm apart, as it tried to eat through the truck's sides to get in. Snakes fell as they were unable to find purchase, or as they were blasted off by Ras in his shotgun turret, and the pellets scored lines in the armor that were well worth the cost. The hood cleared in moments under the force of acceleration, Jill's fears proven wrong.

"How'd she get a chain gun?!" Babu screamed, his voice crazed. "And can we please, please, please get one?!"

Jill pulled the wheel over again hard, so they could keep circling the school. The defenders weren't nearly as defenseless as she'd assumed them to be, but she would be damned if she was going to stop trying to help. At the very least it kept the terror at bay, one moment at a time. She could keep going for just one more moment.

CHAPTER 12

NURSE GUNNER

After an eternity of chaos and blood, the sun's disc broke the horizon, and its searing light revealed a field of corpses. The school stood, its windows shattered and the lower floor ruined, but the natural chokepoint of the stairways had held. A weary cheer rose from the second floor as a box appeared in Jill's vision:

Local Quest Complete: Survive the first night.
Contribution bonus: +1.7x.
Noncombatant savior bonus: +2.6x.
53,000 Experience Gained!
You are now Level 16!

The rush of gaining four levels at once hit hard—too hard. Jill had been exhausted and at her limit hours before: hours spent driving in never ending circles. Crush one monster, dodge a larger one, reinforce one side of the school before a new wave could breach it, repeat again. Even though not one monster had breached Bertha's armor—they had done their best—more than once the windshield had cracked under their assault. The tension, stress, and terror of it all twisted the level-up high from ecstasy to agony, and Jill's vision went black. She took her foot off the gas as the feeling drained out from her, and she settled into sleep.

A monster stalked her dreams, full of fangs and blood and the promise of death. But then it got pancaked by Bertha, whose horn blared a cheerful, deep bass "Hiiiiiiii" as she blew past, which was nice. Jill slept a lot better after that.

"Hey, Jill."

"No. Comfy seat is comfy," Jill half thought and half didn't.

"Junkmouth!"

"Heh." She liked that nickname. She turned over just a bit, burrowing away from the annoying noises, which continued next to her.

"Do you think she'll hit us if we touch her?" Ras's voice drifted through the fog.

"Only if you do it wrong. I can give you tips if this is your first time," Babu replied. Jill smiled a bit as her dreams turned spicier. The much younger man really could be dead sexy when he had confidence. Too bad she was taken, but hey! Dreams didn't count.

"Just because I don't slut myself out like you, doesn't mean that—" Ras said, but got interrupted.

"I am not a slut! Just skilled, don'tcha know," Babu said with a sniff. "I just happen to be popular, unlike you."

Ras started saying something, but their argument had annoyed Jill enough. "Go nuzzle a grundle somewhere else," Jill said, the words coming out in an annoyed moan. "I'm sleeping here."

"Well, we tried being annoying," Babu said, giving a theatrical sigh, "so time for drastic measures."

There was a flash of light, and ice water soaked Jill from head to toe. "Clitclamps!" she yelled, limbs flailing in shock. She opened her eyes and glowered up at Babu, who was pointing a finger at her. The cold and wet seeping through her clothing vanished the moment he stopped pointing.

"Wakey!" Babu said. "You've got shit to do. He," he pointed at Ras, who looked particularly put out, "can explain. I'm going to go hunt down some breakfast." He started whistling and ducked past his brother to hop out of the cab.

"What's up?" Jill asked.

"Babu was supposed," Ras stressed the word, "to be the one to tell you, but. . . ," he rolled his eyes. "The survivors in the school want to talk with you. There's a committee."

Jill snorted. "Of course there is." She took a look out the windows, which were much thicker than they used to be but somehow clearer. "Any monsters left?"

Ras shook his head. "They stopped at dawn, but Captain Tanner thinks they'll be back. She's the one in charge." He paused. "Well, mostly. She's in the military, but on leave, and some of the others don't want to listen because she's new or something? It's complicated."

"Lord save me from local politics," Jill said under her breath, then turned to her gun rack. All that was left was a 9 mm handgun in a holster, but that was better than nothing, so she took it and strapped it to her hip. She stretched her arms up, expecting the usual sequence of snaps and pops her spine gave these days, but none came. Now that she was awake, she felt alright. Surprisingly and suspiciously so, given that she had slept for just a few hours, but that was a worry for another time. "Where am I heading?"

"Second floor, east side. They're meeting in the library."

Jill nodded. "Mind standing watch? Wouldn't want something to crawl inside my girl when no one was looking."

For a moment Ras looked like he was going to say no, but he just sighed and nodded instead.

It turned out that Bertha's final slide had left her near the main entrance, so there wasn't far to walk. Jill hopped down from the big rig, giving her a pat as she went only for her hand to come away sticky. The big rig was splattered all over with mud and guts. Jill frowned, concentrating for a moment through the customize power, and she willed her truck clean. The outside shivered, little ripples flowing from front to back, and the muck cascaded off to reveal gleaming, waxed paint.

"Woah," said one of the men guarding the front entrance to the school. He was in pajamas but holding a triple-barreled, glowing gun. "That was cool."

Jill winked at him, a satisfied smile on her face. "That she is," she said as she passed.

The bottom floor of the school was still a disaster, but in the few hours since the monster attack, there had at least been a token effort to clean. Glass had been roughly swept into corners, leaving a clear trail down the center of the hallways. The monster bodies had been dragged away, the blood smears contrasting the cheerful pastel colors of the tiles and walls.

But for all that, the bottom floor was still eerily empty, and the survivors were avoiding what had just hours before been a killing ground.

There were more guards at the top of the stairwell, where shotguns and swords had held off the monsters that had survived the longer-ranged weapons' slaughter to make it inside. The floor and walls held the evidence of that battle, with enough slashes and holes to make the stairwell treacherous to walk up. Jill gave a respectful nod to the guards as she passed them; for all that she had had an awful, bloody night, she had the power and safety of Bertha on her side. All these brave souls had were whatever weapons they could scrounge.

The second floor was packed with people, organized, and far cleaner than below. Some of the classrooms had been converted into sleeping areas, with individuals and families claiming little areas as their own. In another there were children playing games and coloring in books under the direction of a young man with a falsely cheerful expression. But it was too quiet, and the red eyes and snot-crusted sleeves told of the night that those children had endured.

"Okay kids, snack time!" the man said, clapping his hands. Jill's gaze snapped to him and, for just a moment, she felt the urge to line up and patiently wait for food before the effects of the magic slid off of her. The children had no such resistance, and they gave a muted cheer as they obediently lined up.

Then she was past, heading towards the east end of the floor and the library. The walls of this section of the school were covered in small animal-shaped cutouts of brightly colored construction paper, each labeled and initialed in shaky handwriting. Jill paused right outside the library to admire a rabbit in a hardhat with a shovel, labeled "Broc by RD." It really was remarkably good.

Through the door came raised voices.

"No! We're safe here now, we can't just abandon that!" It was a man's voice, on the edge of snarling.

"We've gone over this. I'm not saying we abandon this location, just that—" said a woman's, tired but calm.

"That we send half the men with guns away, looking for people that are probably dead? Don't be irrational," the man said, cutting her off.

Jill rolled her eyes, took a fortifying breath, then rapped her knuckles on the door on her way in. "Morning," she said. "You all wanted to see me?" There were four people seated around a table that was meant for children and far too low to the ground.

"Yes, Miss. . . ," the man that had snapped said, his sentence trailing off to ask who she was. He looked to be in his late thirties and was the best dressed of the bunch. He even looked like he had found time to shave. Jill didn't answer, instead shifting her gaze to the others.

"Thanks for coming, Ms. MacLeod. I'm Captain Amelie Tanner," said the calm, tired woman. She was wearing camouflage-pattern pajamas and was very pregnant, with dark circles under her eyes. She was also very armed, with a handgun on each side of her chest in an unbuckled holster, an AR-15 semi-automatic rifle on the table in front of her, and knives on her thighs.

"Andrew Berry. I ran the HOA around here, for all that's fucking worth," a man dressed in torn jeans and a t-shirt obscured with bloodstains said. He kept tapping the fingers of one hand on his thigh, and with the other he kept a tight grip on a glowing sci-fi rifle.

"Nice to meet you, Jill! I'm Mia, Mia Williams," said the last person at the table, a younger woman who looked oddly familiar to Jill. She was on the shorter side, with a tightly woven braid of black hair that fell to her mid back.

"And I'm Vice Principal Lawson," said the better dressed man, who didn't know who Jill was.

Amelie leaned forward. "Thank you for helping out last night. I don't know where the hell you came from, but I've never been happier to see farmer armor rolling in."

"The defenders were doing well enough under my instruction, but yes, thank you for showing up," Lawson said. Judging by the looks that Mia and Andrew threw at him, Jill doubted he had much to do with any fighting.

"Anyone would have done it, and my passengers like to play hero," Jill said with a shrug.

The captain smirked. "Sure they do. Anyhow, we need to figure out what the hell's happened, and none of our cars or phones are working. We want you to take me and a half dozen other grunts west, while the rest stay here. The high school and an armory are just a few miles down the road, over the highway and next to the airport. It's close, but I'm not sending anyone on foot right now if I can help it."

"Or," Lawson said with a glare, "we could not ruin the defenses here. We need to wait for the army to come to us; they'll know what to do."

"What the fuck are you on about, she *is* army!" Andrew said. "We've been over this like a dozen times."

"Not in that condition she's not," Lawson said with a gesture to Amelie's stomach.

Sounds of disgust rang out around the table. Jill met Amelie's eyes and they shared a look of understanding.

"Sure, I can do that," Jill said. "I can't stay around here too long though. A half day at most. My friends need to get to their family in Billings, and then I'm going all the way east to Boston." Mia, who had so far been mostly silent, perked up.

"That's fine," Amelie said. "I'll pick some people and get downstairs. Give us twenty minutes?"

"Look," Lawson said before Jill could respond, spreading his hands wide while addressing Amelie. "This seems really important to you, so how about we just send like half a dozen guys? Then things here will still be okay if the monsters come back."

"Jesus Christ, Oliver," Mia said under her breath, shaking her head.

"Why is he even here?" Jill asked.

"Hey!" Lawson looked constipated.

"The principal's missing, so it's his building," Amelie said with a sigh.

Jill shook her head, pitying the poor children. "Twenty minutes sounds good. I'll see you there."

The meeting broke up with everyone standing. Amelie walked off and started calmly giving orders, Andrew following along behind. Jill moved to go.

"Oh, Jill?" Lawson said. "When you come back, don't tear up the grass so much. You know, if you can. I know driving a 'big rig' can be hard."

Jill stared at him for a moment. "Would anyone mind if I just fucking shot this ass-clown?" she asked loudly. She didn't wait for a response, turning on a heel and stalking away, muttering under her breath. "You're lucky I'm not a psychopath, you Sunday driver. As if I can't fucking dodge grass. . ."

The sound of fast footfalls coming from behind made Jill look over her shoulder; Mia was hurrying to catch up with her. Jill didn't stop, but she did slow down a bit so that the shorter woman wouldn't have to run just to keep up.

"Sorry about Oliver," Mia said, "he's an awful person, but," she paused. "I was going to say he's got the school board's ear and his brother's the police chief so it's best to just go along and keep your head down, but maybe that doesn't matter anymore. Not like they can do anything worse than a million monsters."

"Hooray, there are some sprinkles on this shit donut of a day."

"Right! Haha. Um," Mia put on a bright smile, "anyway, I want to ask you a question, if that's okay. You said you're heading east, right? Do you think I can catch a lift? My family's on the way, just off the thruway in New York. It would only delay you by, like, an hour."

Jill glanced at Mia out of the corner of her eye, sizing the short woman up. She seemed nice enough, but the drive was likely to get rougher the farther they went. Jill could probably afford to take her as a passenger, but it would be better if Mia could help the defense. "You ever fired a gun?"

Mia stopped dead, then burst out laughing.

"What?" Jill looked around in confusion.

Mia held a hand dramatically to the side, fingers wide. Gold light poured out, swirling around her once before congealing into a gigantic chain gun, complete with thick carrying-strap and a crate of ammunition.

"You're fucking chain gun lady?!" Jill yelled. "Of course you can come! That thing is wicked. And you saved my ass like five times last night!" She debated for a second, then decided to keep talking. "I uh, owe you an apology. I thought for a moment you were that lawdick's assistant."

"Oh, God no!" Mia said, face twisting in disgust. Another flick of her hand and her chain gun dissolved back into gold light. "Can you imagine? I'm the school nurse."

They descended the stairs. "The school nurse. With a chain gun. I didn't think that was allowed," Jill said. She shook her head. "And I thought they were crazy in Texas."

Mia laughed. "I didn't have it before. I got it from the system and then made it soulbound, like your truck."

"You know about that?"

"Yeah. Ras said so earlier when he was talking with us. Andrew wanted to know why it was still working."

For a moment Jill was annoyed that Ras had spilled about Bertha, but she pushed that down. It's not as if the information was particularly important after all.

"We'll have to see if the two of them will play nice together. Maybe Bertha can solve your reload problem."

"Who's Bertha? And how? That would be amazing!" Mia said, eyes wide.

They exited the school. "The truck's Bertha," Jill said. "And the turrets are magic and make ammo from pixie farts or something. Here, let me show you." Jill sent Mia the box for the mana substitution power, then decided to check on the rest of her status while the woman read it.

Jill MacLeod
Class: Battle Trucker
Level: 16
HP: 390/390
MP: 570/570
XP: 131,221/136,000
Body: 39   Mind: 36   Spirit: 57

Conditions: Hungry

Class Powers: None
9 points available to assign.
(+) Bonus to Class Power effectiveness.
(+) Bonus to Class Powers that boost Soulbound vehicle.

Soulbound Modular Vehicle "Bertha"
Armor: 7980/7980
Durability: 57,000/57,000   Mana: 57,000/57,000

Upgrades:
Customization (1/2)
Cargo: None
Command: None
Habitation: None
Propulsion (Ground):
Torque Converter (1/1), Utility Wheels (1/3)
Turrets (Small Arms):
Mana Substitution (1/1), Dakka (1/4)
Armor: None

Upgrades Available:
Module Upgrades
Dimensional Customization (1/2)

Exactly as she expected but with higher numbers, except for the last ability:

<table>
<tr><td>Dimensional Customization (1/2):</td></tr>
</table>

<table>
<tr><td>1) The cosmetic and structural configuration of "Bertha" can be slowly changed, as long as module limitations are not exceeded.
2) The external and internal volumes of "Bertha" can be independently changed, as long as the external volume of "Bertha" is not reduced below its starting value.</td></tr>
</table>

A grin spread over Jill's face. "Sweet baby Jesus on a pogo stick. Babu is going to freak the fuck out."

CHAPTER 13

GOT A ROOM

Jill had only spent about three minutes more chatting with Mia after sending Babu the Dimensional Customization power before the young man sprinted into view, a grin on his face.

"That. Is. CRAZY!" He waved his arms about. "You have a TARDIS! Well, except for the time bit and the space bit, but the relative dimensions are there." He clasped his hands together. "You have to let me help you design the internal layout. Please! The turrets could all be next to each other inside, and there could be a maze for invading monsters, and you could have a waterfall!"

"Told you," Jill said to Mia, who was holding back laughter. "A waterfall, huh?" Jill made a "hmming" noise, one finger tapping her chin. "Too messy. You're out."

Babu clutched his chest, a gagging, croaking noise coming from his mouth. "I am dead. Dead!" He sunk to his knees in the mud.

Ras, sitting on the edge of Bertha's roof from his time as a lookout, shook his head. "Stop messing around," he snapped, scowling.

"Lighten up," Jill replied. "Babu, meet Mia. She's riding with us for a while."

Babu sprang back up and waved. "We already met. Hi, Mia! And hell yeah, we got a chain gun!"

Mia tsked. "Blossom is mine, thank you very much. But. . . ," she eyed Bertha's turrets. "I really want to see if she'll work up there."

Jill grinned. "That would be wicked awesome. Go on in."

"I'll show her around!" Babu said, moving to get into Bertha.

"Don't you dare get that mud all over —" Jill began to say, but stopped when Babu shimmered, the muck evaporating off of his knees, leaving his pants as clean as if they'd just been laundered and his body showered. Even his hair was in order. "Well. Okay then."

Babu extended an arm melodramatically, and Mia took hold of it before following him into Bertha. Babu said something Jill couldn't quite make out, and Mia laughed.

Jill tilted her head and tracked them with her eyes as they went. "Huh, well that might become a thing," she said under her breath.

Ras, who apparently had exceptional hearing, snorted. "It always is, until it's very loudly not. It won't last."

"Seriously?" Jill asked, glaring. "You've been ragging on him all day. What porcupine crawled up your ass and flexed?"

Ras opened his mouth, then clamped it shut. "Nothing. I just—he—" he stammered. "I'm just worried about our family. We're going soon, right?"

"Yeah," Jill said. She didn't think he was really telling the truth, to her or to himself. "Just a quick drive and then we're off."

"Okay. Well. Good." Ras retreated across Bertha's roof and out of sight.

Jill rolled her eyes, then dove back into her system notifications. It was time to start thinking about what would help her most. She forced herself to think of the worst moment of the fight last night, when Bertha had been trapped by the elder boa. It hadn't been crushing Bertha fast, as Bertha's slow regeneration had blunted the worst of the constriction, but it had been powerful enough to deal serious damage to the armor, unlike a lot of the smaller monsters. If Mia hadn't opened fire, things could have gone very badly. Jill was definitely going to be adding a turret for her. She needed some way to quickly heal Bertha when they encountered a heavy hitter, and she had just the thing for it.

Hold Together - Active - Spell

Repairs 1400 Durability worth of damage and increases physical and elemental Resistances by 14% for Soulbound Modular Vehicle "Bertha" for 1 minute.

Cost: 10 Mana

Numbers flashed through her head like they never had in Jill's math classes from decades before. Irritation and a hint of fear flashed through her at the system so blatantly altering how she thought, but she got over it fast enough. The magic was invading her body and mind whether she liked it or not, and so far, the changes had been positive. And if they weren't, there was nothing she could do about it anyways. Jill let that depressing realization die and concentrated back on figuring out how good the spell was.

In its base form, "Hold Together" had an efficiency of one hundred durability per mana, the same ratio as Bertha's durability to Jill's mana pool, and they both scaled off of her spirit statistic, so draining her mana completely would heal Bertha from nothing. But with the bonuses to her class from having exceeded its prerequisites, and from having Bertha soulbound in the first place, it would only take 71 percent of her mana pool, which was good? Maybe? Jill sighed in annoyance. She was better now at math, but she didn't have any context to compare to.

She needed repairs whether they were good or not, and she wasn't exactly spoiled for options about it, so Jill bought her first class power. It felt different than upgrading Bertha: where that was like something in the palm of her hand twisting and changing, this was like her hand itself growing an extra finger. She just had to flex the new digit, and the mana would do her bidding. It wasn't a painful change, but it felt like she was becoming less "Jill" when it happened. She didn't like the feeling very much at all.

Remembering something Babu had said about unlocking new abilities, Jill checked her class powers screen again.

<table>
<tr><td>Available Class Powers</td></tr>
</table>

<table>
<tr><td>Hold Together, Upgrade (1)
Increase the effect of Hold Together by 14%.</td></tr>
</table>

<table>
<tr><td>Convoy - Passive - Spell
Allied vehicles within 120 meters of Soulbound Modular Vehicle "Bertha" gain 12% Durability. Requires Level 10 Battle Trucker, Hold Together.</td></tr>
</table>

Blockade Runner - Active - Spell
Increases the speed and decreases the detectability of Soulbound Modular Vehicle "Bertha" by 14% for 1 minute. Requires Level 10 Battle Trucker, Hold Together.
Cost: 10 Mana

A Deal's a Deal - Active - Spell
The next agreement you enter becomes a System Contract. The other party must be of sound mind to enter into a System Contract. If the other party breaks the contract, they will receive a penalty of 12% that lasts for 1 System year. You may waive the penalty at any time.
Cost: 100 Mana

Battle Hardened - Passive
Increase physical, elemental, and mental Resistances by 12%.

Jill sent the new powers to Babu to look at out of habit, but didn't expect an immediate response. He was potentially busy after all.

The new available powers—convoy and blockade runner—didn't strike her as good purchases right now. While they were both potentially useful, the first would only help if they came across other functioning vehicles. The second was more interesting, especially the part about decreasing detectability. Jill snorted as the sudden vision of Bertha done up in boxy ninja clothes popped into her head. But she didn't think that a 14 percent reduction was going to stop anyone from noticing what was now a sixty-ton machine blazing along. Her truck was loud and proud. The power might eventually become something worthwhile, but in the meantime those class power points would do far more good being applied to Bertha directly.

Her thoughts were interrupted by a slight tugging sensation coming from Bertha and a notification:

Level 3 shotgun add-on from "Bertha" Small Arms turret 2 removed.

Babu and Mia were installing her chain gun.

> Integrating add-on to "Bertha" Small Arms turret 2.

> Soulbound Rotary Cannon "Blossom" detected. "Blossom" exceeds maximum supported level: effective level reduced. Mana crossfeed enabled.
> Mana cost per discharge: 10

"Fuck yeah!" Jill said, hurrying to climb into the truck and try the gun out for herself. Right after getting into the cab, she heard the rapid-fire hammering of a machine gun firing. A glance at the mana gauge showed that the draw was about double the regeneration rate, so while Bertha could drive forever, she couldn't sustain the continuous firing of something as powerful as Blossom. With the rate at which the gauge was falling though, it would still last multiple minutes, which had better be enough for whatever they were trying to kill.

Jill scowled at the mana gauge. While that kind of estimation had been alright with her before, it wasn't anymore. Exactly how long they could fire when still, or fire when driving, could be a matter of life and death—and if her thoughts earlier showed anything, it was that her mana-upgraded brain could handle exact numbers. A flex of will, channeled through the Customization power, changed the gauge to a digital display. Bertha had a regeneration of 95 mana per second, with an idling consumption of 9.5, which spiked to 209.5 when the gun was firing. That came out to twenty rounds per second: a healthy rate of fire for a person-portable machine gun, but below what a true multi-barreled weapon could do. As for how long they could shoot: with no other factors, 498 seconds of continuous fire. Which was incredible. But she would have to see how much mana driving and repairs cost to get a more accurate battlefield estimate.

She went to go into the trailer and stopped, staring at her sad little living area. Now that she wasn't in the heat of battle, having to step over her bed to get to the rest of the truck was ridiculous. There was a long road ahead of them and they'd all need to sleep; they needed better than this. She purchased the Habitation Module's basic upgrade.

> Upgrading Habitation Module! Prepare for Mana Integration.

Jill felt the changes happening through her bond to Bertha, but this time she was standing in the epicenter. Waves of gold mana shimmered just below every surface as the interior of the truck shifted and changed. Her bed popped up to its normal height, momentarily blocking the door to the trailer, before it bulged, growing wider until it split in two, like a giant blanket-covered cell undergoing mitosis. The back of the cab ballooned sideways as the beds snapped to the outer walls. Pipes snaked into being, and near each bed, a sink, shower, and toilet grew. Partitioning walls sprung up and doors formed. When the process finished, Jill was left standing in a corridor from the driving area to the trailer, with one door on each side.

Habitation
"Bertha" has a Habitation Module with basic amenities for 2. Life support capacity for 5.
Includes: Single Bed, Washroom, Workspace.
Add-ons (0/1): None.

Habitation Upgrades:
Restful Sleep (0/1): All allies who rest in the Habitation Module receive increased physical and psychological healing rates.
Unseen Servant (0/3): Weak manifestations of force will see to the maintenance of the Habitation Module and residents' possessions.
Bunkroom (0/5): Increases the capacity, life support, and volume of the Habitation Module by 2.4x, and by 1 add-on slot.

She opened the door on her right and peered inside. The bedroom was spartan in appearance and mostly made of bare metal, but the toilet, sink, and shower were in their own little sectioned off room, and next to the bed a small desk with a chair tucked underneath it took up the last available space.

Basic was the right word for it, but as a place to crash and have a little privacy, it was perfect. And there was a power right there to make it even better. Jill selected the restful sleep power and purchased it. The sensation of cool water flowing over her, body and mind, flashed through her bond with Bertha. Nothing physical changed in the room, but to Jill it already felt like home.

She closed the door and reached out with her Customization power to engrave her name onto it. The others would probably want rooms of their own, but that was something to think about when she knew how many people would be staying. Babu and Ras might be leaving her very soon, so it didn't make sense to add more rooms just yet.

"Wait, is this new? I'm not crazy, this wasn't here before!"

"Cockfountain!" Jill swore in surprise, her heart hammering. Mia had gotten right behind her without her noticing.

"Habitation?!" Babu said, as he cataloged the changes the cab had undergone. He darted forward and reached towards Jill's door, hesitated, then opened the one on the other side instead. "Coooool! Well, it's actually kind of bland. Couldn't you have spiced things up a bit?"

"What do I look like, a goddamn interior designer?" Jill said, smacking him on the shoulder. She turned to Mia. "How's the gun working? I got a notice saying it was too high a level and had reduced whatsits."

Mia's eyes went wide. "Oh, that's what it is! I was wondering why the fire rate was so much lower than usual. The unlimited ammo is amazing, but my best stuff is getting restricted. You should upgrade the turret so that I can really hose things down."

"Hey, System," Jill thought, directing it through her mana towards where she felt the system messages coming from, "what's the deal with that 'effective level' vomit? How do I raise that?"

> System information inquiry detected.
> The effective level of the Modules of Soulbound Vehicle "Bertha" are determined by your level and by the number of purchased powers in the Module.

"Well, the good news is that I can cheat it a bit by buying more powers, even if you do out-level the fuck out of me," Jill said with a mock scowl.

Mia winked.

"But the bad news is that I only have, like, ten total powers, so there's a limit," Jill continued.

Mia shrugged. "Blossom got more once I'd bought everything I could in her," she said. "Maybe the same for you?"

"System, will mine do that?" Jill thought.

> System information inquiry detected.
> Abilities are revealed upon being unlocked.

"Well, that's useless."

"We could make our builds so much more efficient if we could just know what powers we had in advance," Babu said. "This right here is why I want to document everything and make a proper guide!"

Mia looked him up and down while he was distracted.

Jill nodded. "That's why I'm sending you all my shit. We'll figure it all out eventually. For now, though, I know just the power to start with to get more firepower." She sent Mia the box for the superchargers upgrade.

"O. M. G," she said the letters aloud, "does it stack with my own upgrades? We have to try it! Please?"

Babu stepped next to her. "Extra pretty please? Think of the bullets! Those poor little bullets, all wanting to go faster but held unjustly back!"

Jill snorted. "Fucking adorable, the pair of you. Fine, I'm buying the first level." She pushed her mana towards the ability. It resisted for the shortest moment, then let go with a rush that dragged even more mana along with it. Something shifted in Bertha's turrets, like a pair of animals perking up on hearing prey.

> Maximum Small Arms turret add-on level increased. Soulbound Rotary Cannon "Blossom" effective level increased. Blossom still exceeds maximum supported level.

"Well," Jill said. "Looks like the expletive level went up, just like we thought."

"Wait, did you just say 'expletive'? Have you run out or something?" Babu asked.

"No time for that!" Mia grabbed Babu's hand and pulled him down the hallway. "I got that notification too; we have to go try it! And the supercharger! Can you imagine if they stack!"

Babu flashed Jill a thumbs up with his free hand. "Be right back! This is going to be amazing!"

Jill waited for them to be through the door to the cargo area, and for it to have sealed itself shut, before whistling and slapping her thigh. "Oh, they are so going to bone," she said to herself with a laugh. Grinning, she went forward through the new door that separated habitation from cab and hopped out the passenger-side door. Just after she did, Blossom fired again into the air; the burst of bullets was coming noticeably faster than it had just a few minutes prior. Without Bertha's insulation between Jill and the gun, it was painfully loud, but Jill still couldn't help but smile. She might tease the younger pair about their love of shooting things, but there was something exciting even to her about excessive firepower, and the tracer-infused stream of bullets arcing away certainly qualified.

"Hooah! Hell of a sight!"

"Sugardick!" Jill yelled as she jumped in shock, her heart set racing for the second time in just a few minutes. She swung her gaze around to see who had spoken and nearly swore again when Amelie suddenly appeared in her vision from nowhere, leaning casually against Bertha like she'd been there all along. Given how the pregnant woman was grinning, she probably had been, using some sort of power to avoid notice.

"We good to roll out? My squad will be here in five."

"Almost," Jill said. "Just a little bit of slimming down to do." She gestured towards the new section of the truck between the cab and the trailer. The truck would probably drive just fine—magic made a lot of bullshit possible after all—but it was now much wider than a single lane: wide enough to block the view from the side mirrors and cause problems if they needed to thread any gaps.

She purchased the Dimensional Customization power, and her connection to Bertha surged yet again. For a moment her vision twisted, and her stomach screamed in protest; Jill nearly puked. Luckily the changes weren't happening to her body, but to Bertha's, and their bond offered a degree of separation. Through it, the truck seemed to be twisting inside out, spinning, and turning to jelly except for the outer skin, which remained firm. From the doors, windows, and turrets a feeling of stability bled inwards, pinning the truck back into reality like a multidimensional shifting worm pinned to a fishing hook.

"You okay?" Amelie asked.

"Yeah. Class power. A weird-ass one," Jill said. Her stomach still felt like it was going to try to crawl out of her mouth, but at least now it would negotiate before doing so. Jill ignored it and pushed mana through to Dimensional Customization, an image of Bertha as she'd been ten minutes before in her mind. The bulge of the habitation section shrank bit by bit, and the truck grew shorter, dragging its wheels through the mud as it went, as the outer dimensions went back to normal.

The new power had amazing potential, but she'd have plenty of time to explore that later. Now it was time to get things done. As for other upgrades, she'd have to wait and see exactly what was needed. As it stood, her girl could take a beating and, with a little help, dish one out right back.

"Ready when you are, Captain."

CHAPTER 14

CONFIDENCE

Amelie put two fingers in her mouth and whistled. Within moments Andrew and six others came trotting into view from the school. Four were men with hair going gray and hairlines either gone or fighting a valiant but losing retreat, dressed in variations of jeans and flannel, each with some sort of hunting rifle. The other two newcomers were similar to each other in appearance: women who looked to Jill to be barely out of high school, but armed to the teeth with semi-automatic rifles and bandoliers bristling with grenades.

"Some old retired farts," Amelie introduced the men with a wink and a dismissive wave, which earned her raised middle fingers, "and my nieces, Sarah and Olivia."

Jill looked from Amelie with her strapped-on handguns and knives to the women with their explosives. "I can see the resemblance."

Amelie smirked. "Let's move out. I'm up front to navigate; grunts in the back." One of the men sketched her a fast salute and off they went.

"There're just some pallets back there and a ladder. Are they going to be alright?"

"They've dealt with worse for transport," Amelie said. "Well, the boys have, and the girls will figure it out. Besides, not like there's anywhere else to go in a semi."

Jill almost nodded in agreement, long years of crusted knowledge hard to change. "Hey, watch this," she said.

She closed her eyes and concentrated on the inside of the trailer, feeling its layout through her bond with Bertha, and pushed mana into her

Customization power. The sounds of crinkling metal and snapping glass filled the air as the armored plates on Bertha's trailer shifted about, and a row of thick armored windows opened up on both sides. Jill then willed the inside of the trailer to change its shape, growing slightly shorter but wide enough to have a bench running down each side under the new windows. As a finishing touch, she made harnesses sprout on the benches at regular intervals.

The sounds of yelling came from the open rear door of the truck. Jill's favorite was the unimaginative but passionate "Shit fuck damn . . . fuck!" that came from one of Amelie's nieces, and Jill made a mental note to try and improve the teen's vocabulary. She opened her eyes and saw Amelie looking back and forth between her and the morphed Bertha.

"Bertha's just a touch above a normal semi," Jill said. "C'mon, let's get out of here." She hopped back into the cab in a single bound, a jump that would make a basketball player green with envy, and Amelie did likewise, her mana enhanced body making light work of the usual awkwardness of pregnancy. A few seconds later Bertha rolled out. Amelie gave directions; the drive would only take ten minutes, even taking it slow to avoid the worst of the rubble.

The town seemed a lot smaller now than it had the night before. Daylight let Jill see that, beyond the small residential development, they were in open grassland, brown this time of year. Given Bertha's upgraded wheels there hadn't been any need for her to follow the twisting suburban streets to get to the elementary school; she could have just looped around and approached from the southwest over the open but muddy fields. But what was done was done, and she had crunched quite a few monsters anyhow.

Amelie's directions took her on the reverse of her path the previous night, heading north to cross the highway. Jill kept an eye out for the giant spider that had dented Bertha the last time she'd driven down these streets, eager for a bit of revenge, but it was nowhere to be found. In fact, the neighborhood was devoid of both monsters and people. Most of the houses were completely wrecked, with walls caved in and fires still smoldering, but a few had escaped unscathed—suspicious islands in the devastation.

The quiet of the drive was shattered when they'd reached just a block farther, the buzzsaw pounding of Mia's chain gun splitting the air as the nurse caught sight of something and opened fire.

"Trouble?" Amelie asked, twisting in her seat to get a better look at where the gun was firing.

The gun cut off, and Jill briefly glanced at her notification box: fifteen percent contribution for a half dozen monsters. She snorted. "Ex-trouble: firewolves. Just one of those things almost killed me last night, and Mia just mowed down six in one burst. That gun is bullshit."

Amelie raised an eyebrow. "Your truck is bullshit too, don'tcha know."

"Bertha's wicked awesome," Jill said, giving the dashboard a pat. "But really, it seems like everything soulbound is just better." She glanced over Amelie's equipment, but it all seemed normal. "You got any perk points?"

Amelie nodded. "One. Some of the boys used theirs on a fancy class, but I saved mine."

"Get yourself a soulbound tank or something, I dunno," Jill said, thinking that she should spend her own leftover point as well.

"Pbbbbt," Amelie blew a raspberry. "I wouldn't know what to do with a tank. I'm infantry."

"Get power armor!" Babu's voice rang down the ladder from the turret above.

"Like the Master Chief!" Mia added.

"How can they even hear us?" Amelie said.

Jill shrugged. "Magic bullshit."

Suddenly a bear twelve feet tall bounded onto the road and reared up to challenge Bertha.

"Shitdicks!" Jill didn't swerve, and Bertha plowed headlong into the massive monster. Even with its size it must have been high level, because the impact was nearly enough to stop Bertha cold. But only nearly. The entire truck lurched and the forward armor bent inwards, but in the end, it was the bear that fell over backward. Bertha heaved like a giant segmented monster truck going over a particularly tough set of cars as she crunched over the monster.

Jill slammed the brakes and turned the wheel, bringing the truck into a long slide that stopped with it facing backward. She stared at the bear, but it was best described as pulpy and probably wasn't a threat anymore. Still, it struggled on broken limbs, suicidally aggressive to the last. The continued cracks of the rifle coincided with little circles of red appearing in its fur, but the small caliber gun just wasn't doing much.

The chain gun fired, its glowing rounds slamming into the bear. It took just seconds for the creature to die; two of its limbs were cut clean off and tossed into the air in a fountain of blood by the stream of magically conjured glowing rounds.

"Well, that's that," Jill said, the now familiar high of mana surging through her body, letting her know even before she checked her notifications that she'd gained a level.

Mega Bear defeated. Bonus experience awarded for: monster kill above your level (+0.8).

Your contribution: 86%

3715 Experience Gained!

You are now Level 17!

She smiled and dismissed the box before willing Bertha to repair faster than her already impressive passive regeneration. Mana surged from Jill to her truck as "Hold Together" activated, the spell bending the armor back into shape. As an afterthought she twitched Customization to fix up the paint and give Bertha a new coat of wax.

There weren't any monsters big enough to challenge Bertha on the rest of their drive, but her guns spoke frequently when something was too slow in running away, giving Jill a steady trickle of experience. At 15 percent contribution she was going to level far slower than her gunners, which would be a major problem if their equipment grew in level faster than she could keep the turrets upgraded to match. Jill had a feeling that the monsters would be getting much stronger—it was only the first day, after all—and she refused to be the one holding everyone else back.

In order for her to level alongside her gunners, Jill was either going to need to keep running down monsters, take some turns shooting herself, or she was going to need more gunners. The first option was working so far, but it was much more dangerous than staying at range. The second meant leaving driving to someone far less capable than Jill, which could be okay in easy situations like straight highway driving, but wouldn't do for anything technical. Plus, Jill just didn't like letting anyone else drive Bertha.

That left the last option of upgrading to get as many turrets as she could. At six gunners, assuming an equal distribution of kills, she would then be getting an effective 90 percent to each gunner's 85 percent. But given Blossom's dominance, an even kill rate between turrets was very unlikely, so she'd need even more to compensate. Jill pulled up her status to see how many points she had left to assign.

Jill MacLeod
Class: Battle Trucker
Level: 17
HP: 410/410
MP: 600/600
XP: 138,249/153,000
Body: 41   Mind: 39   Spirit: 60

Conditions: None

Class Powers:
Hold Together
6 points available to assign.
(+) Bonus to Class Power effectiveness.
(+) Bonus to Class Powers that boost Soulbound vehicle.

Soulbound Modular Vehicle "Bertha"
Armor: 7980/7980
Durability: 57,000/57,000
Mana: 53,232/57,000

Upgrades:
Dimensional Customization (2/2)
Cargo: None
Command: None
Habitation: Bare Minimum (1/1)
Propulsion (Ground): Torque Converter (1/1), Utility Wheels (1/3)
Turrets (Small Arms): Mana Substitution (1/1), Superchargers (1/5), Dakka (1/4)
Armor: None

<table>
<tr><td>

Upgrades Available:
Module Upgrades

</td></tr>
</table>

For a fleeting moment Jill thought of buying four more turrets and telling Amelie's troops to get in, but she shelved that idea as quickly as it had come. They would be leaving just as soon as this quick trip was done. Hell, Babu and Ras would probably be going that night when they got to Billings. At some point she would find more people who wanted to head east for the long haul, and eventually she'd pick up her father and brothers, if she could pry them out of whatever bunker they had undoubtedly converted into a magic-fuckery-backed fortress. And Ciara too.

The ice-cold ball of black dread in Jill's stomach flared, sending tendrils through her body, but she pushed them back. They were all alive; they had to be. Her dad had enough guns to equip a company and was as hardcore a prepper as she'd ever met. Certainly no one here compared, and the Midwesterners were making out okay—for certain "it's the end of the world, magic is here, and everything wants to eat you" definitions of okay, at least.

"Oh, God," Amelie whispered. "No."

While Jill had been stuck in her own head, they had rounded the final bend in their short drive, and the high school came into view. The short, controlled bursts from Blossom turned into a continuous roar, as glowing rounds reached out to cut into a horde of monsters crawling over the two-story structure. Animals of all sorts, grown to monstrous sizes, began to boil out through smashed windows like so many furred, fanged, and scaled ants. There was a ring of monster corpses around the building, like at the elementary school but far fewer, and it was clear that here the defenses had fallen. Jill doubted that anyone was left alive inside.

Kill notifications began to appear in the corner of Jill's vision, but she ignored them and turned Bertha towards the school. Her jaw clenched hard, and she forced herself to look not at the monsters, but at the parking lots and fields around the school. A steady, circular path had worked this morning, and it would work now. She had speed, she had firepower; all she needed to kill the murderous fuckers who had eaten everyone in that building was to avoid getting bogged down.

Without warning something slammed into Bertha, the impact enough to throw Jill against her seat belt, hard; even with her enhanced body she would have bruises.

"Fuck a duuuuuck!!!" Jill screamed as the view out the armored front window changed from a nice, proper horizon to pure sky, the clouds whipping sideways. Bertha was off the ground and in a flipping spin, the Torque Converter glowing madly as it locked down only the roll axis, letting the truck flip and yaw. Jill reached against the force of the spin and pulled out all the Torque Converter's controls, grunting as she was thrown against her seat belt yet again, in the opposite direction as before. A small part of her mind, the part not terrified and clenching to stop herself from making a mess, really hoped that the soldiers in the back had been buckled in.

Bertha slammed rear-first into the ground, the crunch of metal and the sharp cracks of breaking glass announcing yet more damage. The truck balanced there for a long moment—unable to fall without tilting, wheels spinning uselessly—until Jill released the pitch axis. Down came the truck like an angry armored eighteen-wheeled tree, the suspension bottoming out with a great crash and bounce.

Fearing another hit of whatever the fuck had just happened, Jill hit the gas, released the yaw axis, and put Bertha into a fast turn that sent clods of dirt and grass flying. And not a moment too soon, because exploding from the ground right where she'd been was the head of an earthworm a dozen feet across—then another, and another. Each head split open into a tri-part mouth ringed with unending teeth. The monster screamed, the sound an icepick driven into both ears.

Lesser Worm Hydra, Level 68
Status: Feeding

CHAPTER 15

A DANGEROUS GRIND

The hydra's scream continued—beats of sound powerful enough to send spiderweb cracks spreading across Bertha's armored glass. Amelie cried out and slapped her hands over her ears, but Jill had no such luxury, as her hands were busy on the wheel pulling her truck out of its turn. The pain in her ears warred with agony radiating across her soulbond with the badly damaged Bertha; she could feel every crack in the armor plate as if it were a slice in her own flesh. Jill activated her repair spell and the pain from her bond lessened slightly, like a cool cloth placed on a broken arm. An improvement, but the underlying problem was still there. Throbbing.

> Soulbound Modular Vehicle "Bertha"
> Armor: 2177/7980
> Durability: 38,628/57,000
> Mana: 50,615/57,000

Repairing 1400 points at a time had seemed plenty that morning, but it certainly didn't seem like much now. Jill activated the spell again and, rather than let the mana flow through her like normal, she mentally pushed, straining metaphorical muscles in an effort to fix Bertha faster. She felt a chill settle over her as the power rushed out, and somehow, she knew she'd be paying the price for her haste later.

"Swarm on the right!" Amelie shouted, her words barely audible over the continuing scream, and Jill snapped her attention to what was happening outside. Dozens of knee-high, brightly feathered velociraptors had charged out of the high school. Their taloned feet threw up clods of earth as they dodged and weaved past the other monsters in a blur of speed; in only a few seconds they were close enough that Jill could make out individual yellow-stained teeth. She didn't know if the small creatures could really do anything to an armored bearfucker like Bertha, but she didn't want to find out, so she turned away from them and accelerated.

The guns had gone silent after the truck had been hit into the air, but Mia must have recovered because glowing rounds erupted from above Jill's head, reaching out towards the worm hydra. The first shots hit the carapace and glanced off in a brilliant shower of sparks, the high-level creature's hide seemingly impervious to gunfire. The flashing stream of bullets curved, bending unnaturally as Mia activated one of her powers, and the impact point slid up the hydra's central head and into its mouth. The horrible scream cut off instantly; the cessation of pain sudden enough to make Jill gasp in relief.

As fast as the hydra had emerged, it retreated, with all three heads pulling back underground.

"Oh, thank God," Jill said.

Amelie twisted in her seat to look out the window where it had been. "It can't be gone for good. It's going to be coming for us."

And it was. Unlike its previous stealthy approach, this time it favored speed and shallow running over a deep dive. The ground churned as the creature moved through the earth, a wave of dirt flung into the air by its passage.

Jill pulled the wheel hard over to the other side and started to race away. She had some room on the high school's athletic fields, but at Bertha's speed the fields were woefully short, and beyond were broken houses that would slow her down if she could even punch through them. A glance in the side mirror showed the dirt wave, pieces flying fifty feet into the air, growing closer. Another turn of the wheel, another hard turn, and the monster lost ground. It was fast on the straightaways but took time turning. Bertha was the same, but with her upgraded tires she was at least a little better than the chasing hydra.

"Can we take it?" Amelie asked.

Jill bit her lip. The hydra was monstrously strong and fifty levels higher than her. She had some measure of its speed, but what really worried her was the possibility of the unknown, of some magic power that would trap Bertha or a ranged attack. So far, the worm had only revealed its scream. Even with all the insulation provided by Bertha's armor, Jill had taken damage from it. If she'd been out in the open it might have been lethal.

"It's all down to Mia," Jill said. "If that gun can hurt the worm, we can kill it eventually."

Amelie nodded, then unbuckled her seat belt and stood, one hand gripping her rifle and the other braced on the ceiling. "I have to check on my people," she said, moving towards the back, "and figure out some way to kick that thing's ass."

Jill flicked her a glance and her eyes fixed on Amelie's semi-automatic rifle. "If you have any magic bullshit to boost your gun, kick Ras out of the turret," she said, "or at least replace that dinky rifle with something better." She pulled Bertha into another turn, pointing her towards the high school and the pack of oncoming monsters. The incoming velociraptors were only two feet tall. No way they would be able to survive getting run over.

"Roger," Amelie said. She moved back, knees bent and a hand on the walls to deal with the jerks and turns.

Babu slid down the ladder to the top turret and landed with a thump. "Mia doesn't think Blossom can hurt that thing bad enough," he said, crushing Jill's hopes. "But she said one of the upper-level gun powers lets it ignore some of the target's armor."

"So what? She wants to unmount it and fire out the window?" Jill asked. She twitched the wheel to run a dino down, but the little thing proved too nimble. It leapt up, feathers flexing this way and that to give it maneuverability in the air. With its mouth open and claws extended, it angled itself straight for Jill's face. Babu gave a little scream and Jill flinched, but she kept the wheel steady, and the creature slammed into the armored windshield and crunched in a bloody red and yellow splatter.

Venomed Velociraptor defeated.
Your contribution: 100%
1400 Experience Gained!

"Huh. For level fourteen that thing was really wimpy." Jill said, turning on the windshield wipers with a flick of her finger. They struggled at first, but it only took a few seconds for them to bat the corpse aside and clear enough of the goo to see again. The rest of the velociraptor pack had split, flowing around Bertha to either side and then turning around to keep up the chase. In the rearview mirrors Jill saw them leaping at the truck's sides, talons seeking out cracks in the armor to get a grip with. Many failed, some even falling into the path of the tires and getting crushed, but more than one succeeded in latching on. That was probably going to be a problem.

"Mia wants you to get more powers for your turrets and raise their maximum level," Babu said. A raptor crawled from the side of the cab onto the front and started scrabbling at the windows. Babu did something, a faint glow encompassing his body, and the raptor abruptly stopped moving.

Jill swerved again to open up distance with the still chasing hydra, and the frozen raptor tumbled off. She pulled up the description for the turrets and shared it with Babu. She was concentrating fully on driving and knew that she didn't have time to read it again herself.

"Gimme what I need so we can kill that shitstain!"

Turrets (Small Arms)
"Bertha" has 2 turrets for Small Arms weaponry.

Includes: Firing station, viewing slits (armored glass).
Add-ons (2/2): Soulbound Rotary Cannon "Blossom" (Level Limited), .243 Rifle.

Turret (Small Arms) Upgrades:
Mana Substitution (1/1): Unloaded Small Arms may fire, drawing Mana from "Bertha" to generate and propel ammunition. Fired ammunition lasts for 84 seconds.
Superchargers (1/5): Increases damage and rate of fire of add-ons by 14%.
Dakka (1/4): Adds 1 turret with 1 Small Arms add-on slot.

Babu stared into space, eyes flicking back and forth as he read. "These are good, but. . . ," Babu bit his lip, "Mia got a whole set of more powerful abilities after she finished upgrading a category. I really think you need to do the same for the turrets, even if the system wouldn't confirm it! You only need seven points!"

"Bollocks, I've got five," Jill said. "So not really an option!"

"Isn't it though?" Babu asked, face set in an evil grin. "You know what those things are out there, with the legs and fangs and screaming?"

"Monsters that would just love to eat us new assholes. Now get to the point!" Jill yelled. She brought Bertha into another sudden turn, one hand flicking on and off the Torque Converter, another spinning the wheel. A green-feathered velociraptor leapt at her and impacted open mouth first on the windscreen, its fangs shattering on the armored glass.

"Those monsters are also little chunks of overeager XP just throwing themselves at us to be killed."

Jill snorted in momentary amusement and for a moment shifted her attention to the dozens of kill notifications that she had been subconsciously suppressing. She had already been close to leveling up, so getting three more class points was really barely more than two full levels.

"Fuck yeah they are," she said. She put three points into the number of turrets, and mana exploded inside Bertha, racing to form not three, but five new turrets. To Jill, it felt like five new arms sprouting out of her torso, and for a moment she felt intense confusion about how she would ever control them, before realizing that of course she didn't have to. That was for whoever was inside. As they were forming, she still forced her will upon the turrets, placing them where they would do the most good. Three more joined the one already on top of the trailer, and two sprouted out of the sides. They wouldn't be able to fire in all directions like the ones on top, but they would be able to fire along its length and scrape off any boarders. Like the feathered velociraptors clawing and biting to little effect right now.

"Get back there and tell those soldiers to get in! And tell them to shoot at anything small, not the worm. If Mia can't hurt it, then they sure as shit can't," Jill said to Babu.

"Right!" Babu said. He snapped a cheeky salute and bounded away.

Jill directed her remaining two class points into superchargers and yet more mana surged, the feeling akin to coffee being injected into her brain. Above her, Blossom's fire kicked up another notch. But the upgrades weren't free, and a faster firing Blossom meant faster mana consumption from the chain gun.

Soulbound Modular Vehicle "Bertha"

Armor: 3273/7980
Durability: 51,222/57,000
Mana: 21,994/57,000

Continuously pushing mana into her repair spell let Jill fix most of the durability damage to Bertha, but the armor was still lagging behind. That wasn't too much of a concern; Jill's mana was still just over four hundred, so she had plenty of magic repairs left in the tank. The problem was Bertha's mana. Normally Jill didn't care about the mana cost of upgrades because the truck recharged so quickly, but six new turrets and two upgrades had drained tens of thousands of mana. And Bertha's mana was still dropping—the chain gun alone consuming hundreds per second.

"Mothermunger," Jill muttered, hoping the mana would last. She had no one left to send a message to Mia and the rest of the gunners to choose their shots with care; she added the Captain Speaking power, which would let her communicate with everyone, to her list of things to buy as soon as she had the points.

Notifications of new guns integrating into the turret began to pop up, but Jill dismissed them without looking. She had a new goal now—to gain levels from these creatures—and she was going to do that faster if she did more damage herself. She turned to throw off the hydra again, but this time she turned into the monster swarm instead of away. Bertha bumped and jerked as the truck went over the curbs and shrubs that had once decorated the school parking lot.

A final turn brought her parallel to the school, and Jill took a quick look inside as they blew past. The windows and doors had been shattered, and she couldn't see any evidence of bodies or blood, nor the telltale strings of holes that automatic weapons would leave. It didn't seem like many people had been fighting or dying in there. Well, at least in the tiny part she could see.

Jill tightened her grip on the steering wheel as the monster horde grew close, fear and excitement rising in anticipation of hitting them dead on, but a wave of addictive power surged through her before she had even reached the monsters. The experience points from her gunners had brought her to level eighteen. Jill assigned the class point straight into superchargers, and the fire rate picked up yet again, the sounds of six rifles and one chain gun blurring together into a roar. With unlimited ammo and a 56 percent increase in fire rate, the gunners were killing lower-level monsters so fast that their main limitation was not firepower. Even with bodies and minds enhanced by the system, it took time for the soldiers to find a new target, and more time for the turrets to swing to that position. Monsters were dying fast, but most of the experience went to the gunners instead of Jill.

It was time to change that. Bertha hit the monsters, crushing small lemmings and wolves and deer under her front grille and tires like bloody grapes underfoot. The kills came so quickly that Jill could feel the experience pouring into her. It was like the mana inside the monsters was boiling out of them as they died and flowing to their killers, an invisible tide of power filling up gunners and driver. Jill realized that she had started laughing, the manic sound filling the cab.

She turned Bertha sharp to the left, not to dodge the hydra, but instead to drive straight at the largest monster she could see—some sort of bear with leathery wings. It reared back and fire came billowing out of its mouth, though if it roared then Jill couldn't hear it over the guns. Jill screamed back at it anyways and pushed the accelerator on the floor. Just before impact she made sure the yaw and roll axis of the Torque Converter were locked and pitch unlocked.

Bertha hit the creature with a crunching thump that shattered more armor and, just like with the last ursine monster, blasted it onto its back before rolling straight over it. While it was under the wheels, Jill released the yaw and threw Bertha into a spin, smearing the caught monster sideways. A fast donut kept her near the pulped creature, and the gunners poured their fire into it.

MF Bearadactyl defeated. Bonus experience awarded for: monster kill above your level (+0.9); monster kill significantly above your level (x2).

Your contribution: 82%

8413 Experience Gained!

> You are now Level 19!

Almost half a level just from one creature and enough to push her over the edge again. Addictive power flowed into Jill, and her grin widened. She assigned her freshly earned point to superchargers, finishing the last small arms turret upgrade.

> Turret (Small Arms) Upgrades:
> Mana Substitution (1/1): Unloaded Small Arms may fire, drawing Mana from "Bertha" to generate and propel ammunition. Fired ammunition lasts for 84 seconds.
> Superchargers (5/5): Increases damage and rate of fire of add-ons by 70%.
> Dakka (4/4): Adds 7 turrets with 1 Small Arms add-on slot each.

> Congratulations! Turret (Small Arms) upgrades complete! Determining most beneficial new abilities.

Babu had been right.

Jill mentally flicked the new power descriptors his way as they appeared, but for just a moment they blocked her vision. "Cuntwaffles!" she yelled, as she willed them away. She scanned her mirrors and realized that she couldn't see the worm anymore: in her moment of distraction, it had dived underground.

The worm hydra erupted under Bertha, slamming the truck into the air. Jill's maneuver had gotten her a fast kill, but it had kept her in one location for too long; in her euphoria, she'd become fixated on leveling, on killing, and she'd momentarily forgotten about the biggest danger on the field. Despite the distraction, she was faster with the Torque Converter—quickly stopping their tumble—but this hit was different from the first. This time Bertha's armor had been worn down, both by the last hydra hit but also from running down monsters and the persistent scrabbling of the raptors crawling on her. This time, when the worm hit, the truck's armor shattered to pieces. Tens of thousands of durability damage hit the truck and the truck lost: the bed bent with a horrible shriek, as the bulbous worm head punched upwards, its hundreds of teeth gouging through metal as it thrashed back and forth, finally releasing Bertha to fly sideways.

When the truck hit the ground the bed bent again, the structure beginning to fail. The all-important drive wheels under the cab could still grip the ground and haul her away from the hydra, but she was slower than before, broken spars of metal hanging from the trailer and digging into the earth. And worse than that, there were gaping holes in the trailer's sides, shimmering kaleidoscope rifts where the dimensionally twisted interior of Bertha was exposed to the outside.

Venomed velociraptors that had been pacing Bertha, clever things that they were, seized the opportunity and they joined those that had already latched on. They had plenty of talon holds in the broken armor now, and they swarmed over and into the truck. To Jill it was like her back had been broken, her skin flayed open, and rats were crawling into her intestines from the outside, biting all the way.

"Mother trucker!"

CHAPTER 16

SPECIAL DELIVERY

Jill gasped and slumped forward, barely seeing the horrors right outside the windscreen, as the worst pain she had ever felt slammed through her bond with Bertha. She blindly turned to evade the hydra's next attack, her foot slamming down on the accelerator in a desperate spasm. She tried to block out the sensations coming through her soulbond, but it was like trying to stop a flood with just her hands. Her mana stirred in anticipation as she forced herself to do something more.

"Dad-pegging avocado-popping donkey's sub!" With every word the pain faded a bit more and her voice grew stronger, ending the invective in a shout.

Malediction Bard cross-class spell discovered!
Swampwater Vitality: Your words are so foul that harmful conditions wither before them. Each word in your spell reduces a harmful condition's effect on a target that can hear and understand you by 21.4%, multiplicatively.
Costs 100 Mana per word.

The outside world came back into focus just in time for Jill to scream "shit dicks!" in surprise as another raptor splattered itself on her windshield. The vicious things were still swarming.

The door at the back of the cab opened, bringing with it the sudden sound of gunfire, and reptilian and human screams mixed in a chorus of brutal survival. A second later Amelie backed through, rifle up, firing in deafening bursts. "Too many are getting in! We need to retreat!" she yelled, then opened fire again.

"Fuck!" Jill agreed, desperately searching for a route out.

"I'll hold them here. You get us out of here!" Amelie said, advancing out of the cab. The door slid closed behind her, muting the sounds of battle.

At least those coming from the trailer: the hydra worm's screams still rattled Jill's bones every time one of its heads breached the surface. It chased directly behind Bertha, not smart enough to attempt an intercept but too powerful to overcome and too fast to outrun once it built up speed in a straight line.

"We can lose it in those cloaca-licking twisty suburb streets. . . ," Jill muttered, and she put Bertha into a sliding spin. She meant to cut through the school parking lot and take its access road out, but that way was filled with a new horde of monsters streaming towards the hydra's siren scream. The monsters formed a deadly barrier of fang and claw that Bertha was in no shape to punch through now.

The spin continued; the centripetal force was strong enough to throw off a few of the raptors. Others were caught in the wheels and pulped, but Jill took no notice of the kills, instead still scanning for her way out. In front of the truck was a thick line of decorative but solid trees that were planted as a natural fence between the school grounds and a line of houses. There was one break: the site of a collapsed one-story ranch house where the trees had been cut down in favor of a miraculously intact wooden fence and a swimming pool.

Jill clenched her teeth and grimaced. There was no way for her to get through the property without going through the ruins of the house. Bertha was a big girl though, and burnt-out wood-frame construction would be easier to break through than the line of thick trees, so she decided to go for it.

She ended the spin and pushed harder with her right foot, but the accelerator was down all the way already. Parts of Bertha dragged on the ground, carving furrows and throwing dirt into the air as they stopped the truck from reaching anywhere near its top speed. Jill cast her repair spell as fast as she could. Every time she did, the drag reduced a little bit more as metal wreckage snapped back into its proper place. Bertha smashed through the fence, its slats snapping and flying into the air in a fountain of wood that didn't slow the eighteen-wheeler down in the slightest.

Something solid must have been hidden behind, because Bertha hit it like a ramp and launched into the air. Jill's hand shot out to grab the Torque Converter to stop Bertha from spinning as they soared over the pool. In the blink of time before they were over, Jill swore she saw the fin of a great white shark in it.

With a series of thuds, they landed in the front lawn, and Jill threw the truck into a short slide and onto the suburban street. They had managed to get out of the high school grounds. Jill's jaw unclenched the smallest amount and she breathed a sigh of relief.

As they rounded the next corner, the screaming sound of tearing metal filled the cab, followed by a surge in the sounds of fighting and gunfire. Jill snapped her head around, and time seemed to slow: a raptor had gotten past everyone and torn the door between the cab and trailer out of its track. Its claws were red with some unfortunate's blood, its eyes crazed, and its teeth yellowed and cracked. There was no armored glass between her and the monster, and no turret spitting out fire at an untouchable range. Panic gripped Jill as its gaze locked on her, and it coiled its legs to surge forward.

But in mid lunge it froze, eyes rolling in their sockets and muscles locking. It had just enough forward momentum to topple over forward, its oversized teeth carving gouges in the cab floor.

Babu staggered into the cab, one hand extended in a claw towards the venomed velociraptor. He had on his face fresh blood instead of his usual sly grin, courtesy of a deep gash that exposed the bone of his forehead, and his eyes glowed red with rage and magic power. Mana pulsed in his hand, black and red motes flaring in short bursts of light, and Babu's luscious, curly black hair blew back as if in a gale. A corona of power surrounded the enchanter: a nimbus of desire that sucked Jill's gaze in like a black hole.

His power flared, and the velociraptor's neck twisted fully around, the snapping crack of its spine a rifle shot in time with its exploding eyes.

Babu wobbled on his feet and blinked in confusion; the dark sexy wizard was replaced in an instant with his usual goofy, improbably attractive self. "Oop!" he said. "Looks like I'm outta mana . . . don'tcha know. . ." He leaned onto the wall and slid down, head lolling to one side and eyes closing. "Just gonna sit for a little. . ." His voice trailed off, as the enchanter lost consciousness.

Jill, her heart still pounding with terror, stared between the raptor and Babu. "Well shit." Bertha lurched as the truck ran over the curb, and Jill snapped her attention back front, wrenching the wheel over to get back onto the road. The hydra worm screeched from behind as it erupted from below a house, shattering the construction as it emerged.

Amelie ran into the cab, rifle raised with one arm and the other curled protectively against her chest, muscle and bone visible through a great trench of a claw wound. She scanned the tiny room and fired a deafening three-shot burst into the dead monster's head. "Clear! Cover the door." Coming up behind her were her nieces, one of them soaked head to toe in off-colored monster blood, and they took up positions in opposite bedroom doorways, weapons pointed at the trailer.

"I think we got them all," Amelie said. With a groan of pain, she slid into the passenger seat. A pulse of mana and azure light surrounded her for an instant as she activated a spell, and the flesh of her arm began to knit together.

"G-good," Jill replied, her voice catching. "It was fucking close in here."

Amelie nodded as she kept repeating her healing spell, then winced as another hydra scream rattled the windows. "Is that thing still chasing us?"

Jill took a hard turn at the next intersection. "Yeah. I'm keeping ahead, but we can't fucking kill this dick, and it just won't give up."

"Head to the armory," Amelie said after a moment's thought. "If there's anyone around with big enough guns to kill that thing, it will be them."

"Where the ass is that?"

Amelie pointed wearily with her good arm, then turned to talk to her nieces. "Sarah, get me a report on the wounded. Make sure that everyone's still alive. Olivia, drag Babu into one of the bedrooms so we don't trip on him."

The next few minutes were alternatively boring and terrifying. The smaller monsters had either given up, been outpaced, or died, but the hydra worm kept up its unending chase—its every appearance heralded by a gut-clenching scream and yet more holes in the neighborhood. Sarah returned first and leaned down to speak privately into Amelie's ear. Olivia was hot on her sister's heels, and with the repeated application of teal mana she sealed Amelie's arm shut.

"We're almost there," Amelie said, testing the range of motion of her newly healed arm. "If anyone's left, they should have eyes on us by now." She pointed to the CB radio, lifeless and forgotten since the night before when the Batis had called for help. "That thing still work?"

"Yup. It's in Bertha's status, so it's probably magic bullshit too."

Amelie scooped up the handset. "This is Baker One heading north on Third Street. Anyone out there?"

The ensuing silence was broken only by the sound of Bertha skidding around a tight turn as Jill took another hard maneuver to stay ahead of the hydra.

"This is Baker One. Anyone?" Amelie tried again, her breath held afterwards in nervous anticipation.

The CB's speaker crackled to life. "Baker One, this is Vulture Two with eyes on you and tango on your six. Do you copy, over."

"Vulture Two this is Baker One, we copy five by five. Requesting any assistance, over!"

There was a long pause.

"Baker One, head north at the next crossroad and don't slow down. Incoming arty to scrape off your stragglers. Over."

"Vulture Two, roger. Over," Amelie said. She set down the CB handset and punched the air. "Yes!"

Jill took a moment to find north and glanced at Amelie out the corner of her eye. There was a vindictive smile on her face that sent a shiver of anticipation down Jill's spine. Jill pulled a fast double juke to lure the hydra off without changing her own course too much.

The radio crackled back to life; the spotter had stayed on the same channel to let Jill and Amelie hear the orders they were giving. "Gun-bunny, this is Vulture Two. Fire for effect, grid E2764. Time on target twenty seconds . . . now. Danger close! Over."

"Uhh, translate for the class?" Jill asked. "Danger close?"

"Explosions right behind where we're going to be," Amelie said. "So don't stop."

Jill smirked and old instincts kicked in. "That's what she said." Her smile faltered, however, when she looked in the side mirror where the hydra-thrown spray of broken asphalt was growing larger and larger. In a straight line it was faster than them, and it had already proven that it could break Bertha with ease.

She pushed nearly the last of her mana into a repair spell to see if it would help Bertha move any faster, but enough of the damage had already been repaired that it didn't help. Twenty seconds stretched on forever as she kept her foot all the way down on the accelerator. The hydra grew closer and closer, and its scream went from loud to painful.

"Hold on to your butts—this is going to be close!" Jill screamed out in the final few seconds. The hydra worm launched itself fully out of the ground; its three maws stretching forward to latch onto the trailer, just as Bertha sped through the target zone.

The back of Bertha's trailer lifted into the air as an explosion tore through the street right behind them. The world slapped Jill in both ears and everything went completely, impossibly silent. Light and fire poured around the truck, the flash hitting her eyes at the same time as the pain through her soulbond. Bertha's armor dented and buckled, but held. Sound came back to Jill in a sudden wave as her eardrums healed: a rumbling boom reverberating through Bertha's frame and the hard pings of debris falling onto the roof.

The artillery had missed Bertha by the closest margin to land a devastating hit on the hydra. Jill looked back and saw one head had been blown apart, that neck now acting as a useless anchor dragging on the ground. The creature reared up before bringing its two remaining heads down into the ground, trying to burrow down, but another explosion—this time thankfully farther back—lit up the mirror as more rounds smashed into the hydra's body. The monster writhed as it tried to pull itself underground, but too much of it was maimed to uselessness, and all it managed to do was carve a black-blood encrusted trench in the roadway. More artillery rounds slammed into and around the creature, each accompanied by a flash and a shower of debris and guts.

Jill's bloodlust rose, and her hands twitched on the wheel; for an instant, moving it to throw Bertha around to run the hydra down herself and get revenge for all the pain that it had caused. But with a scowl she wrenched them back on a straight course. That kind of lack of thinking, of giving into her base feelings, was what had gotten them so in trouble to begin with.

Her knuckles tightened on the wheel as she plotted their course away from the stricken, feebly twitching monster that still somehow clung to life. Bullets of every sort, with magical tracers of every color, flew out from Bertha's many turrets in a continuous roar. Most still pinged uselessly off of the hydra's armored scales, but some found their way into gaps opened by the artillery strikes, pulverizing the holes larger and larger. Mia's chain gun led the way, its thundering report a drum of revenge.

Jill's mouth quirked in a smile as she realized that what she needed to do to keep everyone safe wasn't to be a gung-ho warrior ramming into the enemy: she was the owner, the driver, the direction, and the support that kept her armored fortress out of trouble. In just a day she'd changed so much, but she was still moving things from point A to B to keep everything running.

Lesser Worm Hydra defeated. Bonus experience awarded for: monster kill above your level (+4.8); monster kill significantly above your level (x3).
Your contribution: 23%
27,214 Experience Gained!
You are now Level 21!

"Hooah!" Amelie yelled, pumping her fist in the air. Sarah and Olivia yelled the same in unison a moment later. "That's what I'm talking about!" Shouts of joy echoed from the back of the truck through the damaged door as the other soldiers saw that the fight was over.

CHAPTER 17

DON'T BLOW IT

Jill's heart thundered in her chest even after the concussive blasts of exploding artillery shells had faded away. The hydra worm, once a terrifying monster far beyond her and Bertha, had been reduced to so much broken meat. That such a powerful creature was now dead was a testament to the focused power of the explosives that had rained down on it.

Jill slowed Bertha to a stop. With all the monsters chasing them slain, the truck's guns had fallen silent in their turrets. Their desperate thunder was replaced by the cheers of the soldiers, the pings and cracks of metal and glass snapping back into place, and, beneath it all, the quiet hum of Bertha's mana engine refilling. Jill realized that she had been holding the wheel in a white-knuckled death grip. It took more effort than she expected to force her hands to unclench and come off the wheel. She stared in the mirror at the smoking corpse of the hydra worm; the terror she had been suppressing surged up her spine, then slowly faded to reveal an underlying anger as the end of the fight truly sunk in.

She snarled, then turned Bertha around and drove back towards the monster.

"Armory's that way," Amelie said. "Where are you going?"

"Bertha bled because of that wanking worm. You know, metaphorically speaking. I'm looting the fucker."

Amelie eyed Jill sideways, then nodded. "Do it fast."

There was a crunching squelch as Jill drove onto a pile of the hydra's spilled guts. "Loot this dingle," she commanded the system, and a surge of golden mana erupted into the air. Streams of it poured into Bertha's cab and condensed into a blindingly bright shape on the dashboard.

Jill turned her head away and shielded her eyes with an arm. As the light began to fade, she risked first a quick peek, then a longer look. Sitting on the dashboard was a long, old-fashioned trumpet made of silver, its flaring metal bell inscribed with an abstract hydra pattern.

"Huh," Jill said, "I thought monsters shit animal parts and gems."

"Who knows," Amelie said, shrugging. Her voice changed tone to one of command. "Now get us out of here. We have wounded."

"Yes, sir!" Jill said, her hands and feet moving of their own accord to bring Bertha back into motion. "Wait," she said, but didn't slow down. "Did you just use a power on me?"

Amelie smirked. "Never! Just keep your eyes on the road."

The CB radio crackled to life just a few minutes later as Jill turned Bertha onto the street containing the armory. "Baker One, you are approaching the security perimeter. Good to see more survivors."

"Roger," Amelie responded. The captain leaned back in the passenger seat. Her arm was no longer shredded, courtesy of repeated healing spells from Olivia, but she radiated exhaustion.

"You okay?" Jill asked. She was feeling the aftereffects of stress and adrenaline herself, but the sight of the tall chain-link fence and strangely alien lookout towers ringing the armory was a balm on her nerves.

As Bertha rolled up to the gate, a soldier standing in front with a rifle across his chest raised a hand half in a wave, half in a gesture to stop, and walked towards the truck. Jill slowed Bertha to a stop.

"Fine, I'm just fine," Amelie said, a wan smile on her lips. "I always crash after combat." She slapped her cheeks, then closed her eyes; a glow briefly pulsed on her skin. When she opened her eyes again, they were alert. "Powers still work though, so I'm good to go."

Jill rolled down the window as the soldier approached, idly noting as it slid downwards that the door had grown noticeably thicker to accommodate the armored bulk on the glass.

"Do you have any firearms, explosives, or other hazardous material on board?" the soldier asked.

Jill stared at him. "Sure as pope-shit we do! What kind of numb-nuts question is that?"

Amelie leaned forward and sighed. "Jim, call a damn replacement and get some sleep. You're useless right now."

Jim straightened and snapped a salute. "Captain! Oh, thank Jesus you're back! No offense to Buckman."

"Buckman?" Amelie asked. "What's he doing in charge? Where's Santana?"

"No one knows," Jim said with a shrug. "Probably eaten." He gave Amelie a hopeful look. "Captain, we need you on top."

Jill snorted in amusement.

"Not like that!" Jim said, cheeks turning red. "Can I please let you in now, sir?"

Amelie nodded and pointed a finger at him. "Get some sleep, soldier!"

Jill laughed as she rolled up the window, a bit more of her adrenaline fading away.

Amelie punched Jill in the shoulder, hard. "Lay off Jim, yeah? He's one of mine."

Jill nodded and winced, noting that she had actually lost a few hit points. "Noted. He another relation?"

Amelie laughed. "No, but close enough. He was in my unit, and we saw some action together. He's damn solid but not really good with words."

Jill nodded. She knew the type.

Amelie whistled as they pulled through the gate. "Would you look at that."

The fence and gate appeared to be made of flimsy chain link, but the moment Bertha's nose began to cross into the armory an iridescent shimmer of magic rippled into view along the boundary. Jill felt Bertha struggle against it for a moment; the massive truck slowed noticeably before the barrier peeled back around them and let the truck pass. Bertha finished crossing through the gate, and the barrier snapped back, a distortion rebounding and racing across the surface like tiny waves on a glass-smooth pond.

"Dancing dandy dicks, that's cool," Jill said.

The inside of the armory was a hive of activity, its grounds packed with people moving with purpose. At the far end of the short driveway were old permanent buildings that looked like they had been there for decades. On the field in front of them, refugees were constructing a burgeoning tent city. Heads turned as Bertha rolled by, and some tearful faces gained a sudden spark of hope. In the parking lot a crowd of civilian volunteers, easily identifiable thanks to their lack of uniforms, were being drilled in how to handle rifles.

"Where am I headed?" Jill asked.

"It looks like they already have a medical tent set up," Amelie said, as she pointed to a large tent with a red cross on its canopy. There was a note of respect in her voice. "Let's get the wounded off."

Jill nodded, then swung Bertha around and backed the trailer close to the tent. She and Amelie unbuckled and jumped out to help, but by the time they reached the back of the truck the cargo doors were open, and medics were helping the wounded to leave.

Jill swallowed hard. All of the volunteers who had fought in Bertha's defense were in bloodstained clothes; for the lucky ones, it was mostly not their blood. Through the miracle of Olivia's healing powers no one had died, but it was a near thing, and one of the older men hadn't woken up yet. Another had lost his right arm at the elbow and had the glassy eyed look of someone on heavy painkillers. Jill felt her guts clench as they were taken away.

Amelie leaned against the side of the trailer and closed her eyes, her breathing deep and a look of pain on her face.

"Hey," Jill said. She hesitated, then patted Amelie on the arm. "Not your fault."

Amelie opened her eyes and gazed at Jill for a long moment. Her face showed not the pain that Jill had been expecting, nor any gratitude for the sentiment, but rather a cold assessment.

"I was in command," she said, pronouncing each word with care. "I could have ordered you to drive away the instant we saw that there was no one holed up at the school. But I made the call that we needed to get closer and make sure. I could have ordered Sims to fall back when he was first wounded. But I made the call that if he did, we wouldn't be able to cover all the holes in the trailer walls. We would have been flanked. Whether or not those calls were right or wrong, I made them, so yes, it is my fault. Any commanding officer bears the ultimate responsibility for soldiers in their care."

"Balls, that sounds awful," Jill said. She swallowed hard. "Glad I don't have to deal with that."

"You will sooner than you think, what with the crew you're assembling," Amelie said. "The first time someone dies, it's going to be hard. The times after that. . . ," she shook her head. "Well, those had better be hard too. Got it?"

A heavy, cold weight settled onto Jill's shoulders, pressing her down. She nodded slowly. "I think so."

"Good," Amelie nodded. "I need to get an update from the acting commander and maybe take command if no one more senior is here. Hold tight for a bit." With that she strode off towards the main armory building.

Jill sighed and leaned against Bertha's side. Responsibility for herself was nothing new to her: the fate of her, and her business, had long rested solely on her decisions and driving skill. But she had never truly had responsibility for someone else. Ciara was Jill's partner, but she had her own life and career. She didn't rely on Jill for support. What Amelie had laid out was beyond anything Jill had ever considered: if she was in command of those that went with her, then in a very real way their lives were hers to ruin or end.

Jill took a deep breath in, then out, and pushed those feelings down. She would deal with them later.

"Sweet! Special loot for boss monsters!" a loud voice said right behind her.

"Jizz curtain!" Jill yelled, spinning around.

Babu was there, bouncing up and down on the balls of his feet in excitement, with the silver hydra horn in his grasp. He was still disheveled and had dried blood all over him, but the deep gash on his head had been reduced to a scar that was fading before Jill's eyes. In the distance behind him, Sarah and Olivia had finished helping the wounded and were staring at the excited enchanter like lionesses at a tasty zebra.

"I swear to god you enjoy scaring me, don't you?" Jill asked. "And weren't you out fucking cold?"

Babu shrugged. "I got better," he said. "But no time for jokes. This right here," he tapped the horn, "could be really powerful." He extended the trumpet towards her. "Blow that horn!"

Jill glared at Babu, annoyed enough that she refrained from making the obvious joke.

"Pretty please?" He said, his smile bright. "Just don't point it at me."

"Fine." Jill said, throwing up her hands. Babu thrust the horn into her hands.

It was long and heavy. Far heavier than it should have been—before her system upgrades she would have struggled to even lift it. After a moment of awkward fumbling, she was ready. She took a deep breath, pursed her lips, and blew.

An ear-shattering blast of sonic energy poured out of the far end as Jill felt an enormous amount of mana flow out of her. A cone of destruction shot forward at the speed of sound, throwing up clods of earth as it carved a trench in the ground. It slapped off of the buildings, shattering windows and blowing down the less sturdy tents. Jill's eardrums burst and, despite being the source of the destruction, she staggered backward, battered and stunned.

Unidentified Item (Level 68, Rare) Activated!
Mana Cost: 500

Shouts of alarm echoed around the base. The drilling civilians dove for the dubious cover of their parking lot. Running towards Jill was a squad of armed soldiers.

Babu was half collapsed on the ground, blood coming out of his ears. Despite being out of the direct line of fire, the backblast of the high-level item had hurt him too.

Sarah and Olivia, already watching, were far enough away to be merely stunned. They ran towards the source of the destruction with alarm on their faces. Olivia blurred forward, teal mana swirling around her hands as she closed the distance to Babu's side in an instant.

Jill lowered the horn with caution, far more respectful of it than she had been a moment before. Her hearing recovered with a faint "pop" as her regeneration caught up the light damage she had taken. "Slap me sideways and call me senator," she said, to no one in particular.

The soldiers skidded to a stop in a semi-circle around her, weapons raised. "Drop the weapon!" one with extra stripes on her uniform yelled.

"Oh, for fuck's sake! This goddamn day!"

CHAPTER 18

NEW ADMIRERS

I said drop it!" the ranking soldier repeated herself. While she had her weapon raised, her finger was off the trigger.

"Fine, but if this fucker blows up, I'm blaming you," Jill said. She lowered her arms slowly to her sides and let the hydra horn drop to the ground. It landed with a dull thud and not a single shattering explosion. "There, happy?"

Babu groaned in pain and struggled to stand. "That was—that's too powerful for us to use right now!"

Olivia put a finger under his nose, tipped his head back, and forced him fully onto the ground. "Lie down and let me work. You're more injured than you think."

"Hey!" the soldier shouted to gain their attention. Her expression had changed to one of annoyance. "You pay attention to me, not him. Now, all of you are under arrest until this is sorted out, so get down on the ground and—"

Anger surged through Jill and she snapped. "Oh, suck my twat you limp-dicked, sore-kneed excuse for a pony. Of all the things that have tried to kill me, you are the least scary shit-stain that's leaked from this pro-lapsed, diarrhetic elephant anus of a day, so don't point that peashooter at me, or you'll have to have it pulled out of your own urethra! While I've been out killing monsters and getting my truck's vag kicked in, you sorry-excuse-for-toddlers are just standing around with one thumb up your own asses and the other stuffed down each other's pants! Are you gonna piss me off more or go do something useful?!"

Jill's outburst extended to her mana, which surged out of her in a blast that consumed nearly all of her already low reserves. Her vision narrowed and she stumbled forward, barely stopping herself from falling face first on the ground.

Malediction Bard cross-class advanced spell discovered!
That Which Is Unholy Reveals the Divine: Your words are beyond mortal comprehension in their foulness. For the duration of the incantation, all who can hear and understand you are fascinated. Afterwards, those you view as neutral or allies are overcome with awe, while those you oppose are overcome with fear. Effects are strongly dependent on level: all higher-level beings suffer reduced effects and enemies lower in level take psychic damage. Effects scale based upon invested Mana.
Mana cost: Variable

(+) Enhancement Requirement: Fulfill base requirements 10 times over.
Bonus to Class Power effectiveness.

Malediction Bard cross-class dedication unlocked!
Requirements: Level 21+
Earn an enhancement for the desired class.

You have one dedication slot available.

The lead soldier blinked at Jill and swayed, her gun hanging limply by its carrying strap and an expression of empty wonder on her face. To a person the other soldiers fell to their knees. One began crying tears of joy as they began mouthing Jill's diatribe, committing the revelatory words to memory.

"That. . . ," the lead soldier shook her head rapidly, "that was the most amazing chewing out I've ever heard in all my years." She extended a hand. "Sergeant Anderson at your service, ma'am. Let me just send a runner to the brass and get all this cleared up, hey? Then we're going monster hunting, hooah!"

"Uh. Yeah," Jill said. The vacant expressions and changed attitudes were disturbing. She could feel the lingering tendrils of the mana she had used reaching into the soldiers' minds and knew that it had blasted past their defenses and scrambled their will. She struggled to keep the horror she felt off her face. "That would be, uh, great."

"Cooper!" Anderson barked at the crying soldier. "Get your lazy ass up and over to command!"

"Y-Yes, sir!" The soldier stood, but hesitated before leaving. "Ma'am," he said to Jill, "If I don't see you again, it was truly an honor!" He took off running.

Jill's skin crawled; the thought of anyone doing to her what she had just accidentally done to these people made her sick. She turned to Babu and Olivia with dread, but while they both looked a little stunned, their expressions were still their own. Concentrating on the last lingering wisps of mana, Jill was able to tell that it hadn't penetrated into their minds very far before being stopped.

Jill clapped her hands and forced out a single fake laugh. "Right. So," she said, gathering her thoughts. "All a misunderstanding, right? Let's just . . . wait right here." She staggered a few steps over to Bertha's nearest wheel, cleaned it with a passing thought, and let herself slide to sitting. Her mana was recovering quickly, but the shock and exhaustion from being so close to empty still lingered in her system. "Fuck," she said to herself.

"Shit," Anderson replied. She seemed to be getting back to some semblance of normal faster than the others, but wasn't quite there yet.

"Damn."

"Fuck."

"No repeats!" Jill scolded. She idly noted that the other soldiers kept switching their attention from her to Anderson like they were following the ball at a tennis match.

"Uhh . . . ," Anderson paused. "Dicks?"

"Better. Autofellatio."

"That can't be a real word," Anderson replied.

Jill shook her head. Anderson was woefully uneducated in expletives for her rank. "It is," she said. "Your turn."

"Knocker juggler!"

"Ball-cheese connoisseur, are we allowing compounds now?" Jill asked. She turned her head as a young girl came running up with blinding speed. She couldn't have been older than twelve and had entirely too much energy.

"Message from the captain!" she said, sketching a terrible salute. She unfolded a piece of paper. "F. F. S," she read, pronouncing each letter, "I leave you alone for two minutes and you blow something up. Stop it. Anderson, you are ordered to let Jill go without charges." She zipped forward, thrust the paper into Anderson's hand, and blurred away.

"Are all the kids around here that fast?" Jill asked. She stood and stretched. Her outburst had been cathartic, but she really needed a proper rest sometime soon.

"The LT's idea," Anderson replied. "He wanted them to be able to run from monsters, so had them all run notes around until they qualified to be messengers. Anything else you need to know, ma'am?"

"Uhh. No. I'm good."

"Then it was an honor to meet you. Squad! Move out!" The soldiers obeyed and jogged off, mostly managing to keep moving in a straight line.

Babu whistled softly as the soldiers jogged away. "How did you manage to snooker that lot so bad? I don't remember you having anything like that. Unlock something new?"

Jill swallowed and sent the notification box over. "This is terrifying."

Babu's eyes flickered as he sped read the message. He shrugged. "I doubt it's permanent. And they still waited for orders before letting you go, so I don't think you totally dominated them." He hesitated, swallowed, then squared his shoulders. "You want to see something really worrying? I got this gem after popping the raptor that was going for you."

Jill felt the barest connection in her mana, like two friends whispering to each other across a room, and a box popped up in her vision.

Enchanter evolution, Dark Dominator advanced spell learned!
Devourer of Puppets: Your domination goes beyond the mind and body and extends to the soul. Execute and reap the soul of a creature that you have total control over. The more creatures you slay with this ability the more powerful it becomes, but beware of whispers in the dark. Mana cost scales with level and remaining hit points of the target.
Mana Cost: Variable
You do not meet the prerequisites to evolve Enchanter into Dark Dominator.

"Bouncy bits in heaven, that's messed up."

"Ope, I know right? I'm never using it." He shrugged. "Yours just makes people impressed or afraid. Scary to mess with people's minds, and if you don't want to use it, well, you don't have to. But it's not like we can't do that without magic anyways. I've got this little spin-shimmy-shake I used to do that got people doing what I wanted." He smirked. "Good times."

Jill eyed Babu, somehow more intrigued at this latest revelation than the dark magic. "You had a what now?"

"Uhh, I'll tell you some other time!" Babu said with a nervous laugh, his eyes darting to Olivia, who was looking at him with a confused expression on her face. "Have you seen the trailer yet?" he said hurriedly. "Those monsters really tore things up, don'tcha know. Total mess. You should go fix Bertha up."

"Leaky tits!" Jill said. She strode over to the still open trailer and looked inside. "Crotch goblins on coke, that's just a mess. . . ," she muttered.

Nearly every surface in the widened cargo trailer had some sort of fluid or crusted gunk on it. Monster blood and guts were the most common and stood out with their odd neon colors, but there was enough red human blood starting to turn brown to make Jill feel another pang of guilt. The canned food that she had been hauling had been torn from the wrapping on their pallets; cans and boxes were strewn about, some crushed and leaking. The sight of beef stew mixing with human blood was one that Jill could do without. The pile of loot from the various monsters was noticeably cleaner than everything else despite being mostly a pile of monster parts; after all, they were artificially created in a mana surge after the messy business of killing had already been done.

The physical structure of the trailer was sound—Bertha's automatic healing had taken care of the gross repairs. But the bench and harnesses were completely shredded, and along the walls where the raptors had clawed their way inside were raised and discolored lines in the metal. The inside of the trailer was now scarred, just like flesh would be after a nasty injury.

Jill frowned; none of this was okay for her girl. Her previous worries faded into the background as she focused on Bertha. With a flex of her Customization power, she began cleaning and repairing.

The blood and bile were the first to go, evaporating off with the sparkles of golden mana. When Jill had cleaned the seats in the cab or given the truck a wax coat the mana cost had been minimal, but this time she could feel the pull from the sheer quantity she was dealing with, and it nearly drained her of mana yet again. She paused for a minute, hands on her knees and taking deep breaths, then forced herself to continue. The scars were thankfully easier, fading and recessing as Jill soothed Bertha back to a pristine state. A discomfort that Jill hadn't been consciously aware of in her soulbond faded, and Jill let out a sigh of relief. It was like a headache she had grown used to had suddenly gone away.

The broken food cans remained. "Those are trash too." Jill directed her thoughts towards the system, and they melted into golden puddles that evaporated away.

Her mind expanded to cover the entire truck, and with a final satisfying flex she evaporated the dirt off of every floor, fixed up the upholstery, and added a lavender scent to the bedroom toilet stalls.

Jill jumped out of the back of the truck and closed its doors. She caught her reflection in the gleaming metal and was shocked to see that she was smiling.

While she had been fixing Bertha up, Mia and Ras had come and were talking with Babu, who had the hydra horn in hand and was waving it around in excitement. At the sight of Jill, Ras detached himself from the group and walked over.

"Finally free?" Ras asked. He handed Jill a small package wrapped in wax paper.

"Yeah. What's this?"

"Sandwich. They're handing them out to everyone while supplies last."

"Thanks, Ras," Jill said with a smile. She unwrapped the paper to reveal two pieces of white bread with one slice of bologna and one slice of American "cheese." She looked back up at him, unimpressed. "I take back the thanks."

"Food is food, and they're running low."

Jill glanced back at her trailer, with 80 percent of its load still good, and nodded. "I guess it is. Maybe we can do something about that." She took a bite and before she knew it the sandwich was gone.

"So," Ras said, "are we heading out soon? This has already taken too long."

Jill shrugged. "Sure, pretty soon."

A flash of anger crossed Ras's face. "That's not good enough. You said this would only take a little while. Honor your sugaring word, and let's get going!"

Jill stared him dead in the eye. "Excuse me? You giving me orders now?"

Ras clenched his teeth, then deflated. "Sorry. That was uncalled for."

Jill nodded. "Apology accepted. What the hell's going on, Ras?"

"I'm just worried about the family," he sighed, and the words started spilling out. "Everything's ruined and on fire and mom is sick. I just don't know what's going to happen if the hospital—"

"Mom is what?" Babu asked, striding over. "What's wrong with mom?"

Ras hesitated and let out a fake laugh. "I'm just worrying like you always say I—"

"Ras, please!" Babu said. His face was filled with worry. "Tell me."

"It's her heart," Ras swallowed. "The doctors found a murmur that they're worried about, so she went in last night to get scans and have overnight observation."

"Oh, my God. . ."

"She's not dying! It was just a precaution!"

"But you're worried."

"I'm always worried, right?"

Babu let out hollow laugh. "You're always something. I can't believe you didn't tell me this. Mom's in the hospital, and I didn't know. I can't believe it. Why would you do this to me?"

Ras swallowed. "She. . . ," his voice trailed off. "After your last argument she said she doesn't want to see you again. I know she's going to change her mind, she always does, but if you knew she was sick, you'd go to see her, and then you would fight, and then everything would get worse! I'm just trying to look out for you. To look out for the family!"

Babu clenched his teeth and took a deep breath as if to scream, but instead let it out slowly. His anger deflated along with his breath, leaving him a sad husk. "That wasn't your call, Ras." He opened his mouth to say something else, hesitated, and then finally ground out, "I need to be away from you." He walked to the trailer, opened the driver door, and jumped inside.

Jill and Mia shared a wide-eyed glance. "That's messed up, Ras," the gunner said. She followed after Babu.

Ras stared after them, body frozen in place.

CHAPTER 19

LEGENDARY PINK BEAST OF ARRRGHHH

That's rough, buddy," Jill said. "This sure is a shit sandwich."

"No matter what I do," Ras said, his voice harsher and louder than Jill had ever heard from him, "nothing ever goes right! Mom and Dad start ragging on Babu? I get them to stop, only for Babu to act out! I get Babu to stop, and they threaten to disown him for something tiny! Always one or the other just fucking everything up!" Ras paced back and forth. "And you aren't helping right now! Every time Babu's stressed, he just gets more reckless, more impulsive. He's going to get himself killed one of these days, damnit! Next time he asks you to do something stupid like blow that horn, don't sugaring do it!" He turned to face Bertha, the determination on his face twisted by anger. "I can still fix this. I'm going in there, and I'm going to make him see sense whether he wants me to or not."

He stormed over to Bertha and tugged on the door, but it didn't budge. Jill had sealed the entrance shut with a solid plate of metal over where the door should be.

She shook her head. "That sounds like piss in your cereal bowl, but trust me, you don't want to talk to him this angry."

Ras whirled on her. "What do you know? You don't even know us!"

Jill quirked an eyebrow. "I'm like twice your age. You think I've never had someone in the family leave a floater? You two've got to hash things out, but that's not going to happen right now. Not until you've both cooled down."

Ras clenched his jaw, and he pulsed with magic. He drew his soul-bound sword and flicked it down to his side; an afterimage of mana and the cracking sound of a whip accompanied the idle motion. "Bullshit. If you don't open this door, I'm opening it myself!"

Jill glared at Ras in annoyance. There was no way a sword was going to get through Bertha's armor, but with none of her class points invested in herself personally fighting, she also wouldn't be able to stop him from gouging up the paint.

"You do what you have to do, Ras," she said, her voice level. "But do you think I'm wrong? For real?"

Ras stared at her for a long moment, and the mana around Jill responded to his emotions. It twisted and writhed, alternatively pulling into him like a whirlpool and blasting out in uncontrolled spikes. With a scream he grabbed his sword with both hands, knuckles white, and slammed it into the ground in front of him.

There was no explosion. No earth flew into the air, no lighting blasted out. Instead, a perfect slice opened in the ground: it was only two feet long, but with edges so clean that, despite being made of dirt, they looked sharp enough to cut. The strike had severed through the mana in its way, and the remaining magic had yet to heal itself. For just a moment Jill wondered if Ras really could have gotten into Bertha, then she dismissed the ridiculous thought.

Ras deflated, his arms and head hanging limply. "Fuck." He raised his head and tears sparkled in the corner of his eyes. He sheathed his sword, sniffed, and wiped the tears away before meeting Jill's eyes again. "I apologize for the profanity," he said. "That was uncalled for."

Jill couldn't help it: she burst out laughing. After a moment Ras's face cracked, and he joined her. But when he was finished his face was filled with sadness again.

Jill walked over to him and punched him on the shoulder. "You want some advice? You might not like it."

Ras nodded.

"Okay then,' Jill said. "Babu isn't you. He's his own person and can make his own decisions, including if he's willing to change to meet expectations. Keeping him from making those is never going to end well. You want to give him advice? Fine. But he gets the final say."

"But he's my little brother," Ras said. With the anger drained out of him he looked like he had nothing left. "I have to look out for him."

"And you can. But he's an adult now, even if he's a silly shit sometimes."

Ras took a deep breath and blew it out, then nodded.

Jill stared at the cut in the ground; mana had yet to return to it. "Did I tell you about what I did just a minute ago?" she asked. Ras shook his head and she kept talking. "I mind-fucked a whole bunch of people just doing their jobs. I didn't even mean to do it, but the mana reached into their brains and now they like me more than tits! This magic bullshit is dangerous." She pointed at the ground. "We need to be more careful than that. I feel like I know you, Ras. I know you're not going to go all Sith and kill children, not on purpose, but fuck me if it's not easy to do by accident. I need to rein in my mana, to stop it from doing things without permission, and to do that I'm going to need to experiment, to figure out how the hell it works." She looked him in the eye. "I need Babu's help with that, and we're probably going to do some stupid shit, but I promise you that I'm going to be as careful as I can. That good enough for you?"

Ras grimaced, then nodded. "Okay. I'll just have to deal with it, I guess." He looked over his shoulder at the truck. "Do you think he'll forgive me?"

Jill nodded. "I haven't known you two long, but I don't think Babu has it in him to stay mad at anyone for very long."

"I hope you're right."

Jill clapped her hands together. "Right. Good talk. Now how about we stop standing around with our dicks out and do what needs to be done so we can get out of here?"

Ras snorted a laugh. "I'd like that."

"Then get your uptight ass over to whoever they have managing food and tell them we have most of a shipment for them. Keep . . . oh, hell, I don't know. Keep like a quarter of it and give the rest over. Maybe see if they have anything that goes 'boom' they'll give us in trade."

Ras nodded, gave one final look at Bertha, and walked away.

Jill waited for him to be out of sight, then exhaled hard. "Fuck me, I can't handle all these kiddos. Goddamn drama-llama bullshit." She looked around for the next emergency to kick her in the nuts, just in time to yelp in surprise as a series of explosions sounded across the base. Five blasts rang out, each a sharp thud followed by a roar.

Jill instinctively ran towards Bertha and safety but stopped when she realized that no one else had gone for cover.

"Hey!" Jill said, flagging down a passing messenger boy.

He zipped to a stop and scowled at her. "Yeah?"

"What the ass-burger were those bangs?"

He rolled his eyes. "Never heard a cannon go off? You suck." He stuck out his tongue and ran away.

"What a shithead! I like him," Jill said. The explosions roared again, and this time Jill saw the muzzle flash on the other side of the armory, and her mana-enhanced eyes just barely caught the streak of outbound artillery shells. "I've got some debts to pay," she muttered to herself. She scooped up the hydra horn and started walking.

The direct path took Jill through the tents. While from the outside it looked like chaos, from the inside it was more like a choreographed ballet, with each person moving out of the others' way just in time. Dirty faces with tear tracks were the norm, but there was a spark of hope in the air. As she moved through, Jill felt herself enter the dance, and her steps guided her around a pair of women carrying a long table without any effort.

It had to be a power of some kind making the work smoother. Jill stretched out with her senses and felt subtle tendrils of it on her, but she somehow knew she could break them with a thought. They were different from those of the spell she had just learned: supportive rather than coercive. It felt familiar to Jill; similar to the meditative, but active, state she could slip into during the hours of a long-haul drive. She sunk into the feeling, and before she knew it, she was on the other side of the tents.

What had been a garage for doing routine, occasional maintenance work on the armory's vehicles had been turned into a bustling workshop, with the sound of hammering accompanied by flashes of multicolored light pouring from the building's open roller door. A trio of fighting vehicles were parked outside, sitting cold next to a pile of looted monster parts. Two civilians were busy sorting the parts into bins by type, with a third picking the bins up when full and bringing back empties.

A horn honk from behind her had Jill stepping aside by instinct. A badly dented infantry fighting vehicle—the guard plate on its mounted machine gun bearing distinct bite marks—rolled past, its engine a stuttering growl. Jill stared at it: a working vehicle other than Bertha. "Nitro!" hollered the gunner. "Get out here! We need to get fixed up and back out there ASAP! Do your magic voodoo!"

"I told you to call me Mike!" came the annoyed shouted reply from inside the garage. "Pull it by the others, and I'll get to it in a minute!"

The fighting vehicle pulled into a parking spot next to three others that Jill had previously assumed were inoperable because of the system. Jill watched it for a long moment, then nodded to herself. It wasn't self-repairing, so it couldn't be soulbound. The base mechanics must have figured out some other way to get them running despite the system's interference with technology.

Jill flinched as the artillery piece fired again, its report deafeningly close, and she walked up to the vehicle. As she got close, a door on the side opened and out jumped the crew.

"Hey," she shouted, her ears ringing, "where's the big-ass gun?"

"Out back. You can't miss it," replied a woman wearing a sleeveless, camouflage-pattern top despite the chill.

"Thanks," Jill said, and she circled around the building. The gun was, indeed, impossible to miss.

There sat a huge, bright-pink howitzer, its barrel pointed skywards with smoke still drifting outwards and upwards in a lazy wavering line. Near its base was a supersized decal of a rabbit in a helmet holding a grenade. A man wearing green-tinted goggles ran out of the workshop past Jill holding a glowing bar with a pair of tongs. A crew member rotated a wheel on the howitzer's back to open the breach door, and out spat a dull gray, cracked rod. A shove, close, and turn had the new one installed.

"Loaded!" the wheel-turner yelled.

"No targets! Clear!" was the response from a tall older man with a buzz cut who had a huge, chrome-plated walkie-talkie up to his ear. The two loaders exchanged a fist bump, then started talking to each other while walking back to the workshop.

Jill sauntered up to the buzz cut man, who was staring off into the distance with his eyes flickering back and forth. Reading system messages, most likely.

"You in charge of this beauty?" Jill asked.

"That I am," he said, extending a hand. "Staff Sergeant Jackson, at your service. You're the trucker, right?"

"Jill MacLeod," she said, shaking his hand. "Heard of me already?"

"Rumor mill says you might cuss good enough to be a marine."

Jill snorted. "Only when I'm drunk." She gestured at the pink artillery piece. "You, uhh, saved my ass out there. So, thanks."

"This old girl's saved lots of folks," Jackson replied, giving his gun an affectionate pat, "me included." He gestured with a hand and a notification appeared in Jill's vision.

Soulbound Heavy Weapon "Caerbannog"
Durability: 6400/6400
Mana: External
Upgrades:
Reloading (1/1)
Ammunition: Homing Shells (5/5), Armor Piercing (4/5), Adaptive
Ordinance (5/5)
Armor: None
Command: None
Propulsion: None
Rangefinder: Precision Targeting (4/5), Teamwork Makes the Dream
Work (3/5)

Jill whistled at the number of points invested into offense. "All-in on making monsters taste their elbows through their assholes, huh? Looks like a stiff breeze will make your little bunny fall over though." She sent over an abbreviated status for Bertha.

Jackson grinned. "I have a type, and it's always gone 'boom.'" His eyes flickered as he read. "Not bad, but why bother with guns on the bastard lovechild of a Pinto and a shipping crate?"

"Suck on a corpse flower."

"Bless your heart."

Jill chuckled. She looked to the side, grimaced, and extended the hydra horn out to him. "Pleasantries aside, I came over here because this belongs to you. It came from a wicked big fucker you killed that had already ripped me a new one. Twice."

Jackson took the horn and turned it back and forth under a critical eye. There was a flash of pink mana, and he shook his head. "That's mighty generous of you, but it's wasted on me. It's too close range to be a good add-on for Caerbannog, if I could even attach it, and breaking it down into mana for ammo would just be a waste." He tossed the horn back to Jill and a system box came along with it.

Scream of the Hydra Worm

Level 68, Rare

On activation, projects a short-ranged cone of highly destructive sound that ignores half of a target's physical Resistances.

Mana cost: 500

Mad Scientist analysis:

Classification: Offensive, Close Range, Sonic, Piercing, Unlimited Use

Customization remaining: 12%

Fusion: High compatibility required.

"You sure?" Jill asked. She turned the horn in her hands, imagining what it could do if backed by Bertha's massive mana supply.

"Sure as shootin'. Now—" he cut off speaking mid-sentence when the radio in his hand chirped. He put it to his ear to listen, and when he spoke again his voice was all business. "Gunbunny, Vulture Four, fire mission acknowledged." He turned to Jill and extended a hand. "It's been a pleasure, but I've work to do. Drive safe and kick ass."

Jill shook his hand, nodded, and with no more words needed, she walked away. Behind her a rabbit roared.

CHAPTER 20

I'LL HAVE THE CHICKEN

Jill was intercepted by the same snot-nosed brat that had insulted her earlier. "You again, twerp?" she asked, raising her eyebrow.

"Message for you, hag," he said without missing a beat. "Captain says: 'Get your old crusty ass back to Bertha right now.'"

"I feel like you paraphrased that."

"Para-what?"

"Read a book, ass-clown" Jill said, rolling her eyes. "Tell her I'll be right there."

"Maybe if you read less books, you'd be younger!" the boy responded. He flipped her off and sped away.

"That doesn't even make sense!"

For a mana-churning moment Jill considered that she probably shouldn't have sworn in front of a child, but she quickly dismissed the thought. He was on a military base, and he needed education in how to swear better anyways. Her mana settled back down, and she started jogging to Bertha. After a few moments she realized that jogging didn't even make her heart speed up anymore, so with a laugh and a grin, she accelerated into a sprint.

In no time flat she skidded to a stop in front of her truck. Ras, Amelie, and a short, uniformed, clipboard-carrying man were waiting for her.

"There you are," Amelie said. "Buckman, this is Jill MacLeod. Jill, LT Buckman."

"Pleasure to meet you, ma'am," Buckman said. From the five o'clock shadow on his face he looked like he hadn't slept all night, but his uniform was still crisp, and he radiated energy. "You've really saved the day. That food is going to tide us over until we get our own production up."

Jill glanced around. "No shit? With all these people?"

Buckman flipped the pages on his clipboard in a blur, eyes scanning back and forth faster than Jill could track. Far more pages were going past than should be physically possible for the thickness of the stack on the clipboard. "Yes," he said with a nod. "We have some stockpiled reserves, and with the number of people assigned to agricultural classes, we'll be at even food production in two days." His grip on his clipboard tightened. "Unless the system changes. That would be aggravating."

Jill nodded. "Well, fuck yeah, then. Go me." She turned to Amelie. "Now let's talk payment."

Ras frowned. "Ope, are we really going to charge them for food? You did say 'maybe' and, well, it would be wrong. Right?"

Jill shook her head. "That 'maybe' was a figure of speech. You can't run a business giving everything away, and I don't think the end of the world changes that." Jill raised a hand to forestall further objections from the swordsman, then addressed Amelie. "I'm not going to gouge you though. That would just be stupid." She jerked a thumb over her shoulder, towards the garage. "You've got people who can work on vehicles and equipment despite system bullshittery. Hook me up with some upgrades for my girl, and we'll call it even." She raised the Scream of the Hydra Worm. "I can't wait to have Bertha blast some fucker to pieces."

Amelie nodded. "We can do that. You've done right by us, we'll do right by you. I can't authorize the release of materiel from the armory, but anything we've collected from monsters today is fair game."

Buckman cleared his throat. "I feel it's my responsibility to bring up the fact that we have no idea if the current influx of, uhh, magical materiel will continue," he said, "and it is possible that giving up anything that reduces our combat effectiveness may, in the future, be disastrous."

Jill leveled a flat glare at him.

"I still advise paying!" he said, half hiding behind his clipboard. "It's just my duty to say it!"

Amelie nodded. "Don't rip him apart, Jill: it was," she said. She cleared her throat and continued in her command voice, "Despite the current situation, it would be deleterious for future cooperation between the US Military and Highlander Shipping were we to appropriate food supplies without compensation." She switched back to her normal tone. "So get the grease monkeys, who used to just be regularly insane and are now magically insane, to slap monster parts on Bertha until she can't take anymore."

"Sweet thigh-highs and collars, you are my new favorite person," Jill said.

For the first time since they had met, Jill saw Amelie blush. Jill grinned as she mentally ticked off a box on her daily goals.

The captain coughed. "Y-yes. Right. Before you leave for that, though, I have another job for you, if you'll take it. Buckman, please give us the brief."

"Yes, sir!" Buckman said. He stood straight, hands clasped behind the small of his back, and began to speak. "As of midnight local time last night, an unidentified magical 'system' imposed itself —"

"I noticed," Jill interrupted. She considered meetings a special kind of hell. "What do you need me to do?" She glanced at Ras. "If it's picking everyone up from the elementary school, I can't. I promised to get going soon and don't have time to do lots of trips." Ras gave her a small smile in thanks.

"No, not that. There's a group out salvaging the school busses, so as soon as they are back, we'll convoy everyone over with a full escort of IFVs and artillery cover," Amelie said. "Lieutenant: continue, but only include what's relevant to the proposed mission."

"Understood. One of the first actions I took last night after fighting my way here was to implement a modified version of our EMP—electronic warfare contingency plans—and attempt to re-establish command and control communications. With a class power that can transform pre-system equipment, I've created a medium-distance communication network. I've reached out to bases farther away with another power that lets me send messages only, but not receive them. It's mana intensive, so I can only use it every once in a while, and bandwidth is limited, but I instructed other bases on which powers to take to get their own C2 up and running and requested that they contact us when they had."

"Let me guess: not everyone checked in."

Buckman nodded. "Yes. A number of sites are still dark. We don't know if they just don't have anyone of the right class to respond or if they're dead."

"Thank you, Buckman," Amelie said. "Jill, we'll be sending out a convoy to check some of the bases ourselves once the situation here is stable, but there are two dark bases near your route that are too far away for us.

One is ten miles off your route, the other fifteen. We would like to employ you as a contractor to scout those bases and either establish communications or report that they are destroyed."

Jill chewed her lip. A ten- and fifteen-mile detour wouldn't take Bertha very long, even if she didn't take any speed upgrades, but accepting the mission would mean getting near potentially high-danger locations. She didn't know if the high school was typical or not, but there the monsters had stuck around after they had won, forming a kind of sick nest complete with deadly alpha predator. Then again, there was going to be danger everywhere, and she wasn't promising to clear the bases out, only to take a look.

"I can do that," she decided. "What are you offering?"

"You mean besides giving Bertha an all-you-can-upgrade buffet?" Amelie asked, raising an eyebrow.

"That was payment for the last job. This is a new contract."

Amelie drummed her fingers on her thigh, thinking. "Buckman?" she prompted.

He flipped through his clipboard again. "As a contractor, we can release funds. Considering hazard, your company size, and need," he paused, doing a mental calculation. "Rounding up: twenty thousand USD."

Jill stopped herself from immediately agreeing. "For an hour's work? Arsebadger, I'd have jumped for that yesterday. But I don't really think cash is what I need right now. And will it even be worth anything soon? Pass on that. Are you sure you can't give me any weapons?" Her eyes lit up. "Bertha gives infinite ammo! I bet my left ass cheek I could mount a rocket launcher and just keep firing away!"

Buckman's eyebrows rose. "That would be significantly more valuable than twenty grand, but in aggregate, that would be a good use of resources. Captain, could we induct the company as an allied militia, or similar?"

Jill turned a hopeful, rocket-seeking gaze to Amelie.

Amelie shook her head. "I'm sorry, Jill, but in a situation like this I'm prohibited from dispersing ordinance that could prove critical to our survival without an order from command. Which we won't be able to contact for—" she looked to Buckman.

"Five hours, nineteen minutes, sir."

"Well, shitshack."

Ras, who had been looking at Bertha with narrowed eyes, chimed in. "What you need is something to help cover the blind spots, so things can't swarm you. Something automatic."

"How about some M4s?" Jill said. "You must have crates of them, and they pack a hell of a lot more punch than my old piece."

Amelie thought for a moment. "Buckman, what are the odds there was an inventory issue and," she counted turrets, "six M4s were missing when we went to equip the new recruits?"

"Sir, that would be impossible! I checked them myself!" Buckman said, looking insulted at the mere thought of a supply discrepancy.

Amelie glared at him and pointed at Jill, then Bertha. "Are you absolutely sure?"

"Oh! Understood." He again flipped through his clipboard at blinding speed, but when he stopped, he had a grin on his face. "Why, Captain, I am happy to report that all M4s are accounted for," he said, then hurriedly kept speaking as storm clouds gathered on Amelie's face. "But! I regret to inform you that six surplus M2HBs are missing." He turned to Jill. "You did say you can generate ammunition from mana, yes? We don't have enough rounds for heavy combat operation as it stands."

"LT Buckman, that's terrible!" Amelie said, wagging a finger in mock anger. "You're lucky you've held down the fort so well here or else I'd report you." She looked to Jill. "If you happen to find six fifty-cals lying around, you will let us know, won't you?"

"Fifty-cals?! Sweet sexy Satan, it's like Christmas morning, only with machine guns," Jill said with a laugh. She replied with a mock serious, "Of course, Captain."

"Make it happen then, Buckman," Amelie said, "and do your radio upgrade so Jill can communicate with us. Jill, I have to get back to work. Don't leave without saying goodbye." Amelie turned and walked back to the main building.

"So," Jill said to Buckman, "guns?"

He closed his eyes for a moment and his lips moved in silent speech. "Getting taken off the shelves as we speak. They'll be waiting for you inside in five minutes." He pointed at Bertha's cab. "Permission to enter to upgrade your radio?"

"Oh, pull that stick out of your ass. Anyone who gets me this much dakka is alright by me." She turned to Ras. "Could you handle getting those over here? And if you supervise the food unloading while I'm doing upgrades it will help us leave faster."

"I can do that," Ras said. He gave Buckman a nod and left.

Jill strode towards Bertha, Buckman hurrying after her. "C'mon inside," she said, leading the way into the cab. She slid into the driver's seat and Buckman followed into the passenger spot. He looked around for a moment, his gaze lingering on the system-modified gauges and controls, then scooped up the radio handset. Mana pulsed down his hand, flowing down the handset cord and into the electronics box, and it began to transmute from matte plastic to shiny chrome.

"Well, that's sweet," Jill said. "Very retro."

They sat in silence for a moment as the transformation continued.

"So," Jill said. "You, uh, organized this whole place?"

"Yes, ma'am!"

"Well, nice job; you sorted the balls off this place. And you're okay with Amelie taking over?"

"Absolutely. Being in charge is awful. Now I can get everything orderly without that distraction," Buckman said, a satisfied smile on his face. "The new logistics were a challenge, but the system wasn't too complicated once I started collating everything."

"You look pretty happy about that."

Buckman shrugged. "It's satisfying. I've saved a lot of lives already and proper organization is going to save more, so why shouldn't I be proud of the job I did?"

"No reason, just," Jill gestured outside, "there's a lot of suffering out there right now. A lot of dead neighbors."

Buckman nodded. "I am ninety-nine percent sure that the system is heavily altering the mental state of people as they gain levels to mitigate trauma. I wonder if the suppression will continue this way or if there will be a backlash."

Jill laughed, but there was no humor in it. "Yeah, me too. Our brains are fucked. Hey, speaking of mental state and collating data, I have someone that I really want you to meet. Stay here for a minute, okay?"

Buckman nodded. "Yes, ma'am! This power takes a while to do its job anyways."

Jill punched him on the shoulder and set off to find Babu. There were only two private spaces on the truck and one of them was her off-limits bedroom, so she decided to start with the other. Her hand paused on the handle to Mia's quarters, and she decided that just this once she'd knock.

The door slid open to the side a moment later, and Mia was standing there with an angry expression on her face. Babu lay face down on the bed, head pressed fully into the pillow and arms limp at his sides.

Mia's expression softened. "Oh. I thought you were Ras for a moment. Come in?"

"Nah, I won't be here long," Jill said. She leaned past Mia, glancing at Babu. "Babu, how're you doing?"

The enchanter shrugged.

"Well, tough shit. Time for you to get back to work."

Babu moaned, but didn't move.

Mia stepped close to Jill and whispered, "Are you doing bad cop?"

"Only a bit," Jill said. "Trust me, he's going to love this." She continued in an exaggerated volume, "There's someone up front who's collected a metric fuckton of information on the system from everyone here. You could flush his brain like a fire hydrant enema if you wanted to, but . . . I guess you're going to miss him."

Babu sat up. His eyes were red and angry. "You're trying to manipulate me. I'm not a kid you know."

Jill snorted. "Both of you are kids to me, and you bet your kidney I am. But I'm also not lying, so get up, bonk your nerd heads together, and figure this magic bullshit out before some monster turns us all into cuntpuddles."

Babu cracked a smile and sighed. "Fine. I suppose if the choice is cake or death, I'll choose cake."

"Oh, thank fuck," Jill said, "I really didn't want to have to sort all that out myself. I've got new turret powers for you to look at soon too, but not for a bit. It's time for me to see a mad scientist about an air horn."

CHAPTER 21

MAGICAL GIRL TRUCK TRANSFORMATION SEQUENCE PART 1

Jill pulled Bertha up in front of the workshop and shut the engine off. Mia was riding with her, but the brothers were busy; Ras was dealing with food logistics and Babu was up in the front turret with Buckman, comparing notes in relative privacy.

"Want me to keep watch up top?" Mia asked, as Jill unbuckled her seat belt and moved to leave the cab.

"Nah, it's safe enough here. Come along and let's see what crazy toys we're going to get."

Jill jumped out of the cab and walked to the workshop's open roller door, Mia walking by her side, and peered inside. The shop was a riot of color and activity, with auto parts and monster loot spread out over every available surface. What had been a pit to allow for fast oil changes now had a dozen insectile, purple legs lining the side, each holding a normal looking power tool. An engine block hung suspended on chains with glowing fuchsia tubing winding in and out, which looked suspiciously like intestines. Half a dozen people were there working, including two who were throwing loot into a glowing furnace whose fuel chute was styled to look like a demon's maw.

"Hey! Is there a Nitro here?" Jill shouted to be heard over the noise.

A man who was working on the engine block looked up with an annoyed expression. He looked to be in his late fifties, with fierce gray whiskers and a body that could best be described as a muffin that had been left in the sun too long, had gained sentience, and had gone on to dominate the local wilderness through sheer force of personality. "The name's Mike! Who are you?"

"I'm Jill, and this is Mia. How do you feel about turning an eighteen-wheeler into a death machine?"

"Oh, you came in on the truck," he said, calming down. "That sounds fun, but we're a little busy here!"

"Well, I've got one captain who says to, and I quote, 'slap monster parts on until she can't take anymore.' And I'm in a hurry."

"For real? With all we have to do?" He picked up a chrome-plated radio sitting on his work bench and spoke into it. After a moment an indistinct response came through. Mike sighed and tossed it back down, then stuck two fingers into his mouth and let out an ear-piercing whistle. "Drop what you're doing and follow me outside!" he yelled to the other technicians, as he began walking out of the shop. To Jill he said, "Goddamn brass and their goddamn ideas. Not that I'm blaming you. Us blue collar schmucks have got to work toge—" He stopped talking in mid-sentence upon seeing Bertha. "Hoooly shiiit," he said, drawing out the words. "Well, look at that beauty!"

"Damn right. Bertha is a hell of a truck; always has been," Jill said. She upgraded Mike to a person worth saving if monsters were to suddenly breach the base perimeter.

"Sure, sure, but I was talking about that minigun on top!" Mike replied, gesturing up at Blossom.

Mia grinned. "You, sir, are a man of culture and taste." She stuck out her tongue at Jill, who faux scowled back.

"Hah!" he said. "I wouldn't go that far." He turned to the two women and three men who'd followed them out of the garage. They stood in a semi-circle, looking at Bertha and making appreciative comments to each other. "Alright, you sorry excuses for wrench holders: listen up! We've got a rush job. All of the ridiculous magic you've been fucking around with instead of getting good old-fashioned gasoline burners working again— well, now it's worth something! Pick out whatever is going to make the nice truck meaner. Now, people!"

There was a subtle green flare of mana from Mike, which slithered out and sunk into the rest. Immediately they perked up as if they'd chugged a whole pot of coffee, and as a group they started loudly arguing with each other as they ran back inside.

"Little bit of that 'ridiculous' magic for yourself, I see," Mia said.

"Even an old dog learns new tricks when they're constantly shoved in his face. Literally. Goddamn boxes. . . ," Mike said, grumbling to himself.

Mia looked between Jill and Mike. "Are all old people actually the same person?"

"Fuck off!" Jill said with a laugh. She extended the Scream of the Hydra Worm to Mike. "Since you seem to be the one in charge, you must have plenty of experience holding your wrench. I want to make this Bertha's new air horn."

Mike took the horn; his eyes flashed green, and he gave a whistle. "Good shit." He looked up to Bertha's air horn. "Yeah, I can see it. I still haven't worked out entirely how this 'compatibility' and 'customization' nonsense is supposed to work, but if replacing one horn with another isn't easy, then I give up."

"We want it to run off Bertha's mana too," Mia added.

"Ah," Mike said. He scratched his cheek, the sound akin to metal on sandpaper. "I think I've figured that bit out. Maybe." He closed his eyes, and his hands started to glow. The light flowed down onto the horn, and after a few seconds, it began to morph. The mouthpiece that Jill had blown into sealed shut, then flared out into a squat box with a six-pronged plug. The horn itself grew wider and stouter. The light died down and Mike gestured to Jill and Mia, sending over the item's modified information.

Scream of the Hydra Worm (Vehicle Add-On)

Level 68, Rare

On activation, projects a short-ranged cone of highly destructive sound that ignores half of a target's physical Resistances.

Mana cost: 500 (Vehicle only)

Customization remaining: 10%

"There!" Mike said. "That barely took any effort. Anything else you want it to do?"

"What are the options?" Mia asked.

Mike shrugged. "Hell if I know. This is all new. Come up with something, and I'll try it."

Jill shuddered as she remembered the feeling of the velociraptors slashing their way into Bertha's sides and burrowing in. "How about having the sound blast out all around? Maybe blow things away?"

Mike nodded and his mana flowed out from his hands. This time when it touched the horn, the green light rebounded. He winced and shook his head. "No good. Too big a change; the sound's got to go forward."

"Wasptits," Jill said.

"How about something like a snowplow?" Mia asked. "Big blades of sound that push enemies out of the way?"

Jill nodded. "Good idea. Go for it."

Again green mana flowed and again it seemed to rebound, but Mike growled, his grip tightened, and inch by inch the magic advanced. The bell of the air horn folded in a sharp crease and curled, looking something like an open-mouthed plow itself. Sweat formed on Mike's brow, and with a final grunt of effort, the transformation finished.

"Woooof," he said. "That nearly drained me dry. But hot damn, I got enough from it to level!" He sent over the new item description.

Blast Wave of the Hydra Worm (Vehicle Add-On)

Level 68, Epic Crafted

On activation, projects a short-ranged cone of highly destructive sound that ignores half of a target's physical Resistances and pushes enemies up and away. Continuous activation causes the cone to settle into a 5-meter wedge with enhanced damage and force.

Mana cost: 500 + 100/second (Vehicle only)

This item cannot be modified further.

"Now that is a proper fuck-trumpet," Jill said. She grabbed it and moved to go over to Bertha and install it, but hesitated on seeing the other mechanics emerging from the garage, their hands chock full of weirdly colorful and deadly toys.

Mia clapped her hands together, eyes alight, and chuckled darkly. "You go get that installed. I'll pick out the best stuff for us."

Jill eyed the younger woman. They'd be sharing the road for at least a day, and most likely much more, before they reached where Mia's family might be, if their current progress was any indication. On top of that, Mia was responsible for nearly all of their firepower. Without a doubt, the former nurse was going to be critical to getting where Jill wanted to go, or at least getting there quickly. But at the same time, Bertha was hers: always had been, always would be.

"It would be helpful," Jill said, keeping her tone light, "for you to weed out the worst and give me your ideas. But what goes on Bertha is my call."

"Yeah, of course," Mia said, giving her a confused look. "She's your truck."

"Okay. Great. I'll just put this on then."

Jill leapt from the ground to the top of the engine in one huge bound so that she could be up close and personal with the old air horn above the driver's seat. She detached it with her Customization power and shunted it inside; there was a resistance as it crossed the dimensional barrier where outside and inside didn't quite match, but with a flex of will, Jill pushed it through, and the horn dropped from the cab's ceiling to land in the driver's seat.

Part of Command Module functionality detached!

Recalculating module statistics.

Projector add-on slot recognized.

Warning! Projector add-on slot is only functional if Command Module is adjacent to the exterior dimensional membrane. Installed add-on projects through the membrane.

"Huh. Neat." She pressed the new horn into place and willed it to connect. It felt through her bond like putting a glove on a phantom limb; a glove that crackled with lightning and sent tingles rushing through her body. For a moment she felt as if the horn was fighting her, but then it settled, ready to blow death. It was larger than the old air horn and its silver bell extended two feet out over the hood—a constant visible reminder to the driver of the power just a pull away.

Integrating add-on to "Bertha" Command Module.

Level 68 Blast Wave of the Hydra Worm detected. Blast Wave of the Hydra Worm exceeds maximum supported level: effective level reduced. Mana crossfeed enabled.

Mana cost per discharge: 500 + 100/second

Jill scowled at the reminder that the new item would be less powerful than it could be and looked over her Command Module options to see if there were any powers worth taking to boost its effective level.

Command Module:
"Bertha" has a Command Module with 1 control station and 1 observer station.
Includes: Seat belts (rare technology), air bags (rare technology), openable windows, mirrors, doors.
Add-ons (2/2): Medium Range Radio, Blast Wave of the Hydra Worm (Projector).

Command Upgrades:
Captain Speaking (0/1): Jill MacLeod can speak to and receive replies from anyone within "Bertha" or within 14 meters.
Sensor Upgrade (0/5): Effectiveness of any installed perception devices increased 14%.
Capacity (0/3): Add 1 control station, 2 observer stations, and 1 command add-on slot.

While the new radio was sure to prove useful, again and again Jill had felt blind and deaf to what was unfolding within her own truck, because she couldn't speak to anyone and get updates. With her one free class power point she selected the Captain Speaking upgrade. Her sense of hearing expanded through her truck, as her new mana zipped to every corner and brought back with it every bit of noise. Luckily no individual sound was very loud right now, but the sum total was an overwhelming cacophony that had Jill clapping her hands to her ears. As suddenly as they had come, the sounds fled, and Jill's mana no longer raced to and fro.

"Fuck you, System. Stop making everything suck when it turns on," Jill said under her breath, taking her hands from her ears.

Command Module add-on level increased. Blast Wave of the Hydra Worm effective level increased. Blast Wave of the Hydra Worm still exceeds maximum supported level.
0 Class Power points remaining.

> System Inquiry detected.
> Class power activation side effects are dependent upon the fortitude of the user.

Jill blinked and read the box again. "I'd forgotten what a sassy bugger you are." She shook her head. The possible sentience of the magic voice in her head was a problem for another time, one that she was first going to try and solve with booze. Lots of booze.

In the meantime, she needed to test out her new power now, rather than when in deadly danger. Jill activated the Captain Speaking power with the tiniest bit of mana, threading it through Bertha to her frontmost turret where Babu and Buckman were. When nothing happened, Jill pushed just a bit more mana into it, and the threads snapped into place.

"—found that the rate of fire increases were additive rather than multiplicative," Buckman said, "so we can speculate that other fire rate increasing powers will be as well."

"That may be true, but we know that the system does have different categories for additive and multiplicative bonuses from the experience notifications. It may be that different. . . ," Babu trailed off. "Do you feel that? Like we're being watched?"

"More like listened to. This feels like a communication power."

"Hello, small squishy mortals," Jill said. "It is I, Bertha the magnificent! Bow before me!"

"Great Bertha!" Babu said, voice pleading, "please, you must save us from your foul-mouthed, despicably evil mistress! Only your mighty wheels can crush her magic!"

Jill snorted. "So you know it's me?"

"Next time change your voice."

"Hello, ma'am," Buckman said. "Is there anything we can do for you?"

"No, just testing out a new power. It's a bit disorienting," Jill said. The sounds from the power were skipping her ears entirely and appearing directly in her brain, almost as if she were imagining them to herself.

"I still close my eyes sometimes," Buckman said. Jill imagined him checking his clipboard to note the exact frequency. "I have found that people know when they are being communicated with, and they find it disconcerting. I have mine make a little chime to announce myself."

Jill grinned, cut the power, and reactivated it while imagining the perfect sound. The base roar of Bertha's old air horn, thankfully reduced in volume to a manageable level, rang out inside the turret.

"Well, everyone will know Jill is calling."

"Perfect." Jill cut the power off, gave the new horn one last critical glance to make sure it was aligned, and leapt to the ground.

The technicians had emerged from the garage hauling contraptions of various sizes, half of which looked like they would slaughter a cow by accident if it wandered by. One of them was arguing with Mia loudly about slugs, while another was just sitting bored on a stool-height sealed metal drum.

Jill strode over, eyeing each potential upgrade with growing excitement for what they could do for Bertha. They were still arguing when she reached them so she put two fingers in her mouth, blew, and then sighed to herself when no sounds came out. Even with magic, she still couldn't get that to work.

"Hey, waffle lickers!" she shouted, investing a single mana point into her mind control power. Everyone glanced her way and, seeing that she was back, stopped talking after just a few seconds.

Jill clapped her hands together. "Show me what you've got."

CHAPTER 22

MAGICAL GIRL TRUCK TRANSFORMATION SEQUENCE PART 2

I think you're going to like this!" Mia said to Jill, her eyes alight. "Jim, get your orc ass up here!"

The bored-looking man looked at Mia with a confused expression on his face, rolled his eyes, and presented the metal can he'd been sitting on. "Tada," he managed to say without a hint of enthusiasm.

Jill took it and hoisted it up to get a better look. She gave it a tentative tilt and the insides slowly but smoothly shifted. "This feels like a big paint can."

"That's because it is."

Red Eel Paint (Vehicle Add-On)
Level 19, Rare
Any vehicle painted with this extract of electric eels receives a passive speed boost. Upon activation, the exterior of the vehicle becomes electrified for 1 minute. Any enemy creature that contacts the vehicle in this time takes moderate electricity damage.
Mana cost: 190
This item cannot be modified further.

"Wait," Jill said, "if I paint Bertha red she'll go faster?"
"It's shockingly effective."

His deadpan statement was met by a chorus of groans and boos, but Jill snorted a laugh. "I'll take it!"

She turned to her truck and tilted her head, considering. A brief check of Bertha's status revealed that she had four add-on slots available: one each from armor, cargo, habitation, and propulsion. As she'd just learned from installing the new horn, there was some wiggle room in those limits if she took off something that Bertha already had that the system hadn't recognized.

Jill flexed her Customization power and stripped the paint off of Bertha.

> Part of Armor Module functionality detached!
> Recalculating module statistics.
> Coating add-on slot recognized.
> Warning! Armor Module environmental corrosion increased by 1000%.

She grinned and made a note to go over Bertha and strip out everything she could to make room for more magic upgrades. Removing the paint had made Bertha much more prone to rusting out, but that was something that either the truck's auto-repairing or Jill's Customization power would take care of. For other components the downside might be much more severe, and Jill would have to balance that against whatever it was the magic part did.

"Hey!" she thought towards the system. "Give me some more details. How much is this going to speed Bertha up?"

> System Inquiry detected.
> Inquiry may be solved via system interface optimization. Display future item Statistics using Soulbound Modular Vehicle "Bertha" as the target?

"What else would I be putting things on?"

> System Inquiry detected.
> Multiple other eligible vehicles detected within range.

The response notification was a more eye-searing shade of blue than usual. Jill smirked. "Use Bertha as the target then."

A new version of the paint's statistics popped up in her vision.

Red Eel Paint (Armor Module Add-On)

Level 19, Rare

If painted with this extract of electric eels, Soulbound Modular Vehicle "Bertha" will receive a passive speed boost of 27%. Upon activation, the exterior of the vehicle becomes electrified for 1 minute. Any enemy creature that contacts the vehicle in this time takes 80 electricity damage per second before Resistances.

Mana cost: 190

This item cannot be modified further.

"Twenty-seven percent faster?!" Jill yelled, fumbling and almost dropping the can in her shock. "Flabbertyflutterflyfuck!"

Mike raised an eyebrow. "Jim, I think you broke her."

"No, she just does that sometimes," Mia said.

Jill ignored them both and reached into her pocket, pulling out her key ring. The actual keys to Bertha were useless now, and she had no idea if her apartment was still in one piece, but the big rig novelty bottle opener on the ring would always be useful.

She levered open the paint can. Tiny sparks flashed under the paint's surface, like lightning bolts hopping between clouds in a storm, and it slowly churned under its own power as if the eels that made it were still swimming inside.

She gently directed her mana through her Customization power and into the paint, trickling more in until she felt the liquid become fully saturated with magic. She then jerked the can at Bertha's bare flank. The paint flew in a sideways red waterfall, ignoring any suggestions from gravity that it should fall. Rather than splashing off or running down, it stretched and grew until it covered the truck's entire outer surface. The alien feeling of Bertha evolving slipped down her bond, becoming more familiar every time Jill felt it. This time it was like being dipped in liquid excitement; the paint seemed eager to cooperate and help.

> Integrating add-on to "Bertha" Armor Module.
> Level 19 Red Eel Paint detected. Armor Module environmental corrosion reset. Mana crossfeed enabled. Activated Mana cost per minute: 190

A final twist of will for shine, and a few chrome highlights, finished the job. For just a moment Jill considered adding a spoiler to Bertha to go along with the go-fast red color, but she dismissed the idea as too tacky.

Jill clapped her hands together, chucked the can back to Jim, and spoke to Mia. "Wicked cool. Anything else make the grade?"

"A few things, like—" Mia said, only to be cut off as a woman with bright green hair barged forward.

"Behold the power of slugs!" she said, and from behind her back she pulled a puke-green suction cup that pulsed with inner life.

> Slug Feet (Vehicle Add-On)
> Level 22, Rare
> On toggle, converts the wheel elements of the Propulsion Module into gastropod feet, allowing "Bertha" to adhere to nearly any surface. Reduces speed by 95%.
> Toggle Mana cost: 1100
> Customization remaining: 8%

"Isn't this amazing? You could drive your truck up the side of a building! Or up a mountain! And rain death on your enemies like a true slug king!"

"That sounds," Jill hesitated, "useful. Yeah. It's not going to make Bertha leave a slime trail, is it?"

"It might!"

"Well, good enough," Jill said.

She took the suction cup and turned to put it on Bertha but was interrupted by Mike coughing pointedly. "This is a fun break and all, but we've got shit to do, so how about we finish the show and tell and then you put it all on?"

"Fine, fine, ruin my fun," Jill said, "but yeah, I'll let you get back to it. Everyone with stuff Mia accepted, come on up."

"Everyone else, back to work!" Mike added, and was met with a chorus of complaints.

A short man came up and presented an enormous, taxidermied wolf head.

Breath of the Winter Wolf (Flexible Add-On)
Level 3, Common
When integrated into one of "Bertha's" Modules and activated, cold air continually pours from the jaws of this wolf.
Mana cost: 3/minute
Customization remaining: 70%

"I figured you could use an air conditioner with style," he said.

"I've already got AC," Jill said, "and it's still freezing at night."

"For the trailer in the summer then," the man said, then shrugged. "With seventy percent Customization left I could look around for some sort of fire thingy and slap it on for heat though."

The memory of Jill's first loot smacked her in the brain. She fished around in her right pocket and pulled out the gem she had collected from the lesser firewolf right after the system had struck. "This should work, right? It even came from a wolf."

The man took the gem and rolled it between his fingers. "It's worth a shot!" he said. There was a pulse of mana, and he jammed his hand up the wolf's open mouth. "Aaaaaand . . . there!"

Hearth of the Wolf (Flexible Add-On)
Level 9, Common
When integrated into one of "Bertha's" Modules and activated, this snarling wolf projects cold or hot air from its jaws to maintain a comfortable environment.
Mana cost: 9/minute
Customization remaining: 27%

Jill nodded. "Thanks."

The man waved in reply, then jogged to catch up to the rest of the crowd going back into the workshop.

Jill turned to Mia and punched her on the shoulder. "Sorry for giving you shit earlier. You did good with these."

Mia beamed, then looked away. "I've uh, got one more thing." From the ground beside her she picked up and held out a pelt.

> Dire Bobcat Belly Fur
> Level 11, Common
> Soft enough to be worth any danger.
> Customization remaining: 100%

"We need this as bedding."

Jill reached out and touched it. "Yes," she said, tone dead serious, "we do. Mike, this needs to be, like, blankets or sheets or something. Can you do it?"

Mike took the fur; his hands glowed, and the pelt stretched and thinned, folding back on itself into a set of bedding.

"Easy peasy," Mike said. He handed back the fur and stuck out a hand. "Pleasure to meet you, but that's all we've got, and I've got to get back to it too."

Jill shook Mike's hand. "See you around, Nitro."

Mike shook his head, flipped her off, and left.

Jill tossed the fur to Mia. "You deal with this one; I'll handle the others."

First up was the slug foot. Jill pressed it up against one of Bertha's wheels, not quite certain what was going to happen. After a moment, the slug foot glowed brighter and turned gelatinous, then sank into the wheel, which flashed once before turning bright green. For a moment it felt like Jill's feet were covered in slime.

> Integrating add-on to "Bertha" Propulsion Module.
> Level 22 Slug Feet detected.
> Toggle Mana cost: 1100

Jill scowled at the new wheel color and attempted to change them back to a proper black. When nothing happened, she poured more and more mana in, fighting with the add-on until it finally capitulated.

She went around the back of her truck, opened the door with an expert heave, and jumped inside. With far fewer pallets of food tied down in the center, and the benches on the sides, it was starting to look less like a cargo area and more like an undecorated and awkwardly arranged bus. Worse yet, Jill realized that the only way that the gunners had been getting into the top turrets had been by climbing on top of the cargo—there hadn't been any room for ladders.

That was easy enough to fix; metal rungs grew out of the floor, shooting upwards until they touched the ceiling. Jill scowled at how much the ladders blocked Bertha's ability to carry cargo and put redesigning the cab layout on her mental to-do list.

The wolf head, at least, she knew what she was going to do with now. A careful throw and the application of intent was enough to stick the head right over the door leading to the Habitation Module.

> Integrating add-on to "Bertha" Cargo Module.
> Level 9 Hearth of the Wolf detected.
> Mana cost: 9/minute

Jill smirked and went to go check on Mia's progress. Right before she opened the door, another box appeared.

> Integrating add-on to "Bertha" Habitation Module.
> Level 11 Dire Bobcat Fur Bedding detected.
> This module has replication capabilities. Duplicate Dire Bobcat Fur Bedding in all sleeping areas?

"Flaming-tits, yes!" Jill thought.

She passed through the door and walked down the Habitation Module hallways, a bounce in her step. Once in the cab she slipped into the driver's seat and activated her Captain Speaking power, letting her mana flow throughout the truck so people could hear no matter where they were. The sound of Bertha's horn rang out. "Alright everyone, we're saying goodbye and then hitting the road! So, if anyone needs to pee . . . well, actually, you can just do it here." She thumbed the mana engine back on and brought her truck back to the main armory building.

Buckman slid down the ladder from the turret, Babu close behind him. "I let the captain know that we're here," the lieutenant told Jill. He pointed at the radio. "Please report in when you get to those bases."

Jill nodded. "Will do. Thanks for the guns."

"Use them well, and good luck, ma'am," Buckman said. He extended a fist to Babu, bumped it, then opened a door and dropped down.

Babu slid into the seat next to Jill. "That man is a genius," he said. "They're lucky he was here."

Jill snorted. "Nerds."

"That's a compliment, don'tcha know. Nerds are going to rule the world pretty soon."

"Probably," Jill agreed. She spotted Amelie and her nieces exiting the armory. "C'mon, time to get going."

They exited Bertha. Amelie gave them a nod of greeting. "Taking off?"

"Yup. It's been," Jill paused, "well, kind of awful actually, but it would have been worse without you. Have fun telling everyone what to do."

"It's what I live for," Amelie said, deadpan. She continued in her normal voice. "Don't be a stranger; I expect regular status updates. And if you're ever passing through this way again, you'd better stop by." She extended a hand, and Jill shook it.

Amelie turned and walked back into the armory, but Sarah and Olivia hesitated before following. "We just wanted to say bye too," Sarah said. "You fucking rock!" She extended a fist.

Jill grinned and bumped it. The young woman had somehow strapped even more grenades on her than before. "You too. Blow something up for me."

Babu waved goodbye to Olivia. "Thanks for patching me up!"

"Your butt is always welcome!" the medic stammered out. Then, realizing what she had just said, she turned bright pink and ran back inside. Sarah sighed, gave one more wave, and followed.

Babu smirked. "Oop, been a while since that's happened. Good times."

"Are you ever going to let me in on what the hell you're talking about?" Jill asked.

"Sure, sure. You see—" Babu started to say, but then cut himself off as Ras came out of the armory. The enchanter's face turned from jovial to angry, then sad, then determined. "Hey, could you give me and Ras just a minute? We need to talk in private."

"Sure," Jill said, then hesitated. "I'm butting into your business here, but if you rip him a new asshole, try to make it a wound that will heal, okay?"

Babu sighed. "We'll see." He walked forward to meet Ras.

Jill went back into Bertha and closed the cab door. She had no desire to snoop.

"Hey, Mia," she projected through the truck, "you good to go?"

"Mmmmph," echoed back in her head, a complaint muffled through fluffy cloth.

"Well, we're going. So get up top," Jill said.

The cab door opened and the Bati brothers got in. Ras gave Jill a nod but didn't stop to chat, instead heading straight back into the Cargo Module. Babu slid into the passenger seat.

"Not going to stab each other?" Jill asked.

"Not today," Babu said. He was a bit more relaxed than he had been earlier, but also sadder.

"Then buckle up!" Jill said. The excitement of getting on the road again, of feeling a big rig move under her guidance, surged through her, and she couldn't help but grin. She reached up to give the air horn a celebratory pull but stopped herself just in time. That would have been a very bad move. The city horn wouldn't be enough for a proper celebration, so instead she concentrated on her communication power. The sound of the old air horn vibrated through the truck, loud and proud.

Bertha trundled through the base, out of the gates and their barrier field, and onto the local roads. Only once did the turrets fire—the unfamiliar sound of a 50-caliber machine gun rattling the air—as Ras dispatched a monster who didn't do a good enough job of hiding from the multi-axled predator that was Bertha prowling by. In just a few minutes they were back on the highway, heading east.

"Hey, Mia, Ras," Jill asked the two in their turrets, "anything around that would mind getting shitwrecked?" Jill grinned as they told her no.

Her right foot sank all the way to the floor. The mana engine's hum grew loud as Bertha accelerated, her armored mass thundering down the highway. Jill pulled on the new horn at the same time as she pushed mana into the electric coating. A thundering blast of sound exploded forward as Bertha's new horn roared for the first time, and a moment later the snaps and cracks of arcing lightning joined it.

"One hour to Billings," Jill said, "and nothing's going to stop us."

CHAPTER 23

GETTING SMARTER

As much as Jill had loved the sound of her big rig Bertha's old air horn, she had to admit that the new one was better. With a grin on her face and adrenaline surging through her veins, she raised one hand to the horn's chain in preparation, but she didn't pull it yet. With the other hand she steered Bertha straight towards a pack of deer standing in the eastbound lane of Interstate 90. Their massive serrated teeth and glowing green eyes betrayed their true nature as fear deer.

Jill snarled, pressing down on the accelerator. She might have promised herself just hours earlier that she would stop ramming monsters, and let the turret-mounted machine guns on Bertha take care of them instead, but she was making a special exception for fear deer. She might, just might, still bear a grudge towards the creatures for almost eating her.

"Who's afraid now, beanflicker?!" Jill yelled, as she pulled the horn's chain.

The horn roared, pulling magic from Bertha's mana reserves to fuel itself. A blast of sound bellowed out in a cone, the air distorting from its raw power, and struck the pack of deer. All but the largest one died on the spot, their flesh shearing off of their bones in an explosion of gore. The last, a large buck that must have been a higher level than the others, lowered its antlers and charged.

Even before Jill had used her system-granted powers to bond Bertha to her soul, the deer's actions would have only resulted in profuse profanity and a repair bill. The overlapping bands of armor that now covered the truck's exterior would easily absorb Bertha smashing into a charging deer, but even that was unnecessary.

As Jill held down the horn's chain, the blast wave retracted closer to Bertha until it formed into a roiling plow of sound distortions. The deer hit it head on. Its antlers were blasted upwards with enough force to snap the deer's neck, and its body soon followed. It tumbled through the air, already dead. By the time the sound of the carcass hitting the ground crunched out, Bertha was long past.

A blue box popped up in Jill's vision: a system notification registering the slaughter.

Fear Deer (x7) defeated.
Your contribution: 100%
5300 Experience Gained!
You are now Level 22!

A narcotic surge of pleasure rushed through Jill, and mana flowed into her body, mind, and spirit, rebuilding them bit-by-bit into something stronger. She closed her eyes for just a moment and suppressed the urge to swerve her truck off the road in search of more monsters, more experience, and more levels. She refused to become addicted to power and transform into something other than herself.

Jill skimmed the box's contents and frowned at the amount of experience she'd gained. With a push of her mana, she sent the box to Babu and activated Captain Speaking.

The sound of Bertha's horn rang out next to him, and Jill heard him speak in her mind. "Are we allowed to shoot again?" he asked. "It's rude to hog all the XP, don'tcha know."

"It's rude for those deer to exist. But yeah, go nuts and get some levels for yourself," Jill replied. "Speaking of, did those seem higher level to you than before?"

"They didn't last long enough for me to tell by looking, but the experience numbers say they are. About level seven and a half on average."

Jill digested that for a moment. The deer that had come so close to ending her had only been level four. "Half a day and they've doubled in strength," she said to Babu. "How worried should we be?"

"I dunno," he said, and Jill imagined him shaking his head. "It's impossible to know if they'll keep up the growth. We've gained a lot more than four levels in the same period, so if things stay the same, I don't think the deer will catch up."

"But something out there is stronger than us already, and it's only getting stronger," Jill said with grim certainty. The hydra worm had been a staggering level sixty-eight after all, and it had nearly broken Bertha in half. She didn't want to think about what it would be like with time to grow.

"That's what I'm for," Mia said. "You bring the mobility and armor; I'll bring the damage."

"Well, as long as the mana keeps flowing," Babu said.

"Speaking of magic bullshit," Jill said, "I've been meaning to show you two the new stuff that unlocked when I finished buying all of the turret module's powers." She had only read them briefly before being distracted by Bertha being launched, broken, into the air and hadn't made any decisions on what to take yet. "Hold on," she said, "let me get Ras in on this too."

She threaded her mana backward through her truck, first to the Habitation Module right behind the cab with its twin bedrooms, then through a door and into the trailer, and finally up a ladder into the rearmost turret. Ras had taken it upon himself to man the 50-caliber machine gun at the back of the truck that could fire in Blossom's blind spots.

"Everything's clear back here," he said in Jill's mind.

"Great. I'm all done with catharizing my ass, so feel free to fuck up any monster you see," Jill said. Even though she was speaking with her mind and mana rather than her voice, she still cleared her throat before continuing. "We're all, uh . . . here, sorta. So, time for a talk. I've got a big choice to make for Bertha's powers so hit me with what you think."

She called up the description of the next set of turret class powers she could unlock and sent them along.

Advanced Turrets (Small Arms) unlocked!
Two Custom Powers have been determined to be the most beneficial for Soulbound Modular Vehicle "Bertha." Before module Upgrades may be purchased, one Custom Power must be selected. The selection is final and the other power will not be available in the future.

Advanced Turrets (Small Arms) Custom Powers:
Turret Specialization: One turret becomes optimized for supporting one specific weapon and mounts it semi-permanently. The turret counts as double its level for the purposes of the specified weapon; consumes 44% of normal Mana costs; and grants a 56% bonus to fire rate, range, damage, and penetration. No other weapon may be mounted in this turret, and the weapon may not be removed as long as it assigned to this power. The selected turret and weapon may be separated over a period of 1 week, during which both will be inoperable.
Or:
Adaptive Mounts: All turrets become better at supporting mounted weapons. All weapons below the turret's level receive boosts to their fire rate, range, damage, and penetration sufficient to make them match an uncommon weapon of the turret's level, while retaining their defining characteristics.

Advanced Turrets (Small Arms) Upgrades:
Gunner Enhancement: Boosted Reflexes (0/3): All gunners' nervous systems are modified to have 28% decreased response time.
Ammo Adaption (0/5): Unlocks ammo types that may be selected depending on the situation. Any weapon add-on may fire any purchased ammo. Select from the following: Knockback, Mana-Thief, Explosive, Phasic, Acid, Arcane, Entangling.

Turrets (Small Arms) Completed Upgrades:
Mana Substitution (1/1): Unloaded Small Arms may fire, drawing Mana from "Bertha" to generate and propel ammunition. Fired ammunition lasts for 84 seconds.
Superchargers (5/5): Increases damage and rate of fire of add-ons by 70%.
Dakka (4/4): Adds 6 turrets with 1 Small Arms add-on slot each.

There was a minute of silence as everyone read the box. Mia broke it first. "Another fifty-six percent boost to everything? Blossom would be so sick with that!"

"The mana cost reduction caught my eye," Jill said. "You suck down more than Bertha makes, and I still need it to drive."

"The Adaptive Mounts power doesn't give any numbers," Ras said, "but what level did the system say these M2HBs are? And what level are your turrets?"

"Hey, System," Jill thought through her mana, towards the source of all their powers, "same questions."

System Inquiry detected.
Integrated heavy machine gun level: 18
Effective level of Advanced Turrets (Small Arms): 33

"So they'd be, what, twice as powerful?" Ras asked.

"I was talking with Buckman about that, and we think that some kind of sum of raw statistics scales linearly with level," Babu said. He had spent much of their last stop on a military base holed up with a logistics officer who had a much larger pool of people to pull system information from.

"So twice as powerful, like I said," Ras replied, sounding impatient.

"Maybe, but actual effectiveness can vary a lot more than just raw statistics say."

"Sugar, I know that. Stop thinking I'm an idiot."

"Hey!" Jill snapped. "Stop dripping your armpit cheese all over the place. I'm trying to make a choice here."

There was an awkward silence over their mental chat, broken a few seconds later by the distinctive thudding chatter of Ras firing his machine gun in short bursts.

Dazzling Dilophosaurus defeated.
Your contribution: 15%
255 Experience Gained!

"Nice kill," Mia said. "Blossom's still going to be way more powerful than a machine gun, even one that's boosted in level. I've put enough powers in her that she's effective level," Mia paused for a moment, "forty-three. With special powers too."

"Fuck a duck," Jill said.

"But how long are you going to maintain that advantage?" Babu asked. "Jill gets some experience from every kill we make, and Bertha has seven guns and a blast horn now. If she starts to out-level us, then the Adaptive Mounts might give you a bigger bonus than the turret specialization would."

"I think a more important question for you, Mia," Jill said, "is if you're willing to attach Blossom to Bertha permanently, and if you're willing to commit to going where I go. Because I can't wait around for a week if you decide that there's somewhere else you have to be."

"No," Mia said without hesitation. "I can't commit to that."

Jill nodded, though no one could see it. "Then I think the answer is clear. And hey, if I end up getting stronger than all you jerkasses and it becomes better numbers-wise, then win-win."

> Advanced Turrets Custom Power selected. Applying Adaptive Mounts.

Mana surged through Jill and Bertha, flowing to all seven of the truck's turrets like water released from a dam. The frontmost turret that housed Blossom took very little, but thousands of points poured into the others, frothing, churning, and changing.

"H. E. double hockey sticks!" Ras yelled. "My gun's growing all sorts of glowy bits!"

"Give it a fire," Jill said. The gunfire when Ras did so was louder, deeper, and faster than it had been just a minute before. "Hell ye—"

"Heads up!" Mia interrupted her. "There's a whole bunch of monsters off to our left, and they're moving in fast!"

Jill turned her head for a moment to look. Dozens upon dozens of bison were charging towards them on an intercept course. Their horns were distended to what would have been comically impractical lengths before mana had come, and they were on fire.

> Blazing Bison, Level 20
> Status: Stampeding

"Babu, get in your own turret!" Jill said, her voice snapping with authority. "Everyone else, open fire."

The hatch of the turret behind and above Jill's head sprang open, and Babu slid down the ladder at breakneck speed. He took off running for the trailer. A roaring tear sounded as Blossom opened fire, spitting bullets so fast that it was impossible to distinguish one discharge from another. Ras's gun joined in a moment later in more controlled bursts. Tracer rounds flashed across the brown grass-covered rolling hills, as the two gunners dealt death. For now, Jill just kept driving forward at a steady speed so that she wouldn't throw off their aim. When the stampede got closer, she would pull her big rig off-road to evade them, relying on the mana-boosted all-terrain tires to keep them heading where she needed them to go.

"Haha, my turn you—" Babu said as he reached a turret of his own, then cut himself off. "Wait, they're running away. Come back here my little chunks of XP!"

Jill risked another glance away from watching the road. The bison were wheeling around en masse, leaving their dead and dying behind as flaming hairy lumps and fleeing from Bertha's wrath.

"That's new," Jill said. All of the monsters they had encountered previously had been suicidally bent on attacking above all else, which had made them both implacable foes but also easy to manipulate.

"That's smarter," Ras said, "which is worrying."

"Should we chase them down?" Mia asked, her voice excited. "I bet we could harvest tons of loot from that many level-twenty monsters and probably level ourselves up too!"

Jill looked one more time, trying to decide if the delay would be worth it, but what she saw made her blood run cold. The hill on the horizon that the bison were running to had just stood up.

The monster in the distance was shaped like a bison itself, but it was more than fifty feet tall, and its horns stretched another fifty feet above that. They glittered in the afternoon sunlight like precision cut diamonds, and clouds swirled around their tips. Even though they were separated by miles, Jill swore that the monster made eye contact with her.

"Dip me in syrup and tie me to an anthill!" Jill swore. "I think we're going to leave that herd alone."

CHAPTER 24

SNIP SNAP

The guns fell silent as they sped away from the towering bison. It gave a snort—storm clouds billowed from gigantic nostrils—and turned its head away from Bertha.

"Thank fuck," Jill said, letting out a held breath.

"If the big one's not going to chase us, we should loop back and loot the ones we killed," Ras said in her mind. Jill's Captain Speaking power used little enough mana that she had started to keep renewing it by reflex.

"You okay with that delay?" Jill asked. "Last I remember, there was a lot of 'sugaring' about getting back home."

"I did apologize about that already," Ras grumbled. He was silent for a moment, then sighed. "I do want to get home, but half an hour isn't going to change much at this point. Those monsters were around level twenty each. The loot they might give is worth it."

Jill nodded. "Well, alright then. Hold on to your butts!"

She put Bertha into a spin, flicking on the magical Torque Converter to stop the truck from rolling over, and slammed her foot down on the accelerator once they were facing the opposite direction. Tires screamed as the sudden change in direction overcame even their magically enhanced traction, and Jill was pressed back into her seat. With a jerk and sudden relative silence, the wheels gripped the pavement, and Bertha rocketed back up to speed.

"Was that really necessary?" Mia asked.

"Yes," Jill said. "For dodging practice and no other reason."

"Right. . ."

A minute later Jill slowed the truck just a bit as she took Bertha off road; the Utility Wheels power was good at letting her drive in places an eighteen-wheeler would normally never dare, but they weren't perfect. She wanted to be able to turn at a moment's notice if something horrible appeared and tried to eat her.

Cold tingles spread down Jill's spine as they reached the killing field. Lying on the ground with their flames extinguished, the bison looked almost like regular animals. As monsters infused with mana, they were supernaturally tough, but they still hadn't fared well versus the high-caliber, equally magical gunfire that had killed them; great bloody holes had been punched clean through their flesh, and many of them had multiple limbs blown clean off.

She was jolted out of her horrified fascination by the roaring tear of Blossom firing into the ground a hundred yards away. The gun stopped firing, but no kill notification popped up.

"You see something?" she asked.

"Movement, I thought. . . ," Mia replied, her voice trailing off.

Jill brought Bertha to a stop as they reached the first bison, just barely nosing into the chest-high corpse with the front armored grille. She reached out with her mana and triggered the system's looting mechanic; motes of gold mana exploded outwards as the body disintegrated, leaving behind a single curved, gleaming horn.

"Ras, this was your idea so go out and get it," Jill said. "Babu, Mia, keep your eyes peeled and cover Ras. This place twists my tits."

A moment later the door to the trailer opened and Ras came through. He gave Jill a nod, opened the passenger door, and leapt to the ground. He landed in a crouch and drew his soulbound sword in an arc that left a glowing trail behind in the air. For a long moment he stayed crouched, only standing when it was clear that nothing was going to ambush him.

His twenty-foot walk to the looted horn and back was rather anticlimactic after that.

"That's one down," Jill said. There were another two dozen corpses strewn over a half mile of field.

Ras laid the horn down gently and nodded. "Let's get to it then."

The next two bison gave pelts instead of horns, but the gathering was otherwise uneventful. For the next they weren't so lucky.

Ras tensed the moment his feet touched the ground. "Something isn't right," he said, turning in a slow sweep of the plain. "But I don't see any—" The ground exploded underneath his feet, great clods of dirt flying into the air and smacking into Bertha's armored windows.

"Tickdicks!" Jill yelled, putting Bertha into reverse. She built up just a bit of speed and then jerked the wheel, throwing the truck into a circular slide around the explosion, still going backward. "Do you see anything?" she asked Mia and Babu. Both turrets were trained on where Ras had been, but the view was obscured by a wall of kicked up dust.

"There!" Babu said. "He's in the air!"

Jill looked up, and her jaw dropped.

Ras flashed downwards head first, his sword extended before him. A pulse of mana exploded from the tip of the weapon, and a shockwave blasted the dust away, revealing an enormous iridescent bobbit worm waving its mandibles in the air. Before Mia or Babu could open fire on the creature, Ras struck; his downward momentum halted in an instant as he blasted out a cutting arc of mana.

It hit the monster right in its fang-lined mouth, and the magic slipped effortlessly through hardened carapace. The monster gave one jerk then split in two, each half falling to the side in an eruption of blue, glowing blood. Ras landed softly an instant later, flicked his sword to the side, and sheathed it.

With another spin of the wheel, Jill whipped Bertha around, the cab sliding to a stop next to the new corpse. Ras looted both of the monsters, leapt up to the side of the cab, opened the door, and darted in.

"I think there might be some ambush predators here," he said, a small smile on his face. He slid into the passenger seat with a sigh, the blood splattered over him smearing against black leather.

"Fuck, really? I hadn't noticed," Jill said, flipping him off. She used her Customization power to clean the seat underneath the swordsman, but to her annoyance, she couldn't extend the power over his body to stop him from spreading gunk around. She would give him a pass for now though; he had just almost gotten killed. "I have to admit, you handled the shit out of that. You ready to get the next bison? We'll shoot the ground first for what that's worth."

Ras grimaced. "I need to recover my mana first," he said. "My escape power uses a lot."

Jill tapped her fingers on the wheel, gazing out at the next dead lump of treasure. "That's going to take a while, isn't it? We need a better way of doing this," she said.

"I could go out," Babu said. "I can turn myself invisible if need be."

"Really? Then why was I going outside?" Ras asked, sounding affronted. "I almost got eaten, and you can just waltz around risk free?"

"You enjoyed looking cool. Don't complain now just because—"

Jill flooded their mental connection with Bertha's horn noise cranked up to maximum volume. Once the others' annoyed yelling had died down, she spoke. "Having you two alternate would be safer, and so would blasting the ground, but this is taking too long." She flicked through Bertha's available upgrades in her mind's eye, reading text far faster than she would have been able to do the day before. Her Cargo Module description caught her attention.

"Bertha" has a cargo bay with base volume 90.625 cubic meters, total volume 90.625 cubic meters, internal dimensions of 14.5 meters by 2.5 meters by 2.5 meters.

Includes: Doors.

Add-ons (0/1): None installed.

Cargo Upgrades:

Cargokinesis (0/1): Objects inside of the cargo bay and within 14 meters of the cargo bay doors can be slowly moved.

Climate Control (0/2): Control the temperature and humidity of the cargo bay.

Volume (0/5): The volume of the cargo bay is set to 2.4x base volume and 1 add-on slot is added.

She sent the Cargokinesis power to the others.

"How fast is 'slowly'?" Mia asked. Jill forwarded the question to the system.

System Inquiry detected.

Cargokinesis maximum velocity magnitude: 1.4 meters per second.

"You could have just said that in the first place," Jill mentally grumbled at it, but received no reply as she sent the answer to the others. "That's a decent speed," she said. "It won't take long to float things inside. With the back doors open we'll still need Ras on guard to kill anything that tries to get in, but he'll be inside, at least. Babu should be able to shoot the spines out of the asses of any monster that tries to get in."

Ras nodded. "That sounds much safer to me."

"Wait," Babu said, his voice betraying a growing excitement. "What is the Cargokinesis speed measured from? The ground or the truck?"

Once again Jill repeated the question to the system, and an answer popped back.

System Inquiry detected.
Cargokinesis velocity is relative to the center of mass of the Cargo Module.

Babu started laughing. "I knew it! We don't need to stop!"

"We can just drive past and scoop things up," Mia said, catching on to Babu's idea. "The loot should just tag along and float in!"

"Nice," Jill said. She almost selected the power on the spot, but hesitated. It would help them get value out of the monsters they killed more safely, but it wouldn't help them in surviving their fights in the first place. Putting the class point into speed or armor upgrades would. On the other hand, this kind of ability was something that Jill would have killed for before. Being able to load and unload cargo with just a flex of her mind was incredible and would have saved her a lot of sore days.

Without warning a sense of longing welled up within Jill: an intense desire to be able to go back to the day before, when what she worried about was making her deliveries on time and earning enough money to keep Bertha in good shape. In her heart she was a truck driver, not a tank commander, and she didn't want that to change if she could help it.

"Hey," Ras said beside her, breaking her out of her funk, "you okay? You were just staring off into space."

"Yeah," Jill said. She put a point into Cargokinesis. "I'm good."

The resulting feedback from her soulbond with Bertha was more subtle than the usual feeling from purchasing something new. Normally, whatever new thing had arrived would announce itself with alien feelings, desires, or a phantom limb-like presence, all pushing in on Jill. But this time it was her projecting outwards, giving Bertha her arms to move things with.

Rather than dwell on the feeling, Jill got them moving again. She drove over to the next bison and kicked Bertha around in a half donut; the big rig swung to the new position with unnatural agility for such a large vehicle.

"We're going to try it still first," she said. "So, Ras, get back and cover the doors. Mia, Babu, keep looking for things to shoot."

The first piece of loot wobbled in the air as Jill used her new power for the first time. She couldn't actually see anything happening, but when the power was active, she could feel where everything was instead. After a few moments of practice, moving objects around became natural, and it was time to try and collect the next corpse at speed. The hard part was in flexing these new mental muscles rather than the driving: fourteen meters around the doors was a huge distance, even when barreling along at highway speeds. She levitated the bison corpses inside and let Ras activate the looting, rather than trying to do both at once herself.

Only one other time did another bobbit worm attack, snapping its jaws closed on the truck as it passed. The monster gouged a deep groove in Bertha's flank armor but failed to penetrate, and it was ripped partially from the ground, stunned and exposed, as it tried and failed to pull the massive truck to a stop. Bullets from Mia and Babu shredded it to pieces before it could burrow back down to safety.

Just a few minutes later they were back on the highway with a stack of horns, pelts, pincers, and gems glowing with mana neatly tucked away in the trailer. Jill sent Ras to clean up so that he would stop getting blood everywhere, and she settled in to the drive, the familiar drone of asphalt under tires a comforting hum.

Torn up countryside and fire in the distance marked much of their journey—obvious signs that monsters had taken a bloody toll. Some of the small towns bordering the highway were nothing more than rubble, but others had high walls and glowing barrier shields just like the armory had. Jill called out with the enhanced CB radio to them as they passed, but didn't get any replies.

"I didn't think I'd be back here for a while," Babu said. He had come into the cab to guide Jill once they reached the city and was staring out the window.

"You, uh," Jill said, "don't sound very happy about it."

He shrugged. "It is what it is, don'tcha know."

Jill didn't press. She knew all too well the kinds of things that could drive a person out of a small town, and Babu didn't seem to want to talk about it anymore anyways.

"We're coming up on Laurel," he said, pointing to a town ahead of them.

Mia's voice popped into their heads. "Something's coming from up ahead, fast. Wait, I think it's a group of cars!"

A vintage Thunderbird convertible, a Corvette, and a Model T driving in formation flashed past, then screamed around in a turn. They fell in behind Bertha, and her radio came to life. "Hey, big fella! You listening?"

Jill grinned and scooped up the handset. "Ten four good buddy! Glad to see someone else on the road. You folks doing okay?"

The Thunderbird drew up alongside the cab, and Jill looked down. The driver was an old woman wearing giant sunglasses and a dress that had been scandalous fifty years prior. An elderly man next to her looked up at Jill and waved enthusiastically. He had a radio handset in his other hand, and there was a stack of rifles in easy reach on the back seat. "Well, the rapture is a little different than I thought it would be, but I haven't felt this alive in thirty years! Some young'un's got us some nice glowy walls up around home, and I've got both my loves right here. We'll do alright."

Jill laughed. "Glad to hear it. We're passing through to Billings, heard anything?"

The man sucked on his teeth. "Well, I know they're alive, but the only people they sent out were assholes." The woman smacked him on the leg with a blazing fast slap. "What? It's the truth! Ma'am," he said, talking to Jill again, "you might want to be careful with that truck of yours. They tried to take my Stella," he slapped the dash of the car, "from me cause she's still running and I had to show them off with my belt."

A surge of anger rose in Jill's heart. "Thanks for the warning," she said. "But if they try that with me it's them who should be careful. I've got a few upgrades."

The man grinned. "All are equal in the eyes of Saint Browning." He glanced forward, where the interchanges leading into Billings were visible poking over the flat plains. "This is where I turn around. You take care, young lady."

"You too, gramps."

The car dropped back, falling back into formation with the others. They slowed, crossed the median, and headed back west.

"Well, here we are," Babu said, as the flat plains gave way to low slung buildings. "Home sweet fucking home."

CHAPTER 25

WITH APOLOGIES TO BILLINGS

Walls of energy rose into the air around the city and its surrounding suburbs, stretching miles across. Unlike the armory where they had been invisible until disturbed, the walls surrounding Billings were an opaque, misty white; a long narrow eggshell that spanned from a narrow river in the southeast to a ridge on the north. The interstate followed the river, set back by about a mile, until the eastern limit of the city where it crossed with a pair of bridges.

Jill slowed Bertha to a stop as they rolled up to the barrier. The way was blocked by a police car and a pickup truck parked sideways across the lanes. A man wearing hunting camouflage and sporting a mullet stood up in the bed of the pickup truck, a semi-automatic rifle in his hands. From the higher vantage point afforded by being in a big rig, Jill could see another man and woman in the pickup truck using the bed's sides as cover against anything that would approach at ground level.

The man shouted something, but wasn't loud enough for Jill to be able to make it out through all of Bertha's armor. Her hand moved by instinct to the window controls so that she could lower one and shout back, but she stopped herself from toggling it. She had magic powers now after all, and he was within range of her Captain Speaking power. She activated it and stretched her mana out to the man, but decided to be nice and not startle the man with Bertha's horn straight to the brain.

"Hey there, mullet," Jill said.

"The fuck!?"

"What, never had someone shout in your head?" Jill asked. "Anyhow, I'm coming in to drop some folks off, so would you mind moving your truck? Or I could go around if it's dead."

"Wait, just stop talking. Who are you and what are you doing here? The city isn't taking in strays."

Jill swallowed down a surge of anger, letting it pass before she spoke again. "The name's Jill, Jill MacLeod. Like I said, I'm dropping some people off who wanted to get back to their family, then I'm passing through. Might do some trading," Jill said. She shifted her mana to Mia to speak with her. "Hey, you're okay with spending a few hours here, right?"

Mia was silent for a few seconds. "Yeah, if we need to do something to help people, or if it's going to help us down the road."

"Peachy," Jill said, then swapped back to the man blocking her way.

It turned out he'd been trying to talk to her; her mana brought his words into her mind mid-sentence: "—there? I'm not letting you in until you tell me exactly where you're heading!"

Jill sighed. She wasn't as exhausted as she should have been, but the past half day of death and destruction on top of almost no sleep had left her short on patience. She snapped the thread of mana to mullet-man so she wouldn't hear him, then turned to Babu. "This assclown wants to know where we're heading. Where do your folks live?"

"Up by the university. Cotton Street," Babu said. He tilted his head to the side and frowned. "Ope, I think I know that guy! We went to high school together."

"I guess I should be nicer to him, then?"

"Oh, hell no! He's an asshole."

Jill snorted, but decided to tell the man what he wanted anyways. If he was guarding the highway entrance to the city, he was probably of at least some importance to whoever was in charge, after all. She resumed broadcasting her thoughts to the outside. "We're going up to Cotton Street; I've got a local to show me the way, so don't worry about me getting lost. Now are you getting out of my way or not?"

"You can come in, but you have to uh, pay a toll," the man said.

"Jerry, what are you talking about?" the woman next to him asked.

"Shhh, she might be able to hear you!" he whispered back.

"Of course I can hear you, dipwad," Jill said. "And fuck right off with that toll shake-down bullshit." Official or not, she wasn't going to listen to someone who tried to extort her. "I'm going in now." She cut off the communication, then eased her foot down and nudged Bertha into a slow roll, turning her truck off the highway. There was plenty of room on the flat ground to go around the roadblock.

A muffled bang and a sharp plinking noise startled Jill, and a tiny divot appeared in the glass of the windshield. The man had his rifle aimed at Bertha, though not directly at Babu or Jill themselves, and a wisp of smoke curled upwards from the muzzle. Jill slammed on the brakes and stared at the chip in the glass. It healed itself with a tiny snapping sound of shifting glass.

"Did he just shoot us?!" Babu said, disbelief in his voice. "I knew he was an asshole, but what the fuck!"

"And an idiot too," Jill said, her voice carefully controlled to cover her fury. "We have him outgunned by enough fucktons to break a bridge. Oh, Mia," she asked the heavy gunner, "could you do me a favor and put a stop to his nonsense?"

"You want me to kill them?" Mia asked back, her voice hesitant. "Isn't that a bit extreme? That bullet didn't really do any harm."

"No! Don't kill them just, I dunno, fire a warning shot into the air or into their engine block. I'm not putting up with any Rambo wannabes putting holes in my girl, but I'm not a psychopath."

There was a brief pause, then a roaring cough as Blossom fired for a half second into the air. The man in the truck flinched, his mouth open in terror, then he leapt off the truck and ran for the barrier shield. The other two people dropped their guns and stuck their hands into the air.

"Babu, your hometown sucks," Jill said, ignoring the pair surrendering and resuming her drive. Bertha's nose breached the shield, which offered no resistance. A notification appeared in Jill's vision.

> You have invaded the Settlement of Billings!
> Invasion progress: 0%

"Oh, fuck all the ducks. What do you mean invaded?"

System Inquiry detected.

Unless a settlement is classified as Open, all unauthorized entrants are classified as invaders. Secure the area around the settlement's central control crystal and imprison/exile/kill all current executives in order to claim the settlement for yourself. Secondary fortifications may also need to be overcome if they are present.

Invaders do not gain benefits from settlement abilities keyed to residents and may suffer penalties.

"System, I'm not going to—you know what, forget it," Jill said out loud, then cut herself off and sent both messages to Babu and Ras. "Either of you want to become king of Billings?"

Babu laughed. "Not for a million dollars and a plane ticket out the very next day. I bet Ras would do it in a heartbeat though."

"You say that like it's a bad thing!" Ras replied, indignant. "I could do a lot of good in charge!"

Jill shook her head and kept driving as the brothers settled into a new argument; as annoying as their spats could be, she would miss their antics after they left. The opaque barrier swept over her truck as it rolled through, blocking her view until it had passed the cab. On the other side, the city of Billings revealed itself.

Or at least a stretch of road virtually identical to that outside the city, fields of brown grass, and some low-slung buildings did. Between the flat terrain, the miles to go before reaching the city center, and the relatively short height of the buildings, there really wasn't much to see yet. The density of buildings increased as they went, however, and when at Babu's direction they took an off ramp, they found themselves on a typical low-density commercial street, with car dealerships, supermarkets, and abutting neighborhoods.

To Jill's surprise there were a few other cars on the road, giving a false sense of normalcy to the city. Some were sporting glowing pipes, animal parts, or other obviously magical augmentations, but most looked exactly like what Jill would have expected to see. The illusion was shattered by the number of people walking on the road, huddled together in packs for safety, with dazed and fearful looks on their faces.

Babu whistled as they drove past the supermarket where an angry-looking, armed crowd had gathered in front of its locked doors. A muscular woman, wearing nothing but shorts and a tank top despite the cold, had picked up a bench and was swinging it into the doors as a makeshift battering ram. There were cracks in the glass, but she seemed to be having trouble breaking through.

"I didn't think things would fall apart so quickly," Babu said.

Jill glanced at him and cut off her initial sarcastic reply. For all that he seemed to have mixed feelings about the place, Billings was Babu's home, and she didn't want to rub in how poorly it seemed to be coping. "I've seen looting before. Things will calm down once whoever is in charge gets organized," she said instead. "There must be someone in charge, right?"

There was a chime in Jill's mind and a notification appeared.

Settlement alert!

A monster has breached the barrier. Estimated level 3–11. Kill the monster to earn a bounty of 100 Billibucks.

Current monsters in settlement: 273

Current invaders in settlement: 1033

"Yeah, there's someone in charge," she said, "because it takes a person to come up with a name as stupid as 'Billibucks' for money."

"It's a big city," Babu said, a note of desperation in his voice, "two hundred and seventy-three isn't that many, divided by dozens of square miles! And I bet the monsters are, like, dire rats or something. No problem."

Jill kept silent and kept driving. She had to swerve once to avoid someone running into the street, but the few cars on the road didn't make for enough traffic to slow her down much. Another left turn had them off of the commercial strip and driving through neighborhoods of single-story, mainly ranch-style houses. There were some signs of damage—a few bullet holes here, broken windows there—but for the most part the neighborhoods had been spared the devastation that they had found in Bozeman.

They passed a park teeming with activity, and a stage and tents as if an outdoor performance had been planned for today. Instead, it had turned into a cross between a farmers' market, car rally, and gun show, as people bought and bartered for the necessities that they found themselves lacking in this new world. There was even a clear area where a pair of young women were showing off some sort of monster-part-made flamethrower.

Jill made a note to stop by on the way back and see if anyone would purchase the bison loot in exchange for more upgrades.

"Maybe you're right," Jill said. "This area seems to be doing pretty well. Not many monster attacks here either, from the state of things."

The market passed out of sight and they took a turn into a more commercial area. A block later she slammed on the brakes as a brown delivery van rolled in front of her and then crashed, slowly, into a dead parked car, blocking the road. Jill pressed on Bertha's city horn, not wanting to shake the offending vehicle to pieces. "Typical," she said. "The world ends and everyone forgets how to drive."

"Jill," Ras's voice spoke in her mind, still connected to her via magic even though he was in the back turret, "we have a problem. Someone just blocked us in from behind too."

"These gosh darned turbo-fappers!" Jill said, realizing that they were being attacked. She checked her side mirrors, and a beat-up old flatbed truck was diagonally across the street behind them. The driver leapt away from it, stumbled, and sprinted away. "Hundreds of monsters in the city, and they're attacking us? Ras, I said this to Babu and I'll say it to you: your hometown sucks." A series of cracks sounded as a burst of automatic weapons fire hit the trailer. A glance at Bertha's status showed Jill that the attack hadn't managed to inflict any damage; the small caliber bullets weren't powerful enough to get through hardened armor.

The radio crackled to life. "Hey, darling, I don't suppose you can hear me, can you?" A male voice said, oozing with fake charm. "Why don't you just hand over that nice rig of yours and no one gets hurt?"

Jill snatched the handset up and poured mana into one of the powers she had earned rather than bought: a profanity-fueled spell to inflict awe upon her allies and terror in her enemies. "What kind of an ass-pimpled idiotic cum-stain attacks a ride covered in machine guns?" she yelled. "I'm going to give you ten seconds to run, you bleach-guzzling rat-licking excuse for an artificial cow vagina, and then I'm blowing up that shitbox of a van that's in my way."

There was a silence, then screams from over the radio. "Run, you sons of bitches! Run! She's going to kill us all!" The side door of the delivery van opened and a half dozen people, dressed head to toe in tacticool gear, sprinted away.

Babu looked at Jill with a raised eyebrow. "I thought that spell freaked you out?"

Jill winced. "It did! Does. But it sure beats killing them, right?"

Babu nodded. "Yes. It does," he said.

"I see someone who thinks they're sneaky setting up a sugaring pirate cannon!" Ras interjected, sounding alarmed.

"That could actually hurt us," Jill said. "Let's just go before we have to kill them." Her right foot went down, spurring Bertha into motion, and her left hand pulled the air horn's chain. Her truck's deafening roar thundered forward, the distorted blast wave of sound hitting the delivery van and punching a six-foot wide dent in its panels. The van rocked sideways and spun partially out of the way and rolled onto its side. The blast wave settled into a plow just before Bertha made contact. There was a lurch as Bertha's armored mass fought briefly with the van's inertia, and then the van's rear was thrown sideways and up into the air. It tumbled once, then crashed to the ground, off the road.

Jill pressed the talk button on her radio as she drove away. "Any shitbag who's out there, listen up! I've got no issue with you, not yet, because you all suck so badly that I haven't even lost time. But if this keeps going it's going to end in your blood. So just fuck off. Got it?"

"Would you actually ask us to do it? To kill people?" Ras asked her.

"If I had to? If they attack us again, and we can't afford to show mercy because they're actually dangerous?" Jill said, partly to ask him and partly to ask herself. She paused, then made up her mind. "Yeah. Yeah, I would. Are you okay with that? Cause I'm sure as shootin' not, but it's what we have to do if they push us."

Mia broke the ensuing silence. "If we have to, we have to. Just try not to get us into those situations if you can help it, okay? I don't want to be a killer unless I have no choice." Babu and Ras murmured their agreement.

Jill swallowed, a weight settling in the pit of her stomach. "I'll try. That's the best I can promise." Even as the words left her mouth, she expected that sooner or later she would fail.

CHAPTER 26

ALL GOOD THINGS

Jill turned Bertha down the narrow street where the Batis lived, being careful not to let her oversized truck ride up onto the tree-lined sidewalk. She doubted if the trees could stop her at this point, or even do more than scuff the paint, but it was the principle of the thing. The neighborhood was filled with one- and two-story houses on individual plots. It was an older suburb, and the houses were smaller and more unique than those made in new developments.

A crowd of around a dozen people had gathered and were following behind Bertha, but while some of them were armed, they looked like curious residents rather than bandits. No one had shot at her yet, at least—or thrown themselves in front of her—so Jill was happy to ignore them for now.

"We're here," Ras said. He had joined Jill and Babu in the cab for the final stretch of road and was standing between the two seats. He leaned forward to get a better look at the house. "I just saw the curtains move; they're home!"

Babu took a deep breath and let it out slowly. "A happy ending for us then," he said. He turned to Jill. "Come inside with us?"

Jill shook her head. "Maybe once the reunion is over," she said. "Something tells me I'll be in the way until then."

"Please stay for at least a little while," Ras said to Jill. "I'm sure my parents will want to thank you for getting us home."

"I was passing through," she said. "Not really a big deal."

Babu laughed, but it was an ugly sound. "I'm sure Ma and Pa will dis-agree, what with you returning their pride and joy to them." He unbuckled his seat belt and opened the passenger door. "C'mon Ras, let's make sure the cousins are alright, at least. They like me."

A surge of anger welled up inside Jill, and she narrowed her eyes at Babu. "Don't be a dipshit," she said to him. "You have family problems, fine, but you're home. Some of us don't even know if our families are alive. Like me. So pull your head out of your ass."

Babu had the grace to look ashamed. "Right. Sorry," he said, failing to meet Jill's eyes.

She sighed. "Just go inside and talk with them you idiot. I swear every-one your age has a hamster inside their heads fapping away."

Babu jumped down from the cab, Ras following behind. The swords-man paused before leaving. "'Everyone your age'?" he quoted her, one eye-brow raising. "I'm shocked you didn't shake your cane at us."

"Bitchdicks! No more sass from you!" Jill said with a laugh. She made a shooing gesture with her hand, and Ras jumped down to join his brother.

The front door of the house slammed open and a black-haired missile shot out of it. "Babu, Babu!" screamed a child who looked to be about nine years old. He leapt at the last second and threw his arms around Babu's neck, then looked up, disappointed. "You didn't fall over!"

"Sorry, little cuz, but I'm super strong now."

"Aww, that's no fun," the child said. He waved at Ras. "Hi, Ras."

"Hello, Kevin," Ras said, a grin on his face. He reached over and ruffled the kid's hair.

A blonde-haired woman appeared in the door. "Kevin, don't run out-side right now!" She smiled at Babu and Ras. "Boys, thank the Lord! I'm so glad you're home. Come inside and tell us what's happening out there." She glanced up at Jill, then Bertha, her eyes flickering as they took in the armored, turreted truck. "And tell us who your new friend is."

Babu looked over his shoulder at Jill, Kevin still in his arms, but she just waved him off. She had no intention of exposing herself to any more of their family business than she had to. The brothers entered their home and shut the door behind them.

Jill leaned over and closed the passenger door, then sagged back into her seat with a sigh. She closed her eyes and rubbed them, trying to will her weariness away, then projected her voice up to Mia. "How are you doing? Need a break? This looks like a pretty safe place."

"I'm fine. I had a nap earlier," Mia said. "And between the hundreds of monsters and the people, I don't think anywhere in this city is safe, so I'm just going to stay right up here."

"Suit yourself. I'm going to conk out here," Jill said. "If you see anything nasty, shoot it." She considered going to her newly upgraded bed, but the seat was comfortable and already warm. Plus, she wasn't exactly clean. She breathed out a long sigh and, despite the sunlight shining on her face through the window, drifted off to sleep.

"Hey," Mia's voice startled Jill back to wakefulness. She glanced at the clock on the dashboard; she had only been out for ten minutes—not nearly enough time for a proper rest. She craned her head back, looking up towards the hatch to the turret in the roof. Mia had opened it and stuck her head through, upside down, to talk to her.

"Buggerbutts," Jill mumbled. "What is it?"

"Someone from that crowd is coming over. Looks like they want to talk."

Jill blew out her cheeks and shook her head side to side, fast, to wake herself up. "Great. That's—yeah," she said. "God, I would kill for a coffee."

"See if you can get the system to make you some," Mia said. "If it can make water in the bathroom sinks it can make other stuff, right?"

"Huh," Jill said. "That's not a bad idea."

She was about to dive into her system messages and ask it questions, but a tapping noise interrupted her. There was an older man, still in good shape but with graying hair, outside of the driver's side door with his knuckles still raised from rapping on the window.

Jill raised a hand at him and made a "one second" gesture, then spoke to Mia. "Mind staying on watch while I deal with him?"

"Sure," said Mia. "Try not to swear him to death." She withdrew her head and closed the hatch behind her.

"No promises," Jill muttered, then rolled down her window. "Howdy."

"Hi, there," the man said. He hesitated, then continued. "Nice weather we're having, eh?"

"Are you trying to piss in my cornflakes here? The world is bent over for a good old-fashioned monster pegging, magic boxes keep popping up in your vision, and you're talking to me about the weather?"

He blinked, mouth hanging open. "Cornflakes?" He turned his head to the crowd of people, who were watching their exchange with trepidation, closed and open his mouth a few times as if he wanted to say something but couldn't come up with what, then turned back to Jill. "Are you saying those weird blue things are more than just a prank? They must be some sort of VR meta thingy, right?"

"Oh, fuck me," Jill said, slumping forward so that her forehead thudded onto the steering wheel.

"Are you okay, miss?"

"Mia!" Jill called out with her communication power active, "I'm stepping out to explain things. If they try to abduct me," she paused, "I dunno, do something with bullets." She made a shooing gesture at the man, rolled up the window, opened her door, and jumped out of Bertha.

Without waiting she walked towards the group of people. "You're all going to want to hear this."

It took her five minutes to summarize how her last day had gone. The looks of confusion and disbelief that the start of her story brought quickly morphed into panic as she described the utter devastation that she had seen in some places.

"How do we know you're telling the truth?" said a man in his early thirties. He was dressed in a suit, as if he had woken up that morning expecting to go into work.

"I mean, you don't really. But you think I somehow made you all hallucinate boxes in your vision?" Jill said, then she gestured at Bertha. "Do you think those guns are standard issue? Actually, hold on." She flexed her Customization power and changed Bertha's paint scheme, making the words "this is magic, gutbrain" appear on the side of the trailer, flash bright green, then fade away. "Tada! Magic truck powers."

"Oh, my God," the business man said, his face draining of blood as he finally accepted the truth. "Those messages we see about monsters in the city . . . are they going to come here too?!"

Jill nodded. "Yup. You really haven't heard about all this from the people in charge?"

"Nope, nothing" an elderly woman said. She had a shiny double-barreled shotgun clasped across her chest. "You'd think the mayor would have put out an announcement; he's always been a good, handsome boy."

Jill refrained from mentioning that the mayor might be dead. The crowd didn't seem ready for that yet. "Well," she said instead, "you should all think hard about how you're going to defend yourselves. Ras and Babu," she gestured at the house, "have been through a lot. Babu knows all about the magic stuff. He can help you pick powers."

"Babu?" asked the old woman, her mouth splitting into a gap-toothed grin. "The boy with the sexy bubble-butt? I thought he was only good for shaking his money maker!"

"Grandma!" a shocked woman said, putting her hand on the old woman's elbow. "Don't say that kind of thing!"

Jill narrowed her eyes. "Don't think you're too old for me to kick your ass, granny," she said. "He saved my life at least once today, and he'd do the same for you if I have any read on him. Show some decency."

"Bah, I'm feeling great today," the old woman said. She spat on the ground. "I could bend you over my knee if I wanted to, little missy!"

Jill sighed. "I could be sleeping right now. Why am I not sleeping right now?" She turned to go back to Bertha.

"Wait!" said the man who had gotten her in the first place. "What are we supposed to do?"

"That's not up to me!" Jill called over her shoulder. "But I'd focus on guns, magic powers, and food. And if you see monsters, kill them!"

She found Ras waiting for her next to Bertha. "Jill," he said, a smile on his face. He was the most relaxed that Jill had ever seen him. "Please, come inside. My parents would like to speak to you."

Jill groaned, but veered towards his house. "Is everyone okay?" she asked.

"Better than okay!" Ras said, then gave a little laugh. "Everyone is here and safe. Mother's heart is just fine, and she and Babu are even getting along!" He scanned his gaze over the neighborhood. "We can make this work. I just know it."

Jill smiled, but inside she felt empty dread. She hoped her own family had been as lucky. For a moment she wanted nothing more than to run back into her truck and drive as fast as she could until she was home, but she pushed that thought away. They would be okay for a few days—they had to be.

As they went inside, Ras took his shoes off and placed them in a rack next to the door. Jill grimaced, then did the same. "Uh," she said as the smell hit her, "should I just leave the door open to air this out? I've had those on for a while now."

Ras made a face and nodded. "Maybe for a bit," he said. "It will let more light in too."

It was a bit dim inside, despite it being a sunny day. The sun was in the wrong place to shine inside, and all the lights were off.

"Power out?" Jill asked.

Ras nodded. "Since midnight," he said. "Come on, they're waiting for you."

In the Batis' living room was Babu—sitting on the couch with a mug of steaming tea in his hands and a bamboozled expression on his face—and four other people: The blonde woman Jill had seen at the door was seated next to Babu and was holding hands with a man on her other side; in a recliner was a man with a big smile on his face and rough hands; and a woman, who looked suspiciously like the Bati brothers, stood up as Jill entered the room.

Jill found herself enveloped in a hug. "Thank you," said the woman hugging her. "Thank you for bringing my boys home." She stepped back. "How can I ever repay you?"

"Uh," Jill said, stalling for time. "Have any coffee?"

"Yes! Well, I can make some," she said, hurrying away.

"We've been using a camp stove for water," said the man sitting in the recliner. He stood up, looked Jill up and down, then extended a hand. "Aman Bati, at your service. You look like you know a hard day's work."

"You could say that," Jill said. She looked him in the eye, took his hand to shake, and squeezed. She made sure to squeeze hard enough so that Aman knew not to mess with her, but not hard enough to break anything. She had never been a fainting violet when it came to moving cargo herself, and the system had only enhanced her strength since.

Aman grinned. "Welcome to our home. You met my wife Sangita. This is Taran," he gestured to the seated man, who nodded at Jill, "my brother-in-law. And his lovely wife Karen."

Karen rolled her eyes but stood and gave Jill another hug. Jill moved her arms in a vaguely hug-like gesture, hoping that she had gotten enough of the blood off of her so that the other woman wouldn't get too dirty. "You've seen my youngest already," Karen said, releasing Jill, "but I've got three more upstairs. If they get in your hair just yell at them."

"I, uh, will," Jill said. "I'm going to be hitting the road soon though."

"You're not staying for dinner?" Karen asked.

"Sorry, but no," Jill said. She fought down a yawn. "I might take a rest after checking out that market we saw, but I can't stop." She eyed Babu, who still looked lost. "Want to come trading? I could use an informed opinion, and I owe you two your share of the loot."

"Huh?" Babu said. "Oh, yeah." He looked up at his father. "I can get us some supplies. Guns and food."

Aman nodded in approval. "Good thinking. Ras will stay here and help us plan," he announced.

Jill clapped her hands together and started drifting towards the door. "Well, great. I'll just be. . . ," her voice trailed off, as the scent of heaven on Earth reached her nose. Sangita came into the room holding a cup of steaming coffee in her hands. "Maybe I can stay for just a few minutes."

CHAPTER 27

JILL'S USUAL SHOPPING EXPERIENCE

A few minutes had turned into ten and a second cup of coffee, this time in a disposable cup for Jill to take with her. After a slight delay where Babu had to climb up Bertha after Kevin and return the child to his mother, they set off towards the makeshift market in a park they had seen on their drive in.

Babu slid into the passenger seat, but Jill shook her head. "Rear turret, if you please," she said to him. "If those creeps have stopped shitting themselves and take another swing at us, I want another gun able to shoot."

The precaution proved unnecessary; the drive took just a few minutes, and this time no one got in their way.

The park was even busier than before, with around two hundred people milling about. Most were clustered near a line of open-faced tent stalls. At the end of the line was a stage, where a harassed looking man holding a clipboard addressed the small parts of the crowd that were paying attention. It would have looked like a normal farmer's market except for the way that people moved: there was an air of tension that Jill could sense even from inside her truck. That, and the sheer number of weapons people were carrying.

Heads turned their way as Jill pulled Bertha up to the curb. There were a few other cars there, and Jill spotted someone elbow deep in another, presumably fixing it, but her truck was easily the meanest thing around.

"Okay, kiddos," Jill said via her communication power. "Let's go get shit. Babu, bring the loot from the back, would you?"

"Aren't you, uh, worried about someone taking Bertha?" Mia asked. "I'll stay up here and keep watch."

Jill sighed, then excluded Babu from her mana's grasp so he wouldn't hear her reply. "Are you staying up there all day for a reason? Like, say, avoiding someone?" she asked Mia.

"Is it really that obvious?"

"Yes. Now get down here."

The hatch popped open a moment later, and Mia slid down the ladder. "Let me guess," she said to Jill, before the older woman could say anything, "you don't want to deal with my bullshit, so suck it up?"

"Well, I was going to be nicer about it," Jill said, then scrunched her face. "Actually, no I wasn't." She sighed, then asked with a dead voice, "Do you want to talk about it?"

"No. I want to shoot something."

"Thank fuck. I'm sure something will try to eat us soon enough," Jill said. She pinged Babu. "Did you get stuck back there?"

The door to the trailer opened and Babu stumbled through, his arms full of monster loot. He held the bison hides, horns, gems, and a few other bits of lesser creatures like fear deer and dire lemmings that they'd collected along the way. They formed a precarious pile that looked like it was one stiff breeze away from tumbling out of his arms.

"Huh," Jill said. "More of that than I thought there was." She scooped up half a dozen hides, tossing them onto her shoulder, and stuffed a few gems into her pockets. She jumped down from the cab, Mia and Babu following close behind. With a flex of Customization Jill sealed Bertha's doors shut and coated the gaps with armor. "Alright," she said, clapping her hands together in excitement, "let's go shopping."

"Ope, are you excited?" Babu asked, disbelieving. "To go shopping?"

"What?" Jill said, shooting him a glare. "What's wrong with shopping?"

"Just. . . ," he said, voice trailing off. "Tough as nails Jill MacLeod? Likes shopping?"

"It's just getting stuff! We need stuff!"

"Oh, my God," Mia said, voice shaking with laughter. "I bet you used to hang out in a mall!"

"It was the early nineties! What else was I supposed to do?"

"I bet she got kicked out for swearing," Babu said.

"I bet someone tried, and she beat them up," Mia added. Her voice almost, but not quite, held the same tone of light banter that it had with Babu earlier in the day.

"I hope a snapping turtle takes off both of your thumbs," Jill said, refusing to acknowledge that their scenario was exactly what had happened to her teenage self. She strode forward, scanning the stalls for anything interesting enough to stop the current conversation. While no one was running away from the trio, there was a conspicuous lack of people in their way.

> Settlement alert!
> A monster has breached the barrier. Estimated level 5–13. Kill the monster to earn a bounty of 100 Billibucks.
> Current monsters in settlement: 332
> Current invaders in settlement: 1061

The crowd stilled for a moment; conversations paused and eyes flickered as everyone read the message. "Guns," the cry of a stall owner waving a shotgun in the air broke the silence. "I've got guns for sale!" The crowd's voice came back, louder and angrier than it had been before.

"I bet he's going to be busy," Mia said.

"We should get some," Babu replied, his voice serious.

Jill turned her head back to look at him and raised an eyebrow. "I never say no to a good gun, but we're pretty well stocked at the moment."

"Not for us," the enchanter replied. "For my folks." He chewed on his bottom lip. "I'm worried about them," he admitted.

"Yeah," said Jill, "me too. They seem too . . . well, relaxed about all of this. You and Ras will set them straight, though, right?"

"Hah!" Babu laughed without humor. "Oh, I tried already. Want to know what level they all are?"

"I get the feeling you're going to tell me anyways."

"Zero! Well, one for my pa because he was curious. And I bet Kevin picked something because he's Kevin. But the rest of the so-called adults are stalling because they have no idea what to do, and they told the other cousins not to take anything. And they won't listen to me about what's going on, even if it's 'so wonderful I'm looking out for the family'!" Babu took a breath, his rant over for the moment.

"And what are you going to do about it?" Jill asked.

Babu stared at her. "What?"

"You want the situation to change? Do something. Just," she said, "I don't know, pretend you're someone else in the same situation for a second, and tell me what they should do."

Babu took a breath. "Fuck. Fuckity damn shit fuck!" he said, voice growing louder with every exclamation. "I'm going to buy all the guns, and when we get back, I'm telling them what the hell they need to do." He marched off.

"I think he was pretending to be you," Mia said.

"Of course he was," Jill said. "I'm awesome. Now," she pointed at a stall where a red-headed woman was transforming a green hoodie into a cloak with glowing hands, "time to get some clothes."

"Oh, hell no, I am not going clothes shopping right now."

"Fine! Armor shopping," Jill said. "You can't say no to armor."

Jill went over to the stall without waiting for a reply, and Mia followed behind. The crowd instinctually gave them space. "Hi, there," she said to the redhead, "I'm Jill. You want to make me something cool?"

"Depends," the woman replied, "you don't look like you're from around here."

"I'm not," Jill said, her eyebrows raising. "That going to be a problem?"

The woman hesitated. "Not if you can pay. The card machines are all busted, so cash only. You can call me Kayla."

Jill nodded. "Alright, Kayla. How about a trade?" She held out the stack of bison hide. "These are level twenty from monsters outside town. You make me two sets of biker leathers for us," she gestured at Mia and herself, "and I'll give you two hides as payment. Sound fair? I don't think anyone else here has anything like them, and you can't get them yourself without risking getting killed."

Kayla clicked her tongue. "By pay I meant money. Why would I want skins?"

"How about this," Jill said with a grin. "You try to make something from it, say, a tough biker jacket, and if you don't understand afterwards why this is a good trade, you can keep it for yourself."

The tailor looked skeptical, but she snatched a hide out of Jill's hands. Kayla closed her eyes and called on her mana, which bubbled out of her in a fiery red wave the same color as her hair. The bison hide sucked it up over the course of thirty seconds, glowing brighter and brighter until it finally started to shift and change. It only took another five seconds after that for it to form into a basic leather jacket.

> Bison Bomber Jacket
> Level 20, Common
> When worn, passively protects the wearer from harm. Increases physical and elemental Resistance by 30%. May be fused with leg and head coverings for enhanced protection.
> Customization remaining: 80%
> Item cannot be equipped to Soulbound Modular Vehicle "Bertha."

The woman staggered. "I—" she stammered, "I got a level! Dear Lord in heaven that felt good. And the jacket's some sort of magic armor thing now?"

"So, we have a deal?" Jill asked. "Or I could just take the rest of these away. . ."

"Don't you dare!" The woman held out a hand to shake. "It's a deal. You give me two for myself, and I'll make two sets of leathers. Pants too."

"Pleasure doing business with you!" Jill said, shaking her hand. She handed over the hides. "You need our measurements?"

There was another pulse of mana, and this time the woman's eyes flashed. She grinned. "Oh, I know exactly what shape you two are."

"That's not creepy at all," Mia grumbled. "This is a new reason why I hate clothes shopping."

"Make mine badass, please," Jill said.

"Sure, sure," said Kayla, all her attention devoted to checking every hide for the smallest imperfection. She "I need to get my magic stuff back before I can transform two more. It'll take twenty minutes."

Babu came staggering up to them, his pile of loot partially replaced with a pile of rifles resting atop a crate of ammo. "Hey, Jill," he said, "could you let me into Bertha? I want to drop these off then buy more. I'm getting a good deal on monster parts."

"Yeah, sure, I've got time to kill," Jill said. "Remember," she said to Kayla, "badass."

Mia and Jill escorted Babu back to Bertha. A tow truck sat in front of the big rig, a pot-bellied man leaning against the smaller vehicle's back and looking skeptically at the much larger truck. A pair of men, both sporting sheriff's deputy badges pinned to denim jackets, leaned on Bertha. They had semi-automatic rifles slung across their chests and handguns on their belts, and were blocking the way to the cab. One was chewing on something; upon seeing Jill he stood straight, put his hands on his rifle, and glared.

"Hey, there," Jill said, stopping out of arm's length from them. "You outside my truck for a reason?"

"Afternoon, ma'am," said the one whose mouth wasn't busy, "you made a bit of a splash coming into the city. We're going to have to impound your truck."

Jill turned her head to the tow truck driver. He nodded at her, pointed at the two deputies, and, after making sure they weren't looking, made the universal sign of them jerking off.

She laughed. "Bullshit you are. You can't be dumb enough to think that would work, so why are you really here?"

The first man's face turned beet red, but the chewer chuckled right back at Jill. He turned his head and spat out a wad of tobacco, which splattered onto Bertha's wheel well and dripped down the paint, leaving a foul trail.

"Personally, I just think you should pay for all the shit you've done," he said. Jill's blood chilled, and she prepared herself to fight. She recognized his voice from the ambush earlier. "But the new mayor wants to hire you. Apparently, he thinks that you can do something that we can't. We're here to, ah, invite you to come to City Hall."

"Wait, the new mayor?" said Babu, stepping up beside Jill. "What happened to the old one?"

"Didn't show up to work today," he said with a voice dripping with fake innocence.

"Uh-huh," said Jill. She glanced back, noting that they were drawing a crowd with their confrontation. As much as she wanted to draw on the man, she didn't want to provoke him into shooting at her. Even though she suspected she might be able to take a bullet or two and not go down thanks to the magic running through her veins, the crowd acting as a backstop behind her wasn't so tough. "And what if I tell you and your new mayor to shove an ostrich egg up your asses? All of it, uncooked. Then clench."

The chewer bared his stained teeth in what could only technically be called a smile. "Then once you're gone, I think some darkie friends of yours who live here might be in for some trouble." He winked at Babu. "I hear you've got a lovely family. It would be a sh—"

Babu's hand shot out, his supplies crashing to the ground, and with it came a surge of black mana filled with pain and desire. Dark tendrils blasted into both men, gripping them around the neck and burning their skin. They were lifted off their feet and pinned, choking, against Bertha's side.

"Oh, you're really, really dumb," said Jill to them.

There was a flash and a pop of displaced air, and Mia held Blossom in her hands. She turned away from the pinned men and scanned the surroundings, looking for anyone who might be sneaking up on them. There was an awed, collective gasp from the crowd, which surged away from the massive weapon and display of dark magic. The tow truck driver looked up, smiled, and pulled out a cigarette.

Jill stalked up to the two pinned men. "I gave you a warning. A clear damn warning to just stay away. Now what the fuck am I supposed to do?" She waved her arms wildly in the air. "If you'd have pulled that shit yesterday, I'd have had to grin and bear it—or maybe report you to the police, if you weren't already the beardsplitting police—because otherwise it's a murder charge." A dam of rage and fear that Jill had been holding inside broke. "Do you have any idea how many things I've killed since yesterday? How many bodies there are out there?" She gestured to the wider world. "You just proved there's no laws here, so why shouldn't I kill you right now?"

The two men gurgled as they tried to speak, and their limbs thrashed, but they were held too tightly to get any sound out.

"Babu, you need to ease up a bit for them to answer," said Mia. She was clenching her jaw hard, and her voice wobbled, but her hands were steady on her chain gun, and her finger was ready to pull the trigger.

"You don't kill them," said Babu, rage filling his voice, "because ants like these always come in swarms. If you want them to stay away, you need to poison the hive." His mana flared and the tendrils from his spell forced the men's jaws open and shot down their throats. No longer supported, they slid down Bertha's side to the ground where they crumpled into a heap, twitching despite being unconscious. Babu staggered into Mia and nearly fell to the ground himself; only the gunner reaching out and snagging him by the upper arm kept him standing.

"What did you do?" Jill asked, her rage fading into a horrified curiosity.

"Mind virus," Babu said. "It only works on people a lot lower level than me, but," he swallowed, "it's going to spread to everyone they come in contact with for the next day that they consider allies and make them scared of attacking my family."

"That's terrifying," Mia said, but there was approval in her voice.

"That's from your whacked out class evolution, isn't it?" Jill asked. She bent down and grabbed the first man by his ankles and dragged him away from Bertha, so he wouldn't get run over when they left. "I thought you were staying away from that?"

Babu shrugged. "Only the more messed up stuff. If I'm going to compete with all you soulbound people, I figured I needed to dig around in the system for options and, well," he gestured at the two unconscious men. "Tada."

Jill shuddered. "This whole world is just going to be absolutely fucked with mind control, isn't it? C'mon, Mia, let's go lets go poke Kayla to hurry it up. We should get back to Babu's folks and warn them about what might be coming."

CHAPTER 28

GETTING READY

Excuse me? Ma'am?" a man in a timid voice asked Jill, wearing a bright yellow "volunteer" shirt and holding a clipboard. She and Mia were waiting next to Kayla's stall as the tailor worked, a twenty-foot circle around them devoid of people. No one was willing to be near them anymore after Babu's violent display.

"Yeah?" Jill replied. She had taken her old shotgun out of Bertha and held it propped against her shoulder.

"My name's, um, Jacob. We," Jacob gestured up at the performers' stage, where three other volunteers had gathered in an anxious knot observing Jill and Mia, "we're, um, wondering if you and your colleague were going to, ah, finish your shopping soon? Not to rush you!"

Jill rolled her eyes. "Oh, unclamp your nipples," she said. "I'm not going to eat you or anyone else that's just minding their own business." She caught a glimpse of Babu. He was rushing to make a few more purchases before they left, darting through the crowd like a fish through water. A crowd that didn't seem to mind him at all. "We'll be gone soon enough."

"Oh. Well, good," he said, relaxing the smallest amount. "It's just that you're scaring folks some, don'tcha know. What with the big guns and the knocking out cops."

Jill stared at him, wondering how long he'd keep talking.

"Not that guns are bad! We like guns here!" he rambled, some of his nerves coming back. "And you'd be welcome to come back some other time when folks have calmed down. The market's here every week."

Settlement alert!

A monster has breached the barrier. Estimated level 6–14. Kill the monster to earn a bounty of 100 Billibucks.

Current monsters in settlement: 343

Current invaders in settlement: 1062

"You might not want to count on that," Jill muttered under her breath. The frequency of alerts had gone up over the time that she'd been in Billings, and the monster numbers hadn't dropped either.

"Don't worry about us," Mia said. "Worry about monsters. Get yourself armed and stay that way."

"Oh," Jacob said, swallowing. "Okay. Thanks." He backed away and disappeared into the crowd, heading towards the stage.

"I don't get it," Mia said, frustration in her voice. "Why is it that the people here are so dumb?"

"I don't think they're dumb, they're just," Jill said, "normal. Everyone in Bozeman got attacked right away, right? Fires and teeth everywhere?"

"Yeah. But we all rallied together and had weapons to fight them off!"

"Everyone who lived did. How many never made it to safety at all?"

Mia grimaced and shut her eyes for a moment. "I try not to think about them."

"The people here haven't had any of that yet. They're still trying to live mostly normal lives."

"Shouldn't we be helping more then? Getting them ready?"

Jill sighed. "I can warn them, same as I did outside Babu's place. But that's it." She pointed an accusing finger at Mia. "You have to convince the next group. If I have to do this kind of bullshit everywhere we stop, so do you."

She turned and strode to the stage, people scattering out of her way like leaves from a whirlwind. She casually hopped the four feet up to the platform and spun to address the crowd with her shotgun still propped against her shoulder.

"I've only got enough caffeine in me to say this once, so listen up!" she shouted. Those of the crowd who hadn't been warily watching her turned to look, but the noise of their chatter only increased. "Thumbs out of your asses and into your mouths!" Jill shouted, threading just a little bit of mana through one of her malediction bard spells to force people to pay attention. Silence followed.

"Right, so," she said, the undivided attention of so many people on her triggering a burst of anxiety. "I'm going to tell you how things are now." She began pacing. "All of you need to find some place defensible to hole up, preferably together. The monsters in the warnings? Real, and deadly. All this magic bullshit might seem like fun and games, but things are coming that are going to want to kill you." She gestured to the magical barrier around the city, just visible in the distance. "I think the wall is supposed to be protecting you, but it's letting more monsters through than a screen door on a shit ship."

Her spell had faded at this point, but the crowd was still quiet, watching her. It was Kayla, leaning out of her stall, who broke the silence. "How do you know?"

"This morning I saw a town get its teeth kicked in. Hundreds—maybe thousands—of monsters all running straight at anyone they could find, or burrowing up from underground. Most of Bozeman is gone, though the survivors have their heads on straight in the armory."

Shock raced through the crowd and sounds of horror and disbelief.

"Are you saying we're going to die?" asked one of the volunteers on stage, an older woman with strawberry blonde hair.

Jill shook her head. "No. You have a head start, and if you use it, you'll do okay. Read the messages from the system and ask it questions, pick up some guns and powers, and get somewhere safe."

"Where should we go?" someone shouted from the crowd.

Jill threw up her hands. "Do I look like a local to you? Bang your heads together until the rocks fall out and then you tell me! I'm done warning you all, so," she pointed at Jacob, who was clutching his clipboard to his chest for comfort, "Jacob's in charge. Go bother him."

"Me?!" her victim yelled, voice squeaking. "Why me?!"

"You're organizing something already. Might as well make it important," Jill said. She jumped from the stage, ignoring the sudden surge of people moving forward to question the man she'd "voluntold" into authority, and made her way back to Mia. "There," she said, glaring at the younger woman. "That sucked donkey clits, but their asses are in gear and some schmuck other than me is in charge."

"I thought you did pretty good!" Mia said. "Very decisive, got everyone to listen. What more could you want?"

"To not have everyone's judging eyes looking at me," Jill said with a shudder.

"You get used to it," said Babu from beside them, his arms filled this time with a crate of MREs. He paused for a moment, then frowned. "What, no jump scare?"

"I got used to you," Jill said, a pang of melancholy accompanying the words at their imminent separation.

"I noticed you coming," Mia added.

"Ope, there goes my fun," Babu said, voice filled with mock sadness.

Jill rolled her eyes. "Are you ready to go?"

"Guns and food, what else could a family need?" Babu replied. He smiled, but there was a tension underlying it.

"Then we're just waiting on—" Jill cut herself off as Kayla turned from where she was working, the glow of mana fading from her hands, and walked over. She tossed a set of bulky leather clothes, neatly folded, onto the stall's table in front of Jill.

"Done!" the tailor said, exhaustion plain on her face. "Want to try them on?"

"Does the pope commit crimes in the woods?" Jill replied. She unfolded her modified jacket to get a better look at it. There were spikes on the shoulders, and on the back was a stylized patch of Bertha spewing fire from her exhaust pipes. She put her shotgun on top of Babu's crate and shrugged the jacket on. It was a perfect fit. "Yeah. Yeah, this will do. Actually, it's fantastic." She dug into her pocket, pulled out a glowing mana gem, and tossed it to Kayla. "You might want to make yourself some armor too. Or trade for a gun. I dunno, but—"

She interrupted herself as another notification box popped into her vision.

Settlement alert!

A monster has breached the barrier. Estimated level 19–27. Kill the monster to earn a bounty of 100 Billibucks.

Current monsters in settlement: 384

Current invaders in settlement: 1062

"Those are getting worse," Mia said, glancing at Babu. "Much worse."

The enchanter swallowed. "I'd like to get back home now, please."

"I think it's time for me to close up shop," Kayla said. "Maybe help Jacob up there keep things together." She nodded up to the stage.

"Get someplace safe," Jill said to Kayla, reaching out to take the rest of her and Mia's armor, "and good luck." They hurried back to Bertha. Around them the farmer's market was shutting down, and Jill could hear Jacob's voice shouting orders from the stage for people to go home, get everyone they could, and make their way to the airport. It seemed that despite his terror, the man was actually taking charge, and had picked someplace for everyone to rally.

The drive back went quickly. There was more foot traffic on the road— the beginnings of an exodus of people heading north. Most seemed to be traveling fast and light, but some weren't quite so smart; Jill had to swerve to avoid one man pushing a seventy-inch television in a wheelbarrow.

Babu leapt out of Bertha's cab the moment they pulled up to his house, not even waiting for the truck to come to a full stop. The muted sound of gunfire in the distance echoed through the open passenger door. There was fighting not very far away.

"So," Jill projected up to Mia, "do you still want to shoot something, or are you coming inside? I don't think we can stay here long."

"I think I'm going to need to shoot something," Mia replied. "Like that over there." The ripping roar of Blossom filled the cab as a stream of bullets smashed their way into a black-and-white monster that had trundled into view.

Lesser Skunk defeated.
Your contribution: 15%
210 Experience Gained! 15 Billibucks Gained!

"Right, like something the size of a horse is 'lesser'," Mia muttered.

"Barkstripping ass bandits," Jill said. "Looks like this neighborhood isn't safe anymore." She glanced at the house. "I think Babu might need some backup getting everyone going. Keep, uhh, shooting stuff."

She entered the house to the sound of Babu's raised voice.

"We need to go!" he half yelled, a finger pointing northwards. "You heard that, right? Monsters are here right now."

"Your father and I, and Taran and Karen, are all in agreement, Babu," Babu's mother Sangita said. "This is our home, and we are staying put for now, at least until there is an official order to evacuate." Taran and Karen looked uncomfortable, but didn't say anything.

"If the monsters come, we'll shoot them," Aman said. "You did a great job bringing back so many guns."

"Jill!" Babu said as Jill entered the living room, desperation in his voice. "What level was it? The thing Mia just killed?"

Jill did a quick bit of mental math. "Fourteen."

Ras winced.

Babu pointed at his brother. "Ras, say something! Don't just sit there!"

Ras swallowed. "Dad, Babu is right. The house isn't strong enough. We should leave."

"You told us monsters are just mutated animals," Aman replied. "How could the house not be strong enough? I know you love your brother Ras, but he is just overreacting, right?"

Jill couldn't help herself: she gave a large snort and shook her head.

"Yes?" Sangita said, turning to Jill with narrowed eyed. "You have something to add?"

"Want to know how much magic I've taken to make me stronger?" Jill asked, walking over to the wall. She ran a hand up and down its surface, admiring the flowered wallpaper.

"How does that matter? I don't know, probably lots."

"Absolutely fuck all," Jill said. She turned to look Sangita in the eye, then put her hand through the drywall without any particular effort. Her hand fished about for just a moment until she found a stud. With a terrible crunching snap, she wrenched the two-by-four piece of lumber out of the wall, broken drywall and wires trailing after it. "A level fourteen monster, like the one that was just right outside? It wouldn't even slow down going through your lovely house."

"Ms. MacLeod," Aman said in the ensuing shocked silence. "I'd appreciate if you didn't tear apart my house. This is a family discussion, so please leave."

Jill nodded. "Fair enough. If I were you, I'd get my ass to the airport though. I know some other people have settled on it as the safest place." With that parting shot she turned and left. Once out of sight she shook out her hand and rubbed her shoulder. Her demonstration had been a bit harder to do than she had been expecting. The sounds of further shouting followed her out.

Jill took a centering breath on the doorstep while staring at her truck and thinking of her own family. There was no way that they would be as head-in-the-sand as the Batis were being, but she worried about them all the same. If things had gone well for them, her father would be happily firing off his arsenal of ammunition from his bunker of a prepper house and drowning in experience points. If things had gone badly, then some boss monster would have killed everyone in moments.

Her eyes traced Bertha's new lines, coming to rest on the gun mounts devoid of people to fire them. They had been essential when she had bought them, but now were just dead weight. "I need a crew," she said under her breath. She felt bad for the thought a moment later. What right would she have asking people to abandon their homes and families just to help her get to her family more easily? What could she offer someone that would be worth that?

With Babu, Ras, and Mia the situation was clearer. They got safe transportation to where they needed to go, and in return, they helped defend Bertha. There were probably more people who wanted to travel east, but she didn't have time to find them. Every person meant another detour, and every stop she took only revealed more complications.

Jill flinched as another hail of bullets erupted from Blossom.

Giant Black Widow defeated.
Your contribution: 15%
180 Experience Gained! 15 Billibucks Gained!

"Fuck me, that's loud," she said. She stared at the notification of the death of what had almost certainly been a horrifically deadly spider, then at Bertha. Then she smacked herself on the forehead for being an idiot. What she had to offer in exchange for long-term help was obvious. She marched back into the house, squashing down the tiniest bit of guilt as she did. What she was about to do was manipulative, but it was also for everyone's benefit.

The voices cut off as she entered the living room yet again. Both Babu and Ras were standing now, side by side and facing the others. Babu's face was flushed red, and Sangita pointedly wasn't looking in his direction.

"Ms. MacLeod," Aman said, rubbing his forehead, "we haven't made a decision yet."

"Well tough shit, you're about to have it made for you," Jill said. She turned to Karen, who had been sitting next to her husband with a worried expression on her face. She hadn't said much so far in the conversation. "You want your kids to be safe?" Jill asked her.

"Yes," Karen replied without hesitation.

"Well then, because Babu and Ras have helped out so much, I'll give you an offer: you all come along with me and help out, and your kids get a fuck-off-strong layer of armor between them and anything that wants to eat them. You get to keep them safe with big-ass magic machine guns. I get help reaching my family. And when everyone we care about is safe, then we can decide where you lot want to settle down. How does that sound?"

Sangita started to say something, but Karen cut her off. "Ras? How much safer would we be with Jill in her truck? Safer than heading to the airport or staying here?"

"Much," Ras said without hesitation. "We could all get more magic without being in danger, including the cousins." He looked at Jill with a message in his eyes. "Jill can keep us all out of the worst danger if she's careful."

"I will be," Jill said.

"Kids!" Karen shouted, standing up. "Pack what you can't leave behind! We're going!" She marched out of the room.

Taran stood and smiled after his wife. "I was wondering when she would start acting normally again," he said. "Are you going to be coming?" he asked Aman and Sangita. "Family should stick together."

"I am," said Babu before his parents could speak. "Ma, Pa, I've had enough. I'm going to protect the cousins and that's that. If you care enough to want to see me again, that's up to you." He spun on his heels and left.

"I suppose it really is decided then," Sangita said. She looked at Jill with a complicated expression on her face, full of a mixture of both anger and gratitude. "We'll all be going with you, it seems."

CHAPTER 29

MUST COME TO AN END

Kevin ran into the room, a dinosaur backpack stuffed to the seams on his back. "Road trip!" he yelled, bouncing up and down, "The truck's real big. Are we gonna get bunk beds?!"

Jill smiled. "Sure," she said, "why not? I'll make all of you some bedrooms. It's only fair if you're riding with me long term."

Sangita blinked. "Bedrooms?"

Jill smirked. "Bertha's got a few surprises in her," she said. "Try to be quick about packing; things are getting dangerous. I want to be gone in fifteen minutes."

She strode out of the room, Babu falling into step beside her outside the threshold. He had been just outside, listening in. They walked in silence until they were out of the house. "Bit of a dramatic exit you had there," Jill said, sweeping her gaze up and down the street to check for danger. There were no monsters, but scared looking people were peeking out of the windows of their houses.

"Fuck you," Babu replied, but there was no heat in it.

"Attaboy," Jill said. She stared at the surrounding houses. "How much do you like your neighbors?"

"They were fine. Nice, I guess."

"Tell them to get their nice asses up to the airport then. I don't think this place is going to last much longer."

As if the system had been listening to her and just waiting for the right dramatic moment, another notification came through from the settlement.

> Settlement alert!
> A monster has breached the barrier. Estimated level 1–9. Kill the monster to earn a bounty of 100 Billibucks.
> Current monsters in settlement: 472
> Current invaders in settlement: 1055
> Warning! Settlement approaching Infested status!

Babu grimaced. "Right," he said. He closed his eyes and a surge of mana blasted out from him. "There, they should all know."

"Handy power, that," Jill said. She leapt up to the driver side door, but paused before entering. Just to see if she could, she used her Customization power to remove the door instead of opening it. The armored metal folded into itself and peeled away, leaving just the shimmering barrier that separated the inside of Bertha's dimensional space from the outside.

"Wicked," she said under her breath. She stepped through, shivering slightly at the tingling sensation of the barrier sweeping over her skin. Babu followed her, then she put the door back in place.

Jill clapped her hands together. "First up," she said, "some rooms for them. If I'm pressuring people to join up, least I can do is give them their own crappers." She pulled up the description of the Habitation Module.

> Habitation
> "Bertha" has a Habitation Module with basic amenities for 2. Life support capacity for 5.
> Includes: Single Bed, Washroom, Workspace.
> Add-ons (1/1): Bobcat Belly-Fur Bedding.

> Habitation Upgrades:
> Restful Sleep (1/1): All allies who rest in the Habitation Module receive increased physical and psychological healing rates.
> Unseen Servant (0/3): Weak manifestations of force will see to the maintenance of the Habitation Module and residents' possessions.
> Bunkroom (0/5): Increases the capacity, life support, and volume of the Habitation Module by 2.4x, and by 1 add-on slot.

She braced herself for whatever sensations were about to come and put a point into the bunkroom ability. Golden mana surged from her and Bertha and flowed into the Habitation Module's hallway between the cab and trailer, which stretched away from her with the groans and metallic pops of shifting steel. It was as if new vertebra were popping into existence in Jill's neck, forcing it to grow longer and longer. Faint lines carved themselves on the bare metal walls, growing deeper as the mana settled. They resolved into four new doors.

Jill rubbed the back of her neck, then twisted her head sideways to crack it. Buying new powers for Bertha was rarely comfortable, but wasn't painful either.

"Jill," Babu said, excitement rising in his voice, "there are four new doors and not three."

"Huh," said Jill. A long-forgotten math lesson resurfaced in her mind like a particularly disgruntled whale. "The progression is geometric? Neon tits on a donkey, four more points and I'll be up to one hundred and ninety-one rooms?! And bubbling hobbit farts, it is weird that I can do that in my head!"

Babu started laughing. "What if your Cargo Module progresses like that? Its power is worded the same way!"

Blood rushed to Jill's head, and her breath caught. "I'm going to be able to haul so damn much!" she said in awe. She slapped the wall near her. "Sweet slippery thighs, my girl is just the best damn truck ever! An entire damn trainload at a time." She shook her head. "I need to get more levels—"

A notification cut her off.

Settlement alert!

A bounty has been placed on Mia Williams, Babu Bati, and Jill MacLeod. Capture or kill them to earn 10,000 Billibucks each. Additional information: Seen driving a large, red semi-truck.

Danger estimate:

Mia Williams: Extreme

Babu Bati: Extreme

Jill MacLeod: Minimal

"Minimal?!" Jill yelled. "Minimal? I'll show you minimal, you gopher-stuffing paper pusher! Fucking bounty on us for protecting ourselves: Babu, your hometown sucks."

Babu tssked. "It's run like shit now," he said, "but this place used to be okay, I guess. I can't believe the," he raised his finger in scare quotes, "'new mayor' is doing things like this when there are monsters pouring in! It's just a terrible build, don'tcha know? Can you imagine putting settlement points into size and taxes and bounties instead of . . . of . . . ," Babu's voice trailed off. He blinked a few times. "Jill, can I use the radio? I need to ask Buckman some questions. It might take some mana."

"Yeah sure, go for—"

"Jill!" Ras's voice interrupted her as the swordsman burst into the cab. "Jill, we have to go now!"

Jill ran down the now longer Habitation hallway and vaulted over the back of the driver's seat. "What's going on? Monsters?" she asked, as she jammed her thumb into the ignition button for the mana engine. Bertha's propulsion system hummed to life, but Jill didn't hear any of the gunfire that she would have expected if a horde were approaching.

"Our cousin Nihal is gone! She left a note saying she's going to save her friend, but—" Ras's eyes were wide in panic, "Jill, there are so many monsters!" The rest of the family piled out of the house hauling suitcases and duffel bags packed full.

"Goddamnit, why is your family so full of protagonists?" Jill said. "Babu, Ras, get your family in, get me someone up front to navigate, then teach the rest how to use the turrets." With a moment of concentration, she created a new door to the Habitation Module so that the family wouldn't have to climb over her. "Go!"

The brothers bolted off. Jill tapped her fingers on the steering wheel, then activated her Captain Speaking power. "Mia, we're heading out ASAP on a rescue mission. Everyone else: welcome aboard the baddest truck in the goddamn universe. When shit goes down, stay inside and shoot the guns."

Jill felt Ras close the door; she could hear the family's confused exclamations as they saw the inside of the truck.

"Please tell them not to select a class yet," Babu asked her.

"Oh, and don't take any classes yet, just shoot shit! Babu's going to make you kick ass later," Jill said. "That work?" she directed to just Babu.

"Perfect."

Karen stepped into the cab, hands shaking but gaze filled with fire. "Where am I heading?" Jill asked.

"Off of Hallowell," Karen said, gripping the back of the passenger seat.

"Directions!" Jill snapped. "I don't live here, remember?"

"South, just a few miles," Karen said. She staggered as Jill hit the accelerator, throwing Bertha into motion.

"Better sit down," Jill said to Karen, then broadcast to everyone. "Hold on to something, this is going to be awesome!" Bertha rounded the corner at the end of the street, fast enough that Jill had to use the Torque Converter to keep the truck from tilting, and brought them onto a longer, straight, north-south road.

Jill hit the accelerator at the same time that Mia fired her chain gun from above. A stream of glowing tracer fire slashed across ahead and blasted into a storm drain. The monstrous spider crawling out died in a burst of purple gore; its barbed, severed legs launched into the air from the force of its execution.

"Oh, my God! What was that?!" Karen screamed.

"We keep telling you there are monsters."

"No, no, no. . . She's already dead, isn't she?!"

"Hey," Jill said, snapping her fingers in front of Karen's face, "I said your kids are gonna be safe with me. Now get your shit together and tell me where to go."

"L-left up ahead," Karen said. "We need to get onto Sixth to cross the highway."

"Cross the highway, got it," Jill replied, blowing past the indicated turn without slowing.

Settlement alert!

A monster has breached the barrier. Estimated level 33–41. Kill the monster to earn a bounty of 100 Billibucks.

Current monsters in settlement: 501

Current invaders in settlement: 1032

Danger! Settlement has become Infested! Monsters may now evolve inside the settlement! Monsters may now spawn inside the settlement! Danger!

"Fucking fabulous," Jill muttered, dismissing the box so she could focus on driving. The other machine guns opened fire as more than a dozen more spider monsters leapt in front of Bertha from a side street, their fangs already coated in blood. Karen said something, but the rapid-fire, deep reports of the 50-caliber guns merged together into a blast of sound that, even with the sound insulation of the armor, was enough to drown out her voice.

The gunfire tore through the spiders, tearing great holes in swollen abdomens and blasting most of the creatures to pieces.

Lesser Silkweaver Spider (x17) defeated.
Your contribution: 15%
1785 Experience Gained!

Through sheer numbers some survived, and the spiders skittered around the corpses of their siblings. Jill drove faster and pulled her horn. The cab shook from the noise as the blast wave shot forward, scouring the street in an explosion of dirt and dust that Bertha burst through. The monsters were low level and looked spindly; Jill doubted they would even slow her down.

She was right. She netted herself another five kills in an explosion of legs and purple ichor as the blast wave, now settled into its plow shape, struck the spiders. Most of the gore sprayed away, but a few large chunks splattered onto the windshield.

"So," Jill asked, affecting a bored tone as she flipped on the windshield wipers, "where to after crossing the highway?"

"You're crazy!"

Jill laughed. "You get used to it! Now, where to?"

"Left for one block on the access road, then south, and we're there," Karen said. She pointed forward. "Watch out!"

In front of them, running northeast-southeast, was Interstate 90, and on its far side was a chain-link fence separating the highway from a set of railroad tracks and the parallel access road beyond. Bertha leapt across the highway and burst through the chain-link like tissue paper. The railway tracks were a minor bump but gave Jill enough clear space to throw Bertha into a sliding turn. They skidded onto the access road still at speed.

"Almost there!" Karen said, a bit of hope breaking through her terror.

They took a slight right turn to follow the road, and Jill slammed on the brakes. The shriek of tires on pavement rang out as the truck slid to a stop.

Three semi-trucks formed a barricade blocking the turn onto Hallow-ell, placed across not just the road, but also the parking lots of a hardware store and thrift shop on either side. Five police cars, lights flashing, were arrayed in front of the trucks. Uniformed officers and civilians with gleaming badges leaned over open doors, their pistols and rifles trained on Bertha.

"How the fuck did they know where we were going?" Jill asked herself.

The radio crackled to life. "Jill MacLee-odd!" a woman's voice came through, mispronouncing Jill's name. "Give yourself up, or we will open fire!"

Jill grabbed the radio handset and pressed the talk button while pouring mana into her fear ability. "Get the fuck out of my way, you shit-smeared, unwashed Fleshlights, or I'll smash right through you!"

Two people ran, but the rest stood their ground.

"That won't work on us anymore. We're protected!" The woman over the radio gloated.

"Jill," Mia's voice echoed in Jill's mind, "I can see over them. There's a whole horde of monsters tearing up everything! The cops aren't even shooting at them!"

Before Karen could turn her pleading expression on her, Jill hit the accelerator. Bertha surged forward, and Jill aimed the armored battering ram of the truck for the gap between two semi-trailers. The police opened fire and bullets pinged off of Bertha's armor like so much ineffective rain. "Move!" Jill shouted into the radio. She switched to projecting her voice to the whole truck. "Brace for impact!"

The cops had parked a police cruiser in front of the gap, and while there was enough time before the impact for the officers to have leapt away, they didn't. Instead, they stayed put, firing their handguns at their onrushing death in a futile last stand. The cruiser was lifted up and back by the speed of the impact, and the doors caught the officers in their chests, crushing them backward. With system-enhanced toughness, they might have survived if flung clear—if it weren't for the semi-trucks behind them. With a crunch of metal and bone, they were smashed between car and truck by forty tons of Bertha's armored bulk. This time the spatters on the windshield were red.

Mathew West defeated.
Your contribution: 100%
7000 Experience Gained.

> Tiffany Kaufman defeated.
> Your contribution: 100%
> 8000 Experience Gained.

> Killing other sapients is not recommended.

The impact slowed Bertha briefly, but then the semi-trailers parted from each other like the opening gates of hell.

"Fuck!" Jill screamed, a surge of anger and shame overwhelming her. She held the wheel steady as Bertha blew through the roadblock.

On the far side dozens upon dozens of monsters erupted from the ground. Most were mutated bugs: ants, crickets, praying mantises, spiders, centipedes, and more. They swelled in size as mana rushed into them, transforming them into monsters. Jill hauled on her horn, and the blast shredded the low-level monsters unlucky enough to be in her path. All of Bertha's guns fired, bright lead cutting through the air in unending streams. A quick glance at the mana gauge showed it falling, but Jill didn't tell them to stop firing.

For every monster that died, another skittered away in fear from Bertha; they crashed into houses through windows and, for the larger monsters, walls. Some buildings were already on fire. A gigantic wolf spider leapt from a tidy suburban home, a silk-wrapped body clutched in its pedipalps, only for it to be cut to pieces by gunfire. Just like the last time Bertha had slaughtered so many monsters so quickly, Jill could feel the flow of mana surging into her as the experience points mounted.

The high of leveling hit her fast and hard, her heart pounding a joyful rhythm of power. Jill grinned.

"There! I can see them. There they are!" shouted Karen, pointing.

Three people stood on the roof of a small ranch-style house: an older woman and two teens. They crouched in a tight triangle, guns clutched in their hands. A gigantic cricket leapt from the ground and smashed down onto the roof, cracking the shingles, only to be met with a hail of gunfire from the trio that ripped it apart. Freshly engorged ants burst from the ground and started to climb the walls.

Jill slammed on the brakes, bringing Bertha to a stop broadside-on to the house. "Protect the house!" she said in everyone's mind. A flicker of movement caught her eye; Karen had picked up a shotgun and was reaching for the window controls.

Jill sealed the window. "I like your spirit, but don't you dare let things in the fucking truck," she said. "Your shotgun isn't doing shit compared to the fifty-cals."

She jerked as a spider leapt onto the hood and sprayed acid onto the windshield right in front of her face. "Fry, fucker," she said, activating the red eel paint's electricity aura. The spider jerked and twitched as lightning danced off of its spiny hairs. It tried to flee but was dead before it could make it off the hood. Notifications for even more monsters dying flickered in Jill's vision; they were present for the barest second, before she instinctively dismissed them as the other bugs that had crawled up onto Bertha's trailer met the same end.

Jill started to worry about Bertha's mana, but before it got too low the surge of emerging monsters ended. The house upon which Nihal and the others crouched was utterly wrecked. Its wood-frame construction wasn't even close to being tough enough to stand up to high-caliber, magically enhanced gunfire that had over-penetrated the monsters. It was a miracle that the structure still even stood.

Jill eyeballed the distance to the trio, then nudged Bertha forward so that they would be within the fourteen-meter range of her communication power. "Nihal! Whoever the fuck you two are! Get in the truck before more monsters come!" To Babu and Ras, she projected, "Jump out and help them!" Each was in their own turret, so Jill flexed Customization and opened a hole in each of them so they wouldn't have to run through the whole truck to get out.

The brothers leapt the entire distance from Bertha's trailer roof onto the house in a single leap; the impulse of their landing was enough to make the weakened structure sway. Without stopping, Ras scooped up Nihal and the other teen, one in each arm. Babu lowered his shoulder and tipped the older woman into a fireman's carry. They nodded at each other and leapt back in unison. The house crumbled sideways and collapsed behind them.

Jill reached over and punched Karen in the shoulder, being careful to do so as lightly as she could, so as not to injure the level zero woman. "Told you they'd be safe. Go hug your kid."

CHAPTER 30

RESCUES

Jill stretched in her seat, allowing herself just a bit of time to decompress. The guns were silent, for the moment, and nothing outside was moving. She reached down and picked up Karen's shotgun to stow it in the gun rack; the woman had dropped it on her run towards the trailer.

"Well, now what?" Jill asked herself. She supposed it was time to leave Billings, before the city became even more of a shitshow. The face of one of the dead cops flashed across Jill's mind: a rictus of horror, pain, and regret as the life was crushed from his body. Jill shook her head, banishing the image. It was made up anyways, a figment of her imagination; she had been focusing on the semi-trailers ahead and hadn't even seen the poor bastards during their final moments. Before she'd killed them.

A surge of hot anger roared up inside of Jill, banishing any regret. She had warned them. More than once she had told the authorities here that she wasn't playing around, that she would defend herself. It wasn't her fault that people had died; it was the fault of the idiots who just wouldn't get out of her way.

"They made their choices," Jill said, trying to convince herself that she really believed that. The anger faded in an instant, replaced by the shakes of a fading adrenaline high. "Get your shit together," she said to herself, gripping the steering wheel to steady herself.

Jill's hands clenched hard enough to turn her knuckles white, and her gaze snapped to movement outside the truck, but it wasn't a monster. A woman holding a giant claymore in her hands had kicked open a house's door and stepped outside. Her exhausted, bloodshot eyes met Jill's for a moment. Jill waved at her to come; the woman nodded and started moving, her head on a swivel for any sort of threat. Two children and an injured man followed her out of the house, picking their way through the field of dead monsters towards Bertha.

"Oh, shit, that dude's missing an arm!" Jill said, grimacing at the bloody, hasty tourniquet where an elbow should have been. "People are fucking dying out there," she continued, the sound of her voice an anchor dragging her back to action, "so get your shit together and do something."

She took one more breath and banished her doubts. "Babu," she projected to the enchanter. Through the connection she heard the sounds of crying and celebration in the background.

"Hold on a sec, bud," Babu said softly before replying, "Yeah, Jill?"

"I need you to let everyone in the houses around us know that it's safe to get out of wherever they are hiding and that they should run for the kickass truck," Jill said.

"Done," Babu said after a moment's pause. "We're picking everyone up?"

"Everyone?" Jill heard Kevin's voice over the connection, "Awww, I'm going to have to share my room, aren't I?"

"Little cuz, you love sleepovers," Babu said. "Now, how about you go join your mom's hug pile, okay?"

"Okay!"

Jill smiled. Some things were worth fighting for.

The sounds through the link shifted as Babu relocated to a quieter place. "Are we really going to try and save everyone?"

"We'll get as many as we can out of this pissplosive death trap of a neighborhood. We'll shuttle them to the airport." Left unsaid was if those up north were in any position to be taking on more refugees. Those that had made it to the airport had the advantage of numbers, warning, and good terrain, but there had doubtless been many people caught on the road. Jill hoped that they had found some means to defend themselves.

"Hey, listen up," Jill said, opening her projection to everyone in the truck. "We'll get wasted over all being alive some other time. Right now, we're picking up more survivors. So, I need people in their turrets and ready to shoot any monsters dumb enough to mess with us."

The sword-carrying woman and her family had almost made it to Bertha. Jill cranked the wheel over and nudged forward, lining up the back of the trailer with the approaching refugees.

"Ras," Jill said, "I'm opening the cargo door a bit so that survivors can get in. Make sure no monsters get in with them."

"On it," the swordsman replied.

Out of the side mirror Jill caught a closer look at the injured man staggering over. He looked like he could barely walk, and he had other claw marks on him, which were oozing blood in addition to the more obvious missing limb.

"Anyone on board know how to stop people from dying if they've been gnawed on too much?" Jill asked. Through the link Jill could hear people rushing around, climbing the ladders in the trailer to get back into the turret, and no one responded for a few moments.

"I do," Mia said. "Healing isn't my focus now, but yesterday I was a nurse. I took a basic power for it too, just in case."

Jill hesitated. Mia was Bertha's best offense by a wide margin, and if they got into serious trouble, she wanted the woman firing. But on the other hand, they weren't in serious trouble at the moment, and the other guns were more than enough to deal with the type of low-level monster that had been spawning around them. "Mia, could you set up, I dunno, a medical station in the trailer? Someplace to patch people up."

"I'll take a look," Mia said.

The hatch above Jill opened, and Mia leapt down. She had changed into the new leather armor. Practical, bulky, and unadorned, it gave the former nurse the air of a hardened veteran. Jill whistled. "How is it that yours looks even more badass than mine? You don't even have spikes!"

Mia laughed. "It's all about who's wearing it."

Jill flipped her off. "Get outta my cab, you plucky chicken," she said. Mia gave an exaggerated, sloppy salute and left, chuckling to herself. Jill's own smile faded, her humor leaching out. She doubted the younger woman knew that Jill had crushed two people to death— either that, or Mia had suddenly become a much better actor than she'd been just an hour before. Again, a face flashed in her vision, and again, she pushed it away.

There was a burst of gunfire, as one of the side turrets opened up on a monster.

> Terrible Tunneling Termite defeated.
> Your contribution: 15%
> 150 Experience Gained!

"Jill," Mia's voice rang in Jill's head, levity gone, "the trailer isn't good enough for medicine. I need someplace less busy, with beds, and with some way to keep clean, at the very least. I don't think we have medical supplies either."

"Aw, overcooked cumcakes," Jill said back. She had a small first aid kit stuck in a corner of the cab, but she hadn't actually needed it since the system had arrived; her magical regeneration had taken care of all of the minor, and not so minor, wounds she'd taken over the course of the day.

Jill considered shifting some of the rooms from the Habitation Module to the back of the truck. They had beds, sinks, and showers already; it wouldn't be beyond her abilities to turn it into a makeshift infirmary by removing extra walls and changing the layout. But that wouldn't help with the lack of medical supplies. Semi-trucks didn't normally come with medical facilities, but then again, they didn't come with turrets or dimensional barriers either. She bet she could do a lot better than just rearranged rooms.

"Hey, System," Jill thought towards her mana. "Can you make a Hospital Module?"

> System Inquiry detected.
> Soulbound Modules are available based upon Compatibility.
> Evaluate suitability of medical facilities? This will consume Mana.

"Hell yes! Go for it." There was a sucking sensation as mana flowed from Jill's head. Her vision swam as mental fatigue struck; it was as if she had answered a hundred hard questions in an instant. It took longer than usual for the system to reply to her.

> Gathering information on medical practices and requirements.
> Medbay Module Compatibility: 91%
> Estimated Mana cost for Module synthesis: 55,000
> Class Point cost: 1

> New Module Available:
> Medbay: Creates a basic medical facility where the injured can recuperate.

Relief hit Jill like an icy balm on the back of her neck, and her hands started shaking again. She swallowed down a sudden lump in her throat. It was just a module, like all the rest. There really wasn't a need to get worked up over it.

Jill purchased the module with her last free class point.

> Medbay Module added!
> 0 Class Power points remaining.
> Prepare for Integration.

The steady purr of the mana engine stuttered and the mana gauge dropped drastically as most of Bertha's stored magic surged backward through the truck. Jill felt the trailer swell and shift as the module formed; metal warped and twisted with shrieks and echoing clangs as a new material emerged into existence beside the old. Jill closed her eyes and took control of the process, willing the new module to shunt off to the left side of the trailer, rather than appear in the middle of it. The trailer snapped back to its normal shape with an ear rattling pop of displaced air, and a double set of swinging doors emerged from the left-side wall.

The new configuration left Jill feeling strange, as if she were seeing double inside of her own mind. Even with all the changes she had made before, the inside of the truck had at least matched the shape of the outside. The volume and proportions might have been different, and turrets were a bit of a stretch conceptually, but the truck had still been a truck inside and out. Now there was an entire extra set of rooms sticking out sideways on Bertha's insides, while on the outside she was just as sleek as ever.

Was Bertha still really a truck anymore? Jill's soulbond grew taut, almost painful, at the thought. Bertha was shifting and changing, her original purpose skewed by magic into something new, something more—something that could take lives or save lives. "Just like me," Jill muttered to herself. She chuckled once, without humor, and gave the wheel a pat. "I guess we're still in sync after all, old girl." Her soulbond settled, the tension dissolving into a calm, steady force.

Integration complete!

Medbay
"Bertha" has a Medbay Module with basic medical facilities for 1 examination room, 1 surgical suite, and care of 1 long-term patient. Generates medical supplies sufficient to treat common ailments at the cost of Mana. Add-ons (0/1): None installed.

Medbay Upgrades:
Stasis (0/1): While being treated in surgical suites, patients do not suffer HP damage from ongoing conditions.
Mana Prosthetics (0/2): Missing body parts may be replaced by prosthetics made of Mana. Draws Mana from "Bertha's" reserves to generate, but ongoing maintenance Mana is supplied by the patient.
Ward Expansion (0/5): Increases the number of examination rooms and surgical suites by 1 and by 1 add-on slot. Increases the number of long-term patient beds by 2.4x.

"Nice job, System," Jill sent. She read through the upgrades, and a thought struck her. "Did you pick prosthetics for that guy?"

System Inquiry detected.
Class Powers and Upgrades follow certain patterns, which depend on what is most beneficial for the user.

"So that's a yes, then. It sucks for him he'll have to wait for me to level again."

System Inquiry detected.
Bonus experience is awarded for completing Quests. Active Quests: Preserve the life of newly transitioned sapients in Billings; Save the settlement of Billings from the monster infestation; Survive the first day.

Newly transitioned sapients from Billings currently preserved: 15

"Huh," Jill thought. "I didn't really ask you a question, but thanks for the info. Who comes up with the quests?"

Information denied. Classified access request has been logged.

"Helpful."

A tendril of mana, dark and silky, slinked into the cab and Babu's voice spoke, panicked. "Things just went crazy back here! Is everything okay?" Unlike her own communication power, this one made actual sound instead of being a purely mental communication.

"Everything's great! Bertha just got a sugaring Medbay!"

"Sugaring? Okay, Ras. Wait, wait—a Medbay? Did you get a new module?!" Babu's voice rang out with excitement. "Send me everything!"

Jill did, then got up, deciding that she wanted to see the Medbay for herself.

She stopped short, still in the hallway of the Habitation Module, as the door to the trailer opened. Taran walked through with his arms piled high with stuffed suitcases. "Oh!" he said, hesitating. "Sorry for intruding on you, Ms. MacLeod. Sangita said you had mentioned making a room for us? I admit, I'm a little lost. When we agreed to come along, I thought we'd be sleeping in the back!"

"Bertha's full of surprises," Jill said. She opened her mouth to keep speaking, but was interrupted for a moment by a machine gun firing again. This time there was no notification of a kill; whatever the target was, it had gotten away. "Speaking of, I expected you to be shooting," she continued. She left the unspoken question of why he wasn't hanging in the air.

"Babu showed me how, and I was on lookout for a bit, but with so little to shoot at and so many people in the back, I decided to clear our bags away," Taran said. He picked out his next words with care. "I know that we are your guests, but I have to ask: do you expect us to follow your orders to the letter?"

Jill almost blurted out a "no" on instinct, but stopped herself. Maybe it was because she was older than Babu, Ras, and Mia, or maybe it was because she had rescued the brothers, but Jill had fallen into the role of boss over all of them. When she gave them orders, they obeyed, and Jill had, without realizing it, expected the rest of the family to do likewise.

"Shit, I don't know! Until last night I worked alone," Jill said. "I won't force people to do anything. But," she paused, gathering her thoughts,

"I'm going to keep deciding what we're doing because Bertha's my truck. Sometimes that might mean me giving orders. Other times it might mean people just helping out how they can. That's the price of the ride."

"I think I can live with that. In the interest of helping the best I can," he smiled and shook his head, "I am an absolutely awful shot. Always have been. But my day job is designing hydroponic systems. If you give me some space to work with, and if we can find some equipment, I might be able to get something growing here to feed us all."

"You want to farm in my truck," Jill said, not quite believing that the sentence was coming out of her mouth.

"Yes?"

"Oh, fuck me. Why not," Jill said, throwing her hands in the air, "she's got a new magic bullshit hospital in her; I'm sure I can get something with glowing magical plants going. But not right now." She pointed at one of the new doors to a bedroom. "That one's for you and Karen. It isn't big, but I can move stuff around inside if you need it."

"Thank you," Taran said. He leaned his stack of bags against the wall for balance, opened the door, and went inside.

Jill rubbed her forehead; she had a feeling more awkward conversations were coming. With a flick of her will she raised a wall and door between the Habitation Module and the cab. At least with that she would have some privacy when driving.

She finally entered the trailer and stopped dead still, blinking in shock. More than two dozen people were inside, and every one of them was staring right at her. There was a moment of silence, and then they all started asking her questions at once, the noise of overlapping voices growing louder by the second.

____

CHAPTER 31

A MONSTER OR NOT

Shut it!" Jill yelled, threading some mana into her awe and fear power. The power balked, and she knew that she had miscast the spell; it was based on profanity, and so tame a phrase wasn't proper fuel. The magic still swept out from her, but its tendrils were frayed, weaker than they should have been.

It was enough for a moment's pause in the noise. "Listen up," Jill said before anyone could start shouting again. "I'm Jill, and this," she slapped the truck, "is Bertha. This city looks like it's going to shit, but last I knew a bunch of people were heading to the airport to hole up. I'm dropping you off there. Questions?"

"Whose fault is all this?" The woman with the claymore asked, a look of fury on her face. "What made all this happen?"

Jill shrugged. "Fucked if I know! Feel free to ask the system, but it doesn't seem allowed to talk about that." She looked the woman up and down. "You look like you want to kill something. We'll take care of your family in here; you go and hang out with Ras, the guy who met you outside, and slice some shit up."

"What about the rest of us?" asked a man in overalls, blood smeared on his face. He had a gnarled and fresh, but fading, scar on his forehead where some monster had managed to claw him.

"Sit tight or help, your choice. I'm heading to the airport either way," Jill replied. She snapped her fingers as a thought bloomed in her mind. "Wait, scratch that. Everyone take a turn in a turret: climb up those ladders, sit your asses down, then point and shoot. Trust me, you're all going to be a lot safer once you have a few levels. And you get to kill some mouth-breathing chode-chomping monsters too!"

There was a rumble of approval from the crowd at that, and a shift in body language. More than one pair of eyes lit up at the thought of getting revenge.

A piercing whistle turned everyone's attention to the far end of the trailer: Babu had just come back inside through the shimmering dimensional barrier. "Make some room everyone," he said, some power of his own making his voice perfectly audible. "There are more people coming in. Oh, and don't freak out!"

Jill took a breath to ask Babu what he meant, but her words died in her mouth as a snout, with jaws open to reveal gleaming white teeth, poked into the trailer at shoulder height. Her gut clenched in instinctive fear, flashes of her several near-death experiences that day hammering into her. A collective gasp of alarm swept through the crowd, and people scrambled for weapons.

But then the creature came in more fully, revealing a pony-sized Bernese Mountain Dog with a young child riding on its shoulders.

The dog's eyes lit up, and its tongue lolled out. "Look! Look! So many newfriends!" it barked, the meaning clear despite no actual words being formed. "Hi, newfriends! Packmaster, can I go play?!"

"Say hello but behave, Sander," the child said, her high-pitched voice contrasted with a firm tone of command. She had one hand gripping the hair on the dog's haunches to keep herself balanced; the other held a stuffed animal version of the massive dog close to her chest.

Sander trotted forward to the closest sitting person and lowered his huge nose onto their lap. "Hi, hi! I'm a good boy! Pets, please?" he barked, looking up with giant, friendly eyes.

The collective blood pressure of the trailer plummeted, many laughing with relief. More refugees followed the dog inside. Babu directed the worst injured of them to the Medbay, and the rest squeezed into the few seats that were remaining. It was standing room only now in the trailer.

Jill swallowed. She would have to be extra careful to not let any monsters swarm Bertha and get inside, or it would be a slaughter; even if the refugees weren't so low level, there was no way they could fight effectively with so little room.

"Anyone else coming?" Jill projected to the gunners and Ras.

Instead of getting a verbal answer, first one and then another of the guns on the trailer roof opened fire. The other weapons joined in just a moment later. The sound was even louder in the trailer than it was in the cab: a deafening staccato drumbeat. Many of the refugees clamped hands over their ears, and poor Sander buried his snout inside the sitting person's coat, but was too big to get his ears in. The gunfire lasted a long ten seconds, then tapered off one gun at a time.

Experience points flowed into Jill, the system recognizing and rewarding her for being the one providing Bertha as a firing platform.

6237 Experience Gained!
You are now Level 24!

Jill closed her eyes as the pleasure of leveling hit, only opening them once the feeling had subsided. The refugees were watching her, worried. She raised a hand up to them, signaling that everything was alright.

"That was a lot of experience," she broadcast to the gunners, looping in Mia and the rest of what she considered her new permanent crew. She made sure to say the words only in her head and not aloud, so as not to alarm the refugees any further. "Are we in trouble?"

"Something weird, Ms. MacLeod," came a male teenage voice through the link. Jill thought it was Ras and Babu's eldest cousin. "A big pack of monsters just," he paused, "just walking down the street. They only started running once we fired. All dead now, but that was super fucking weird!"

"Language, Mahesh Jhakar!" Taran's voice spoke in their minds. "We don't speak like that!"

"Sorry, Dad," Mahesh said, sounding contrite.

"You're right, that is, uh, weird. I'm going to get us moving," Jill said, casting one longing look at the unseen Medbay. She would have to visit it some other time. "But first, we really need more room for people back here."

She invested the class point she had just earned by leveling into expanding the volume of the Cargo Module. The metal walls and floor rippled as if they were the surface of a lake, before stretching in all directions. To Jill, it was as if her stomach was overfull from a meal but growing larger to fit everything in. Shouts of alarm filled the trailer as seats shifted away from one another, and there was the sound of a great inhalation as a blast of air rushed through the open cargo doors to fill the new volume.

> Cargo:
> "Bertha" has a cargo bay with total volume 217.5 cubic meters, a spatial compression factor of 2.4, and internal dimensions of 19.43 meters by 3.35 meters by 3.35 meters.
> Includes: Doors.
> Add-ons (1/2): Hearth of the Wolf.

> Cargo Upgrades:
> Cargokinesis (1/1): Objects inside of the cargo bay and within 14 meters of the cargo bay doors can be slowly moved.
> Climate Control (0/2): Control the temperature and humidity of the cargo bay.
> Volume (1/5): Increases the volume of the Cargo Module by 2.4x and 1 add-on slot is added.

The transformation finished and Jill took a moment to examine the larger space. Even aside from the seating being messed up now, the new dimensions weren't ideal. While having a tall ceiling was nice in terms of headroom, it wasn't going to help her pack more people inside. With a flex of Customization she stretched the trailer wider and shorter, bringing it back to its original height. She took inspiration from airliners and willed new seats with proper seat belts to emerge from the floor in rows, with an aisle down the center and along each wall. The Medbay stayed on the left side, but she shifted all the ladders and turret access hatches to lie along the right-hand wall instead of dropping down in the center. The inside and outside of Bertha were even less matched than before, but that didn't seem to matter much beyond giving Jill a headache if she thought about it too hard.

"Welcome to Highlander Airlines," Jill said to the crowd, the new configuration of the trailer inspiring a fit of levity in her. "We don't fly, but we kick a lot more ass. There's going to be turbulence all the fucking time, so strap in. Or don't. Either way, don't complain to me!"

She spun on her heel and jogged back through the doors into the cab. "Talk to me, people," she projected to the crew. "Anyone else out there we need to wait for?"

"I don't see anyone," Aman said. "There should be so many more people in this neighborhood. . . ," his voice trailed off, lost.

"We don't know they are dead for sure, but it's time for us to move" Jill said, settling into the driver's seat. "Babu, manage the crowd. Ras, get back inside. Everyone else—"

Sangita's voice interrupted her. "I see monsters by the access road. It looks like a herd of cattle, only with their horns on fire!"

"Doublebutt," Jill said. "Those things are a lot stronger than all of these bugs. Let's deal with them before they tear through whatever defenses this city has left."

Bertha was parked facing south, and the access road was to the north. Jill spotted a park a block ahead that would serve as a place to turn the massive truck around in. With a silent apology to the city's parks department, she drove Bertha over the curb, burst through the fence around a kiddie-league baseball diamond, and spun the truck around in a donut that carved furrows into the dirt. Jill pulled back onto the road, now heading in the correct direction.

"I can't see them anymore," said Sangita, "but they were heading northeast."

The remains of small bug monsters littered the roadway. Jill's first instinct was to try and avoid them so that Bertha wouldn't be splattered with their insides, but she remembered that as gross as the things looked, every monster they had looted so far had contained something valuable. "Ras, I'm opening the door to float the dead monsters in. You loot them, okay?"

"On it," Ras said back.

Jill opened the cargo doors and activated Cargokinesis, extending a dozen arms of mana out from Bertha to grab on to the corpses as she drove into range of them. The sudden jerk of acceleration as they matched Bertha's speed made ichor spray into the air, and Jill struggled to control so many objects at once; over around a dozen, and she would lose track. Some monsters dropped to the ground and were soon out of range of the speeding truck. Jill decided not to slow, and just picked up as many monsters as she could, flinging them into the trailer one after another in a gore-spattering, chitinous assembly line. She could feel through the power that Ras was looting them as fast as they went in, their forms dissolving into clouds of mana that she no longer needed to keep a hold of.

They reached the roadblock; it had been abandoned. The semi-trailers remained where they had been thrown, alongside the cop car Bertha had smashed, but the rest of the system-compatible vehicles were gone. There were signs that the police and deputies had fought a hard battle: no monster bodies, but plenty of bullet holes in the semi-trailers, and splatters of purple and green blood abounded alongside pools of human red. The roadblock personnel may have been ignoring the monsters in favor of targeting Bertha, but the spawning monsters had had no such respect for them.

The door to the cab opened and Mia stepped inside. "Everyone's stable," she said. "I'm heading back to Blossom."

Jill nodded without replying, her attention needed for driving as she turned Bertha to the right, onto the access road. Mia jumped up the ladder, opened the hatch with one hand, and pulled herself inside with the other in a one-handed pull-up.

While Jill couldn't see the bison yet, she could tell they had passed. The roadway was torn up, with holes punched into it and broken slabs shifted on top of each other. The monsters' mana-enhanced weight and strength, concentrated on diamond-tough hooves, had been too much for simple asphalt to handle. Bertha's wheels had no trouble dealing with the broken ground, but a rumbling vibration filled the truck as Jill pushed it faster.

They rounded a slight bend and the monsters came into view. When she had seen monsterized bison outside the city they had been running, either charging towards Bertha to kill or away in fear. But now they were just trotting, moving steadily along and ignoring everything around them.

"What is going on with them?" Jill asked herself. She shook her head. It didn't really matter—she knew that they were monsters, and high-level ones at that. The residents of Billings were struggling with those under level ten, and these were twenty or higher.

"Light 'em up!" she projected to the gunners.

Blossom spoke first, her tearing roar filling the cab, and her blazing tracers cutting through the air. The side guns joined with their chattering a moment later, but no others. The bison were directly ahead, and the firing arcs of the turrets on top of the trailer were blocked. Still, two 50-caliber machine guns boosted by all the powers Jill had invested in her turrets, plus Blossom, were more than enough to carve a bloody trench into the back of the bison herd.

As the first bison fell dead, the rest started to run, heading away from Bertha and to the northeast, towards the center of Billings' downtown area. Jill pushed down on the accelerator, easily keeping pace. Most of her attention was on floating the bison corpses around her truck and into the trailer. Again, experience flowed into Jill, and before long, half the bison were slain, leaving only the fastest and luckiest.

Blazing Bison (x41) defeated.
Your contribution: 15%
13,530 Experience Gained!

The remains of the herd took a sharp left turn towards downtown. Jill continued her chase, rumbling past four-story, brick-lined buildings, and the occasional glass-clad tower. The four-lane-wide street gave the bison plenty of room to dodge from side to side as they ran, but they continued to die one after the other.

"The fuck?!" Jill swore. Another swarm of monsters, raptors this time, leapt out of a cross street and joined the bison, ignoring Bertha in favor of charging towards the city center. As a group, they all took a sharp turn, and again Jill followed. What she saw made her slam on the brakes, her instincts screaming at her that she had made a terrible mistake.

Standing in the street in front of City Hall, tendrils of dark energy flowing out of him like so many snakes, was a man in a sleek, black business suit. The monsters ran towards him, the faster scrambling over the slower in their haste, and he killed them all with a whirling forest of black blades. A trio of snowplows, cops at the wheel, circled him, pushing dead monsters out of the way and onto the sidewalk, where more police and deputies looted them and collected the resulting treasure.

Jill stared, uncertain as to what she was seeing. The thunder of the guns filled her ears as the turrets kept harvesting monsters, but Jill blocked out the sounds as best she could, focusing on her mana sense. Right at the edge of her perception, centered on City Hall, was a towering column of mana. Thin streams broke off from it, each connecting to one of the monsters in the street.

"Dip me in a vat of tarantulas on crack, that's mind control!" Jill said, recognizing the power as reaching out in the same way hers did. But while her ability inspired awe and fear in those it connected to, this soothed and inspired desire—it was luring monsters in to be slaughtered.

"Tssk," a rich, dark, cruel voice bloomed in Jill's mind. The man had ceased in his killing, the tide of monsters heading towards him stemmed by Bertha's firepower, and turned his attention to the truck. "I can't abide people who steal what's mine."

He reached into his pocket and pulled out a sleek, jet-black handgun, which he pointed straight at Jill. She kicked Bertha into reverse and turned the wheel hard over, but the man fired before she could get out of the line of sight. The bullet left a black line in the air, as if a crack had opened in the fabric of reality. It cut a perfect circular hole through the windshield and Jill grunted. Something had punched into the right side of her chest, hard. Two more bullets blasted through the windshield, but Jill's desperate turn had moved the truck enough that they missed her.

Jill tried to pull Bertha straight once the truck had fully wheeled around, but for the first time in years, she missed a turn; for some reason her right arm wasn't working correctly, and she couldn't get the steering wheel to spin fast enough. The armored truck backed sideways over the curb and smashed into the glass facade of an office building, sinking a dozen feet in before the impact managed to stop it. Jill desperately turned the wheel with just her left arm and jammed her foot on the accelerator. Bertha lurched out of the building, her armored sides scraping on bent metal beams.

"Well, boys," the cruel voice echoed in her mind, "she's all yours!"

CHAPTER 32

HOLY SHIRT

Jill tried to curse, but all that came out was an odd rasping, gurgling noise. Her body spasmed, her arm tugging on the steering wheel, and Bertha veered dangerously close to a dead car on the side of the road.

"Jill!" Mia's voice spoke in Jill's mind. "Are you alright? Did that fucker actually hit you?!" The heavy gunner was still spraying down monsters with Blossom, keeping the horde of low-level enemies away.

Jill glanced down. There was a hole in her brand-new leather armor on her upper right chest; blood pulsed out of the wound in time with her pounding heart. "I just got this jacket!" she projected. "Also, my arm isn't working." She tried to move her right arm again, hoping her enhanced healing would have dealt with the injury. Pain lanced through her, radiating from her collar bone. Jill grimaced, but didn't let it distract her. The pain was bad, but not as bad as when Bertha had been smashed.

"Hold on, I'll be right—" Mia said, but cut off just as Jill felt a hot needle stab into Bertha through her soulbond. Another shot from the man had pierced the truck, this time lancing into the turret where Mia sat. "Shit! Well, if you want to play that way: eat lead!"

Jill looked at the side mirror just as Blossom roared above her. The soulbound weapon, boosted by the powers of a soulbound truck, fired a stream of glowing bullets that tore through the air, blasting into and around the suited man. He staggered as the rounds hit him, the sheer force of the multiple impacts driving him back several steps. But as each bullet hit, patches of his skin and suit turned for an instant into an obsidian-black liquid. The bullets sank into the liquid, rather than pierced through him, causing only the smallest ripples.

While the chain gun didn't tear him to pieces like it did so many monsters, it did force him to stop shooting. He recalled his mana tendrils, forming a black sphere around himself. Bullets slammed into it, causing overlapping ripples in its liquid surface.

The truck reached the next cross street, and Jill turned Bertha down it, the tires skidding not because they lacked traction, but because the force of the massive truck taking the turn was just too much for the broken road to handle.

The line of sight to her target broken, Mia cut off her fire. "That shut him up," she said with a snarl.

Jill pushed down on the accelerator, risking more speed despite the narrow roads. A moment later, the CB radio crackled to life and a garbled, twisted voice spoke in rapid bass cackles. "Finally! Finally I'm off my leash! No more sending out the pawns to bring me that sweet truck of yours. No, no, no. . . I'm going to kill you, and your truck will be so tasty. Or maybe I'll make it a part of me? So stop running from me and say your—"

Jill let go of the wheel for just a moment, reaching across her body to turn the radio off. "Fuck monologues," she said. Her body pulsed with pain, but she forced herself to stay alert; if some dipshit was going to warn her they were coming, she wasn't going to let herself get surprised. She wrenched Bertha into a turn at the next street, dodging a bolt of glowing plasma that she had seen coming out of the corner of her eye. It missed Bertha by mere feet and hit a house, burning through the wall in an instant, then detonating in a spray of fire, glass, and wood debris.

The source of the attack came charging in from a side street. With its red and blue flashing lights and wailing siren, from a distance it could have been mistaken for the police cruiser it had once been. But now it was an abomination: a fusion of person and machine, to form a literal monster car. The chassis had been ripped out and thick bones lay in its place, supporting oversized wheels that raised the vehicle four feet higher than it had been. The lights were still in their usual place, but behind them, sticking up out of the back seat, was a weapon emplacement. Instead of a gun were the lashed-together horns of a dozen blazing bison, their tips curled outwards to form a mouth housing an incandescent flame.

The cruiser's grille had been replaced with a gaping mouth, replete with bloody fangs. The car swerved into a monstrous praying mantis;

the mouth distended forward, teeth leading the way, to impale it. With a crunching explosion of gore, the teeth retracted, pulping the insect into the mouth.

But worse of all was the driver. He was melted into the vehicle, his skin peeled off his bones to fuse into and form the upholstery, leaving his face a leaking, bloody rictus of meat. His teeth matched those of the grille, and mantis ichor spilled from his mouth down his plaid shirt, as the two chewed in unison.

"Gross," Jill said.

"What in the sugaring fuck is that?!" Ras yelled over the mental link, just a moment before similar exclamations from the others echoed in Jill's mind.

Jill gritted her teeth. "Does it matter?! Shoot it!"

One after another the guns fired, all but the turret on Bertha's opposite side turning to walk their shots into the monster car. But its chassis cracked open, rib-like bones spreading to form four wheel-tipped limbs, and the thing skittered sideways, dodging the bullets with erratic but preternaturally precise movements. The bison cannon on its roof fired, and a ball of plasma shot out in a spiraling vortex of flame. Jill attempted to swerve Bertha sideways again, but the range was too short, and the flame hit the trailer. She felt the gouge it carved in the armor like an ice cream scooper serving up her own flesh.

"Aaaaah," Mahesh—in the turret closest to the impact point—started screaming in terror. Jill hoped that the armor had held, that he hadn't been burned, but couldn't tell. The throbbing pain in her chest was getting worse, drowning out her ability to feel Bertha with precision. She activated her truck repair power and funneled her own magic into helping her girl regenerate faster.

The horror car accelerated forward and darted sideways, rib-wheels crossing over each other like a four-legged roller skater. It ending up facing backward, ahead and to the side of Bertha. It had been hit by the turrets several times, but its latest move had been quick enough that they hadn't yet turned to retarget it. The man's ichor-stained teeth opened in a grin, and the plasma gun started to glow, pointing directly at Jill. She swerved to point Bertha directly at the abomination; it was in range of the hydra horn.

With one arm out of action, she couldn't let go of the wheel to pull the horn and, at the same time, keep her truck pointed in the right direction.

But her hands weren't the only way she had of moving things. She willed an arm of metal to sprout out of the ceiling, and crude fingers caught the horn's cord and pulled it down. Sound blasted forward, rocking the monster car back just as it fired so that the plasma ball shot upwards, over Bertha and into the sky. The monster skidded sideways as the wave crushed over it, its traction lost for a moment.

Jill followed without mercy and rammed as the now plow-shaped blast wave caused the thing to flip into the air, where it couldn't dodge. By now the turrets had finally skewed around enough to fire again, and hundreds of rounds of high-caliber ammunition pounded into the monstrous vehicle; those coming from Blossom changed in color and size as Mia activated some power of hers, each now exploding after piercing. The abomination let out an atonal scream that rattled the armored windows. It crashed to the ground at Bertha's side and attempted to drive away, but the bone limbs on its right side had been shattered, leaving it flailing as it dragged its body slowly across the ground in a shower of sparks. Jill jerked the wheel and pulled the Torque Converter to put Bertha into a sliding turn, keeping the monster to the side of the truck where nearly all the turrets could shoot it. Automatic fire poured in, finally shredding the former person to pieces.

Corrupted Liam Jones defeated. Bonus experience awarded for: corrupted sapients kill above your level (+0.9); killing a corrupted sapients (x2).
Your contribution: 65%
81,510 Experience Gained!

You are now level 27!

The immense amount of experience slammed into Jill; the thrill of gaining three levels at once blotted out the pain for a heavenly five seconds. Then the reality of her wounds crashed back onto her, eliciting an agonized moan.

"That—that was pretty messed up," Jill said. Her breathing was coming harder now, and a quick look down showed that she was bleeding even more now than before. She checked her status in the system to see if there was a reason it wasn't healing her this time.

Jill MacLeod
Class: Battle Trucker
Level: 27
HP: 103/610
MP: 830/900
XP: 361,771/378,000
Body: 61   Mind: 58   Spirit: 90

Conditions: Wound of the Shadow Assassin (-92 HP/minute)

"Mia," she projected upwards, sending her status along with it, "I need some of that nurse power, right now!"

The hatch above her slammed open and Mia jumped down, skipping the ladder entirely. She took one look at Jill, then slapped a glowing hand on the wound. The mana pulsed, then died. "Shit, that condition is too strong!" she said. "I can keep up with the HP loss, but that's going to drain my mana quick." She bit her lip. "Call one of the boys up here to drive. I need to get the bullet out, and I can't do that with you sitting here."

"I need you in the cab," Jill sent to both Bati brothers. She had a feeling there would be more shooting to do before they managed to get out of town, and they would need someone up top with Blossom.

The evasive turns had stopped Jill from putting as much distance as she wanted between herself and the city center, but they had still managed to make it a good way east. She turned Bertha to the right, heading north on the same street she had raced down just an hour before to save Nihal. The houses lining the road looked much the same as they had then, with no evidence of an explosion of monsters devastating the area like she had been expecting. The corpses of monsters lay scattered in isolated ones and twos on the street amid bullet holes and spatters of odd-colored blood. A herd of fear deer leapt from a side street, distended teeth punched through lips dripping with blood, only to be cut to pieces by Bertha's guns. The survivors didn't charge her, though; instead, they ran towards the city center.

"That scumbag must be luring every monster for miles," Mia said. "Good thing they don't seem to be stopping for people-snacks." Her tone was light and conversational, but there was deep worry on her face.

The door to the Habitation Module opened, and Ras and Babu rushed in.

"What's going—oh, sugar, that's a lot of blood!" Ras said, eyes wide.

"This thing has tendrils digging their way into you," Mia said to Jill. "I need to cut into you, so pull over and let Ras drive."

"Cops are coming" Jill said. It was getting harder to speak. She nodded at the side mirror, where red and blue flashing lights signaled police cars closing in from behind them. Her arm slipped, and Bertha jerked sideways.

Ras grabbed the wheel and straightened it. He had squeezed between the driver seat and door. "Get her back to the Medbay!" he ordered the other two. "I've got this."

Jill tried to push herself up, but failed—she was still wearing her seat belt. Mia reached down and undid the buckle, then hauled the older woman upright. With Babu on one side and Mia on the other, Jill staggered backward through Bertha. She had wanted to visit the Medbay, but not like this.

Babu opened the door to the trailer, and they shuffled sideways through the narrow opening. The refugees were seated in rows, buckled in with seat belts, and many had their heads down between their knees in the crash position. The sound of wailing babies filled the compartment, and there were two flickering beams of sunlight from perfectly circular bullet holes. Luckily the shots had been high up the trailer walls; Jill's gut clenched at the thought of what one of the rounds would have done to someone low level, or a child.

Just like before when she had come into the trailer, all eyes snapped to her—but this time there were shouts of alarm rather than questions. Jill smiled feebly at everyone as she half shambled, and was half dragged, towards the Medbay. "Settle the fuck down," she said, threading a little mana into her power to let everyone hear her, despite not being able to get much volume out. She tried, but failed, to suppress the gurgling rasp of her voice. "It takes more than this to kill me."

They entered the Medbay before Jill had a chance to see how the refugees reacted. It was a hyper-clean space, with an outer waiting room that looked exactly like the one in Jill's hometown hospital, only on a much smaller scale. One stub of a hallway, labeled *Wards* and sporting just one door, led off to the left, while to the right was another stub hallway labeled *Operating Suites*.

Mia dragged them through a swinging double door into the suite. In the center of the room was an operating table, with a cloth-covered rolling cart next to it. The walls were lined with cabinets, their glass doors revealing organized stocks of medical equipment that Jill couldn't identify.

With Babu's help, Jill collapsed onto the operating table.

"Any upgrades to this place?" Mia asked. "Now would be the time." She pulled the cloth covering off of the cart, revealing a set of gleaming surgical tools. Her hand hovered over the selection of cutting implements.

"Yeah," Jill muttered, then purchased the Medbay's Stasis power. Mana surged from Bertha, swirling around the table and condensing into a crystal-studded chandelier hanging above it. A blanket of cold pressed down on Jill, comforting and smothering at the same time. The throbbing from her shoulder froze, and she gasped in relief. "No more hit point loss," she said.

Mia sighed with relief. "Thank God." Bertha lurched, and Mia staggered into the table. A shuddering crash reverberated through the floor as the truck smashed through something. "Not helping!" she yelled at no one. To Jill, she said, "Get ready: this is going to suck."

CHAPTER 33

DIGGING DEEP

Coyote taint," Jill said through clenched teeth, as Mia cut into her yet again.

"Your tissue keeps knitting itself closed," Mia said, annoyance clear in her voice. "I keep needing to cut it open over and over. Are you sure you don't want drugs for the pain?" The muffled sound of machine guns reverberated through the floor; the sound insulation in the Medbay was better than in the rest of the truck.

Jill shook her head. "There's no time for me to be loopy." She groaned as Mia stuck a gloved finger into the wound to hold it open. "Can't you get some magic to help with that?"

"Can't you find a real doctor? The city has a hospital," Mia replied. She picked up a pair of gleaming steel tongs from the cart and slid them into the open wound.

Bertha swerved, avoiding some obstacle or another. While Mia managed to stay still, her feet spread wide and one hand braced on the table, Jill wasn't so stable. She slid on the table and the tongs pressed deeper, pushing on her broken collar bone.

"Bidet," Jill moaned, her vision turning black from the pain.

"We need straps," Mia muttered. "There must be some way to—okay, here." She toggled something underneath the table, and a trio of cloth bands shot out, wrapping around Jill and holding her steady.

Jill closed her eyes and breathed deeply, focusing on the bond that connected her to Bertha to try and figure out what was going on outside.

She couldn't see what was happening around Bertha: her sense wasn't that precise. With her Cargokinesis, she could sense the objects near the back of the truck, but beyond that she only had a vague awareness.

The asphalt was a blurred, cracked ribbon underneath Bertha as the truck sped down a street. Small obstacles, what might be monsters or might be debris, flashed in and out of Jill's limited perception in fractions of a second. Something larger—a car—closed in from behind. A burst of pain flashed through the bond as some sort of weapon carved a line in the armor covering the trailer's doors.

"Babu, Ras," Jill projected to the two men, "we're taking damage! Talk to me!"

Pulses of deafening sound raced back along the mana she had sent to Babu; he was in the front top turret, firing Blossom. "The cops have more of those fire guns!"

Claudia Hayes defeated.
Your contribution: 15%
1950 Experience Gained.

Michael Desmire defeated.
Your contribution: 15%
2700 Experience Gained.

Killing other sapients is not recommended.

"I just killed two people," Babu said, shocked. He wasn't firing Blossom anymore.

"Oh, shit," Mia said at the same time, not included in the communications Jill had opened. "Did you get that?" She asked Jill. "I think we just killed people." Her hands had frozen in place.

Jill grimaced. "They were attacking us. They made their choices," she said, pushing down her own horror. "Can you speed this up? I need to get back out there."

Mia swallowed. "I'll try," she said. She took a breath, then kept digging.

Somehow, it hurt even more than before. A tense minute passed; the occasional maneuver of the truck rocked them both and forced Mia to stop in her work. A sudden, alien tugging gripped the right side of Jill's chest.

"What the shit was that?" she gasped.

"Don't talk anymore," Mia said. "I've found the bullet."

The nurse-turned-gunner began to pull, and a horrible sliding, tearing pain caused Jill's vision to narrow again. She clenched her eyes shut and groaned. On her next breath, her right lung burned and failed to draw in air.

"What kind of sick power did this?" Mia muttered.

Jill opened her eyes again and glanced down. Mia had drawn the tongs free of her body, the bullet clamped in their jaws, but trailing behind them was a mass of taut, dull-gray strands: lead tendrils that had grown from the bullet to dig into her flesh. Mia let up on the tension for just a second and they flared out, trying to pull the bullet back in. The few tendrils that had been pulled out entirely writhed wildly, their tips seeking more flesh to burrow into.

"I have to go slow," Mia said. "If these break, then," she paused, "I don't know what happens, but it could be real bad." She resumed her pulling. Jill felt more flesh inside of her right chest shred. She clamped her teeth down hard and squeezed her eyes shut, tears leaking from her eyes against her will. She pushed more and more of her awareness along her bond and into Bertha, taking sanctuary in the solid mass of her soulbound truck. The sensations of her meat body faded, but didn't disappear. It was bearable, if only just. Her sense of time warped: seconds took an eternity, while minutes passed in an instant.

Bertha slowed, coming to a stop. The guns had been mostly silent for the last little while, with only the occasional short burst of fire and notification of a dead monster breaking the peace. The rear doors opened, and someone jumped out the back. Only a few moments later a crowd of people approached, huddled together in Jill's senses. She tried to activate her communications power again but found that part of her abilities far away. She trembled as she drew back into her body, but the pain was less than it had been before. Her eyes were still closed, and only a few stubborn threads of fiery pain remained inside of her.

"What's going on?" she projected to Babu. She could feel that the enchanter was in the driver's seat. Ras wasn't in range.

"Jill! You're awake!" Babu said back. "Are you okay?"

"No, I'm not okaaaaa—!" Jill's words morphed into a scream. The very last tendrils had wrapped around bone and sprouted barbed hooks, refusing to let go. Mia had to yank hard to pull them free, and like a malicious rope saw, the tendrils carved their way into Jill's bones, leaving one last poisoned gift of agony.

"That's the last of them," Mia said, sounding exhausted. She dropped first the bullet, then her tools into a metal pan with a clang. A faint metallic slithering sound filled the Medbay, as the metal worms writhed away against the pan.

"Oh, thank fuck," Jill said. Her body shuddered, and she let herself cry properly for a minute, great wet sobs wracking her body. Mia awkwardly patted her on the shoulder, and the straps holding her down retracted back into the table. "Okay," she said, breathing in, then out. "Okay. Remind me next time to not get shot." With Mia's help, she sat up. Her chest ached and crawled as her insides knit themselves back together, and her displaced bones shifted back into place.

"Don't get shot," Mia said. "I'm. . . I'm not qualified to do this kind of surgery. If it weren't for the system regeneration, I would have killed you a dozen times over."

"But you didn't," Jill said. She tried to raise her right arm and failed. The burst of pain that followed was nothing compared to what she had just endured.

"Don't fucking do that!" Mia said. She slapped Jill on the back of the head and went to one of the cabinets on the walls.

"Your bedside manner sucks," Jill said.

"Only when my patient is an idiot," Mia replied. "You'll probably be fine in like an hour, which is ridiculous, but until then I'm putting you in a sling." She turned from the cabinet with a white contraption held in her hands.

"Mia," Babu's voice sounded in the room, "is Jill awake?"

"Yeah," Jill replied before Mia could. "What do you need?"

"Do you have the points to make more space in the back? We're evacuating more people, and there are too many of them to fit inside."

Mia lowered the sling over Jill's head and strapped the trucker's arm into it.

"I think I can do that," Jill said. Her memories after getting shot were a bit hazy, but she remembered having leveled more than once. She checked, and she had leveled again while she had dissociated into Bertha, bringing her total level to twenty-eight and her free class points to three.

She purchased the next two upgrades for the volume of the Cargo Module and felt something inside of herself shift. Two shards of crystallized power raced from some nebulous part of herself, through the soulbond, and into Bertha. A vertiginous feeling of growth slammed into her, as the part of her body's senses that insisted it was Bertha exploded in size. The dimensional membrane that separated Bertha's inside from outside stretched thin and felt for just an instant like it would snap, but then a torrent of mana flowed from the truck's reserves to fuel the growth, and it settled.

Jill blinked, finding herself collapsed back on the operating table again. "Horny Mouseketeers," she said, "that was worse than usual. How big did I make that?"

Cargo:
"Bertha" has a cargo bay with total volume 1252.8 cubic meters, a spatial compression factor of 13.82, and internal dimensions of 41.76 meters by 10 meters by 3 meters.
Includes: Doors.
Add-ons (1/4): Hearth of the Wolf.

Cargo Upgrades:
Cargokinesis (1/1): Objects inside of the cargo bay and within 14 meters of the cargo bay doors can be slowly moved.
Climate Control (0/2): Control the temperature and humidity of the cargo bay.
Volume (3/5): Increases the volume of the Cargo Module by 2.4x and 1 add-on slot is added.

"Trap me in a five-hour meeting!" Jill swore. "Help me up?" She asked Mia. "I need to see this."

Jill's head swam for the first few steps and she leaned on Mia's arm, but she adapted quickly. By the time they exited the surgical suite she could walk on her own, if only at a slow pace. There were half a dozen people in the waiting area: some cradling limbs carved with deep defensive wounds, others just covered in blood.

Mia sighed. "I wanted to stop being a nurse," she said to Jill, quietly enough that no one else in the room heard.

"And I want to be home with my girlfriend," Jill projected back with her communication power so that it would be silent to everyone else, "not having clingy bullets pulled out of me. We both have to suck it up and deal."

"I hate when you're right," she sent back without heat. "I'm going to try and recruit some assistants. Someone out there must be able to help."

"Sounds like a plan. Can you deal with this lot first?" She gestured with her head at the waiting refugees.

"Who here is the most hurt?" Mia said aloud in lieu of responding to Jill. "There's just me in here right now," she flashed a bright, fake smile at the group, "but I've got magic on my side to help patch you up!"

Jill left her to it, making her way with deliberate steps out of the Medbay. She felt awful. All she wanted to do was crawl into her new bed and pass out for a week. But if Babu and Ras had decided to pick up more people, then she was going to have to keep going.

She pushed the swinging Medbay doors open and stopped in shock. The trailer was a dozen times larger than it had been just hours before: a single enormous room over 130 feet long, and 30 feet wide. The rows of airline-style seats now took up an island in the center of the trailer room; the few palettes of preserved food, all that remained of her pre-system shipping contract, were a lonely pile shoved into a corner by the door to the Habitation Module.

But more surprising was the transformation that had taken place with the refugees. When she had staggered past them—leaking blood onto the floor—they had been cowering, scared. Now there was a sense of purpose to them. Lines of people stood next to the ladders and hatches leading to the turrets; each person was waiting their turn to protect the truck and harvest some experience for themselves. A man dressed so stereotypically like a gym coach that Jill rubbed her eyes to make sure he was real was staring at a stop watch, a whistle in his mouth. The watch must have ticked to zero, because he blew on the whistle, hard. No sound came out, but half of the turret hatches opened and out came the occupants, who all stepped to the side and started talking with each other.

The sheer number of people in the cargo bay had also grown drastically. A crowd of over a hundred people stood just inside the cargo doors, and small groups broke off to head further inside when called. A dozen people, Sangita among them, had scrounged up paper from somewhere and were interviewing those that came inside, taking notes and directing people further inside. There were enough people waiting that Jill couldn't see out the cargo doors to tell if there were even more outside or not.

Jill glanced around the room: it had just been a few minutes since she had massively expanded the trailer, but she could already tell that they would need more space. She put her good hand against the wall to steady herself, then spent her last point on yet another volume expansion.

The trailer groaned and a hurricane of air rushed in, the room a massive lung taking a deep breath as it expanded. Jill focused on the expanding sensation inside of her, guiding it into width rather than length.

> "Bertha" has a cargo bay with total volume 3002.7 cubic meters, a spatial compression factor of 33.18, and internal dimensions of 41.76 meters by 24 meters by 3 meters.

The activity in the trailer paused during the expansion, and then to Jill's shock, a cheer broke out. Everyone picked right back up where they had left off.

"Hey," Jill projected to Sangita, not wanting to draw attention to herself by crossing across the cargo bay, "what do all these people need?"

Sangita jumped, then held up a hand to the person in front of her. "Ms. MacLeod," she sent back, "I'm glad you're back up." She paused, then sighed. "How about a rebuilt city, without a psychopath in charge? Can you magic that up for us?"

Jill snorted. "I can't guarantee the second, but it looks like I'm working on the first." Looking over the crowd, she realized that her joke was closer to truth than humor. "I meant in terms of space though. More seats? Beds?"

"More seating for now, thank you, but in clusters so families can be near each other."

"Gotcha," Jill said. She concentrated on sprouting new rows of seats from the floor, half facing forward and half backward. Every fourth seat, she raised a low, circular table between the rows. "Thanks for, uh, checking everyone in?" she said to Sangita.

"I'm creating a census to find out who has died and to reunite survivors."

Jill grimaced. "Fuck. How bad is it?"

There was a pause. "I don't know. People are dead. More people could be dead, I suppose." Sangita's voice was melancholy.

"Yeah, I don't know either," Jill said. She looked over the survivors again. "But I'm going to do my best to keep these people alive."

"I think we all will."

CHAPTER 34

PRECISELY 577 GOOD DEEDS

The door between cab and habitation slid shut behind Jill, and the swish of its movement was echoed in her sigh of exhaustion. Behind her were hundreds of people fleeing their homes, who were depending on her and Bertha for temporary safety. She leaned against the wall and closed her eyes. The discomfort from her wound had settled to a pervasive itch; her regeneration had sealed the gross damage, but the muscles in her chest were still healing.

"Thanks for the info, Charles," Babu, sitting in the driver's seat, said into the handset of the radio. "I'll check in tomorrow." He released the talk button and slid the handset back into its holster. He twisted to look around the seat, saw Jill, and leapt up.

"Jill!" he said. "How's the," he broke off, gesturing at his own shoulder and grimacing.

"It's like rats are having a combination of an all-you-can-eat buffet and an orgy under my skin," Jill said, "so I guess it could be worse." She levered herself off the wall with her good arm and walked over. "Thanks for taking care of things here."

She looked out the armored windows. They were in the parking lot of an outdoor mall, surrounded by a sprawl of tall, single-story grocery stores, assorted shops, and restaurants that would fit in anywhere in the United States. Most of the windows were broken, and there were bullet holes in the asphalt. Beside puddles of multi-colored blood were long tears where mon-ster claws had rent walls and the ground. Even now people were filtering out of the building; some had weapons and others were clutching bags. All were heading towards Bertha to join the crowd lined up behind the trailer. The sky to the east was a clear, darkening blue, but to the west, rather than the beginnings of sunset, were storm clouds.

"Where even are we, anyways?" Jill asked.

"Westdrive Shops. Ras figured that we should loop west before cutting north to the airport; that way avoids downtown, don'tcha know. But we saw all these people were in trouble and, well," Babu shrugged, "we figured you wouldn't mind."

Jill snorted. "If I ever do, tell me to go fuck myself and do it anyways." She walked past him and slid into the passenger seat with a groan of relief. She shut her eyes, as the familiar feel of the seat beneath her relaxed her more than the act of sitting itself.

"You, uh, don't want to drive?" Babu asked, alarm in his voice.

"Don't sound so freaked out. If you're going to be driving, I'm giving you lessons before you wreck something. I can't do that if I'm driving."

"You do know we were in a high-speed chase with the cops and got away, right?"

Jill opened her eyes so that she could glare at Babu. "Yeah, and every time you Sunday drivers ball-slapped a turn, I got stabbed more."

Babu pouted, and Jill rolled her eyes.

"I suppose you two did good enough," she said. "I'm just tired. Besides, can you really say you don't want to drive?"

Babu slid back into the driver's seat. "I'm just shocked you're letting me put my hands all over your—"

Jill leaned over and smacked him, shutting Babu up before he could finish his innuendo.

They sat in silence for a few moments. Jill closed her eyes again and concentrated on Bertha through her bond. There was a layer of grime on the truck: ordinary road gunk and exploded monster viscera commingling in a collage of past mayhem. Jill willed it away and smiled in satisfaction as the filth evaporated into golden light. She shifted her senses to the inside of the truck. The cargo area was remarkably clean, with only the usual amount of dirt to be expected from so many people walking into Bertha from the outside. Her opinion of the refugees rose. Anyone who treated her big girl with respect was alright in her books.

"So, what's been happening while I was taking a vacation?" Jill asked, breaking the silence.

"Eruptions of new monsters, like down south. The good news is that the big ones from out of town are ignoring people. The bad news is that the new little ones are going for the kill against anyone they can find."

Jill looked towards the city center. Now that she knew it was there, she could feel the spell pulling monsters in.

"I managed to get through to someone at the airport," Babu continued. "A guy in air traffic control also got a radio power. They got hit hard by monsters trying to go through them and into the city."

"Shit, are they okay?" Jill asked. "And wait: 'through them into the city'? Isn't the airport inside?"

Babu shook his head. "It's on a ridge above the city; the shield stops short. They're holding strong now, but not everyone survived the first wave. They just weren't prepared."

Jill blew out a long breath. "I might hate that creepy tendril bastard more for that than for shooting me."

"Really?"

The pain of digging the bullet out flashed through her body and she shivered. "No. We've been stopped for a while now," she said. "How many people are we picking up?"

"Lots. Ras is outside managing that."

Jill nodded. "Everyone's really stepping up. Even the folks who just got picked up are trying to help out."

"People around here will rally for anyone they think deserves it. And hey, who deserves things more than them?"

Jill shot him a hard glance. "That's a bit harsh."

Babu shrugged. "You didn't grow up here. They don't deserve to be left to the monsters, but," he paused, "well, there was a reason I was moving away, don'tcha know."

Jill scowled. "I can imagine. Those people can suck my truck nuts."

Babu laughed, but there was little mirth in it. He was silent for a long moment, then spoke in a rush. "If you die, we're in deep trouble. You know that right?"

"Buddha with a chainsaw, Babu. Way to care about me for who I am."

"Be serious for a moment," he said, an uncharacteristic frown on his face.

"Okay, okay," she said. "If I die," she swallowed, "well, would you all lose Bertha?"

Babu nodded. "I think she would just become a truck. One that wouldn't work unless someone else fixed her. I was talking with Charles—Buckman—just now, and that's what he thinks too."

Jill stared out the window at the ruined buildings around them. The crowd getting into Bertha had shrunk to the point where she could barely see them in the side mirror. "Everyone we've picked up would be pretty well fucked, huh?"

"Somewhat," Babu said. "The stronger people could make it out, I think. It's not that many miles to the airport, or even to those towns we passed outside the city proper. But lots of people would get killed on the way."

"So, what?" Jill asked. "How do we keep me safe without locking me up? It's kind of dangerous for everyone these days, if you hadn't noticed, and I'm not going to live in a cage." She rolled her right shoulder; it was starting to move naturally again.

Babu leaned over to look Jill in the eyes, a determined fire in his own. "We're going to power level the fuck out of you."

There was a beat of silence. "I get that was probably supposed to be a big dramatic moment, but I don't know what 'power level' means."

Babu threw his hands in the air. "Aw, c'mon! It means we get you levels, fast, even if the rest of us have to give up on growth." Jill opened her mouth to object, but he talked faster, not letting her interrupt. "We don't have to do it for very long! Just until you have enough defenses to not die from a single bullet—a bullet that got slowed down by armor—or from some random monster outside jumping on you."

Jill pulled a face, but she couldn't deny that she was too vulnerable. Part of her stirred at the memory of how pleasurable leveling was; a hunger that she both feared and looked forward to satisfying. "Fine. If that's what we have to do, let's do it," she said. "You're in charge of planning this, so what are we doing?"

"The most important thing is to feed you experience. The next time we see a big swarm of monsters, you need to be the one killing them. You get on a gun and start shooting; everyone else only chips in if the monsters are getting too close. And you can't use Blossom! Mia gets XP for that."

Jill nodded. "What if there aren't monsters around?"

"Then we focus on quests," Babu said without hesitation.

"Any idea how much those are worth? I've got one going right now for saving people," Jill said. She pulled up the notification for it, sending it to Babu as well.

Active Quests: Preserve the life of newly transitioned sapients in Billings; Save the settlement of Billings from the monster infestation; Survive the first day.

Newly transitioned sapients from Billings currently preserved: 531

"Grandma naked on the couch! That many people are in Bertha?!"

"We might," Babu stressed the word, "have stopped at a place or two other than here."

"I just—that's—" Jill swallowed and slid down in her seat, as if the metaphorical weight pressing down on her shoulders were physical. "That's so many people!"

Babu grinned. "I can't wait to see how much experience you get! I wonder what will trigger it as complete and give it to you?"

"Fucked if I know!"

The door to the Habitation Module opened; Jill twisted in her seat to see Ras coming in through the doorway, tension on his face. Behind him was a line of people stretching off into the trailer, waiting against the walls of the Habitation hallways.

"Jill!" he said. His face relaxed fractionally, but remained etched with worry. "Should you be up so soon?"

"I'm not made of glass," Jill said back, rolling her eyes. "What are all those people waiting for?"

"The bathrooms," Ras said. "Everyone from the shops who wants to come along is inside."

"Did many people stay behind?" Jill asked, with a worried glance to the west. The storm was getting closer; flashes of lightning and great black thunder clouds were harbingers of a truly nasty night.

"No," Ras said, leaning against the back of the driver's seat. "A few just didn't trust that I was telling them the truth."

Babu reached forward and pressed the ignition button, and the mana engine hummed to life. "Where to?" he asked, looking at Jill.

"The airport," she said. "But if we see more people, let them in."

"Right," Babu agreed, spurring Bertha into motion. Ras clapped his brother once on the shoulder, then climbed up the ladder into the cab's turret. Jill leaned back, closing her eyes, and hoped that the growl of the engine and drone of tires on asphalt would lull her to sleep—but a jolt and crunch had her eyes snapping open just seconds later. Babu had driven over a curb, and the truck had flattened a pair of decorative saplings on its way back to the main road.

Babu coughed, his face turning red. "Ras might have done all the driving so far."

"Clear out your ears, 'cause it's learning time," Jill said. She didn't care if she was tired; no one was going to be allowed to drive Bertha if they couldn't drive their way out of a parking lot.

Once Babu had learned the basics of handling a massive vehicle, the drive out of the city was—compared to the chaos they had all dealt with before—uneventful. Three times during the short drive they stopped the truck to let a group of survivors on, and occasionally a gunner would open fire to mow down a monster that stuck its head onto the road, but there were no enemies strong enough to make the truck need to change its course. Some of the tension bled out of Jill, but she was still too on edge to be able to sleep.

In what seemed like no time at all they were winding their way up the Zimmerman Trail, a short, but treacherous, two-lane switchback road that rose from the city to the top of a cliff. Babu's knuckles turned white from how hard he was gripping the wheel as he threaded the massive truck up the narrow road, but Jill wasn't worried. She had yet to try out the Slug Feet upgrade to the tires, but if the truck went over the road's edge, she would activate them and see if they truly could make Bertha climb walls. If not, well, the truck had survived worse than a slide, and the Torque Converter would stop them from rolling.

Towering above them was Billings's barrier shield, which touched the ground on the ridgeline itself. The settlement barrier that was supposed to keep out monsters was weak; a flickering curtain that had thinned to the point of no longer being opaque. Jill closed her eyes and traced the flows of mana around her. Luring strands from the city center arced over her head, each one connected to some monster in the distance. Where they passed the shield, it recoiled; its protective nature melted away by antithetical magic.

"That donkey diddler is tearing the shield apart with that lure," Jill said.

"Don't worry, Ras and I have plans for him," Babu said. He still clenched the wheel far too tightly, but his eyes had a vindictive gleam to them.

"Better you than me," Jill muttered, an aftershock of pain racing through her.

"Yes," Babu said. "We have combat builds. You don't."

"Just don't underestimate him, okay?"

"We won't. I ran the numbers for his level, based on what we saw of him farming monsters, and he's beyond us. For now."

They crept around the final bend, the rear of the trailer sticking out over empty space, and the left side of the truck scraped the sandy cliff face. In front of them was a T intersection with Montana Highway 3 and the barrier shield. Babu accelerated them just a bit, and Bertha nosed through the shield.

Jill's perception of reality shattered as an inrush of mana overwhelmed her. A tidal wave of magic greater than all that she had so far earned—combined—blasted into her, weaving itself into her being. She struggled with the power, forcing it to bend to her will to reinforce who she was, rather than rewrite her in its own image.

When she opened her eyes, her vision was clear and her thoughts sharp. She was Jill MacLeod, and she was heading home.

Local Quest Complete: Preserve the life of newly transitioned sapients in Billings. Sapients preserved: 577
Your contribution: 82%
473,140 Experience Gained!
You are now Level 29! . . . You are now Level 42!

CHAPTER 35

GET THOSE GAINS

Fuckstronauts in orbit!" Jill gasped. Aftershocks of pleasure pulsed through her body, the mere echoes of the mind-blanking sensation making her shiver.

They were just outside the barrier, when Babu stopped the truck. "Uffda! What just happened?" he said, staring at Jill with his mouth open and concern in his eyes.

"Fourteen levels just happened! From that quest we were just talking about." She began to laugh, a slightly crazed edge creeping in. "It turns out that the levels were inside me all along!" she said, slapping her leg at her own joke. "Well, inside Bertha. You get the idea." She chuckled a few more times and, once the mania had faded enough, sent Babu the notification of the quest completion.

"You only got the equivalent of a level one monster per person, but," he shook his head, "I don't think that quest had something like Bertha in mind."

"That's my girl," Jill said, grinning. "Let's keep moving."

Babu nodded, and Bertha rumbled into motion, heading east towards the airport. The road followed the ridgeline above the city; the settlement shield touched the ground just to their right as they drove. Despite the visual distortions from the weakened barrier, there were clear spokes of destruction leading inwards from the city edges, converging on City Hall. The high-level, lured monsters followed the roads that let them go towards their killer; when there were no roads in that direction, they made their own.

"Well, it seems as if you've gotten this power leveling thing under control for now. But if I'm going to plan your build," Babu said, eyes fixed forward on the road, "we should see what more of your class powers are by unlocking them."

Jill willed the system to show her the base powers from her class that she hadn't taken yet.

A Deal's a Deal - Active - Spell
The next agreement you enter becomes a System Contract. The other party must be of sound mind to enter into a System Contract. If the other party breaks the Contract, they will receive a penalty of 12% that lasts for 1 System year. You may waive the penalty at any time.
Cost: 100 Mana

Battle Hardened - Passive
Increase physical, elemental, and mental Resistances by 12%.

"Is twelve percent resistance even worth buying? I could be making the cargo bay twice as big," she said, rolling her right shoulder again. It almost felt good as new.

"I know it doesn't seem like much, but if we want to make you tougher, it's where you need to start. And I think I know what this power tree is from Buckman's notes, but confirming that would be worth a lot for planning."

Jill nodded and purchased Battle Hardened. A sliver of power detached from the roiling mass inside of her and dispersed over her skin, and fine bands of magic settled in place to resist any attack. A notification popped up:

Battle Hardened, Upgrade (1)
Increase the physical, elemental, and mental Resistances granted by Battle Hardened by a further 12%.

Mana Strike - Active - Spell
Invest Mana into your next attack with a weapon or unarmed strike. Increases damage by 12. Requires Level 10 Battle Trucker, Battle Hardened (1).
Cost: 10 Mana

> Hustle - Active - Spell
> Increases speed by 4.8 meters per second for 1 minute. Requires Level
> 10 Battle Trucker, Battle Hardened (1).
> Cost: 10 Mana

"These new powers seem a bit lame," Jill said, sending the box to Babu.

"They're okay. People usually get them when they're level five or earlier, don'tcha know," he said back. "But good news: I've seen these abilities before! Ras has them, and so did a lot of the soldiers that Buckman interviewed, so I'm ninety percent certain of what the next few progressions in the skill tree are."

"Huh, ten points for Ravenclaw," Jill said. "Are any of them must-have amazing?"

"If you wanted to be a frontline fighter, sure. For you I'd concentrate on the defensive stuff," he said. He shot her a look out of the corner of his eye and grinned. "Harry Potter, huh? I knew you were at least a little bit of a nerd."

"I sleep in a truck sometimes, not under a rock," Jill said, rolling her eyes. "What about the contract power; any idea what comes next after that?" Jill asked. "I don't really see myself making deals with monsters any time soon. I've never needed magic to do business with people before either, so I don't know if that's worth it."

Babu shrugged. "I have no idea what's next for that one; no one in the survey had that power! But it's not just monsters out here, and I think a lot of the people who gain powers are going to be opportunistic assholes. I'd take that power just so that they know in advance—even if they think you won't shoot them—that they can't get away with screwing you over on a delivery."

"I wouldn't mind a nice, boring shipping contract after today," she said with longing in her voice. Into her mind popped the movie of her and Bertha blasting through a horde of monsters and skidding sideways up to a loading dock, before unloading an entire train's worth of crates. She smiled; that felt right. She purchased "A Deal's a Deal" without a second thought, and her mana shot out towards the system, a beacon seeking its attention. For a moment it was as if some part of a vast machine had turned its eyes on her, judging her every intention and waiting for its tithe of mana to make her will law. The feeling faded and Jill shivered.

Another notification appeared in her vision:

> Synergy - Passive
> Disrupt the static paradigm with groundbreaking synergy! Designate 12 sapients under your command. They receive 12% of experience you would gain, divided amongst them, after other modifiers. You receive 12% of experience they would gain, after other modifiers. This ability is non-recursive. Requires Level 10 Battle Trucker, A Deal's a Deal (1).

> Subliminal Messaging - Toggle - Spell
> Sapients within 120 meters of you gain a general knowledge of your business, including goods/services available and typical prices.
> Cost: 10 Mana/minute

> Requires Level 10 Battle Trucker, A Deal's a Deal (1).

As she read the latest abilities, a new box popped up in front of them and flashed once at her.

> Congratulations on purchasing your starting powers! New powers will unlock when you reach Level 10. Don't worry, you'll get there soon!

"Pfff," Jill laughed. "Fucking system is getting sassier. Get a load of this." She sent Babu both the new powers and also the congratulatory message. "Parrot tits!" she swore a moment later, as Bertha jerked sideways; the truck swerved far too close to the edge of the ridge for comfort. "Watch where you're driving!"

"That is completely broken!" Babu yelled, bouncing up and down in the driver's seat and punching the wheel with one hand. "Please, you have to take synergy right now!"

"Alright, what's the big—oh," Jill said. She had turned her thoughts to calculating just how much of an impact the ability might have on her experience growth, and her mind had given her the answer with lightning speed.

Her usual 15 percent cut of a gunner's kill left them with 85 percent; synergy would take 10.2 percent of the original amount and give it to her as well, increasing her net take to 25.2 percent. With seven gunners, she would be getting more experience than any one of them in a given fight, even without getting kills of her own. And that was just fighting: it didn't count quests, or experience from crafting, or any experience-gaining methods that they hadn't discovered yet.

"That is wicked unfair," Jill said. "Talk about a fatberg of CEO pay bullshit." Her mood wasn't improved by the speed she'd done the calculations at: it was an unwelcome reminder that the system-wrought changes weren't purely physical.

"Mom always said I should go into business," Babu said ruefully, shaking his head. "Though with the system and people having to be 'under your command' it's more like being a feudal monarch than anything else."

Jill pulled a face. "Gross." She pushed her feelings away and took the power anyway.

Another shard of power bloomed inside of her spirit, and twelve delicate threads reached out from her in search of connections. She instinctively knew that Mia, Babu, Ras, and their family were all people that the threads would latch onto, and she designated them all as targets for the power. But to Jill's shock, there were dozens of others in the Cargo Module, each a glowing presence that the magic recognized as under her command. It was just a small fraction of the hundreds of refugees, but Jill hadn't expected any of them to qualify.

"One problem at a time," she muttered to herself, as the power finished settling in. Another unlocked power appeared before her.

Company Scrip - Passive
You can create a System Currency for your business and can convert any other System Currency you have earned to your own, without conversion fees. Transactions converting your Currency to others suffer from a 12% tax paid directly to you.

It was an interesting enough power in its own exploitive way, but Jill's thoughts were stuck on those under her command. The woman with the claymore—Jill realized she had never even asked the woman her name, despite telling her to fight for her—was one of them, and so was her amputee husband. Jill could sense him in the rear-most turret at that very moment, his lack of one arm doing nothing to stop him aiming the machine gun.

"Problem?" Babu asked. "Did synergy not work?"

"No, it's working better than a good cup of coffee. I'm leeching off of all of you already. The problem is just me being a shitty-ass selfish person," Jill said, scowling. She purchased the Mana Prosthetics upgrade for the Medbay.

Mana Enhanced Prosthetics (1/2):
1) Missing body parts may be replaced by prosthetics made of Mana. Draws Mana from "Bertha's" reserves to generate, but ongoing maintenance Mana is supplied by the patient.
2) Enhanced prosthetics have a Body rating equal to the effective level of the Medbay Module multiplied by 2.8.
Medbay Effective Level: 44

Bertha's mana rushed into the Medbay and into the surgical table. Jill could tell that it had changed, but not exactly how.

"Hey, Mia," she projected, "I just made more work for you. Sorry, not sorry."

"Fucking spider arms tipped with fucking needles grew out of the fucking table!" Mia shouted back. Jill could hear other voices shouting in the background in alarm. "What did you do?!"

Jill laughed and sent Mia the new abilities, making sure that Babu got a copy as well.

"Oh," Mia's voice lost its heat, "well I guess that's good. I'll tell my new helpers to round up everyone who needs it." She sighed. "There must be twenty of them, you know? I suppose it's better that their healing saved them before they bled out, but. . . ," her voice trailed off.

"You, uh, doing okay back there?" Jill asked

"You owe me a lot of shooting after this," Mia said.

"Somehow I don't think that will be a problem," Jill projected. She severed the mana thread, and the voices in the Medbay cut off.

"You should think about putting another point into prosthetics," Babu said. "Can you imagine putting an arm on some low-level person and suddenly they can attack with one hundred and twenty-five strength? That's way more than even I have! But what if the mana cost were too high? What would that do to—"

He was cut off by the radio crackling to life.

"Bertha Three? Are you still out there?" A woman's voice came through the handset, words fast and desperate.

Babu snatched it up. "I'm here! We're only a few minutes out. You should be able to see us soon."

"Who's that?" Jill asked Babu.

"Air traffic control," he said back.

"Thank God! Please hurry, there was just another eruption of monsters, and they're going for the terminals!"

Jill looked at Babu. "Time to show me what you've learned. Floor it."

CHAPTER 36

BURDENS OF COMMAND

The flat ground above the ridge offered no dramatic reveal of the airport, as Bertha thundered down the road; there was no sudden hill to crest over and give a cinematic view from above. Rather, the scattered, low-slung warehouses whizzing by on the left side of the road blocked all sight lines right up until they gave way to the extended parking lot in front of the airport's main building. Scattered groups of people—refugees still heading towards the airport for safety—ran in all directions, their abandoned belongings littering the ground.

The pavement of the parking lot heaved and cracked in dozens of broken mounds. The asphalt had been unable to contain the monsters exploding upwards from below. While the infestations inside Billings were comprised of mixed types of insects, those erupting at the airport were all the same: giant, monsterized locusts. Dog-sized, with mottled green-brown carapaces and long powerful legs, the creatures paused for only the briefest of moments after their emergence before charging towards the building, heedless of the gunfire slamming into them from the airport's defenders, killing them before they could get close. But more of the monsters were emerging every second: a rising tide that threatened to eat all in its path.

Just beyond the parking lot was a modest air traffic control tower and the main airport building: a long, glass-and-brick terminal that had seen better days. The laminated glass windows were spiderwebbed with fractures, both from bullets and from monsters throwing themselves at them. For the most part they still held, but a thirty-foot long segment had been completely destroyed; the twisted panels had torn from the building in one long strip.

The locusts swarmed towards that gap, but defending fighters waited for them in close-packed ranks. A mix of uniformed military, airport security, police, and civilians stood behind a makeshift barricade of tables, check-in kiosks, and heavy pieces of luggage. They had a motley assortment of weapons: guns of all sorts wielded next to medieval weapons and base-ball bats, with half of them sporting some sort of glowing, mana-fueled upgrade. Behind them Jill could see a crowd of hundreds of desperate, unarmed people pressing to get deeper inside.

Bertha's turrets began to fire, heavy rounds flashing towards the monsters. "Fuck," Jill yelled, eyes widening in horror as a dozen defenders staggered and fell. "Don't shoot! Don't shoot!" she yelled, projecting the command to all of the gunners in a deafening blast of sound.

The volunteer gunners had aimed at the monsters, but backstopping the murderous beasts were the very people they were trying to save. Their shots had cut the swarm to pieces, but not every bullet had hit a monster: some misses tore into the asphalt and pierced harmlessly into the artificial rock; others ricocheted into the crowd of defenders.

"Get us in there!" Jill said to Babu, wishing that she had taken the wheel instead of letting him practice. "Right between the barricade and the monsters. Even into the building if you have to!" She longed to tear Babu out of the driver's seat, but even now the enchanter was steering Bertha off the road and towards the terminal; there just wasn't time for her to replace him safely. The urge to buy a Command Module upgrade and make herself a new set of co-pilot controls flashed into her mind, but she pushed it away for the same reason.

"Shiiiit!" Babu yelled, as Bertha exploded through a chain-link fence into the parking lot itself. He swerved to avoid a parked car but clipped its corner, sending the sedan spinning away, its bumper torn clean off.

More locusts had burst from the ground: enough that some were able reach the barricade without being cut down by gunfire. Some of the defenders panicked and broke. Not all, not even most, but enough of them ran that gaps opened up on the barricade, and the locusts piled in without mercy.

Jill took in the scene during an endless few seconds; her eyes snatched up unwanted details, and her mind categorized the horror unfolding with unerring accuracy. Jill's heart leapt into her throat as one locust crouched, then leapt forward with blurred speed, its bizarrely fanged insectile mouth open wide and ready to tear apart a teen whose only defense was a snow shovel gripped in white-knuckled, shaking hands.

And then Bertha smashed through the glass front of the building; the remaining shards of broken laminate were no match for her mass. Jill opened her mouth to yell at Babu to turn, but he had already pulled the wheel over, hard, and slammed on the brakes. It wasn't the prettiest stop: they went through a support pillar that Jill dearly hoped wasn't structural, and the defenders had to leap out of the way as the truck skidded sideways into their barricade, pulping locusts along the way. But in the end, Babu's driving had gotten the job done. Bertha came to rest, a bulwark of magic, guns, and metal between the crowd and the monsters.

"Fuck 'em up!" Jill projected, and the gunners, with no unfortunate people to hit by accident, obeyed.

Just like that, the fight around Bertha turned in the humans' favor. It didn't matter that the volunteers taking their turns in the turrets were low level themselves; the heavy machine guns, boosted to level fifty-nine by Jill's powers even before they received a 70 percent boost to their damage and rate of fire, chewed through the newly-spawned locusts with ease.

Jill scrambled to unbuckle her seat belt and stand. "Mia," she projected to the Medbay, still speaking aloud at the same time, "get ready for more wounded. Gunshots." She purchased an expansion of the Medbay, ignoring the now familiar inflating feeling to instead focus on what had to happen next. "Ras," she switched her power to the swordsman, "I'm opening a hole for you; start getting the wounded into the Medbay."

She willed the turret above them to open, and the armor panels peeled back to allow Ras to exit. He leapt down, and when his feet touched the ground there was a flash of mana. He blurred forward, heading towards one of the fallen. The other turrets kept firing, but more sporadically. Their full firepower wasn't needed to keep the monsters at bay.

She went to open a door from the Medbay to the outside world, but her mana rebounded as Bertha resisted the change. Punching the hole in the truck there was like trying to put her fist through the eye of a needle: the dimensional barrier was so stretched over the Medbay, the internal volume so inflated there, that it couldn't support an opening.

"What a great puss-pissing time to figure that out," Jill muttered. She compromised by opening a door in the trailer right next to the Medbay, rather than inside of it, so that the wounded still wouldn't have far to travel.

The dimensional mismatch fought her, but by pouring nearly half of her mana into her Customization power, she managed to make the opening.

"I'll get people outside to bring the wounded in too!" Babu said, closing his eyes. Wisps of mana exploded off of him, and streamers reached out of the cab. "There," he said. "I hope they listen."

"Okay," Jill said, suddenly aware that her heart was hammering in her chest. "Okay. We can handle—"

Kyle Riley defeated.
Your contribution: 25.2%
1008 Experience Gained.

Killing other sapients is not recommended.

Jill's mouth snapped shut, and she closed her eyes. She counted a long ten seconds, suppressing an internal scream.

"What—what happened?" Babu asked, his face pale. "I just got—" He swallowed. "They were on our side."

"They must have bled out," Jill said, voice dead. She looked upwards. "Fuck you, System," she said aloud. There was no response.

The gunfire had nearly ceased; only the occasional short burst broke the silence.

Jill's eyes scanned the cab and locked onto the radio. She stalked forward and, Babu scrambling out of her way, threw herself into the driver's seat, then grabbed the handset. Hopefully the air traffic controller that had contacted them was still listening. "Hey!" Jill said into the magic-powered radio. "We plugged up the front, but what's going on everywhere else?"

"That was fucking incredible!" the airport employee said back, awe in her voice. "The way you just smashed right through them and started shooting was super sick!"

"Fine," Jill said, the woman's enthusiasm a scourge on her guilty conscience. "Just—please, just tell me what you can see from up there."

"Oh. Okay," she said back. There was a pause, and when the voice came back it was professional. "A lot less bug things are burrowing up, and the runways are clear. No one else on the perimeter called in for more help, so I think you stopped them from breaking through."

Jill let out a breath of relief. "Good. Now—"

"Wait!" she said, and Jill let her head fall forward onto the steering wheel. Of course there was something else. "There's something coming from the north, underneath that huge storm cloud. I can't tell what they are, but I see all these flashes of light on the ground."

"How long until they get here?" Jill asked.

There was another pause. "Maybe fifteen minutes? It's moving fast."

"If you see anything else, you tell me right away, got it?" Jill said. It wasn't really a question. "And warn everyone else off. If those are what I think they are, they're all over level twenty."

"Uh, yes, ma'am!"

Jill put the handset back.

"More bison do you think?" Babu asked, leaning against the back of the passenger seat and biting his lip. "The light could be from their horns."

"Probably," Jill said. "Ras," she projected her voice to him, "we need to move in a few minutes. More monsters are coming, but we have a little while."

"All of the survivors are inside," he replied, voice ice cold. "I'm going to stay back here and help. Jill, I—" His voice cut off.

Jill was struck by the realization that she knew who had fired the fatal shots. Of all the guns firing, one was much more powerful than the others, and Ras had been behind the trigger.

"I'm awful at this guilt shit, but if you want my advice," Jill sent, making sure that she didn't speak it aloud for Babu to hear, "try and keep yourself busy. Fuck, that's what I'm doing. We'll all talk about this later, when things aren't so crazy."

There was no response, so Jill let the power fade.

Jill spent a moment looking for any monsters hiding around the truck. The area seemed clear, and there was already a flow of people getting on and off.

"Listen up," she projected to everyone in and around the truck. The cacophony of sounds rushing back to her was less overwhelming than she expected. "There's a bunch of those hoof-gobbling bison coming, and I'm going to put this truck in the way. We should be fine, and we're going to stay close, but if you want off now is your chance. I'm moving in five minutes."

She broke the connection and leaned back in her chair, letting her mind go blank. For all that she had told Ras to keep busy, she knew that she was near the limit of her own endurance and that she needed at least some rest before the next bit of mayhem struck. She didn't quite sleep, but neither was she fully awake. Exactly five minutes later her mind snapped back into focus.

She stretched, raising her arms up and cracking her neck to each side. "Time to go."

With a crunch of breaking metal, Jill pulled Bertha off of the barricade and out of the building, managing to thread the truck through the hole in the windows without tearing too many new ones open. She circled the building, busting down another chain-link fence, until she was on the north side. There were still a trio of large passenger planes pulled up to the gates, their lights dark. Jill wondered how long it would take for someone with a mechanic-type class to get them flying again, this time fueled by mana instead of jet fuel.

"You should get up top and shoot," Babu said, startling Jill out of her thoughts. "I know you got a ton of levels, but you need more."

Jill thought for a moment, then nodded and unbuckled her seat belt. "Consider yourself a fire-forged driver then. She's yours for now," she said, clapping him on the shoulder.

The climb up the ladder was easy; her weight was no longer any obstacle to her strength. Jill settled into the gunner seat and stared down the sights at the approaching monsters. Before long, she could see the individual members of the herd.

The range was long, but the gun was stuffed full of magic bullshit, so she opened fire anyways. She missed, badly, but she walked her bursts of glowing rounds closer and closer to the group until they were landing in and among them. The heavy machine guns joined her but were less accurate, with only the occasional round landing on target.

Still, the kills started coming, and the experience rolled in. The pleasure of leveling washed over her, but it was more muted than it had been before.

Blazing Bison (x29) defeated.
Your contribution: 22.2%
14,175 Experience Gained!

Blazing Bison (x12) defeated.
Your contribution: 86.8%
23,436 Experience Gained!

You are now level 43!

Then, without warning, the herd turned as one and reversed direction, running away from the city. Their previously straight, predictable charge was broken with zigs and zags that stopped Jill and the rest of the gunners from being able to hit them at such a long range. "Cease fire," Jill projected, a feeling of dread welling up inside of her. She had seen this kind of intelligent behavior from monsters once before.

The bison had been traveling under a storm cloud. Now, despite them having turned and run, the cloud was still coming.

She leapt to her feet and down the ladder, grabbing the radio handset fast enough that she nearly broke the cord. "Hey! Air traffic girl!"

"The name's Stacy," the voice said back, "and that was sick as fuck."

"Right, sure, whatever. I need you to look at that storm again. Is there anything else there?"

"Nah, just a bunch of running bison."

Jill let out a sigh of relief.

"Wait," Stacy said. She sounded confused now. "There's a hill that way that's gotten . . . bigger?"

CHAPTER 37

STORM COMING

Does it have horns?" Jill asked. She had to be sure.

"Does it have," Stacy paused, "what?"

"Does the giant hill have cock-splitting horns? Things that poke out the top!"

"Oh! I thought those were, like, radio towers getting struck by lightning or something. Yeah, the hill has horns. Ooooh, and they just bobbed up and down. That's not a hill, is it?"

"No," Jill said. "It's a fuck-you-we're-all-dead bison that shoots lightning bolts from its head."

Jill stared out the window into the distance, looking for any sign of the beast, but there was nothing to see so close to ground level. She bit her lip, thinking about what she and Bertha's guns could possibly do against a monster that weighed thousands—maybe tens of thousands—of tons.

On the one hand, size could be deceiving. After all, Jill was far stronger than she would have ever thought possible thanks to the mana that now infused her, but she hadn't grown any larger. A lack of mana might mean that even something the size of a mountain would be vulnerable. But this thing shot lightning from its head; it had plenty of magic. Something that size was just beyond Bertha, at least for now.

Just because she couldn't fight it didn't mean that Jill couldn't do anything.

"Brainstorm time," Jill said. "What do we know about that thing?"

"It's different from the little bison," Babu said. "Lightning instead of fire."

"It didn't chase us," Jill said. "The fire ones just went for us like all monsters, but it didn't."

"They did at first, but they ran away when they realized they couldn't kill us. Or maybe. . . ," he frowned. "They ran towards the big one, didn't they? Maybe it called them back, like it didn't want them to die?"

Jill grimaced. She had just killed a dozen of the blazing bison and really didn't want to imagine their protective mountain crushing her under hoof. "It can't be that. It let us go after killing a lot of its . . . what, children? Herd? Anyway, it didn't seem to care. More important for us: why is it coming now?"

"I think it might be coming because it's being called," Babu said, voice quiet. "That mana lure that Mr. Tentacle Assassin set up is drawing all of the smaller monsters in. Why not the giant boss too?"

"If City Hall is the target, it might miss the airport, right?" Jill said. "We need to know exactly where it is and where it's going."

"Uhhh, hello? Dudes?" came Stacy's voice through the radio. "That thing just took another step! It's definitively, positively moving."

Jill pressed the talk button on the handset. "Can you tell exactly where it's going?"

"Sorry, Brosephina, but the radar's not working, so no can do."

Jill's eyelid twitched, but she forced herself not to raise her voice. "How about you use your monkfish-licking eyeballs to look closer?"

"Woah, chill! I thought you wanted exactly, not, like, my best guess," Stacy said. There was a pause, then, "It's west-northwest of us, at two hundred and eighty degrees. Maybe two eighty-two?"

Jill blinked at the specific answer. "That's. . . ," Jill trailed off. She had no idea exactly what direction that was relative to the city. "Is it going to hit the city?"

"No idea! I can't tell where it's moving or how far away it really is. It's just too hard to tell from this angle with the sun going down!" She paused. "Hah, the bossman down in the airport just asked me the same question. Big brains think alike."

"You're talking with someone in charge in the airport?"

"Well, yeah. How else would I have a radio? My class doesn't do nerd stuff."

"Hold on a second," Jill said, letting go of the talk button. To Babu, she said, "Are there any class powers that might help? Some sort of scout option? If the giant thing is coming right at us, we need to get everyone out now. If she can confirm that we've got a little bit of time, well," she took a deep breath and let it out slowly, "then we can do this right."

Jill swung Bertha around and pushed down on the accelerator, speeding the truck back towards the airport. "Can you call her mentally?" Jill asked Babu, gesturing to her head with one hand and wiggling her finger. "I need the radio for whoever's giving Stacy orders."

Babu gave her a sloppy salute and sank into the passenger seat. He closed his eyes, and mana bloomed from his head, reaching out towards the tower.

They crossed over the runway with a barely perceptible bump, heading towards the gates with their dark, motionless airliners. The windows on this side of the terminal were intact; through them, Jill could see that the gates were packed with people. She upped her estimate of the number of people that had sought refuge from hundreds to thousands.

She pulled Bertha to a stop next to a free passenger boarding ramp, a plane on each side of her, then reached for the controls of the radio. Even though the switches and dials of the chrome-plated, mana-enhanced device weren't labeled, her fingers moved with a mind of their own, sweeping the receiver from one frequency to another, searching for anyone else who was using something else compatible. Static gave way to speech with a pop.

"—at do you mean she left?! Damn civilians! McGregor, get your ass up to the tower and get eyes on the area," came a rough male voice.

"Yes, sir!" said a woman.

"Uh, hi there," Jill said into the handset. "This is Jill MacLeod, in the badass truck outside. Are you in charge here?"

"For my sins, I am. Commander Davis, Navy. Now, how did you get on this frequency?" Davis demanded. "This is a military encrypted channel."

"Who do you think I got my shiny radio from?" Jill said. "You need to know there's a giant—and I mean balls-stomping, lip-twisting, giant-ass giant—bison coming."

"So our spotter told us before she went AWOL. Do you have something more important to report beyond 'it's really big,' or do you just like the sound of your own voice?"

"Fuck you too, buddy," Jill said with a laugh. Movement caught her eye outside: a woman in military coveralls had burst out of one of the gate's exterior doors and was running towards the tower. "Look, if you need to evacuate, I can haul people. My girl's a lot bigger on the inside than the outside."

There was a pause and when Davis spoke again his voice was calmer. "I appreciate that. You have room in that truck of yours for ten thousand plus people?"

"Ten thousand?!" Jill shouted.

Babu, mana still connecting him to Stacy, choked. "Ten thousand?" he repeated. "There are ten thousand people here? Already?"

"Do you copy?" Davis asked, impatience entering his voice again. "Ten thousand might be low. Plan for fifteen."

"I can't fit that many. Not yet," Jill said. While the growth rate of the Cargo Module had been incredible, it wasn't going to be that large with the powers she had available. If she invested three more points into the Cargo Module, a new set of powers would unlock, but there was no telling what they would be other than "beneficial." The size enhancement was exactly what she needed, but putting two points into Climate Control seemed a waste, at least for right now. "I could maybe stuff two thousand in if they were really close friends."

Davis sighed. "That's better than I had feared. For now, stick around. If worse comes to worst, at least we can send some of the kids with you."

"Sir!" The woman from before's voice spoke again on the radio, this time out of breath. "Ms. Lee is on the roof!"

"What?!" Davis yelled.

Jill leaned forward in her seat to get a better view of the tower. It wasn't as tall as those at larger airports, but the tower's roof was still over a hundred feet above the ground. Standing on the lip of the roof was a figure, barely visible.

"What is she doing?" Jill asked, alarm in her voice.

"She has an extreme sports class," Babu said, also leaning forward to watch. "Daredevil. We talked it through and, well. . ."

Stacy spread her arms out to the sides: stretched between them and her body was the glowing membrane of a wingsuit. She leapt and plummeted a dozen feet before swooping upwards into the sky.

"Blow me down," Jill said. "She can fly?"

"It's her first time, but yes."

"She leapt from a hundred-foot-tall tower into a storm for her first flight?" Jill asked, much more impressed than she had been. "Badass."

"That's not even a system-provided suit," Babu said. "Just one she's pumping with mana from a class power. She said she wears it to work every day, just in case," Babu massaged his scalp with his fingers. "Why is everyone from my hometown so screwed up?" Babu asked himself. "Is it something in the water?" He froze. "Do I have it too?"

"Yes," Jill said. She craned her neck upwards to follow the woman's progress into the sky. If it weren't for the glittering triangles of the wingsuit's panels, Jill would have lost the woman amongst the dark, twilit clouds.

"Ope, she's talking to me again, not just screaming!" Babu said. "She can see it better from the air." He paused, listening to the voice in his head.

Jill pressed the talk button on the radio handset so Davis would hear what Babu had to say.

"We were right!" Babu continued. "It's heading towards the city, and it's going to miss us by miles! It's about two hours out."

"It's moving that slowly?"

"No. It's just that far away. Stacy couldn't tell before."

"You get that, Davis?" Jill asked the navy commander.

"Copy. It looks like we won't be needing your offer for evac, at least not yet."

He sounded relieved, and Jill felt the same. Those taking refuge at the airport had dodged one lightning-horned bullet. Jill swallowed; a feeling of queasiness was growing in her, welling up from the pit of her stomach. Even if it skipped destroying the airport, anyone in its path inside the city was doomed.

"We have to go back in," she said. "Ohhhh, bungee cord me to a rocket ship and fling my tits to the moon, we have to go back into that goddamn psychopath-infested city and get people out."

Babu hesitated. "What about my cousins?" he asked. "We can't take them back in with that thing coming."

Jill scowled; he had a point. She had made a promise that Babu and Ras's family would be safe, and driving back into the city was the opposite of that. But at the same time, the airport was no guarantee of safety—not at all. "We'll ask your aunt and uncle. Hell, we'll ask everyone. We can spare fifteen minutes for that."

Jill threaded her mana through the truck, back into the medical bay, and connected it to Ras's now familiar mana signature. "Ras," she projected, "how are you doing?" Sounds bloomed in Jill's mind from around the swordsman, a tangled mess of voices; some in pain, others soothing, and one man complaining in a rapid clip about the medical care he'd received.

"Things are stable here," he replied back, tone clipped.

"Yeah. Sure," Jill replied, deciding not to press him. "We've got a big problem, but some time to deal with it. Can you get Mia and come up here? And someone to speak for your folks too."

"What's the situation?" Ras asked.

"The hill-sized-lightning-death bison is heading towards the city."

He took a moment to reply. Jill could hear the complainer in the background growing louder and more authoritative in tone.

"That's the end of the city then," Ras said. "Unless you have a plan to stop it?"

"Not yet, but maybe we can come up with something together."

"I'll be right there," Ras said, voice just a bit more energetic. "Somehow I don't think Mia will—" There was a sharp cracking sound in the background and a male scream. "Ope, gotta go! Mia, stop!"

"Stop?! I'm just getting started! I can put him back together again, this time to his exacting standards!" Mia shouted in the background. There was a flare of mana—from whom, Jill couldn't tell—and her connection to them snapped.

"We're all losing our goddamn minds," she said to herself. She snorted. "At least that explains why we're heading back in." She gave the steering wheel a pat. "Good thing I've still got you, girl."

CHAPTER 38

——————

BERTHA IS ONE THICC LADY

The door to the Habitation Module opened and Ras, his father Aman, and his aunt Karen came into the cab. Following behind them by a few steps was Mia, a spray of dried blood on her face.

"Spill my Dunkin', what did you do to that guy?" Jill asked, alarmed.

"Not enough," Mia said with a huff.

"She broke his fingers," Ras said, brows furrowed. "It was an abuse of power."

"He grabbed me!" Mia said with the impatient air of someone who had explained the same before. "And I put them back together again, even though he's a goddamn Karen whiner!" She paused her tirade to turn to Karen. "No offense?"

"I demand to speak to your manager," Karen said, voice deadpan but the edges of her mouth curling up in a slight smile. She winked at Jill, who snorted out a single laugh.

"Mia, no breaking parts of people we rescue," Jill said. "That's messed up. Though I am just glad that he wasn't, well," she gestured at her face, "the source of that blood."

"Oh," Mia said, flinching, "I'd forgotten about that. I stopped an artery from spraying blood by pinching it shut, and you know that thing where you put your thumb over a hose and it sprays really hard? Yeah. Isn't that just fucking great?" She closed her eyes and shook her head. "I'm going to wash this off." She spun on her heel and went back towards her room and its waiting shower.

Jill pursed her lips but let the younger woman go. They would have to talk more about what had happened, about what it meant to be in a position of power over other people, but that was a conversation that could be done later. She couldn't blame Mia for wanting to get clean, not after the woman had saved so many lives, including her own. For now, she had a rescue operation to plan.

"So, Ms. MacLeod," Aman said, breaking her introspection. "Ras said you needed our help. I'll do what I can of course, but," he shrugged, "I'm really not sure what I can contribute inside of a truck. What do you want us to do?"

"Uh, right," Jill said. She stood up out of her chair, feeling suddenly awkward that she was sitting while others were standing. "A monster's coming to Billings that could spit roast a megalodon. I'm going back with Bertha to save as many people as I can." She ran a hand down her exhausted face. "Because I'm an idiot with a soft spot wider than a pornstar's taint, or some bullshit like that."

"That's not the deal you promised," Karen said, no trace of humor remaining in her voice. She didn't sound disapproving, just concerned. "You said you'd keep our kids safe. I understand that this whole awful," she paused, searching in vain for the right word, "thing makes safety relative. But if this monster really is as bad as you say . . . I can't put them in that kind of danger."

Jill nodded. "I know, and it's shitty of me. But I can't just leave people in the city to die."

"Then we'll leave the kids here, with Taran and Sangita to watch them," she said, then pointed a finger at Jill. "No extra heroics, okay? No tilting at windmills? I want to get back to my kids afterward."

Jill blinked. "Wait, you're coming with us?"

Now Karen looked offended. "Of course I am. What's your plan?"

"Right," Jill looked at them. "Karen, you and Aman know the city better than I do. I need to know where people would go for shelter, and I need a route to follow that avoids downtown."

"We can do that," Karen said.

"We will ask Sangita as well," Aman said. "She knows downtown better than I do. But for planning, I have the perfect thing." He reached into a pocket, pulling out a pocket road atlas; its creased spine and faded cover told a story of decades of use.

"Dad, you still have that?" Babu asked, incredulous. "I thought we got you to throw that out years ago!"

"GPS is overrated," Aman said, shaking his head. "A good printed map is never going to run out of batteries. Besides, I have a—what's it called again? A class power for using maps better."

"What's next, a bonus for wearing socks and sandals?" Babu muttered. But he sidled over closer to his father and, in a quiet voice, began to interrogate him on what options the older man had unlocked.

"Ras," Jill said, calling out the swordsman's name just a bit sharper than she had the others. He had been staring out the window, only half his mind on matters at hand. "You and Mia are the heaviest hitters we have. I'm going to need you outside of Bertha, getting people inside as fast as you can. When Mia gets back, coordinate with her on how she can give you any covering fire you need, without any," she paused for a moment, remembering that it had been him who had killed someone by friendly fire. But it was more important to be clear than to spare his feelings, as much as she wanted to. "Without any of the people you're rescuing getting shot. Yours is the most important job. If we can't get people inside fast, we can't save people."

Ras nodded and swallowed. He didn't say anything, but a fire lit in his eyes: a mixture of dread and pride wrapped together into motivation.

"And finally: Babu, for you and me," Jill said. "We need to get Bertha ready for this. I've got ten class points to spend and I feel like we're going to need every single one of them."

Babu's attention snapped to Jill. "I was born for this."

"Okay," Jill said. "Then . . . break?"

"What are you, a quarterback now?" Babu asked, winking.

"Go fuck yourself," Jill replied without heat. "I hate meetings, so let's just get this shit done."

Ras left to wait for Mia in the Habitation Module, and Aman and Karen followed after him on their way to consult with Sangita.

Jill started to pace back and forth in the small area behind the seats. "We might be picking up a lot of people," she said, "so the last cargo expansion slot is a must. So are some of the armor upgrades; we need to stay in one place picking people up without getting wrecked." She glanced at Babu, who was nodding along. "Probably a few points there. I really don't want to get a murder-squid shot into me again." It had been an endless day since she had last looked at her armor module, so she recalled its information box.

Armor
"Bertha" has an armored exterior with 14% increase in Durability as Armor; damage to this additional Durability does not damage interior systems. Incoming damage is reduced by 14%. Mass increased by 10,000 kg, modified by external dimensions.
Includes: Transparent Aluminum Viewports
Add-ons (1/1): Red Eel Paint.

Armor Upgrades:
Ablative Armor (0/1): Continuous sources of damage affecting "Bertha" decrease by 14% per second.
Face Hardening (0/3): Incoming damage reduced by 14 after other reductions.
Bulwark (0/5): Further 14% increase in Armor Durability and incoming damage reduction. Each upgrade increases mass by 10,000 kg, modified by external dimensions.

Jill grimaced: not a single point invested. She really had been taking her girl's toughness for granted. "How does this damage reduction work?" she asked Babu. "Is it as simple as I think it is? Add it all up, reduce incoming damage by that amount?"

"Mostly," he said. "The source of the damage can also have some amount of extra penetration that counters it. Linearly, we think. If you have ninety percent resistance and they have thirty percent penetration, you take forty percent of the damage."

"I should still take as much of it as I can afford, shouldn't I? More is better, no matter the math."

Babu hesitated, then nodded. "I guess so. But take some face hardening too. It should stop small attacks completely and stop things from tickling you to death from a thousand cuts."

"Two into bulwark and one into face hardening it is," she said. She purchased the powers. Through her soulbond, it felt as if her skin had turned rigid and as if she was being pressed to the floor with a sudden weight. Bertha dipped down as her suspension was compressed under twenty metric tons of extra armor. The armored windows of the cab grew thicker; cubic crystals of mana-saturated glass grew an extra pair of layers but remained perfectly clear.

Jill funneled mana into Customization to thicken the springs and shock absorbers to let them better handle the immense mass of the new armor.

"Damn, Bertha's a fat-bottomed girl now!" she said, straightening up as the feedback from taking the powers faded. "I think it's time to take a propulsion upgrade. Try and keep her moving fast enough to run from that kaiju Bison, even with all this extra weight." She took the first level of the Need for Speed power, and it was as if a gust of anticipatory wind had smacked her in the face.

> Need for Speed (1/5): Increases maximum speed by a further 70 km/h.
> Current maximum speed: 320 km/h
> Note: Acceleration and braking influenced by Soulbound Modular Vehicle "Bertha's" mass.

She nodded in satisfaction and licked her lips, just imagining hitting a straight section of highway after putting a few more points in. But that was fun for another day. "Anything I'm missing, other than doubling down on more armor and speed?" she asked Babu.

"I have two big ideas," he said, leaning forward. He had been waiting for her to ask him for input. "The first is buying the mana-thief rounds. I know we don't know exactly how they work, but if we're going to be stuck defending a position, we can't have Bertha running out of mana. Even a little bit of extra mana gain would help us keep firing. And," a flash of viciousness crossed his face, "I'm pretty sure Mr. Tentacle Assassin's build relies on mana more than strength. And that shield of his relies on tanking hits instead of dodging. This would be perfect for absolutely fucking him if he comes for us, don'tcha know."

An echoing flash of pain made Jill shudder, and she nodded. For all her anguish over the deaths they had caused so far, she would shed no tears if Bertha tore the man a dozen new assholes.

"Agreed," she said, taking the power. Bertha's mana pulsed and surged into the turrets, washing through them and into the guns, waking up a hunger inside of them. Mana was their lifeblood, and they wanted to taste it. "I feel like a vampire," Jill said with a shudder. "You said you had two ideas. What's the second?"

"This is a bigger risk," Babu said, starting to pace himself, "but I think you should take the last two powers for the Cargo Module: the Climate Control and whatever its upgrade is."

Jill frowned. "I don't really see how those are going to help us rescue people."

"They won't, but if cargo works as the turrets did, then it will unlock a new set of powers!" Babu said, waving his hands as he spoke in excitement. "And let's not forget that once-only Customization choice that you got. It was incredible."

"Spend the points, hope the system comes through?" Jill asked, mostly to herself.

"Pretty much," Babu said. "It's weirdly helpful sometimes, despite, you know," he shrugged.

"It bringing the end of the fucking world and the death of who-the-fuck-knows how many people?" Jill said, her mood souring. "Yeah. Other than that, it's a real peach." She leaned her forehead against the cool metal wall of Bertha's cab and extended her senses into her truck. The currents of mana swirling through its solid bulk, waiting patiently to be unleashed, calmed her mind.

"But you're right," she said, raising her head. "The gamble's worth it."

Before she could second guess herself, she purchased the final cargo volume upgrade. Her vision swam as the sensation of inhaling, or growing, blasted through her bond with Bertha. Each upgrade was more than a doubling of volume, and this last one was enough of a change to nearly overwhelm her. The barrier between the Cargo Module's inside and outside, the dimensional warping that allowed it to be so large, thrummed with tension. Jill cried out as a spike of pain hit her through her soulbond. The door she had opened in the trailer wall, next to the Medbay, slammed closed; the force was enough to buckle the metal surrounding it.

"Are you okay?" Babu asked. He reached a tentative hand out to her shoulder but dropped it before touching her.

"Yeah," Jill gasped, "just a bit of growing pains." She purchased the first Climate Control upgrade before she could think better of it and braced for another debilitating change. But this one was more subtle; all she felt was a cool breeze in one part of her bond and a warm one in another. She pulsed mana down the cold path, and the cold of early spring rushed through the cargo bay.

She willed the system to show her what the next stage of the Climate Control ability was.

> Freezer Control (1/2): Non-living goods spoil at 1/14 the normal rate
> when inside the cargo bay.

Jill grinned, half in real mirth and half to try and wash her discomfort from the last set of upgrades away. She sent the power to Babu. "What I wouldn't have given to have had this before!" she said. "Talk about a great ability."

Babu shrugged. "I guess so."

Jill just shook her head. "Spoken like someone who's never had to unload a truckload of rotting oranges by hand in one-hundred-and-ten-degree heat. Good riddance to dealing with that putrid anal cheese ever again." She purchased the power, the last available in the Cargo Module. For a bizarre moment, she felt as if she were a tree in winter, with the sap in her veins stilled and held in cold stasis until the next spring thaw.

Before the feeling had faded, a notification sprang into her vision.

> Advanced Cargo Unlocked!
> Two Custom Powers have been determined to be the most beneficial
> for Soulbound Modular Vehicle "Bertha." Before module Upgrades
> may be purchased, one Custom Power must be selected. The selection
> is final and the other Power will not be available in the future.

> **Habitation Fusion:** The Cargo Module is specifically configured to
> support the Habitation Module. The Habitation Module's Bunkroom
> upgrade will have its expansion factor increase from 2.4 to 3.4. The
> Cargo Module will retain current upgrades but receive no further
> upgrades. No new Cargo Module may be added.
> Or:
> **Cargo Nexus:** The Cargo Module becomes the central hub for Soul-
> bound Modular Vehicle "Bertha." The Cargo Module receives a Class
> boost (+0.2) for every exclusively attached eligible module. Current
> exclusive Modules: Medbay. Eligible Modules: Habitation, Advanced
> Turrets (Small Arms), Command. Ineligible Modules: Armor, Propul-
> sion. Future Cargo Module powers will be geared towards supporting
> other Modules.

CHAPTER 39

RECONFIGURE

Great, more bonuses. But what in Satan's saggy scrotum are those numbers going to mean?" Jill asked, bending her mana-enhanced mind to the task of figuring that out. "Cargo Nexus has four eligible modules. Hey, System! What about the engine and armor, why don't those count?"

System Inquiry detected.
Armor and Propulsion Modules attach to all Modules and cannot be made exclusive.

"Well, that's a scam. But fine, four modules make for a point-eight boost if I change how they attach, which would give. . . ," she trailed off in shock as her mind gave her the answer. "The trailer would grow from seven thousand two hundred to thirty thousand four hundred cubic meters?! How big even is . . . Three hundred and thirty-five times a regular trailer?!" She shook her head in disbelief. "Two and a half acres of floor space, with high ceilings? This is insane."

"I knew unlocking this was a good call, don'tcha know," Babu said, grinning. "Habitation fusion is crazy too! I know you haven't maxed out that upgrade yet, but if you did, then the fusion would take the module from one hundred and ninety-one rooms to one thousand five hundred and forty-five. That's, like, a hotel for three thousand people! And can you imagine how much more that could grow from habitation's own 'advanced' upgrade?"

"I'm guessing more than a small-town politician's bank account," Jill said. "But Bertha's not a cruise ship, and the fusion locks me out of ever making the Cargo Module bigger. She's a truck, and trucks need to haul cargo, so I'm going to pick nexus," Jill said. "Any huge thing I'm missing that could change my mind?"

Babu scrunched his face in thought. "Not much. It's a choice of specialist versus generalist build, so if you don't want to specialize in carrying people the choice is easy. But what do we do if there really are thousands of people to pick up?"

"Then we shove them inside anyways. We'll have enough room for a few thousand, easy. I'll make more crappy airline seats. It's not like everyone is going to stay inside Bertha for more than a few hours; we just need to get them out of danger and drop them off."

"Ope, I just hope none of them need to poop."

Jill shuddered. She and Bertha were closer than ever, and she really didn't want to feel strangers relieving themselves on her, even if only by proxy. But a little bit of disgust wasn't going to stop her. "Then I'll clean it up with customize. Worse things have happened."

She mulled the choice over in her mind one last time, but couldn't think of any other reason to not take the Nexus upgrade. "I think I have some rearranging to do," Jill said, cracking her knuckles. "Everything needs to connect to the trailer, and the trailer alone, for this to work best."

She pushed her Captain Speaking power to its widest extent, and the sound of a truck horn announced to everyone inside and around Bertha that she was about to say something. "Hey, uh, folks," she projected, a spike of nervousness hitting her at the thought of hundreds of people listening. "I'm about to mess with Bertha's insides a little more than usual. Don't try and move between modules until I'm done. And it might be a good time to find something to hold on to."

It was time. With Customization, she closed and sealed all the hatches and doors, making double sure that those attached to the Command Module were extra secure. She had no idea what would happen to someone stepping through when she rerouted those connections, and she didn't want to find out. Jill took a deep breath, closed her eyes, then began the largest change to Bertha she had ever made.

She wanted the outside of Bertha to stay relatively unchanged: her truck was perfect, after all. But the space inside the truck was already so different from the outside that she visualized them as entirely different places anyways. Thinking of the cab only on the inside, she sliced her mana through the wall connecting it to the Habitation Module, trying to sever and pull the modules apart so that she could reconnect them somewhere else.

The cab shuddered and metal shrieked as the floor, walls, and ceilings deformed in waves, as if they were the water of a lake that had just had a rock thrown into it.

"Uffda!" Babu said, staggering against the wall, "Jill, what's happening?!"

"Gimme a single wanking second; I haven't done this before!" Jill snapped back. She stopped trying to move the cab and instead focused on calming the mana crashing through it. The shrieking descended in volume and pitch as the metal-deforming waves stilled, then died out.

"Alright," Jill said, "note to self: detaching modules doesn't work." She cracked her neck sideways. "You might want to sit down for try number two." She took her own advice and dropped into the driver's seat, buckling her seat belt as well for good measure. Babu scrambled to do likewise.

She concentrated on the wall between modules, willing it to liquify in its center. With a push of mana, she sent the cab sliding over the living spaces, and this time there was no rebound: just a twisting and pulling as the mind-bending geometry that was Bertha's relationship to the outside world shifted. Through her soulbond, the sensation was akin to grabbing her own head and sliding her neck from the top of her torso to the bottom.

Then came the critical moment when the cab reached the trailer. Jill braced, expecting some cataclysm, but the transition was easy. With no more effort than before, the Command Module slipped from Habitation to Cargo. She finalized the new layout by piercing the wall to the trailer to form a doorway, and grew a secure-able hatch over it that wouldn't look out of place on a submarine.

"There," she said.

"That was really weird," Babu said, rubbing his forehead with one hand. "I felt like," he paused, "like I was moving through something, but not. I think I might be motion sick."

"Body horror, for me," Jill said, double-checking that her neck really was in its proper place still. "One turret to move and then I'm done." She took a deep breath and forced herself to keep going.

Jill kept her eyes open this time as she slid the turret along the cab's roof and onto the Cargo Module. From the outside, it still looked like the turret, with Blossom, sat proudly above the cab. From the inside, the hatch leading into the turret zipped along the walls until coming to rest next to the line of other turret access doors in the cargo bay.

"Anything else you can think of before I pick nexus?" she asked when she had finished.

"Is there anything you can do about the air rushing in when the trailer grows? It's going to be like a hurricane in there."

"Butt stuff, you're right," Jill said, frowning. "We don't have time to unload everyone. I'll just do the upgrade slowly."

"Can you do that?" Babu asked, doubt in his voice. "I've never tried to take a power slowly."

"It's my magic. I don't see why not."

Jill pressed her intent into Cargo Nexus as her choice of upgrade. A tidal wave of power rose up from Bertha's mana reserves; the reality-warping magic was bent on following the system's instructions. Jill clamped her will onto it: a fist squeezing a firehose to slow down the flow and make the change more bearable.

A great vibrating groan shook through Bertha, low-pitched but omnipresent. The familiar feeling of expansion pressed itself into Jill's mind, but this time it was so all-encompassing that her awareness of her own body faded away. She was Bertha, and she was growing. She opened her mouth—the rear cargo doors—to let air in as her lungs expanded. Air rushed in; a battering blast only kept in check by Jill's iron will.

To Jill's surprise, the doors weren't the only source of air. Her Climate Control ability tugged at her attention like an insistent friend, asking for more power to keep those inside comfortable. Jill loosened her grip on the flow of mana slightly, giving it what it wanted. The rush of air through the cargo doors lessened to a breeze as Climate Control took up the slack.

Minutes passed, and the trailer grew steadily and safely. Jill stretched it not just sideways but upwards, as the inner space was getting too large to just be a single story any longer. Her mind grew tired, and she allowed more mana through to lessen the strain. With a force that rang Bertha like a bell the trailer surged to its final height.

Bertha's mana stilled, and Jill's perception snapped back to her own body. A notification appeared.

Cargo Nexus:
"Bertha" has a cargo bay with total volume 30,408.7 cubic meters, a spatial compression factor of 335.5, and internal dimensions of 50 meters by 50 meters by 12.16 meters. Effective Boost: +1.2
Includes: Doors.
Add-ons (1/5): Hearth of the Wolf.

Upgrades:
Teamster Enhancement (0/3): All authorized sapients inside of the Cargo Module, and within 22 meters of "Bertha," have their movement speed and spatial reasoning enhanced by 32%.
Reinforced Module Mounting (0/5): Choose one exclusively attached Module. That Module's Class boost increases by +0.2. A Module may only be boosted once with this power.

"Vibrators stuck on overdrive, that was intense," Jill said, her voice a croak. She looked to the side where Babu sat staring at her, his mouth open. "What?" she asked, "I grow an extra ass or something?"

"That was just a lot, and I mean a lot, of mana," he said, pointing at the gauge that had replaced Bertha's gas meter. It read just over forty thousand: she had spent nearly one hundred thousand mana. "If I cast a spell a tenth of that size, I think my head would explode."

"It was Bertha's mana, not mine," Jill said, giving the steering wheel a slap. "My girl's tougher than your head."

"Just a bit," Babu said, "but still—"

Jill interrupted him by sending the notification of the Cargo Nexus's new upgrades. Babu's mouth snapped shut, and his eyes flickered left to right, taking in the new information.

"Alright everyone," Jill projected to the whole truck, "this ride on the Highlander Shipping Hurricane Simulator is over. It's safe to move again." She unsealed the truck's interior doors.

"What do you think of the new abilities?" Jill asked Babu, who had pulled a small notebook out of his pocket to write in.

"Numbers go up," Babu replied, finishing a line of text with a dramatic flourish of his pen. "But numbers could save our lives. A point in the reinforced mounting would raise the turret damage boost from seventy to eighty percent, and—woah, habitation's rooms from a maximum of one hundred and ninety-one to," he paused for a split second as he did the math, "three hundred and nine."

"Exponentials are bullshit," Jill said. "But I'm going to take the teamster upgrade so that the people we're picking up can get in ASAP. The faster we can get in and out of the city, the better."

"It will also let us fight better if the monsters get in."

Jill grimaced. "That too." She purchased the ability, and a new set of mana connections bloomed in her. Threads reached out to everyone inside Bertha's trailer; they didn't connect though, instead waiting on her command.

The power's next-level ability appeared in her vision:

> Teamster Tetris (1/3): All authorized sapients inside of the Cargo Module can teleport non-living objects to other locations inside of the Cargo Module, using "Bertha's" Mana reserves.
> Mana cost: 1 per kilogram or meter

"Holy shit," Babu said, breathless. "Teleportation. Real, actual teleportation. There are so, so many ways to abuse that! And that's only the second ability out of three!"

Jill snorted out a tired laugh. "Never change, Babu. I don't think that's going to help us as much as more armor would though. Not for this job."

"You're probably right," he said with a sigh, "but remember it for later!"

"Will do," Jill said. She put her last free class point into Bulwark, raising the total damage reduction from Bertha's armor to 56 percent. Her truck rocked with the additional weight, then settled.

The hatch behind Jill opened, bringing with it a rush of noise: the echoing sound of hundreds of people, and one giant dog, adapting to the huge space they now found themselves in. Aman and Karen stepped over the threshold, followed by Mia, her hair still wet, and finally, Ras.

Jill unbuckled herself and stood, leaning over her seat to face the others. "Hope it wasn't too rough back there," she said. "I'm good to go save some folks. How are things on your end?"

"I've found half a dozen people for the Medbay who are all more qualified than me," Mia said. "So, I'm going back to shooting." She looked relieved.

"I have some volunteers to help me outside," Ras said. "They aren't all high level, but they all have the melee basics to keep them safe," he said with a nod to Babu, "and monsters don't need to be powerhouses to ambush fleeing level ones."

Jill nodded at the pair of them. "Great. Is there anything in your plan that I can help with?"

"Yes," Mia said. "Once we've stopped to pick people up, can you raise my turret up? Like on a tower?"

"Huh," Jill frowned. "I don't see why not, as long as we aren't driving. That would murder our top speed."

Mia grinned. "Great. I'm going to have sight lines for days."

"Babu, can you make sure they can always talk to each other when things are going down?" Jill asked the mind control specialist.

"As long as I don't have to cast something else really strenuous, then yes," Babu replied.

"Then Ras, I trust whatever you've come up with for your volunteers." Jill turned to Karen and Aman. "How about you two? Know where we're heading?"

"We have a plan, but," Karen answered, casting a nervous glance at Aman, "you might not like it. We're going to need to get close to City Hall. Really close."

CHAPTER 40

CONVICTION

Aman took out his pocket atlas and unfolded an inset showing the city streets of Billings in more detail. A dozen or so red circles had been drawn on the map with a route marked between them that snaked over the length and breadth of the city. Aman stabbed a finger down on a circle. "Each of these is a place where we think people are. Churches, schools, malls, sports arenas, that sort of thing."

He pointed to the same winding trail to the west they had used to climb the ridge above the city just over an hour before. "We'll start from here and loop downwards, first trying to evacuate the places close to where the Boss Bison is coming from."

"We move fast; try to stay ahead of it," Jill said, nodding. She raised an eyebrow. "'Boss Bison?'"

Karen shrugged. "We needed to call it something," she said. "That seemed to fit."

"If by fit you mean like an un-lubed anal plug six sizes too big, I guess so," Jill said, cracking a smirk at the shocked expressions on both Karen and Aman's faces. "But sure, 'Boss Bison.' Why not?"

"R-right," Aman said, "the problem is here at the end." He pointed to an area less than a quarter mile from the City Hall, which had been marked with a black X. "Two churches, a YMCA, and the First Interstate Building."

"The what?"

"It's the tallest building in the city," he said. "Maybe no one went there. Maybe a thousand people tried to pack in."

"But either way," Jill finished for him, scowling, "there's going to be people hiding on that block."

"A lot of people live near there," Karen said, "and we were, ah, being chased by the cops then, so didn't pick anyone up."

"That decides it," Jill said. "We get out as many people as we can." She looked at Mia and Ras. "Babu said you have ideas for dealing with Mr. Tall-Dark-and-Murderous?"

The three looked at each other, some silent communication passing between them.

Mia cracked her knuckles. "You've finally leveled up enough that Blossom's not being held back, so I'm going to tear him a new asshole. Pulling that bullet out of you was, like, super annoying, and he tried to kill me too."

"For countering his mind control I have a power from the, uh, dark dominator," Babu said, coughing the last two words, "class evolution."

"The what?" Ras asked.

"Dark dominator," Babu said, facing his brother.

"That sounds powerful," Ras said, eyebrows rising.

"Babu can share his evil class evolution later," Jill said. She pointed at Babu. "What are you doing if our leaky asshole doesn't have mind-controlled turds around?"

"Communications, area of effect incapacitation, and any counter-spelling I can," he said without missing a beat. "Plus, well, I have some other tricks up my sleeve."

"Fine. Ras?" Jill prompted.

"Ras will hit him really hard if he comes close," Babu answered before Ras could.

"My strategy is more detailed than that!" Ras said, shooting Babu a dirty look.

Babu grinned. "Ras smash!"

"How high level is he?" Jill asked. "Is he going to smash through you like my fist through drywall?" She glanced at Aman. "Sorry about that by the way." To the others, she continued, "How do you know you can take him?"

"From the monster flow we've seen," Babu said, "his leveling rate should be slowing, while we just got a huge boost. It won't be like last time."

"Good," Jill said. "Let's assume we at least make him run back to his shadows. What's the next step of the rescue plan?"

Aman pointed at the furthest-east circle. "Then there's just one more stop. We cut over on Sixth Street to the MetraPark Arena, get everyone there, and complete the circle back to the airport."

"Who's staying up front to help me navigate?" Jill asked. "My eyes are for the road, not a map."

"I will," Aman said. "My powers will help link us to the map."

"I'll be here too," Babu chimed in. "For seeing what's going on."

"Okay then," Jill said. "Anything else?"

"One last thing," Karen said. "We're all talking as if the Boss Bison is this, this force of nature. Something we have no hope of killing! But what if we could? Could we save the city?"

"The thing was fifty feet tall, not even counting the horns, last time I saw it," Jill said, remembering the massive creature's piercing gaze as it had stood, looking at her from miles away. She shuddered.

"Stacey said that it's bigger than that," Babu said, voice quiet. "It could just be the angle from the air, or it could have grown."

"I think the Boss Bison is special and that it really has gotten bigger," Ras said. "I kept asking the system questions, trying to get useful information about the creature. After a little while it answered with this."

A text box appeared in Jill's vision.

System Inquiry detected.

Regional Mana concentrators are beings or objects that absorb the excess Mana flow in a geographical Region.

Warning! It is not recommended to interact with a regional Mana concentrator at your level!

"The system did that thing where it seems like it's answering a totally different question," Ras said.

"But it doesn't do that," Jill added. "What it says is always related somehow. It couldn't just be a normal giant monster; it's some super special one too."

"It really is a boss," Babu said

"One question led to another," Ras continued, "and I found out a little about what's powering it too." He sent another notification.

> You are located in the Big Sky Region
> Mana flow: High
> Status: Wild
> Warning! It is not recommended to enter a high Mana region at your level!

"We're too low-level to even be here?" she asked, incredulous. "No wonder this whole place is going to shit." She shook her head. "We're not going to fight the Boss Bison. If it comes for us, shoot away and hope we tickle it enough to leave. Otherwise, we run and save as many as we can."

Karen sighed. "Then the city really is doomed." Aman leaned over, giving her a hug with one arm around her shoulders.

Jill stood up. "I want us moving out in ten minutes or less," she said. "Babu, you call Davis and tell him we're going. I'm going to go tell everyone still in the trailer the danger that we're going into and give them one last chance to get off. I think I owe them that conversation face-to-face. Anything else to talk about?" She looked around, but no one spoke. "Then let's get to it."

She led the way to the rear of the cab. The reinforced door leading back along the truck moved aside at her approach, the locking mechanisms spinning and sliding to allow it to open outwards. Jill paused on the threshold, staring at the trailer. A mixture of wonder and awe, tinged with a little mania, rose in her at the sight. With a footprint of 2500 square meters, and a four-story-tall ceiling, it was starting to look more like the inside of a stadium than a regular building.

The seating from before stood clustered in a corner and was much more occupied than Jill expected. Families in little clusters, each separated by a pile of what belongings they had managed to run with, rested against each other. Next to them was set up a score of tents. Jill narrowed her eyes at the tent stakes on their corners that had been driven, with superhuman strength, into the trailer's metal floor. But she couldn't really blame their owners for being resourceful, and any holes they made would repair themselves anyways. There was still a line of people coming into and out of the turrets, getting trained in turn on how to fire the truck's guns even without any enemies around to actually shoot at. A pack of children ran screaming laps chased by Sander the dog, who could easily catch them if he wanted, but contented himself loping behind them with his tongue lolling out. On his head sat a new occupant of Bertha that Jill hadn't seen before: a small tortoiseshell cat who looked supremely bored.

If they were going to be packing more people in, Jill figured that she couldn't waste so much volume on an incredibly high ceiling. She drew on Bertha's mana reserves with her mind, willing new metal to flow out from the bay walls, forming a ceiling above her head, then another and another, until the cargo bay had four floors, each with a three-meter ceiling. A wide, parking-garage-style ramp connected them together.

"Ms. MacLeod," Aman, who had followed Jill through the hatch, said from next to her. "I can tell that you are a truck driver, not an architect."

"Pfft, fuck you too, buddy."

"I'll present you with a design sometime tomorrow if things are no longer life and death," he said over his shoulder, as he walked past Jill on his way to Sangita.

Jill shook her head. Tomorrow was for tomorrow. For now, she had a crowd to talk to. The people in front of her hadn't reacted much to the trailer growing more floors; Jill supposed that compared to the rapid-fire changes of the last few hours that had been a minor alteration.

She projected the sound of Bertha's horn through the bay, then her own voice. "Hey, uh, everyone," she said, "listen up. In case the rumors haven't reached you yet, there's a giant monster coming straight for Billings. I'm going to get as many people out as I can. Some of you," she nodded at the knots of people gathering around Ras and Mia, "have already agreed to go back into danger. If another half dozen of you can stay to fire the machine guns, well, you'll be helping to save lives. For the rest of you, well, it's nice to meet you, but this is going to be fucking dangerous, so get your asses off my truck and into the airport where it's safer."

"Hey!" shouted a man from the seating area, just seconds after Jill had finished her speech. He stood on top of a seat, balancing so that everyone could see and hear him. He was one of the first people Jill had rescued in the city, alongside his child and claymore-wielding wife, and from the elbow down he had a chrome-plated prosthetic arm. "Get off your truck? After all you've done for me, you expect me to just leave? Not on your life! You need someone to shoot, I'm here!"

There was a murmur of approval at his words and nods of determination.

"My husband's still in there somewhere," a woman with a tight black braid yelled next. "I'm going back in to find him!"

"Me too!"

"My daughter is missing!" A chorus of voices, some breaking with emotion, joined in.

"If we thought it was safer in the airport, we would have already left!" yelled a man by the Medbay. His face was half covered in bandages, and his clothes bore obvious claw marks. More agreement followed, less intense than before but still sincere.

"You let me shoot a bigass gun!" yelled a teen girl, giving Jill a double thumbs up. Laughter broke out in the crowd.

"Sorry," the chrome-armed man said, grinning. "It looks like you're stuck with us."

"I think you're all a bunch of suicidal idiots," Jill projected, an answering grin forming on her face, "but it seems that I am too. So, what the fuck, let's go save some people."

A roar answered her, voices lifted in determination tempered by loss. Jill added her own voice back, shouting out all of the terror of the day, all of her longing to just be back with her own family, all of her fear for the future, and all of her will to not take the end of the world lying down.

Mana swirled through the trailer, streams of power of every color circling, flowing, connecting.

CHAPTER 41

IN THEIR LANES

The road sped by beneath Bertha as they set off on their rescue mission. The truck was more powerful than ever, and hopefully prepared for anything.

Jill, though, was exhausted. Even with magic flowing through her, strengthening her body and mind, she felt a deep-seated weariness that clouded her thoughts and made her eyelids droop. But this wasn't the first time she'd driven tired, not by a long shot, nor was it the worst. Her eyes patrolled the road and mirrors in a regular rhythm that took no effort on her part, and she held Bertha's wheel with steady hands, her fingers tapping to a rough tune that only she could hear.

"Ms. MacLeod," Aman had pressed himself back into the passenger seat, his knuckles clenched around his road atlas and his eyes wide, "is it really wise to go this fast?"

Babu, standing behind his father, chuckled.

"I don't tell you how to do whatever-the-fuck you do," Jill said, "so don't tell me how to drive." She guided Bertha around a turn in the road with a slight twist of the wheel. The armored behemoth of a truck barreled west on the airport access road at ninety miles an hour, its weight enough that, even on oversized tires, the pavement cracked in places behind it. She let up on the accelerator, letting the truck slow. Not because Aman was right about driving, but just because their turn was coming up.

Jill pressed on the brakes, slowing Bertha to a stop as she turned the truck left onto the same winding road they had taken out of the city in the first place. The cliff offered them a view over the city and intelligence about what was happening below that they wouldn't be able to gather again once they descended. The settlement shield flickered ahead of them, barely holding together.

"There," said Jill, pointing into the city. She could see the telltale signs of successful defenses; monster bodies piled up in macabre barricades were visible from their mile-away vantage point. "Everywhere those things are dying, there are people! Or were. You boys do your thing and get me a route."

Babu stepped forward to get a better view out the front window; a pulse of mana washed over Jill as he activated some sort of power. Next to him, Aman unfolded his marked map of the city.

"I don't feel any people at Albertson's," Babu said.

Aman made a note on his map, then cast a spell. To Jill, his mana felt like the inside of a hardware store: a mixture of plywood and possibilities. In front of Jill's eyes appeared a map of the city, their route marked with a rich, glowing brown telling her exactly where she needed to go.

Babu took a sudden breath in, jerking in unpleasant surprise. "City College is a giant ball of terror and adrenaline. I think they're fighting right now!"

"Hold on, folks," Jill projected to the entire truck. Then her foot went down on the accelerator, driving Bertha forward and through the settlement shield.

You have invaded the Settlement of Billings!
Invasion progress: 21%

Settlement alert!
Monster Infestation in progress.
Current monsters in settlement: 41,735
Current invaders in settlement: 21,994

"Forty thousand monsters?!" Jill said. "Time for us to get the fuck down there!"

Babu's slow trip up the Zimmerman Trail had been a test for him: a pair of hairpin turns abutting a cliff that pushed his ability to handle a big rig to the literal edge. Jill didn't even bother to use the brakes, whipping them around the turns with a combination of magical reflexes and the ability

to sense where her girl was as if the truck were a part of her. The back of
the trailer hung out over open air as she took the first turn, and she had to
toggle on the Torque Converter to stop the rig from flipping. Excess magic
sparked off of Bertha's tires in a shower of gold, as the mana harvested from
the potential roll overflowed from the truck's already-full mana storage.

"I don't like Mario Kart anymore!" Babu said, holding on to the passenger seat to stay upright.

"Hey, I know that one!" Jill said back. "But really, hold on tight. That's
the slowest I'm going on this entire run." A woman of her word, she accelerated into the straightaway at the bottom of the trail, pushing Bertha past
ranch-style and split-level homes in a roaring blur of red-painted steel.

"Look out!" Aman shouted, pointing at a woman who had run onto
the road ahead of them. Following her was an enormous crab: a ten-foot-
tall, brown-and-orange-spiked monster scuttling sideways after its prey.
The woman leapt and spun with mana-enhanced agility, bringing a handgun to bear and squeezing off three shots before landing, all without slowing. The crab hardly seemed to care; the three tiny holes in its shell caused
too little damage to stop it.

Jill twitched the wheel, aiming carefully. She could swear that the crab
had a surprised expression in its eyes the instant before Bertha blasted
straight through the crustacean in a multi-ton explosion of carapace, viscera, and off-white crab meat.

Miniature Heraldic Crab defeated.
Your contribution: 98%
1078 Experience Gained!

The impact barely jarred them, and Bertha's armor didn't take any damage at all. They were in more danger from the thick coating of guts that
now blocked the view out of the windshield.

"The new armor works," Jill said, flicking the wipers on out of habit
before remembering she could simply evaporate the muck away.

"Holy moly!" Aman gasped, recoiling.

"You get used to it," Babu said with a shrug, echoing Jill's words from
earlier in the day.

"Tell that woman to get to one of our later pickup points," Jill said
to Babu, as she put on more speed. They were heading south first, then

jogging east before cutting back north, so if the woman was fast, she could get ahead of them. It was up to her to survive that far: Jill couldn't afford to slow down now, not for just one person.

They sped past Albertson's, the grocery store that would have been their first stop. In the parking lot was a smattering of dead monsters, but not many. The grocery store itself was a writhing hive of broken windows and massive insects. Bertha's guns spoke in a choir, led by the ripping tear that was the voice of Blossom. Concrete, brick, and monsters exploded into a wet dust storm under the onslaught. Mana flowed out of Bertha and experience flowed in, but they were only in range for a scant few seconds before leaving the building behind.

Jill threw the wheel over two blocks later, turning towards the college in an asphalt-tearing, streetlight-crushing slide. A pack of fear deer was crossing the road, heading towards City Hall. Their distended teeth were red with blood. Jill pulled on the horn and the blast wave tore the low-level creatures limb from limb. She let go before the plow could form, saving the mana for the guns. Bertha covered the last block to their destination in a matter of seconds.

The City College main building was a two-story fortress of brick. The front doors stood recessed in a window-free expanse of wall, making a perfect killing funnel. That didn't stop the monsters from trying to get in, and a horde of insects crawled over the bodies of their fellows, charging suicidally ahead.

"Hold fire!" Jill yelled to the gunners, the friendly fire incident from earlier fresh in her mind. "I'm moving in. Once your shot is clear, let 'er rip!"

The front door passed in a flash on their right, revealing a more desperate situation around the corner. This side of the building had a solid line of windows, now broken, at waist height—welcome relief for bored students, but a liability for monster defense. Guns poked out over the sills, and their bullets attempted to hold back a tide of monsters. Jill slammed on the brakes and steered for the wall, the wheels churning grass and dirt into the air in a brown wave as the truck left the paved road.

They came to a stop in a scant fifty yards, her seat belt the only thing stopping Jill from being flung forward. She grimaced, hoping that those in the trailer had been smart enough to buckle themselves in. But the sudden stop had accomplished her goal: Bertha was close to the side of the building, the swarming monsters behind them and on their left, with no possibility of their shots over-penetrating and killing the defenders inside.

A half-heartbeat later, the rear turret fired and was joined an instant later by the rest. Even the turret nearly pressed against the building opened up; its rounds scraped down the wall, cutting any monster who had reached the windows to ribbons.

Jill backed Bertha up, eyes on the side mirror, until the trailer extended past the corner at the front of the building, giving the truck a 270-degree arc of unimpeded fire. Thirty seconds later and the monsters were still coming, but the tide had been pushed back all the way to the road. "Ras, go!" Jill projected to him. With a flex of her mana, she burst the trailer doors open. Mana streamed from Babu's mind without Jill having to prompt him, and the spell-caster reached out to anyone inside who would listen to tell them to evacuate.

Ras sprang out the back in a flash of mana, covering twenty yards in an instant. He was followed by a score of other people: some with swords, most with guns, and one stout man packing a dual-armed flamethrower. The close-ranged fighters spread out in an uncertain line, weapons clenched tight, while those with guns began to shoot. While Bertha's guns claimed the lion's share of kills, the defender's careful fire cut down its fair share more.

Ras stood in front of them all, his sword raised into the air. The soul-bound weapon flew upwards and exploded with magic, splitting again and again until all that was left were flickers of shining edge. They pulsed outwards and formed a flashing barrier of ultra-thin blades, protecting the path from the college's front door to Bertha.

At the same time, Jill pushed Mia's turret upwards one story, two, then three—enough height that the chain gun towered over the top of the building.

"Lower by four feet!" Mia's voice spoke, funneled into the cab by Babu. "I need to shoot across the roof, not down through it!" Jill complied, and Mia opened fire, sweeping bullets in a lethal sideways hail. Even more experience flowed into Jill as all those monsters clever enough to attack from above met their fate.

"Is there anything I can do?" Aman asked. His eyes flickered as he tracked the monsters outside the windows, but there was no fear in his voice.

Jill blew out a breath. "No. Our part in getting here is done. Now it's up to the others." She pointed surreptitiously at Babu, who wasn't paying attention to them at all.

He stood with both hands clutched on the sides of his head; the hundreds of threads emerging from him hummed and buzzed with power. "Uffda!" he said, breathing out hard in annoyance. "The stubborn mules in there don't want to come out." He looked to Jill. "Permission for drastic measures?"

"What are you going to—" Jill said, cutting herself off as she realized exactly what Babu would consider drastic. "Save their lives. Just make it reversible." She swallowed, feeling herself inch just that little bit down a slippery slope, if only by proxy.

Mana swelled and pulsed as Babu built up his power one layer at a time over ten long seconds before he let it explode into the college. The enchanter's hair blew in a ghostly wind, his eyes flashed, and the wave of desire that rolled off of him left Jill feeling thoroughly annoyed. She turned to glare at Babu, but her anger evaporated on seeing Aman's face. Babu's father, so much lower of a level and more susceptible than her, had a look of pure confusion etched into his face deep enough that Jill was concerned it might stick.

"Ooooh," Babu said, wobbling forward to lean against the dash. "That was a doozy, don'tcha know."

"I suddenly understand why you make so much money in your, um, career," Aman said, blinking.

"What did you do to them?" Jill asked. The fire from the turrets had slackened, reduced to just the occasional burst. The monsters had been beaten back, for now, and if the people inside were going to get out, now was the time.

"Mind virus again," Babu said. "It's a ludicrously OP ability, at least against—wait, here they come!"

The front doors of the college opened and through them scrambled bedraggled and bloody people, all trying to get to Bertha. Jill spread her own magic out in a gentle tide around Bertha, authorizing all of them so that her Teamster Enhancement power would apply. Their movements became fast and sharp, and they piled into Bertha in a rush of people too large for Jill to count in the mirror. Seconds turned to minutes, and the tide turned to a trickle. Hundreds, maybe thousands, more people were now safe inside Bertha.

Jill breathed out a sigh of relief and rubbed her eyes. They just might pull this whole thing off. But her day wasn't over, not yet.

CHAPTER 42

SQUASHING A BUG

That's it," Babu said, eyes open but looking at nothing as his mana swept the college, "we've got everyone."

Jill stretched in her seat and cracked her neck. "Then let's move." She put Bertha in reverse to clear the building, cranked the wheel over to start a hard turn, then accelerated forward, pulling the massive truck around in a J-turn that tore the ground to shreds. Jill grinned.

"Did you have to do that?" Babu asked her. The sudden turn had forced him to hang on to the dashboard to stay upright.

Jill snorted out a laugh. "No, but it was fun." She projected her next sentence to the whole truck. "For all the new folks: welcome to Highlander Shipping! I'm Jill, and before the day's out, we're going to be doing crazier shit than that turn, so buckle up or hold on to something."

The noise in the trailer—a mixture of excited chatter, shouted questions, and not a little sobbing—came back through Jill's communication power. She let it wash over her for just a second, taking it all in, before withdrawing her mana and letting the sound fade out.

"Do you think they'll be pissed when they find out you brain fucked them?" Jill asked Babu.

"You did what?" Aman asked in alarm.

"She means the mind virus, not anything sexual," Babu said, rolling his eyes.

"Ah," Aman said. "That's a new one for me. Brain fucked." He said the words slowly and with careful diction.

Jill frowned, uncertain if the man was mocking her language or not.

"I tried to make it subtle," Babu said, "and it should have worn off the instant they got into Bertha. If we're lucky they'll never figure out what happened."

Jill pulled Bertha through a smooth right-hand turn, taking them south and following the map in her vision. She pushed her foot down on the accelerator, and Bertha surged ahead. "We'll be at the next stop in just a minute," she said.

The sky, already dim thanks to the storm clouds, turned fully black as the sun finally set in the west. Without power, Billings was the darkest it had been in decades, with only fires and the occasional flash of mana lighting the underside of the clouds above. Bertha's headlights cut through the murk, golden-yellow beams leading the way. But without light to the sides, the occasional monster-slaying burst of gunfire from the turrets slackened down to almost nothing; the gunners were unable to see any but the most aggressive targets.

The truck screamed to a stop at their next destination: a church whose steeple had fallen in. Again Ras leapt out, but this time there was no surge of monsters to fight. A spiky white sphere of light rose above Bertha and was soon followed by more, as one of Ras's volunteers repeatedly cast a spell to let them all see. One mental announcement from Babu was all it took to convince those hiding in the sanctuary to flee into Jill's far safer, if more profanity-laden, protection.

A bolt of lightning, a pure cerulean blue that couldn't be natural, flashed down from the heavens into a nearby house, setting fire to the roof in an explosion of wooden debris. Jill swallowed, glancing to the west where the Boss Bison was coming from.

"How are we doing on time?" she asked Aman as she took a corner a little too fast, pressing them all to the side with centripetal force. They were almost to the next marked spot to check for survivors, and there were another nine after that to go.

"Another two hours? More, if there are lots of people at each stop."

"And maybe less," Babu said. He sighed. "I'm not feeling anyone ahead."

Out of the darkness emerged a shopping center: parking lots sprinkled with burning cars and low commercial buildings anchored by a movie theater. Smoke from the cars rose in inky pillars, and the car fires lit the scene in flickering red. Jill turned into the parking lot, sweeping the headlights across pitted asphalt and wrecked landscaping. Chunks had been ripped from the pavement and thrown into vehicles, and there were great gouges in the asphalt, their edges melted rather than smashed or cut. Splashes and streaks of blood, both the odd shades of monsters and the familiar red of humans, were everywhere, but Jill couldn't see any bodies. Bertha bounced over a curb as they followed the blood, all leading towards the movie theater.

Lightning flashed, a snapshot of visibility burning its way into Jill's vision: the segments and legs of an enormous millipede wound through gaping holes in the theater's walls, its black carapace and clawed pincers cast in sharp relief.

"Shoot that crawly fucker," Jill projected into the turrets. She reached into Bertha with her magic, twisting one headlight like a searchlight.

The beam of light flashed over the millipede just as it smashed through the theater's ceiling, rearing up into the air. Bodies of humans and monsters adorned its head like a crown, each impaled on a spike of chitin, their leaking insides the only color on the monster. It turned its maw towards Bertha, opened its jaws, and a jet of glowing green liquid blasted out. Jill pulled the wheel over, but it wasn't fast enough; she grunted in pain as the acid splashed over the truck, burning through armor.

Maleficent Myriapoda, Level 51
Status: Crowned in Glory

The stream cut off as Mia returned fire, her shots shattering armor with every hit. The other machine guns joined in; seven glowing streams of magic bullets connected truck to monstrosity. It fell back into the building, but its long body—wound as it was inside and outside of the walls—betrayed it. As fast as it pulled itself along, it couldn't get out of the line of fire for long seconds. Bullet after bullet found their mark, each punching a hole that sprayed out dark ichor. But it was still alive when its bulbous tail sank into the ruins of the theater, taking it completely out of sight.

"We're killing that," Jill said, voice cold. She brought Bertha to a stop, headlights trained forward to where the millipede had disappeared. A moment later a line of acid shot from a dark hole in the side of the building and splashed on the front window with a crashing splat. The crystalline armor of the windshield fogged and bubbled, as the outer layers sloughed off like so much melted sugar.

"Shitdicks!" Jill yelled, feeling as if her face was on fire. She kicked Bertha into reverse and hauled the wheel over as her own turrets returned fire, their burning tracers cutting through concrete to disappear into darkness. The acid stopped, but without the headlights pointing at the movie theater, Jill had no idea what the monster was doing.

She kept Bertha moving, doing the occasional weave to throw off any potential bursts of acid. At the same time, she spread her mana through Bertha searching for Ras. She found him near the rear doors and sent her voice to him. "Ras!" she said, both through her power and aloud. "We need those light spells outside, now!"

"On it."

A surge of mana beside her had Jill snap her head to the side; Babu made a flicking motion with his hand, and outside of Bertha a ball of light hovered in place, soon left behind by Bertha's motion. He repeated the spell another half dozen times. More flashed out from the left side turret, cast by someone inside. The light balls rose upwards, pure white lanterns against a black sky, and cast the destroyed buildings in harsh light.

"There!" Aman yelled, pointing out the passenger-side window.

The millipede had left its hiding place and was sprinting to a new building. Along its dorsal ridge were more corpse-carrying spines; the black and red spikes writhed back and forth as it scurried, giving the impression of waving flags of meat.

"The legs!" Babu's voice boomed out, amplified by magic. "Shoot the legs!" He raised a hand to point at the creature and snapped his fingers. Dark lightning erupted from the ground and raced up and down the millipede. With every spark, the creature's motion faltered as segment after segment was paralyzed for a fraction of a second. Babu staggered forward, catching himself against the dash.

By then Jill had pointed Bertha at the creature, her foot all the way down on the accelerator. The truck reverberated with the sound of machine guns firing: no controlled bursts these, but a constant automatic fire that raked up and down the millipede near ground level. Most of the rounds missed, but those that hit blasted through thin legs, snapping the carapace and pulping the tissue underneath.

"Can't hide from me now," Jill snarled. The monster hauled itself behind the only cover available: a burned-out camper. But one blast of the hydra horn was enough to shatter the lesser vehicle, blowing broken metal into the air. Jill kept the horn pulled, a plow of distorted air building around Bertha's front, and a screaming bass rumble joined the guns in a symphony of destruction.

The millipede's cracked and hobbled body was unable to stand up to a direct hit; ichor sprayed into the air as Bertha cut the monster in two. Jill spun Bertha around in a slide, tires screaming and churning the rear half of the millipede into so much pulp. Before she finished her turn, a kill notification appeared.

> Maleficent Myriapoda defeated. Bonus experience awarded for: monster kill above your level (+0.8).
> Your contribution: 42%
> 3856 Experience Gained!
> You are now Level 44!

They came rocking to a stop facing the dead, but still twitching, insect. For a long few seconds, the only sound in the cab was the crinkling of metal as the armor regrew bit by bit. Pleasure washed through Jill's veins as magic changed her just a bit more, but it wasn't enough to blunt the horror before her of people reduced from living beings to decorations.

Rain began to fall; heavy drops hit the windshield with dull splats, the normal sound muted by the thickness of the armor.

"My God," Aman said, breaking the silence. "I knew the mutated creatures were bad, but that was. . ."

"A monster," Jill said. She advanced Bertha until the truck bumped up against the corpse and looted it. Black flesh burst into gold motes that flew to Jill, congealing into a smoky crystal. She let it fall to the floor. The bodies remained behind, but there was nothing Jill could do for them beyond the revenge she'd already served. "Time to go."

Aman cleared his throat. "Right." The map of their route had disappeared from Jill's vision at some point during the fight. Aman recast his spell, and it popped up again.

"Can you sense the next group?" Jill asked Babu. She pulled Bertha out of the parking lot, heading east.

The enchanter, still leaning against the dashboard, sent his mana racing outwards again. "There are people!" he said, relieved. "A lot of them. A lot of them are absolutely terrified, but most are just scared." He chewed on his lip. "The angry ones don't feel right. Their emotions are all twisted."

"What does that mean?" Aman asked.

Babu shook his head. "I don't know," he said. "I need to conserve mana for a little while. That spell really took a lot, don'tcha know."

"We'll find out when we get there, then," Jill said. A look at Bertha's mana gauge showed that the continuous gunfire had done a number on her mana reserves as well. Nothing that wouldn't come back with a few minutes of rest, but they didn't have those minutes.

A pair of screeching turns had them back on Interstate 90, retracing the same roads they'd taken into the city earlier in the day. The buildings lining the road, a comforting slice of normality just hours before, were jagged shadows, each a potential source of ambush. The next stop on their mission was a grocery store: the same that they had seen being looted.

Jill slowed and turned into the parking lot, eyes scanning for monsters. Lumps in the darkness showed where they had fallen, but nothing moved now. Impacts sounded on the windshield and armor, sharper and louder than rain, and hard enough that Jill felt them stinging through her soul-bond. Bertha was taking damage, but not much. Muzzle flashes from the store told Jill all she needed to know.

"We're being shot," she said, anger and disbelief in her voice. "Those hamster-brained bonobo-shaming assholes are shooting at people instead of monsters!"

"And not for the first time," Aman said, voice flat and finger pointing. "Look more closely at the ground."

A twitch of the wheel brought the headlights to where he had indicated. Some of what Jill had taken for monsters were human. She jerked the wheel to the side, narrowly avoiding running over what had once been a person.

"Fuck," Jill said.

"Maybe they got caught outside by one of those eruptions of new monsters?" Babu asked. "Then got left there?"

Aman shook his head. "Those are bullet wounds. Trust me."

"Most of the people in there are just scared!" Babu said. He flinched as an extra-loud bullet impact hit the window right in front of him, cracking it ever so slightly.

Jill clenched her jaw. "Then those people we need to get. We'll sort out what happened to the people out here later. Babu, tell them about the Boss Bison. Maybe they'll listen."

He nodded, and mana streamed off of him; the tendrils flowed into the grocery store in search of minds to connect to. "I've got one who's acting like their leader," he said. "Hold on a moment."

The gunfire continued, a pitter-patter of hornet stings.

"This is ri-god-damn-diculous," Jill said. "Loop me in so I can yell at these clogged sphincters."

"—just want our food!" a scratchy woman's voice bloomed next to Jill's ear. "We're doing just fine here, so fuck off!"

"Hey, moron," Jill said. "Stop shooting my truck and listen. What's coming is bigger than—"

There was a deep crunch, and spider cracks raced across the windshield. The armored glass had held, but a glowing purple bullet a half-inch wide was lodged in it.

"You clit-clipper!" Jill yelled, putting Bertha back into motion. She turned enough that those in the grocery store didn't have a clear line of sight to the cab anymore. She wasn't eager to get shot for the second time in one day.

"That's right," the voice continued, "you better run, you—"

"You dried up shit-puddle, I'm trying to save your worthless life!" Jill pushed mana into her own mind-influencing ability, flooding it along the pathway that Babu had established into the grocery store. Without the support of his connection, she would never have been able to extend her own mana so far. "Get your mouth unclamped from whatever diseased spunk-nozzle you have in there that you think is going to save you, and use the shriveled remains of your brain! There is a Godzilla-sized monster coming. Stop pissing me off and get everyone out here, now!"

There was a beat of silence at the end of her tirade as the spell waited to make sure she was done before completing with a final surge of magic. Jill's vision wobbled, and she clamped her eyes shut for a moment to recover. She had spent an entire thousand mana trying to bend the other woman to her will. A shrill scream sounded in Jill's ears—the tortured sound of someone whose own brain was rebelling against them.

"She just passed out," Babu said, staring at Jill with wide eyes. "I lost the connection."

Alice Finch defeated.
Your contribution: 100%
11,000 Experience Gained.

Killing other sapients is not recommended.

Jill froze, slamming a lid on her own emotions. Too late she remembered the last part of her power: it was harmless to those neutral to her, but true enemies took damage. She didn't know how the system knew one from the other, but the woman who had shot her had been an enemy. And she had died for it.

"Don't worry about it," Jill said, making the snap decision to not tell him about what his own power had let her do. At least not now. Her hands shook on the steering wheel, so she gripped harder to stop them. "We need to get these people out, whether they want it or not. I'd bet my morning coffee that all the scared people are being held against their will anyways. Do your mind virus thing."

Babu nodded, and his mana flashed out. He shivered. "I need to recharge for a little while after that."

Jill nodded. She turned Bertha, bringing the truck closer to the grocery store, ready to pick up those who left. The occasional bullet still smacked into the armor, but fewer than had been just a minute earlier. Bertha's headlights swept over the front of the store, revealing a line of perforated bodies lying in a pool of blood. Not all were adults.

"Oh, my God," Babu said. "I know him. Oh, my God, and that's his mom, I—" he gagged and ran to the back of the cab. He collapsed to his knees and vomited into the corner by the door, only staying upright because of hands braced against the wall.

Jill's stomach clenched at the smell, but she held it down.

"Ms. MacLeod," Aman said. His voice had a sharp edge to it now, a hint of danger that Jill hadn't heard from him before. "I think we should keep these people separated. Until we sort out who is responsible for this." He unbuckled from his seat and walked back, then kneeled down next to his son. He whispered something in Babu's ear. Jill didn't try to listen in.

Jill flexed her Customization ability and walled off a quarter of the top floor of the Cargo Nexus, with only a single lockable door between it and the rest of the module. She filled it with the same seating she was giving everyone else.

"Done. I'll fill Ras in on the plan before I open the doors," Jill said. She turned in her seat to look at them. Babu, who had nothing but dry heaves left, was standing with Aman's help. She evaporated the vomit into a burst of golden light.

"Justice is going to have to wait for another day," she said, mentally including the price she'd have to pay as well. "For now, we have a mission: save who we can and sort out the monsters tomorrow."

CHAPTER 43

NEW DIMENSIONS

I can't see shit," Jill said, fifteen minutes of weaving through the city later, as they pulled away from an abandoned sporting goods store. The potential pickup site had been eerily empty, with no signs of people—or monsters—having ever been there. It was the second site in a row that had been abandoned.

She leaned forward in her seat as if being two feet closer to the windshield would let her eyes pierce the torrential rain pouring down on them. The clouds above had grown thicker and blacker, and even the lightning flashes were dimmed by their presence. The wind blew in fits and starts: calm one moment and strong enough to push a wall of water sideways the next.

None of the weather was strong enough to inconvenience Bertha, but the truck's driver was another story. Jill pulled the wheel over the instant the headlights revealed a broken-down pickup truck ahead of them, but they were going too fast. Bertha just clipped the pickup's corner, sending a jolt through the big rig, and the pickup spun away, crumpled.

Babu, still standing between the seats, poked Jill's shoulder. His mana flooded through the touch and into Jill's eyes. There was a flash of pain, and then her vision shifted. Color fled, but the black-and-white sight that remained pierced through the darkness as if it were a bright day.

"Balltwist," Jill said, rubbing her stinging eyes. "Warn a girl before you shove shit into her, will you?"

Aman breathed out an exasperated sigh, and Jill laughed.

"Did the spell work?" Babu asked. "I just got it now, don'tcha know."

"Yeah, it did," Jill said, "thanks." She twitched the wheel and Bertha shifted sideways, splattering an unfortunate monsterized cockroach that had wandered onto the road. They took the next left turn, heading north, and accelerated.

"There are people ahead," Babu said, "scared, but no panic. Probably not fighting?"

"That's the Walmart," Aman said, consulting his atlas.

Bertha thundered into the parking lot; Jill had ignored the landscaping in favor of reaching the front doors faster. They skidded to a stop, and out leapt Ras and his team to secure a path to the building. This time there was no argument when Babu contacted those inside, and the refugees came pouring out, pushing shopping carts overflowing with goods. More than one had boxes of ammo stacked under semi-automatic rifles, and many of the rest had packaged food.

"Good shit," Jill said, eyeing the supplies. She sent her magic back through Bertha and extended a ramp to the ground so that the carts could get inside more easily. "Hey, Ras!" she projected to the swordsman, who was close enough to Bertha to still hear her. "I've got a mission for you."

"What do you need?" Ras said back. The sound of torrential rain thundered through the magic connection.

"This Walmart has got to have coffee. I need all of it."

There was a pause. "Do we have time?"

"It's going to take all these people a while to get in anyways!"

Ras sighed. The sound was somehow still perfectly audible despite the rain. "I'm on it."

"Fuck yeah!" said Jill, pumping her fist just a bit in celebration. "Thanks, Ras." With a grin on her face, she turned to Babu and Aman. The younger man was turning the radio's reception dial, searching the magical airwaves for anyone who might be talking. Aman was sketching in a small notebook, making designs for Bertha's interior.

"I've got a spare class point," Jill said, getting their attention. "Ideas for spending it?"

"Command capacity maybe?" Babu said, still fiddling with the radio. "We don't really know what a 'control station' is. And I could sit down."

Jill shook her head. "Seats aren't urgent. A control station," she paused, thinking of all the powers that she could use on Bertha and no one else could. "Well, I guess it could be a big deal. But it could also not."

"Your limitation right now is intelligence," Aman said.

"Suck on my truck nuts, buddy!" Jill said. She knew what he really meant, but the thought of coffee had her in a joking mood. "Yeah, I need some sort of . . . what, monster radar?"

Aman shrugged. "If that is possible, yes. Some way to share your talking power is essential as well."

"Or you could get me a seat, and I would relay commands," Babu said, waggling his eyebrows.

"I'll think about it," Jill said. She had the feeling that everything they said was true, but also that her lone point would be better spent on more armor or speed—something that could tip the balance in their favor, should the worst happen.

"Everyone's inside," Ras said to her through the still-open connection. "And I've got an aisle's worth of coffee for you, plus a few pots that someone is going to need to fix up with magic."

"If you were my type I'd kiss you," Jill said back. "Get that black gold tucked away somewhere safe." She checked the map: the next stop was only a mile away. "We're moving out." She withdrew her mana, letting the communication power fade away, and put Bertha back into motion.

The three of them in the cab lapsed into silence. Jill's excitement faded, and was replaced by wary tension. It grew along with the storm as Bertha roared down deserted streets to the next pickup point: a shopping mall in the center of Billings. Again, there were few monsters in their path; the guns fired only sporadically, and little experience flowed into her.

The next stop was their smoothest yet. Babu's now-practiced announcement of the coming calamity roused the mall's occupants out with little fuss, and Ras's team protected and escorted them inside. A score of Sangita's organizers, pushing looted shopping carts, ran into the mall, escorted by Ras and his volunteers. They came back out minutes later with everything from food to blankets to big-screen TVs. Jill didn't know whether to smack whoever had got that upside the head for having their priorities scrambled or to ask for one and integrate it into the Habitation Module.

"Why do I feel like this can't last?" Aman asked. The map in Jill's vision sharpened as he renewed his spell.

A blast of lightning hit the lightning rod atop the mall's roof, setting it on fire. Whatever engineering specification it had been built for was no match for the power of the unnatural storm.

"Because you're not an idiot," Jill said. "This long without monsters? It's like the calm before the storm, only with teeth instead of water."

But as they turned east, now at the north end of their zig-zag path through the city, no sudden eruptions of mutated insects blocked their path. Not every potential gathering point had refugees, and not every group came willingly, but an hour later Bertha had picked up hundreds more people. The wind was no longer fitful but a hurricane strong enough to push even Bertha.

"Can any—hear—?" came a crackling voice out of the chrome-plated radio. "—elp us!"

Babu picked up the handset. "We can hear you!" he said into it. "Where are you?"

"—igh schoo—! They're in the bui—" the voice cut off.

"It must be the high school," Aman said. "We'll have to change our route."

Babu's mana reached out in tendrils to search ahead of them. "There's a lot of panic in that direction. I think you're right!"

"Always the damn schools under attack," Jill said under her breath. "Where do I go?"

Aman concentrated on his map. In Jill's vision, the route flickered through a dozen configurations, each trying to get them to the school in the shortest amount of time. The brown line stabilized with a turn just twenty feet ahead. Jill cranked the wheel over—flicking on the Torque Converter as she did just in case—and Bertha slid around the bend, side-swiping a sedan on the far side. The small car spun away, half crushed by even an indirect hit.

Bertha surged down Grand Ave. asphalt cracking behind her. "Shit!" Jill said, as a sudden clattering on the armored glass nearly made her swerve, but it had just been a burst of hail.

One of the back turrets started firing, first in bursts and then in a long, drawn-out rattle. None of the other guns joined, and no kill notifications popped into Jill's vision. A flicker of pain slipped through Jill's bond to Bertha: a slice on her top side that scored armor.

Jill juked Bertha side to side on the five-lane road and looked at the side mirrors, but couldn't see anything chasing them. "Hey!" she projected to the firing turret, including Babu and Aman in the communication. "What just hit us?"

The ear-splitting sound of a 50-caliber machine gun firing at close range echoed back through her mana. "In the air!" came a panicked teenage girl's voice. "Up in the clouds, there are dozens of flying . . . things! I think they're swarming us!"

"Fuck," Jill said. She widened the communication net to include the other turrets. "Look up!" she said to them all. "Incoming from above!" She looked again out the window and in the mirrors, but even with her magical night vision, she couldn't see any creatures in the black, storm-covered sky.

She kept juking Bertha from one lane to another, slowing their progress but hopefully making the truck a harder target for any diving creature. "I still don't see—" she started to say to herself, but she was interrupted.

"There!" cried the teenage girl, and Jill saw it.

Riding the hail and rain was a grotesque combination of bat and scorpion, with its rear legs replaced by a wicked muscular tail topped with a stinger. Its body was a mottled dark green and nearly impossible to see in the gloom; Jill had a moment of pure respect for the teen in the back who had spotted it through the clouds.

That young woman was still the only one firing, her bullets a blazing trail converging on the diving monster. Just as the rounds connected though, the creature faded, becoming no more than a blurred outline, and the bullets passed through it with no effect. The creature danced around the bullets, and landed directly on the turret itself so it couldn't be shot. Jill heard a scream as the tail whipped down, and she felt the sting as it connected. The armor held, and whatever fluid the monster tried to inject splashed harmlessly off.

Jill activated the eel paint and electric shocks coursed through the creature. It fled, shrieking, back up into the storm. A few of the other heavy machine guns opened fire at it, but again it faded from reality before they could tear it apart.

Displacer Chiropteracore, Level 35
Status: Out of This World

Jill pushed her mana into her repair power and closed the gouge in the turret's armor. "Tits," she muttered, twitching the wheel to dodge another broken-down car. Her eyes needed to be on the road, not glued to the side mirrors watching for monsters. "You okay back there?" Jill asked the young woman. She sunk her foot all the way down on the accelerator, pushing the truck faster.

"Y-yeah," came back a shaky reply.

"The other gunners can hear you," Jill said. "You can see, so call the shots."

"But none of the bullets are hitting!"

"Try the mana-thief rounds," Babu said. "The disappearance must take mana!"

The gunners listened. That part of Jill connected to the predatory turrets turned from bloodthirsty to something altogether more crafty; from a dog going for the throat to a cat sneaking into a bird's nest.

Before she found out if the magic-stealing rounds would be of any use, they were at the high school. The building was barely standing; its three stories of brick were reduced in places to two by a collapsed roof. The brown lawn by the road was crawling with monsters. Those inside still held the front doors, but the windows had been overwhelmed into shattered holes through which monstrous insects swarmed.

Jill pulled on the horn and Bertha roared; the blast swept out ahead of the truck to wipe the lawn clean. None of the low-level monsters survived the hit, and experience flowed into Jill. She slammed on the brakes but held the wheel steady, bringing Bertha to a skidding stop that threw up a cloud of dirt.

Ras and crew jumped out, this time directly into combat. Mana flashed in the mirrors, and sparks of power of every color leapt out to kill the creatures that would hunt people.

"We're here!" Babu said into the radio handset. At the same time, his mana reached out, ready to connect to people and spread the order to evacuate. But those defending the school were fleeing towards Bertha before it even reached them. There was no response over the radio—just the crackling static of a dead channel.

"Three coming in from the left!" the teen gunner said, and the turrets opened up, firing into the sky. The tearing noise of Blossom going full out echoed through the cab. Jill closed her eyes, trying to sense through magic what she couldn't see in the mirrors. Hungry voids in Bertha's magic shot out of the guns; the converging streams of bullets found monstrous mana and drank it in, even if they couldn't physically touch the fliers. The creatures dipped and weaved, throwing off most of the shots, but eventually their mana ran out as it was sucked away. First one, then another of the chiropteracores died.

> Displacer Chiropteracore (x2) defeated.
> Your contribution: 25.2%
> 1789 Experience Gained!
> You are now Level 45!

But the first two had dodged so well, and taken so much time to kill, that the third had completed its dive. "They just got Jim!" the teenage gunner yelled into Jill's mind. "I can't hit it without hitting him!"

"What do you mean they—" Jill's voice cut off as the top half of a human body smashed into the hood. The man—Jim, she presumed—had been pierced through a dozen times, the holes sizzling and growing before Jill's eyes, before being bitten in half. His torso slid off of Bertha and fell into the dirt even as it dissolved.

"Fuck!" Jill yelled at the same time Babu screamed and fell away from the window. Aman didn't flinch, but his hands balled into fists and he took a deep, hard breath.

"More are coming!" cried another gunner, a man this time.

Jill's mind went into overdrive; horrific images of flying scorpions killing everyone outside, of Ras's torn apart body slamming into the windshield next, flashed through her mind. She shoved all that away. Their problem wasn't firepower. Even with the need to drain mana first, Bertha's turrets had more than enough raw damage to kill the chiropteracores by the dozen. But the creatures were so stealthy, and so agile, that the gunners just couldn't hit them. Jill tapped into a part of her mana-enhanced mind, the encyclopedic knowledge of every class upgrade she had taken and every power still available, and searched at breakneck speed for a solution. She found it.

> Gunner Enhancement:
> Boosted Reflexes (0/3): All gunners' nervous systems are modified to have 28% decreased response time.

Gasps and screams rang out in Jill's mind as mana spiked from the turrets' seats and into the gunners themselves. The upgrade's next evolution appeared in her vision.

> Gunner Enhancement:
> Linked Senses (1/3): All gunners gain an instinctive knowledge of what all other gunners are seeing. All Perception Class abilities are shared between gunners, with the effects scaled by the level difference between donor and recipient.

Jill purchased that as well, and Bertha's mana dipped. Power radiated from one turret to the next as a web of information flowed from person to person. The sounds of vomiting flowed over the communication power, and two of the turrets stopped firing entirely, their gunners incapacitated by the sudden change to their perception.

The third and final gunner enhancement appeared in Jill's sight, but she lacked the class point to take it.

> Gunner Enhancement:
> Hive Mind (2/3): Forms a non-sapients hive mind from the mental contribution of all gunners, allowing for the optimization of target selection and firing patterns. All Class abilities are shared between gunners, with the effects scaled by the level difference between donor and recipient.

Even without that power, the fight shifted. What had been wild gunfire, guided only by the tracer bullets of the one person who could see through the clouds, became disciplined and precise. "I can see them! More coming from behind us!" came the voice of the gym teacher. Five turrets swiveled, and this time all of them could aim. Waves of chiropteracores dove in turn, but with their defenses finally negated, they proved easy prey.

> Displacer Chiropteracore (x19) defeated.
> Your contribution: 25.2%
> 16,758 Experience Gained!

"Eat shit!" Mia yelled, and she was answered with cheers.

"It's not over," Babu said, his face ashen. He extended his communication net to Jill.

"—sters are in the school, coming in from the other side," Ras said, voice stressed. "I'm taking half of my team in to deal with them and get people out."

"Do it," Jill said after a moment's thought. "Babu, you too."

Aman turned an angry face towards her, and he opened his mouth to say something, but Jill cut him off. "Both of them are higher level than these bugs, and we can't move until that building is clear," she said, as she peeled back the armor covering the driver's side door. She popped it open and was hit by a blast of water and wind.

"Dad, I've got this," Babu shouted at Aman over the storm. He leapt out the door without waiting for a reply and ran towards the school. Jill sealed the door behind him.

"Sitting here in safety while someone else orders my boys to their possible deaths," Aman said, his voice trailing off. "I feel . . . powerless. I just want them safe."

Jill kept a firm lid on the mental image of Jim's torn-apart body. "Yeah, me too. But they're the ones with magic that kills monsters," she said. "I get them where they need to be to save people and give them an armored fuck-everything-up-with-bullets battle truck to fall back to if things get rough." As she said the words, she realized they felt right. She might have hidden in the cab before, unable to do anything about the raptors that had clawed their way into Bertha, but that didn't mean she was weak. It just meant she had another role to play. "You say you feel powerless. What are you going to do about it?"

Aman's gaze dropped to his lap, where the map and his sketch notebook lay. "You ever play a tower defense game?" he asked.

Jill blinked. "A what?"

"Babu introduced me to them," he said, leaning back and unclenching just a bit. "I think . . . some of the powers the system has shown me could help your truck be even greater. But I need levels to get them."

Jill reached out and punched him on the shoulder.

"That's the story of the whole vomit-chugging day, isn't it?"

They lapsed into silence. The turrets blasted into the air, cutting down the few chiropteracores that still remained, and Ras's volunteers held the line against any insects unfortunate enough to show their carapaced heads. Refugees still surged from the school and into Bertha; the braver of them joined the line to hold back the monsters. And inside the cab, Jill and Aman waited for Ras and Babu to come back.

CHAPTER 44

KITCHEN APPLIANCES GO BRRRR

Jill wasn't very good at waiting.

"So," she said, "think someone in the back would bring us coffee?"

Aman had been looking out the window, eyes fixed after Babu and Ras. He frowned at Jill's words and turned to her. "Really, Ms. MacLeod?"

"What?" Jill asked. "The more tired I am the more likely I am to make mistakes, and there's no guarantee we're going to get another quiet moment." The turrets roared to life, vibrating the cab, and the death notices for another trio of flying creatures popped into Jill's vision. "You know, sort of quiet."

An explosion of mana in the school momentarily lit the clouds from underneath; a mana conflagration that blasted light from every window like so many unfocused searchlights. The structure shuddered, and more of the top floor collapsed downwards, throwing up a cloud of dust. When it cleared, the building was still standing, but for how long Jill couldn't tell.

Aman's hands were clenched into tight fists. He blew out a breath. "I do not want any coffee right now."

Jill shrugged. "Suit yourself." She reached back into the trailer with her mana, searching for Karen.

She found the woman in the medical module. Jill opened her communication power and the sounds of an emergency room poured back: calls for supplies or to move people away blending into a constant stream of life-saving labor.

"Hey, uh, Karen?" Jill asked, feeling a bit chagrined. "Could you find someone not doing anything important?"

"No!" There was a ripping sound like cloth being torn, and a man groaned in pain nearby.

"Right, sorry about that!" Jill said. She withdrew that thread of mana and searched through the trailer for someone more suitable. She found her target in line for a turn in the turrets: one of Babu's cousins, the one who had run off to save her best friend.

"Hey, Nihal," Jill said, giving herself a mental high-five for remembering the young woman's name.

"Jill!" Nihal said, startled. "I mean Ms. MacLeod. Do you need something?"

"I am going to die without coffee."

"Can it wait? I'm about to shoot things, and Jake's up by three!"

"I'll bully Mia into giving you a turn on Blossom if you manage to make me some goddamn coffee. Two cups! The better it is, the longer you get."

"Done!" came the instant reply, and the sounds of running and indignant shouting filled Jill's mind. A shrill whistle blast sounded out, followed by a shouted "No running young lady!" Jill cut the connection, content that her bribe had been enough.

"Jill, look!!" Aman said in a panic, reaching out to grab her arm.

Jill twitched and, with a twist of her wrist, knocked his hand off of her. Only then did she look to the school.

A gigantic insectile limb, twenty feet long, had burst from the wreckage of the top floor, bright green and covered in hooks and spines. Jill squinted at it and prodded the system, hoping the partial view of the monster was enough to determine how much of a threat it really was.

Major Mantis, Level 37
Status: None

Jill reached magic out to the turrets in a flash. "Top of the school! Fire!" Jill projected to them. And they answered. First one, then another gun swiveled to fire; their 50-caliber rounds shattered carapace. And then Blossom joined in, her stream of death sawing the limb apart. It crashed down, a stream of purple ichor sprayed into the air behind it, and no more of the insect emerged.

"That's fucking right, you better hide!" Jill said, nodding in satisfaction.

"Do they need reinforcements?" Aman asked, half standing in his seat. He took another deep breath and forced himself back down.

"Nah, they'll tear that crusty crap-licker to pieces. It's big," Jill said, "but compared to Babu and Ras combined it isn't high level. And it can't run from Ras's sword. If it gets outside, we'll blow it to pieces with the guns. I'm not worried."

Still, she made a point to check her surroundings, making sure that she had somewhere to drive if something truly nasty reared its head. She grimaced at what she saw: while Bertha had a clean getaway, the crowd of people still shoving their way out of the school, and those remaining of Ras's crew protecting them, would be stranded. And anything powerful enough to chase Bertha away wouldn't have any problem making a meal out of them all.

Jill searched her mind, but she couldn't think of anything she could actually do to make the appearance of a killer monster less likely. She crushed her worries away. They wouldn't do her any good.

Integrating add-on to "Bertha" Habitation Module.

Level 2 Coffee Service detected.

This Module has replication capabilities. Duplicate Coffee Maker in all lounge areas?

Jill's eyebrows raised. "Shit, your niece really wants to fire Blossom," she said, accepting the prompt. A slight drain of Bertha's mana accompanied the scent of roasting coffee beans through her soulbond, and Jill smiled.

Aman chuckled, but it was strained. "Everyone wants to fire it."

Another explosion rocked the school, and the mantis leapt into the air in a streak of green speed, its wings a shining multicolored blur to keep it aloft. The wind from its flight blasted the ground, adding an extra layer to the storm and making those outside stagger. It bore more wounds than just a missing leg: deep slashes had severed one antenna, its forelegs hung in useless tatters, and it leaked from another dozen deep wounds.

Now that Ras and Babu had flushed the creature into the open, Jill expected it to be destroyed in moments. But only Blossom and two other turrets fired; the other four turrets were silent. Jill straightened in her seat and expanded her awareness, and she felt the problem: her gunners were swapping. Only half of them, but one of those staying in was on the wrong side of Bertha to shoot at the mantis.

"I need a command crew," Jill muttered to herself, lamenting the lack of coordination she had with all of the volunteers in the trailer. But she still wasn't worried, not at something below her level.

"Woah," Nihal said from behind Jill. The young woman had gotten into the cab, unnoticed in the commotion. She held two steaming mugs of coffee in her hands and stared, wide-eyed, out the window at the enormous monster hanging in mid-air. Jill reached out and took both mugs; one she put on the dashboard, the other she held up under her nose, taking a deep inhale.

The creature was still alive, but Blossom and two guns were more than enough to blast gaping, oozing holes in it. It opened its mouth, spreading all four palps wide, and a glowing orb of toxic mana congealed there, building a corrosive power that it aimed downwards at the school.

But before the monster could launch its attack, a lance of Babu's mana shot up from below. The creature froze for only an instant before it shook off the enchantment, but that moment was enough: the power in its mouth, suddenly uncontrolled, exploded.

Major Mantis defeated.
Your contribution: 17%
259 Experience Gained!

Rain mixed with vaporized ichor as the mantis, half its head gone, fell. A flashing barrier of blades—courtesy of Ras—rose up to meet it, shredding the monster before its landing could damage the school even further and coating the entire area in a thick layer of insectile monster guts.

Jill took a long, loud slurp of her coffee. "See? Nothing to worry about," she said.

Aman stood. "I need to see. . . ," his voice trailed off, and he gestured to the back. "Will you be alright navigating?"

"Go see your boys," Jill said, waving the mug. "I'm always alright driving, but keep that spell of yours refreshed." She took another, more discerning sip. "Damn, this is fan-fucking-tastic coffee!"

"So, I get to fire the big gun?" Nihal asked, eyes bright with hope. She stood to the side as Aman passed her, then slid into the now-vacant passenger seat.

"Hey, Mia," Jill projected to the heavy gunner, looping Nihal in so she could hear, "nice shooting! I think we're in the clear, at least for now. You want to come up front for some coffee? I've got a replacement all lined up for you to keep Blossom going."

"Oh. My. God," Mia said back, exhaustion in her voice. "You're the damn best Jill. I'll be right there!" Jill cut the connection.

"Wait," Nihal said, eyes narrowed. "You're giving her the coffee I made. So, you just sit there, get coffee and a thanks. For what? Telling me to do stuff?"

"Welcome to business, kid," Jill said, raising the cup in a mock salute.

"I feel like I'm being taken advantage of," Nihal said, but she sounded more admiring than upset.

"And yet you get to fire Blossom," Jill said. She made a shooing motion with the coffee mug. "Go. Shoot anything that threatens us, get some XP, have fun. Follow orders though! No friendly fire!"

Nihal brightened, leapt out of the seat, and took off at a run.

In her head, Jill wished her luck but doubted the teen would get that much target practice in the next few minutes. The surge of monsters outside seemed to be over. She willed her seat to slide back, kicked her feet up onto the dash, and clutched her coffee in both hands, enjoying the moment of quiet.

She woke to Mia shoving her shoulder. "Hey, no sleeping on the job!" The younger woman was in the passenger seat, her own cup drained.

Jill blinked, and the confusion of sleep faded in an instant. A glance at the mirrors showed just a trickle of people running into Bertha; everyone here still living would be onboard in moments.

"Right," Jill said, swinging her feet back to the floor. She was still holding her coffee, so she chugged the remainder in one long pull. It was still warm, almost hot: she couldn't have been asleep for more than a few minutes. In one corner of her vision was a trio of system notifications for monster kills, each detailing her take of the experience. She dismissed them without reading them; if she had leveled, she would have known.

The route ahead still floated in her vision. "Bollocks," Jill muttered, scowling at it. The next stop was their most dangerous, next to the City Hall. Mere blocks from where she had been shot and nearly killed.

The hatch to the trailer opened, and Aman, Babu, and Ras walked through. The two younger men were perfectly clean; Babu had a cleaning spell, after all.

"That's everyone evacuated and inside," Ras said.

Jill tossed him the coffee mug, cracked her knuckles, and put Bertha into motion. The wheels spun for just a moment as they slipped on ichor. A bit of mana had them clean and able to grip again; the gore evaporated off in a puff of gold.

"The next stop is—" Aman said, but Jill cut him off.

"Yup: murder central," she said. "Mia, thanks for being a creeper and watching me sleep, but I need your firepower up top."

Mia bounced to her feet. "Thanks for the coffee," she said. She also threw her mug to Ras, then sauntered past the three men, throwing Babu a wink as she went.

Aman slid back into the passenger seat and pulled out his map. Babu and Ras stood behind them, heads together and talking to each other in quiet, but intense, tones.

The guns fired in bursts, punctuations of floor-shaking sound over muted road noise, as they left the area that they had cleared behind. Jill bit her lip, her pulse accelerating as they neared their destination, but her hands were steady as she whipped the steering wheel around, pulling Bertha around the final corner.

Down the street was the First Interstate Building: a column of concrete and glass stretching twenty stories tall. Broken windows and scarred concrete on the bottom three stories told the story of combat, but the remaining height of the building was pristine, a modest monument to yesterday's world order.

The street was covered in monsters; a parade of mutated animals trotted towards City Hall, drawn by the mana lure. Most were low level, and when Bertha's guns opened fire the bullets ripped through them, killing them by the score.

"Hold fire!" Jill projected to the gunners. The scattering monsters were a resource rather than a threat, but the last thing she wanted was to attract the unwanted attention of their harvester. She slowed Bertha, letting the monsters pull ahead as they charged away. In just a few seconds, the street was clear.

Babu's mana stretched out to the tower, and he whistled. "There must be two thousand people in there!" he said. "They feel," he swallowed, "desperate."

Jill grimaced; she could fit them in, but that many people would take a long time to load.

Parked in front of the office tower were four police cruisers, their lights flashing. Jill narrowed her eyes at them, expecting bullets to slam into the windshield at any moment, but no gunfire came her way: the cars were abandoned. She threaded Bertha through a gap between them, onto the sidewalk, and slammed on the brakes. The truck screeched to a halt, pavement cracking under the force of her tires.

Barely a second after the truck stopped, people came boiling out of the tower, waving their arms at Jill to try and get her attention. Jill willed the rear doors to open, and the volunteers sprang out, ready to defend if any of the mind-controlled monsters turned their way.

"Get your pasty asses inside!" Jill projected to all of the fleeing people within range of her Captain Speaking power, hoping that they would obey and that those following behind them would get the message. She snapped the connection shut, not caring what any of them had to say, and closed her eyes. Her attention was wholly focused on the mana around them, and her senses strained to their limit. The air above them was still filled with streamers of allure reaching out from the city center to draw monsters in, and in the distance, she could feel the tide of monsters flowing around Bertha's position like a school of fish avoiding a shark.

And then she felt it. That same slimy, burrowing, hungry magic that had tortured her; a black hole with grasping limbs. She could feel its presence like a weight in her senses, but not where exactly it was.

"Motherfucker," Jill said, knuckles clenching the wheel. "He's here."

"I'm disappointed," a voice brimming with arrogance wormed its way into Jill's mind. "I thought you had learned your lesson. These people belong to me, and you don't steal what's—"

His voice cut off as Blossom opened fire. A ripping tear of mana-thief chain gun bullets flashed across the street and covered the office building opposite in a hail of explosions. Mia had held nothing back: she activated all of her own mana-intensive class powers in one burst. The rounds multiplied as they flew, one becoming two becoming four, tearing through concrete as if it wasn't even there, and exploding in spheres of annihilation.

Black mana flowed towards Bertha as bullets found their mark; the stolen power faded to gray as it lost its corruptive nature. Within seconds the office building was an unrecognizable and structurally unstable mess. A pulse of rage washed over Jill's mana senses as the assassin activated his escape ability and sank into the earth to escape the onslaught. But Jill could still feel his presence. He hadn't run far.

"Hey, boys?" Jill said. "Be careful, but fuck him up."

CHAPTER 45

TRICKS AND TRAPS

Dark magic pulsed to Jill's left, so she peeled back the armor on her right, over the passenger side door, allowing it to open. Ras and Babu jumped out and ran around Bertha's nose, Ras leading the way with his sword drawn. Pale mana swirled around Babu as he began casting. They each planted their feet to activate a movement ability, ready to spring forward.

"No!" Jill yelled as lines of black mana tore across her vision. The assassin's bullets punched through Babu and Ras as if they weren't even there. He shot six times, three alternating rounds for each man. Exaggerated sprays of blood burst out behind them as the two collapsed to the ground.

"What?" Aman said, blinking in confusion at the sight before his eyes.

Cracks in reality, the leftover tracks from the bullets, connected his sons' still-twitching bodies to the roof of a building one block away where a figure in black stood, gun raised and face smug. He looked into Jill's horrified eyes, and his smile grew wider, hungrier. Mia opened fire, Blossom roaring in rage, and was joined by the other turrets; a broadside of machine guns was ready to cut the man to pieces.

The assassin shifted his attention from Jill to the incoming threat and raised a floating disc of shadows, which caught the bullets in its inky grasp. But even though the bullets hadn't struck him, they still gouged into his magic, eating away at his mana. He grimaced but didn't run. Instead, he raised his gun; mana swirled around it, condensing into the weapon, and he aimed it carefully at Mia's turret.

Then Ras and Babu's bodies faded, their illusion spent to reveal Ras lunging at the assassin in a blur of motion, his sword whipping around in a glowing arc aimed at the monster's neck.

"Hold fire!" Jill projected to the gunners, slamming the words out at maximum volume to stop any friendly fire from hitting Ras. The bullets stopped in an instant, but Jill still felt Bertha's mana flowing into Blossom, as if the gun were still firing.

The assassin's shadow responded at the speed of thought, flowing up from the ground to interpose itself in the way of Ras's blow, and covering the mayor's body on all sides. An instant later the sword struck, its light diving into darkness. The blade flickered, then went out, its power spent. But the blow took its toll: shadows evaporated away like so much smoke upon the breeze.

"A good try," a slimy voice bloomed in Jill's mind, turning feral as it went on, "but not good enough!"

The shadows around the assassin unfurled like a malevolent octopus's arms, then whipped down at Ras one after the other. The air screeched at their passage, and Ras was forced back, his sword blocking blow after blow. One tendril slipped through the swordsman's defense and stabbed forward, carving a bloody line across Ras's face. Ras staggered back, head twisted by the force of the blow, and fell to one knee.

A vortex of mana formed around the assassin as he held his gun aloft, and deadly energies coalesced into the weapon. He pointed it at the downed Ras and pulled the trigger.

Babu flickered into existence in front of his brother, a savage grin on his face. "Surprise!" he said. In front of his outstretched hand was a floating mirror, just two inches in diameter, perfectly positioned in the path of the assassin's shot. The bullet, a black hole of condensed mana, struck the mirror, and the scene exploded into light.

"Shit!" Jill said, throwing up an arm to block the brilliance from blinding her. It was a long few seconds until the light faded enough for her to look again.

Ras stood tall in front of Babu, sword raised in front of him in a guard stance, blood running freely down his face. Now it was the enchanter on one knee, recovering from pushing so much of his mana into one spell. But his face was still triumphant.

"Take that, you hoser," Babu said.

The assassin retreated through the air, running from the brothers while encased in a ball of shadows. Bertha's heavy machine guns opened up on him; the bullets sliced off their toll of mana one impact at a time. He landed on another roof, and the shadows split apart to reveal his furious face.

A hole the size of a fist had been punched straight through his chest; his own attack was too powerful for him to block. Worms of shadows burrowed from one side of the hole to another, sewing the wound shut one wiggle at a time. Black ichor gushed out with each pulse of his exposed heart, staining his otherwise pristine suit.

"I'm going to——" he started to say, the words echoing in Jill's mind even from a hundred feet away, but he was silenced as a ray of power slammed into him.

Only a few dozen seconds had passed since the assassin and Ras had crossed shadow and sword, but in those seconds Mia hadn't been idle. Blossom released all of Bertha's mana that the chain gun had drunk in a single shot whose recoil rocked the massive truck back on its suspension. Jill felt a spike of pain as the turret broke its mounting; the heavy bearings had shattered with sudden force.

A second hole opened in the dark assassin's torso, this time in his stomach, and he staggered back, disbelief on his face. An incoherent, multi-toned scream of rage exploded in Jill's mind, and his eyes met Jill's for a fraction of a second. Then his shadows wrapped around him, and he sunk into the building below. This time, he went far enough away that Jill's senses couldn't detect him.

"Phase two!" Babu's voice boomed through the cab. Babu and Ras vanished, once again invisible.

Jill wished she had asked a few more questions of the brothers about their plan beforehand but trusted that if they hadn't told her, she didn't need to know. She cast her repair spell and remounted Blossom's turret with a squeal of shifting metal. Refugees from the tower kept pouring into Bertha in a solid stream of terrified people.

"Check in," Babu said.

"Health: two-thirds. Mana: one-half," Ras said.

"One-third mana. Full health," Mia snapped.

"Twenty percent mana for me," Babu said, voice grim. "Keep your eyes peeled. He can't be in good shape, but I don't think he's run for good."

There was a pause, a moment of relative peace, and the fleeting hope that Babu was wrong bloomed in Jill's mind. Every second that passed was more people safe inside of Bertha, and one more second closer to when they could run for good. A feeling of wrongness pulsed over her from above, and she gasped.

"Something big just changed," she said, craning her neck to look up out the window. "Something in the mana."

The monster lure still hung above them: mana blasted up from City Hall in a towering column that pierced the clouds and reached outwards beyond the city to draw in more prey. Streams of power dropped from that umbrella of magic, each connected to a monster that it had bewitched.

For a dozen blocks around Bertha, those connections were under attack as slick mana wrapped around them. Jill shuddered as gentle allure changed to rage and hunger as the assassin's mana infected the city-wide spell. Jill's mouth dropped open as the threads, jerking and writhing in protest, descended straight towards her. Like a spider wrapping its prey in silken death, the mayor twisted Billing's mana lure around Bertha.

"Diesel–electric turbodicks!" Jill said. She opened a connection to the gunners and everyone outside in range. "Watch out! We're about to get swarmed with—"

Pain shot through her as impacts cracked the armored windshield—horrible, piercing intent scrabbling to torture her yet again—and her communications spell collapsed. Jill threw herself out of her seat in a desperate bid to dodge any follow-up gunshots, her strength enough to snap the seat belt, but this time the pain had only been through her soulbond. The upgraded armor held.

"There he is!" Babu's voice said in Jill's ear, but from the floor, she couldn't see what was happening. Bertha's guns fired one after another, building up to a continuous roar of noise.

Experience flowed into Jill as monster kill notifications popped up in the corner of her vision, one after another. Her heart pounded in her chest, faster and faster, and black crept in at the edges of her vision. While she hadn't been shot, Bertha had. The rounds, hungry for mana and living flesh alike, were lodged in the windshield; their hooks cracked the crystalline armor as they began their spread. Their intent pulsed down Jill's soulbond, eager for torture, and phantom pain lanced through her.

"Jill!" Aman's voice sounded from far away. "Are you hit?"

"I'm going to wear that cuntless fuckcycle's skin as a coat!" Jill snarled, pushing mana into "Swampwater Vitality." The spell blasted out, circled her once, then dove back into her, drowning out the pain. She shoved herself to her feet and pointed at the bullets. "Those need to get the fuck out!" She pushed with both her Customization power and repair spell; bit by bit, the writhing, hooked, metallic threads of the bullets stopped their advance and were pushed back.

"On it," Aman said, sounding exactly like Ras. He put a hand on the windshield, and his warm mana flowed into Bertha. It was an intruder into Jill's domain and a weak one at that; she could have crushed it in an instant. But instead, she let it pass.

The windshield rippled as if a stone had been dropped into a pond, then a pillar of glass shot out of it with the bullets suspended in its tip.

"Nice one," Jill said, annoyed at herself for not thinking of doing the same. She severed the end of the pillar with a flex of her own power; it bounced off the hood and onto the ground, as Bertha's mana faded from the disconnected chunk of glass. The writhing bullets inside went still.

Jill glared at the windshield, then willed the armor of the cab to flow over it, so opaque metal blocked any light from getting through. The transparent glass made her a target, and she didn't need to see outside right now. Ras and Babu were fighting for their lives outside, but nothing she did was going to impact that battle. Not until everyone was inside, and she could drive again.

Bertha shuddered as something slammed into the truck—something big. The whole time Jill had been dealing with the murder bullets, the machine guns had been firing and killing monsters by the score. But something had gotten through. A moment later it died, and its experience pushed Jill over the edge to the next level.

> Galvanic Goat defeated.
> Your contribution: 25.2%
> 806 Experience Gained!

> You are now Level 46!

"Talk to me!" Jill projected to the gunners. The deafening sound of machine guns thundered back on the link, alongside not a little screaming.

"Our people retreated to the tower to protect the, uh, other people!" the gym teacher said. "But now they're trapped! There are too many monsters, and we can't see inside well enough!"

"Fuck!" Jill swore. She vaulted into the driver's seat, then peeled back just enough armor over the window so that she could see the side mirrors. Bertha's wheels surged to life, and the armored battering ram of a truck smashed backward into the office tower. Jill let up on the accelerator, leaving the truck partially embedded with some turrets firing inwards and others out.

"Kill anything trying to get in!" Jill said to the gunners. She sunk her senses into her Cargokinesis power, using the kinetic sense to get an impression of what was happening around her truck. It was a mess of a battle, with people and monsters tangled in a tight melee. Bullets flashed out from the turrets almost too fast for her to sense, firing not into the scrum but around it, killing monsters running in from the sides.

With that pressure relieved, it only took the defenders a few minutes to kill those monsters next to them—but not without losses. Too many of the motionless bodies on the ground, valid targets as lifeless objects for Cargokinesis, were human.

And then the monsters stopped coming. The assassin had called a horde down upon them, but only from a limited area, and they had run out. In just a few seconds the gunfire slackened, and constant thunder turned to just the occasional burst.

"Is that it?" Aman asked, sweat on his forehead. He had been pushing mana into Bertha for the last minute, repairing the minor damage that the monsters had inflicted.

"It can't be," Jill said. "That would be too—"

"Jill!" Babu's voice, rough and desperate, interrupted her. "It's a trap! He seeded the tower with—" His voice cut off.

"Seeded it with what?" Jill asked the air, wracking her mind for what Babu had meant.

Aman's face paled. "What if it's explosives?" he asked. "Can your truck take an entire tower coming down on it?"

Jill closed her eyes. There were hundreds of people waiting to get inside who had fought and bled for their chance at safety. But at this point, there were thousands inside of Bertha. She made up her mind and opened her eyes.

"We have to—ow. What the shit?" Her soulbond had erupted in pricks of pain coming from inside of Bertha and growing stronger by the moment. She sent her mana racing along the truck, sensing what was happening. What she found horrified her.

Bertha had erupted into violence, inside and out, as people turned on their neighbors with deadly intent. The pain she felt was from the swords, bullets, and spells that had missed people and hit the truck instead.

"Mind control," Jill whispered. "That rat pimp seeded the tower with mind-controlled people!"

Before Jill could think to do anything about it, the hatch to the trailer burst open. Two men and a woman ran through, police-issue AR-15s in their hands. They opened fire.

CHAPTER 46

OVERPOWERED

Terror gripped Jill's heart, and she dove towards the front of the cab as muzzle flashes gave her a stop-motion view of the intruders. Their faces were slack and devoid of any expression; dead eyes stared back at her, with neither malice nor fury in their gazes but only apathy. Their form with the guns was terrible and shots went spraying over the whole cab, tearing gouges and ricocheting in a deafening, clattering roar.

But at this close of a range, they couldn't miss. Bullets slapped into Jill in midair like hornet stings, striking the back of her legs and arms, raising welts. Between her levels and her biker leathers, the deadly, but mundane, semi-automatic rifle rounds couldn't pierce her.

She cleared the driver's seat and crashed to the ground, shocked that she wasn't horribly injured. An abbreviated form of her status flashed up in the corner of her vision, responding to her confusion.

HP: 922/990
MP: 1374/1470

Bertha's dashboard wasn't as tough as Jill's flesh. Acting as the backstop to the dodging target that was Jill, it was struck by dozens of rounds. Glass-covered dials, buttons, and switches shattered under the onslaught; the pain radiated through the soulbond to Jill worse than what she had experienced from getting shot herself. Debris rained down on her in her hiding position.

And then the onslaught was over; all of the rifles' ammunition was expended.

Aman, who had dropped to the floor as the shooting had started, scrambled into a kneeling stance and drew a Beretta M9 from a concealed holster at his hip. Blood poured over his face from a wound on his head, and a red stain bloomed on his chest. Despite not being the ambush's target, stray rounds and ricochets had still found their mark. He opened fire, putting four rapid shots in the chest of the intruder nearest him. They staggered, then kept mechanically reloading their rifle. Aman's next shots took them in the head.

"Fuuuuck!" Jill screamed as she leapt up from her hiding spot and charged forward at the woman, who was closest to finishing her reload. Jill lowered her right shoulder at the last moment, intending to tackle the woman to the ground, but she wasn't used to her new strength. The force of the impact knocked the woman back, cracking her ribs inwards under the blow. Her expression never changed as her ragdolling body hit the wall and slid limply to the ground.

> Tori Scott defeated.
> Your contribution: 95%
> 950 Experience Gained.

> Killing other sapients is not recommended.

Jill dismissed the kill notification without reading it. Squashing her horror in the thick of the action took barely a thought.

The last intruder had finished reloading. From point-blank range he pointed the gun at Jill, but before he could pull the trigger, she had grabbed the barrel of the gun. She ripped it from his grasp with one hand and punched him in the face with the other, pulling the blow at the last second and reducing her power to just a fraction of her full strength. It was still strong enough to shatter the man's nose and snap his head back. In his moment of disorientation, Jill grabbed his arm, twisting and pulling to bring him down to the ground in an effortless takedown.

One of her arms snaked around his neck, and she began to squeeze. He struggled, spasming with his whole body in an inept, but determined, attempt to break free. Despite being smaller and older than the man, Jill handled him with ease—the tyranny of levels in full force. The sounds of yelling, gunshots, and the pounding of feet on metal decking echoed into the cab from the trailer as Jill kept the pressure on, being careful not to squeeze too hard and break the man's neck. Ten long seconds passed, and he went limp.

Jill expected a notification to appear, but there was none.

"If you don't want them dead, give experience for a non-lethal take-down, you catpiss system!" Jill said, releasing her victim. "Thanks for the—" she said, turning her head to talk to Aman, but her thanks died on her lips.

Babu and Ras's father had collapsed against the wall of the cab, one hand pressed hard against a wound on his chest. His breaths came in ragged whistles, and his eyes were wide with shock.

Jill scrambled over to him. Up close she could see that he had been pierced more than once, and it was only his own system-fueled toughness that kept him alive now. The magic would close his wounds, but only if he didn't die from them first. And there was a lot of blood pooled underneath him already.

"Tell—" Aman coughed, blood welling up in his mouth, "Tell my fam-ily that—"

"Fuck that noise," Jill said, scooping him up into a princess carry and jarring him as little as she could in the process. "Tell them yourself. We have magic."

She ran to the hatch, Aman's head lolling on her shoulder, and reached it just in time for another woman to run through, a small paring knife in her hand. She looked at Jill without recognition but still lunged at her with the knife. Jill twisted sideways so that the knife hit her and not Aman. It turned harmlessly off of her flesh, unable to penetrate, and she headbutted the woman, who collapsed to the ground. Aman moaned at the sudden motion, which Jill took as a good sign.

She entered the cavernous space of the trailer in a smooth run, going straight for the Medbay. She was met with a wall of chaos: guns firing, people screaming, and flashes of mana painting the trailer in a strobe of differing colors as people used their new spells. A panicked mob ran up the ramps to the upper level, fleeing from the violence. Others wrestled with their neighbors in a fierce melee, only one side of which was making any sound at all.

A wave passed through the mind-controlled people as Jill ran through them. Some bit of their programming triggered on seeing her, and one after another, they switched targets, abandoning their previous victims to run straight at Jill.

"Balls!" Jill yelled, seeing one of them raise a handgun in her direction. She spun, curling herself down to both protect Aman with her body and also get the back of her head out of the firing line. Bullets pattered off her jacket and leather pants; the handgun rounds were not strong enough to even sting. She spun back around, only to find a score of people blocking her path, running towards her with blank faces.

She bent forward and turned sideways, trying to bowl her way through them without having Aman hit. The first person she hit fell backward, knocking two others down, but then she was surrounded. Some grabbed her, others punched and kicked—the worst used magic.

A burst of mana heralded a power activating, and a line of fire burnt across her cheek as a man caught her face with a stab of a knife. Jill kicked his knee, sending him crashing to the ground on a shattered leg. Another man jumped on her back, trying to drag her down. She elbowed him as hard as she could without thinking and felt his ribs cave under the blow. He slid off of her.

Joel Burke defeated.
Your contribution: 95%
4750 Experience Gained.

Killing other sapients is not recommended.

But still more came; a pressing mass of silent people. She was far, far, more powerful than any one of them, but she needed to get Aman through as fast as she could. She was sure that some of the wild strikes coming her way would hit her charge.

"Back off, you pus-licking corn worshippers!" Jill yelled, slamming everyone coming at her with her mind control power. Hundreds of points of mana blasted out of her, and those near her recoiled as if struck, but they didn't obey. Jill's mana attacked, but couldn't find purchase: some counter-ability was blocking her, just like had happened before.

Still, it was enough time to give Jill a bit of breathing room. She dove through her connection to Bertha, expanding her senses into the structure of the trailer itself, and forced it to change. Metal surged upwards underneath her, pressing her close enough to the ceiling that she had to crouch. It surged forward in a metal wave that flung people away from it and propelled her and Aman towards the Medbay.

Just before she reached safety, a crack rang out louder than any gun had a right to be. A lance of pain tore into Jill's left thigh.

HP: 477/990
MP: 852/1470

She willed the Medbay door to open just in time for her and Aman to be propelled through. She staggered into the reception area, bruised and bloody, and sealed the door behind her. Jill's entry drew startled gasps of concern from some of the dozen people waiting inside with minor wounds. They seemed otherwise oblivious to the chaos that had erupted in the rest of the truck.

"Oh, my Lord in heaven!" a man with a shining, mana-made arm said to her. He was sitting behind the tiny reception desk. "Are you alright?"

"Do I look alright?!" she said. "Get a doctor, now!" She pushed her will outwards with the words, projecting them to the whole Medbay. She struggled to take a step forward, still holding Aman in front of her, and looked down. There was a ragged hole in her leg: a real injury courtesy of someone who was truly dangerous, unlike most of the poor people who had been mindfucked into trying to kill her.

"Aw, fucknuggets, not again," she sighed, an instant before the pain hit. It wasn't even close to the worst that she'd had that day but, combined with her fatigue, was still strong enough to make her vision go black at the edges.

A loud bang behind her coincided with a dent appearing in the door to the trailer. A flex of her Cargokinesis senses revealed that everyone who had been chasing her had formed a crowd just outside the Medbay, standing pressed up against each other, oddly still. A burst of bullets sliced into the group, dropping one of the mind-controlled people. A third of them, those who had guns at all, turned in unison and fired back. It was an overwhelming amount of return fire that silenced the lone shooter who had stopped one of them from completing their mission. The rest of the people waited, except for one at the very front who swung a fist at the door in a mana-fueled blow.

Another bang—this time accompanied by shrieks, as the others waiting in the Medbay realized they were under attack—and another dent appeared in the door. Jill cast her repair spell. The dents smoothed out in an instant. Unless the automatons outside had some more powerful ability, they wouldn't be able to break down the hatch faster than she could repair it.

The doors to the surgical area burst open, and out ran a boy in his early teens, wearing pajamas featuring a pink-haired anime character, his hands covered in blood. He was followed by Karen and another woman, both of whom were also splattered with blood, pushing a gurney.

"Aman!" Karen said with a gasp.

The teen skidded to a stop in front of Jill and slapped a hand onto Aman's chest. Pink mana pulsed around them, swirling like flower blossoms in the wind. Aman's wounds didn't close, but he took a sudden deep, clear breath, as his ruined lungs healed on the inside. The teen swayed on his feet but didn't fall.

"Thank fuck," Jill said, her guts unclenching as some of her fear unwound. "Nice job, kid!"

"The name's Sam!" he said back, putting his index and middle finger over his eye in a peace sign. But he swayed on his feet, out of mana after pumping all of it into one life-saving spell.

The older women reached them, wheeling the gurney up in front of Jill. Twin flashes of mana burst out as both of them cast their own spells onto Aman. Jill slid him out of her arms and onto the waiting bed, gave the unconscious man a pat on the shoulder, then spun herself around and limped towards the exit. The wound in her leg was deep, but her regeneration had taken care of the bleeding. She would be fine.

"You've been shot!" Karen called out behind her. "Where are you going?"

"To finish this," Jill replied. She extended a hand, pressed it against the door, and began to warp Bertha's interior.

In the floor beneath the crowd, Jill pooled her mana and will. Over a dozen seconds it built, with ten thousand of Bertha's mana, alongside a hundred of her own, to guide it. She released it all in one surge. With a scream of bending metal that reverberated through the floor, walls of steel exploded upwards in the trailer, trapping Jill's victims inside like fish in a net. She clenched her fist, sealing the chamber at the top, then flung it sideways, pulling the whole prison cell away from the Medbay.

She probably could have done it without the dramatic gestures, but at the same time, some instinct told her that the close contact had helped.

"Holy shit!" one of the waiting people said, eyes wide. "What was that?!"

Jill nodded to herself. It was nice to be appreciated, but she had work to do.

She willed the door to open ahead of her, and she walked through. The bottom floor of the trailer was a wreck and strewn with bodies. But while she could hear the din of thousands of panicked people on the levels above, this one was quiet—the aftermath of a storm of violence.

"Hey!" she yelled and projected. "I'm right here you assholes, come take your shot!"

Movement caught her eye: a figure carrying a rifle in their hands, running away from her and towards the still-open loading doors. Jill scowled. Whoever they were, they weren't under the same spell that had doomed so many innocent people. She raised a hand, fingers bent inwards in a claw. A giant replica of her hand emerged from the floor, catching the person as they ran. Another sweeping gesture sequestered them away.

> Battle Trucker Advanced power discovered!
> Extreme Customization: The structural configuration of "Bertha" can be changed quickly and with high levels of detail. Doing so consumes Mana from Jill MacLeod and "Bertha" in proportion to the size and speed of any changes.

"Fuck you, 'discovered.' I've been doing that for hours," Jill muttered at the system. She then opened her communication power up to the whole truck. "Anyone that's wounded, get your ass down to the Medbay! Anyone not wounded, help them!"

A bullet whizzed past her head, coming from the cargo door: yet another expressionless person had climbed inside and shot at her. Jill wrapped the floor up and around him, trapping him in his own bubble. For all her snark at the system, having her new level of control codified did make it easier to use. She didn't have to envision every minute detail of how the changes had to happen. She just needed to activate it, funnel mana in, and envision the broad strokes of what she wanted to happen.

Jill stalked towards the door, her limp fading just a bit with every step. Behind her, at the ramp to the upper levels, people began to trickle down, obeying her instructions. Jill's attention was solely on the open cargo doors. She wouldn't let a moment of inattention cost the lives of anyone else depending on her.

She was almost to the doors when a blood-covered pair of people, leaning against each other for support, pulled themselves inside. Jill nearly imprisoned them but managed to stop herself. It was Babu and Ras. Ras was covered in cuts, his clothes nearly shredded, as if he had been dipped into a blender. Babu wasn't as overtly wounded, but his mana flickered and sputtered in a way that Jill had never seen before.

"Shit on a shingle, you two look awful!" Jill said. "Did you get the bastard?" As she asked the question, she knew that the answer was no. She hadn't gotten a kill notification.

"We have to go!" Babu said, instead of answering her. His voice was rough, exhausted. "Right now!" He tried to gesture for emphasis, but nearly fell over.

"The Boss Bison," Ras said. "We can see it, almost at the edge of the city. And it's grown."

A wave of weariness crashed down on Jill. They were out of time. Anyone they hadn't picked up would have to rescue themselves.

"Everyone outside," she projected out to her maximum range, "we're leaving! Get in the truck or get left behind!" To the exhausted brothers, she continued. "Close the doors when the last are inside, then get to the Medbay."

She tried to run back to the cab, but her leg was bothering her too much, so she repeated her wave of metal trick to push herself the fifty-five yards she needed to go. She did make an effort to not knock anyone else down and she crossed through the trailer and into the deserted cab. She slid into the bullet-ridden driver's seat, sighing in dissatisfaction at the bullet-ridden controls. She activated her repair spell and her vision swam; she was nearly out of mana. But she had enough to get the controls working again and to peel back the armor covering the windows to let her see.

Jill gasped. The city, so dark before, was bathed in a soft white light. She craned her head upwards. They were in the eye of the storm; walls of clouds circled the city in a vortex, with a clear center revealing the moon high above.

"Everyone is—go!" Babu's voice crackled in her ear, warbling in and out, his communication spell failing.

Jill's foot went down on the accelerator, and Bertha pulled away from the office tower. Whether the new mayor was hiding or not, she had no intention of getting close to him and letting him shoot her full of tentacle bullets. So she turned the truck west, away from the city center, at the next crossroad.

The moment Bertha rounded the corner, Jill saw the Boss Bison on the horizon. Ten stories tall at the shoulder, with lightning-crowned horns that rose upwards further still, it strode forward with blocks-long strides, not bothering to run but still moving at highway speed. It lowered its head and slammed horns-first into the settlement shield.

To Jill's shock, the weakened barrier repelled the first strike. It was full of holes that smaller monsters could slip through with ease, and so close to collapse that it was transparent, but somehow it was keeping the regional monster out.

Then the Boss Bison began to push. The tips of its horns deformed the barrier; twin dents of madly glowing magic intruded into the smooth, rounded surface of the shields. A pulse of mana greater than anything Jill had ever felt washed over her, and lightning flashed from one horn-tip to another, strike after strike arcing across the weakened barrier from the inside.

The shield failed.

CHAPTER 47

THE DOOM OF BILLINGS

The Boss Bison tossed its head and roared in triumph. Its way into the city was clear. Around its head, hundreds of tendrils of the mana lure circled, trying to take control of its mind to make it docile and ready for slaughter. Instead, they were pulled like water down a whirlpool, disappearing into a bottomless mana drain that they had no hope of pacifying.

"This place is so fucked," Jill muttered.

It took an experimental step into the settlement, fifty feet traveled with the swing of one leg. Its hoof caught a car, launching it tumbling into the air. The creature didn't seem to notice.

Settlement alert!
The barrier shield has been suppressed! Monsters can enter the settlement without resistance!
A monster has breached the barrier. Estimated level: Unavailable. Kill the monster to earn a bounty of 100 Billibucks!

Danger! Settlement has become Infested!
Monsters may now evolve inside the settlement! Monsters may now spawn inside the settlement!

Extreme Danger! A regional concentrator has invaded the settlement! Recommended course of action: flee.

The bison broke into a trot. Every step sent shakes through the ground; the localized earthquakes brought down shops and houses along its path. It thundered east, towards the city center. Jill was directly in its path and heading right for it.

"Nope!" Jill said. "Nope, nope, no fucking way!" She pulled hard-right on the wheel to turn Bertha away from the monster, not even waiting for a cross street. Bertha smashed straight through a ranch-style house in an explosion of plywood, drywall, and insulation in her hurry to be going anywhere but forward. Another right turn had them back on a suburban road, now driving away from the bison. She pushed the accelerator all the way down.

Jill's head whipped around as the hatch to the trailer opened, her mana primed to imprison whoever was coming to kill her within Bertha's walls. But it was just Ras and Babu who entered, Babu leaning on his brother for support.

"Shouldn't you two be in the Medbay?" Jill asked. She made a quick juke to avoid a parked car but didn't let up on the accelerator.

Babu stumbled into the passenger seat, his face pale; Ras grabbed onto the seat from behind. "Others needed treatment more," Ras said. His wounds had closed, but the scars had yet to fade.

Jill looked away from the brothers and back to the mirror: the bison filled the whole reflective surface, close enough now to Bertha that Jill could see nothing but it. "Must go faster," she muttered to herself, before raising her voice to the others. "You better hold on to something!" She invested her last class point into the Propulsion Module's Need for Speed power.

Need for Speed (2/5): Increases maximum speed by 70 km/h.
Current maximum speed: 390 km/h
Note: Acceleration and braking influenced by Soulbound Modular Vehicle "Bertha's" mass.

Excitement coursed through Jill's veins as her truck's engine grew in power. Bertha pulled ahead, widening its lead on the bison bit by bit.

The thunder of guns filled the cab, and tracer fire flashed in the side mirrors, heading towards the monster. The target was bigger than the proverbial barn door: every round hit. Glowing bullets disappeared into cable-thick fur, clipping off the occasional hair.

"Stop! Cease fire!" Jill projected to the gunners. "For fuck's sake, you wank-gnomes, don't make it mad!"

The guns' fire trailed off, but not before one stream of bullets bounced off the bison's eye. It blinked, then snorted; a hurricane of air from its nostrils swept the street in front of it, throwing up dirt and debris. It turned its head towards Bertha, horns starting to glow an electric blue.

"Hold on to your butts," Jill projected to the whole truck. She jerked the wheel, and Bertha's tires screamed against failing pavement as the truck dodged to the side.

Mana surged, lightning flashed, and the world to Bertha's side exploded in light and sound. Bertha lifted into the air and would have tumbled, if not for Jill's inhumanly fast application of the Torque Converter. Debris pelted the truck's side, scoring gouges in the armor. To Jill it was like a flash-bang grenade had gone off in her peripheral vision; without her levels and Bertha's armor she would have been deaf and blind, even if she had survived the blast. As it was, she just had to blink hard to clear the spots, and her ears stopped ringing in seconds.

Bertha landed with a suspension-crushing smash, rear wheels first. For a moment the truck was stuck with its front off the ground, its drive wheels screaming on their axles and grabbing nothing but air. Jill flicked off the Torque Converter, and the truck fell the rest of the way, landing with a jarring thud. Bertha surged ahead, throwing Jill back against her seat with sudden acceleration. She grimaced, hoping the thousands of people in the back managed to find something to brace against.

"This is not a level-appropriate encounter!" Babu screamed, clutching his eyes.

"Blame Shitbag McTentaclebrains!" Jill shouted back, "It's his damn lure that brought it here!" Half of her attention was on the road, the other half on the monster in the mirror. The bison snorted again, blowing up another cloud of debris, but it didn't launch another lightning attack. Its gaze turned instead back towards City Hall and the grasping lure of mana therefrom.

"Turn left at the next intersection," Ras said, pointing.

Jill nodded. She missed Aman's map already. A moment later, Bertha screamed around the turn onto Route 3, heading north out of the city. Insectile monsters boiled out of the side streets: a horde of newly-mutated creatures out for blood. Jill pulled on the air horn, and Bertha's roar swept the way ahead of her clear, as the sound wave sheared the monsters into gore on contact. Monster guts splattered into the air and coated the front windshield; luckily, the wipers still worked.

The guns joined in the slaughter, and monsters to the sides of Bertha died by the score. Experience flowed into Jill, pushing her over the edge to the next level in a surge of pleasure.

You are now Level 47!

She kept her eyes on the road ahead of her, saving the class point in case of an emergency. For now, they were getting away. The thought made Jill tense. Her hands gripped the wheel tighter, as her instincts screamed at her to be ready for anything.

The attack came not from a monster, but from a spell from above. The city's lure, ineffective against the incoming mega-beast, was again being bent by the assassin, creating a new epicenter focused on Bertha. Even now he was trying to swamp them with monsters, and while Jill didn't fear the little ones that were already swarming the road, larger creatures with dozens of levels might be enough to cause real problems.

"Switch to mana-thief rounds and fire upwards!" Jill said to her gunners. The chattering roar of some, but not all, of the guns answered.

"I don't see anything," a male voice said, panicked. "Are there more fliers? Does anyone see anything?!"

"No, but there's magic bullshit up there," Jill snapped. "Fire into the sky and sweep your shots around! Mana-thief rounds, now!" For a moment she wondered why it was that she could sense the working above them so clearly while the gunners couldn't. But then her attention was back on the road, swerving Bertha around a broken-down bus swarming with five-foot-long millipedes. The monsters couldn't slow her, but crushing the bus might.

The rest of the guns joined in firing. Streams of punctuated light reached upwards into the cloudless sky of the eye of the storm, and the mana cost of the ammunition took Bertha's mana reserves with it. There was nothing physical for the rounds to hit, but each bullet cut through the massive spell just a bit, siphoning away some of its mana. The spell shuddered, then broke apart.

Jill exhaled, hard. "Cease fire! Nice job attacking the darkness, people."

Her relief was short-lived: behind her, the bison fired another bolt of lightning, its reflection from the mirror painting the entire cab in harsh blue light. Jill swerved Bertha at the last second, knowing that this time she was too late. But it wasn't her under attack. Rather, something in the city center had offended the boss creature, drawing its deadly ire. The lightning bolt's explosion bucked the ground; its blast wave rocked Bertha and knocked the still-swarming monsters around them off of their feet.

Behind them, the First Interstate Building tilted sideways, its base shattered. In motion that seemed slow only because of the building's size, it collapsed, sending up billowing clouds of dust and debris that blocked Jill's view.

"Sugar," Ras whispered, his eyes wide and face pressed up against the passenger window to get a better look.

Throughout the debris cloud, lightning and shadows clashed, but the darkness only held on for a few seconds before being swept away. A sphere of inky black magic shot out of the cloud: the mayor in retreat. Flickers of lightning ate away at his protection from every direction, and he barely managed to stay ahead of the bison's chasing horns.

"Heh, Mayor Shitstain back there's getting his ass kicked," Jill said.

"We softened him up," Babu said. His mana flickered feebly as he tried to cast some spell, and he winced in pain.

"Sure, you tell yourself that," Jill said. She reached over and punched the miserable enchanter on the shoulder, pulling the blow to a fraction of its strength.

Bertha thundered north up the road but couldn't get up to her maximum speed, thanks to the monsters and debris covering it. Still, they'd be free in just minutes.

Behind them the bison reared up and roared, first shaking the ground with its victorious bellow and then causing another localized earthquake with the force of its landing. It took one more step, lowered its head, and closed its mouth around City Hall.

The mana of the city screamed in Jill's senses, then winked out. The lure vanished.

> The Settlement of Billings has lost its last Settlement Core! The Settlement has been destroyed!

> Quest failed: Save the settlement of Billings from the monster infestation.

The bison roared once more, then froze, its body erupting in blue light. The creature swelled, growing larger as it absorbed the settlement core.

"I have no idea how we're going to fight that," Ras said, resignation in his voice.

Jill shook her head and kept driving. "We don't. Not yet, at least. If it chases us to the airport, well, we pack everyone in and hit the mother-trucking road."

A flicker of putrid shadows racing along the road caught her attention, half from her vision and half through her mana sense, but only for a moment. The mayor was somewhere nearby, hiding.

Jill growled. "Why can't this skidmark just lea—"

"You! I'm going to kill you and make you eat yourself!" She was interrupted by an insane multi-tonal shriek erupting in her mind. "Hahaha! My city is gone, and it's because of you! I'm going to rip your eyes out and stuff them up your ass! Then I'm going to eat them! Wait, no, I'm going to shoot you, yes, yes, yeeees! Then you'll be mine forever, and you can give me back everything you took! Yes, everything, everything, everything! But first, you'll beg me. Yes, yes, no, what do you mean no?! You won't, hahaha, but I'll—"

"Goddamn, he's being more of a cockwomble than ever," Jill said, trying to ignore the ongoing tirade. Her eyes flickered back and forth, and she extended her senses wide, but she couldn't find where he was hiding. "I know he just lost the city or whatever, but what the fuck. How bad did you two mess him up before?"

Ras growled in frustration. "I cut his arm off, but it didn't take. Twice!"

"He was getting crazier as we fought, but," Babu said, shaking his head, "this is something else."

"Hey, Mia," Jill projected, "you have any idea where he is?"

Rather than answer, Mia opened fire. Her chain gun hosed down the buildings, first on one side of the road ahead of them, then the other, in a deliberate sweep. The front of first a house, then a brick-faced bank, collapsed into piles of rubble, their facades unable to withstand the hail of destruction.

Disgusting, warped mana flowing towards Bertha announced when Mia's exploration by force found its mark. She activated her powers and the rounds doubled, quadrupled, in flight, then bloomed in mana-stealing explosions wherever they struck.

The assassin burst into the air, wreathed in writhing tendrils of darkness and his face distorted by a madly grinning mouth too large for his skull. He pointed his gun at Bertha with both hands and fired as fast as he could pull the trigger, each round slamming home in a different part of the truck and cracking, but not piercing, the armor.

Jill grunted as the horrible bullets began their burrowing, torturous attack. "Piss right off, you truck-stop toilet!" Jill yelled, magic flowing through her profane powers to suppress the bullets' pain and fear. She pinched off the armor that held the writhing rounds, letting the containing blocks of metal slam down onto the road behind them as they blazed past.

A storm of magic bullets answered the mayor's shots; six heavy machine guns, and one soulbound rotary cannon, all boosted by Bertha's module powers, threw back a wave of death. The assassin erupted in holes, his body unable to stop the rounds from tearing through him, but the wounds healed as fast as he received them.

"Hahahaha," he laughed, his voice a shrieking scream in Jill's mind. He reloaded his gun with exaggerated, showy motions. "Don't you see?! I'm invincible!" A round took him right through the head, bursting it apart in a shower of brain matter. Worms of black sprouted from his neck stump, weaving together to form the rough shape of a head, but before they'd even finished, he had leveled his gun at Bertha again.

He managed to fire off three more shots, but then the mana flowing from him to Bertha—the tax imposed by the mana-thief bullets— stopped. Out of mana to spend, so did his regeneration. In a split second his body was torn apart for good.

"Good fucking riddance," Jill said, feeling only satisfaction for the death of the monster who had mismanaged Billings so badly.

Corrupted David Beatty defeated. Bonus experience awarded for: corrupted sapients kill above your level (+6.2); killing a corrupted sapients (x2); kill significantly above your level (x2).
Your contribution: 11%
345,312 Experience Gained!
You are now Level 54!

"Clitstorm!" Jill yelled, as the experience slammed into her, and seven levels of power rewrote her body, mind, and spirit. She forced her eyes to stay open, biting her tongue and clamping her hands on the wheel to stay focused. She wouldn't give in, not when passing out would mean their crashing, not when they were so close to getting out of the city.

"Hah!" she shouted in triumph, punching a fist into the air, as the feelings of euphoria faded. "Suck on it, System, I'm still going!"

She glanced to her side when no one else said anything. The Bati brothers, much more responsible for Beatty's death than her, were out cold, mana raging through their bodies.

"Sure, take a nap buddies," Jill said to them, "I'll just keep track of—oh, fuck!" She realized that in the escape from the city and the fight with Beatty, she had somehow lost track of the Boss Bison.

The huge monster was easy to find. It was ambling away to the west, back to wherever it came from, and now thirteen stories tall at the shoulder instead of ten. It didn't seem to care at all about the chaos surrounding it, or the destruction it had left behind. It took the eye of the storm with it, leaving behind pouring rain blown sideways by the wind.

Bertha roared up Route 3, nearly back to the airport. The university to their left, abandoned for hours, had few buildings still standing. As they passed, a monstrous praying mantis burst out of a dormitory, only to be repelled by gunfire. Behind them the former city burned, fires spreading unchecked. Monsters ran rampant, spawning and growing with wild abandon.

Jill shook her head. "Babu, Ras," she said to the unconscious brothers, "your hometown sucks."

CHAPTER 48

ON THE EDGE OF TOMORROW

Jill let out a sigh of exhausted relief as she pulled Bertha up to an empty boarding ramp at the airport. Once finally out of the former settlement of Billings, the drive had been mercifully short and uneventful. The local monster population, depleted by the city lure and subsequent slaughter, seemed to be taking the night off, as only a few especially suicidal, low-level monsters had shown their fanged faces. Bertha's guns had torn them apart without effort, and now the horizon was clear.

"Hey, everyone," Jill projected to the entire truck. "We just got to the airport and, for once, there are no monsters trying to murder everything. So, mission accomplished. All of the volunteers who came along: we just saved a truckload of people." She cracked a smile, despite no one being able to see her. "To everyone we picked up: thanks for riding with Highlander Shipping, your choice for getting thrown around and only nearly killed."

A smatter of laughter and cheering broke out in the trailer, echoing in Jill's mind. Her smile widened, and she leaned back in her seat, closing her eyes and relaxing for the first time in hours. She closed off her communications power and turned off the mana engine, enjoying a moment of silence broken only by Ras's light snores. The swordsman and Babu had yet to wake, but the mana flowing in their bodies had settled from a furious whitewater churn to a steady, powerful flow.

Jill's eyes snapped open as a notification appeared before her.

> Local Quest Complete: Preserve the life of newly transitioned sapients refugees of Billings. Sapients preserved: 4066
> Your contribution: 73%
> 2,968,180 Experience Gained!

The experience slammed into her, an unrelenting torrent of—

"Fuck no!" Jill yelled in her mind, pushing the words towards that part of her magic tied to the system. "Don't you dare. I have had it with you knocking me out at the worst badger-ball-busting times! And while we're at it, knock it off with that drug-high addiction that comes along with it. It's manipulative bullshit. I've seen that game before, and I'm not playing it, you hear me?!"

The flow of experience cut off abruptly.

> User preferences updated: experience growth deferred until activated by user.
> Experience deferred: 2,912,365
> Warning! Euphoria is recommended.

"Make yourself an asshole, coat that recommendation in hot sauce, and shove it deep, deep up there."

> User preferences updated. Preferred activities noted.

Jill narrowed her eyes, but chuckled.

A fast, light knock on the hatch sent her heart pounding. "Calm your tits," she muttered to herself, taking a deep breath.

The knock repeated, a rapid-fire tapping that must be from two hands going at once. "Fine, fine," Jill said. She extended a touch of magic to the hatch, spinning open the locking mechanism and swinging open the door. Kevin ran through with improbable speed, skidding to a stop next to his older cousins.

His aunt Sangita followed him inside at a more leisurely pace. She stopped on seeing the passed-out forms of her sons, one sprawled out on the floor, and leveled a flat glare at Jill.

"Hi, Ms. MacLeod!" Kevin said, waving.

"Hey, squirt," Jill said. "How did you get back onboard so fast?" She looked at Sangita and shrugged.

"I've been waiting for you to get back," Kevin said. "Want me to wake up Cuz Babu and Ras? I'm really good at it!"

Jill unbuckled her seat belt and stretched, her body uncoiling to its maximum extent in one smooth, powerful motion. Her shoulder and thigh burned as scar tissue pulled tight, but considering she had been on the road for more than twenty-four hours, not to mention getting shot twice, she felt great. Just exhausted.

"Sure thing, kid," she said, "just wait for me to go with your aunt first. I don't want to be in the blast zone."

"Okay!" Kevin grinned, bouncing on the balls of his feet.

Jill snorted out a laugh and made her way out of the cab, gesturing for Sangita to follow her. As she crossed the threshold between modules, Kevin screamed "Wake upppppp!" in a high-pitched, piercing voice that rattled the deck plating. She left the hatch open behind her, just in case the little twerp needed to make a running escape.

Jill stopped just inside the trailer. It was still torn apart from the fighting, an irritant like a pebble in her mental shoe, and she idly began cleaning and fixing everything in sight. Sangita was still glaring at her.

"They're fine," Jill said, jerking her thumb back at the now awake and flailing men.

"Obviously," Sangita replied. "But couldn't you have grown a seat or bed under Ras and not just left him on the floor?"

"Oh, huh," Jill said. "Yeah, that would have been decent of me. Anyhow, it is ridiculously late, I've been up for like forty hours, and if nothing else catches on fire in the next five minutes, I am getting my saggy ass some sleep. What do you need?"

Sangita shook her head. "Some other people have approached me about the deal you offered my family: to be able to stay on Bertha if we are helping. Can they stay?"

Jill shrugged. "As long as they're willing to go to Boston, sure. I can make a few extra bedrooms, so why not?"

The mana around Jill exploded in a maelstrom, and connections of loyalty and belonging burst out of the ether to join with Jill and Bertha's own magical presence. More and more power gathered in the truck in a roiling mass of possibility just waiting to do something.

"Ope!" Babu shouted in the cab, releasing Kevin from a playful noogie. "Is it finally happening?!" Other, more confused, exclamations joined his from the trailer, as the more magically attuned sensed the drastic changes happening around them.

A notification popped up in Jill's vision.

Congratulations, Jill MacLeod! You can create a new Settlement!
Requirements:
Fully claim a region with sufficient Mana flow. Region claimed: Soul-bound Modular Vehicle "Bertha." Region Type: Dimensional. Warning: Dimensional regions require more initial willing and accepted inhabitants and a higher investment of experience.
Have 10,000 levels worth of willing and accepted inhabitants supporting the settlement.
Have 1,000,000 experience points to invest. Warning: invested experience points may cause a loss of levels. System Notice: deferred experience points may be invested before incorporated.

Creating this settlement will require the investment of 1,000,000 experience points. Would you like to proceed?

"How the fuck many people is 'some'?!" Jill yelled. She sent the notification to Ras, Mia, and Babu, the latter of whom let out a yell of excitement.

Sangita smirked. "I'm not sure exactly. We ran out of signup sheets."

Jill narrowed her eyes. "Nice prank getting me to agree to take all of them. Here's mine: you get to organize how the face-fucking-flowers people are going to live here, because I don't have thousands of bedrooms, and I can't feed thousands of people."

Sangita's smirk dropped, replaced first by shock, and then fire. She raised her chin. "Challenge accepted."

Babu skidded to a stop next to them. "Jill! You have to do it, please! Just think of the possibilities!"

Jill sighed and rubbed her eyes. "The settlement thing, right? Is it worth a whole million experience?"

"Almost certainly!"

Jill groaned. "Fine, but I am delegating so much shit to all of you, got it? I am not going to be a waffle-iron-up-the-ass politician!"

Threat delivered, she accepted the system's prompt and braced herself for a titanic change.

Nothing happened.

> Proceed to your designated Innermost Sanctum to activate the Settlement Core.
>
> Notice: Innermost Sanctum location assigned based on user preferences.

"And where is that?" Jill asked the system, but she received no response.

"Did you, uh, do it?" Babu asked her.

Jill threw her hands up. "You know what? Nothing's trying to kill us right now, though the system is begging for an ass-kicking. I'm going to bed. I'm figuring this out in the morning."

"We need to get more supplies and living space, right away," Sangita said. "At least toilets!"

"There's a whole airport right there, figure things out," Jill said, gesturing vaguely outside. "I'm done!"

"But what about all the settlement powers?" Babu said.

"In the morning!"

"But I have a dinosaur to show you!" Kevin chimed in, having followed Babu out of the cab. Ras was right behind him.

"That's really great, kid, but you can show me in the—" Jill said, cutting herself off. "Wait, like a toy dinosaur or a living one?"

"It's my new pet!"

Jill looked at Ras meaningfully.

"I'll check it out," he said. "You go to sleep."

"Finally, someone gets it!" Jill said. She turned and stalked away before anyone else could interject.

She made it to the Habitation Module without having to talk to anyone else, her exhausted glare enough to send would-be petitioners scattering. There was a line of people waiting to use the toilets in the other bedrooms, but hers was mercifully reserved for her. She resolved to find out whoever had saved her from excretory intruders and give them a promotion.

Her room was as she had left it: narrow bed covered in luxurious fur bedding, tiny desk with chair, and a combo toilet and shower with a door separating it from the rest of the room. She took two steps forward and collapsed, face down, into the bed.

> Quest Complete: Survive 24 hours.
> Bonus (x3) for surviving in a high Mana flow region! Good job, human!
> 3000 Experience Awarded!

Jill burst out in uncontrollable, stomach-clenching laughter at the tiny reward. Ten seconds later it morphed into sobbing as the horrible events of the last day—all the deaths she'd seen, the worry over her family, and the horrible pain of being shot and operated on—all came slamming into her. Over the next few minutes, it all poured out of her in heaving sobs, leaving her still and hollow when she was done.

Well, nearly hollow. "Truck nuts," she said to no one, "I need to take a dump."

She shuffled into her bathroom, shutting the door behind her. She yelped and leapt to the side, ending up standing on the toilet, as a glowing gold crystal erupted from the floor where she'd been standing.

> Welcome to your Inner Sanctum!
> To continue Settlement creation, please input a Settlement name!

"System," Jill said, "go fuck yourself. I'm going to bed."

ABOUT THE AUTHOR

Tom Goldstein is a physicist-turned-writer with a passion for classic fantasy and science fiction. He and his partner live in Vancouver, where he serves his science-cat, Shiva.

Podium
DISCOVER
STORIES UNBOUND
PodiumAudio.com